Two hours later, Kerry was seated at her _____ ng at a few lines she'd written on her notepad—*What was bothering Nick? Why a hypodermic? Was Diana right that someone else was there? Why did she call me last night and then decide not to talk?*—she plucked her cell phone from her purse and punched in Cole's number quickly before she could lose her nerve. The call went straight to voice mail, so she clicked off, worried that he could see her number and had just chosen not to accept the call.

She sat back in her chair and was lost in thought, remembering snippets of conversation at the memorial service. She wanted to know what was going on.

Who'd killed her brother?

Diana?

Or this mysterious extra person Diana had finally remembered with the help of hypnosis?

Did that seem credible, or a way for Diana to wriggle out of blame . . .

Books by Nancy Bush

Published by Kensington Publishing Corporation

BAD THINGS

NANCY BUSH

ZEBRA BOOKS
KENSINGTON PUBLISHING CORP.
www.kensingtonbooks.com

ZEBRA BOOKS are published by

Kensington Publishing Corp.
119 West 40th Street
New York, NY 10018

All Kensington titles, imprints, and distributed lines are available at special quantity discounts for bulk purchases for sales promotion, premiums, fund-raising, educational, or institutional use.

Special book excerpts or customized printings can also be created to fit specific needs. For details, write or phone the office of the Kensington Sales Manager: Attn.: Sales Department. Kensington Publishing Corp., 119 West 40th Street, New York, NY 10018. Phone: 1-800-221-2647.

Zebra and the Z logo Reg. U.S. Pat. & TM Off.

First Printing: July 2019
ISBN-13: 978-1-4201-4293-8
ISBN-10: 1-4201-4293-3

ISBN-13: 978-1-4201-4294-5 (eBook)
ISBN-10: 1-4201-4294-1 (eBook)

10 9 8 7 6 5 4 3 2 1

Printed in the United States of America

Prologue

Patient: *Bad things happen, Doc. Bad choices. Bad decision-making.*

Doctor: *You think the decisions you made are bad?*

Patient: *If things had turned out differently, I might have made different choices. But fate took the wheel. You know that.*

Doctor: *It's hard to blame what happened on fate.*

Patient: *Oh, don't worry. I know what I did.*

Doctor: *Let's talk about your motivation.*

Patient: *Sure. Then you can write up some notes about my homicidal behavior, look smart and serious, and go on to your next case.*

Doctor: *I'm here to get to the truth.*

Patient: *Sorry, Doc, my story is my story. Not for public consumption.*

Doctor: *Anything you say here is private.*

Patient: *Doctor/patient privilege? Tell me another one.*

Doctor: *I'm your doctor. You're—*

Patient: *You're the brain digger. Digging, digging, digging away. You don't think I know what you're doing?*

Doctor: *Okay. Let's pivot for a minute and talk about those bad decisions you made.*

Patient: *You tell me one bad decision you've made, Brain Digger. Maybe then I'll tell you what you want to know.*

Doctor: *All right. That's fair. Well . . . I've already cheated on my diet this morning.*

Patient (short laugh): *You haven't killed anybody? Hurt them? Called them out?*

Doctor: *No.*

Patient: *Then you're not on the same playing field, Doc. You're not even in the same ballpark.*

Doctor: *Tell me about the bad things that have happened recently.*

Patient: *The ones I caused? That's what you're really thinking. Well, this is going to take a while.*

Doctor: *I'm here as long as it takes.*

Patient: *As long as you get paid, right? Well, fine, Brain Digger. This is a story about Nick Radnor. Some of us believed he was something special. He's certainly always believed it. And the whole damn town bought into his act. But I found him out for the faithless bastard he really is. That's what my story's about, Doc. Bad choices for a bad guy everyone thought was good.*

Chapter One

Diana Conger woke up with a sense of deep dread. Her mouth was a sewer and her head ached. Once again, she'd had too much to drink . . . among other things.

It was dark, the middle of the night, the wee hours of the morning. Throwing her legs over the side of the bed, she stumbled into the bathroom. Her stomach quivered as she leaned over the toilet, spitting. After several minutes and some hard breathing, she sensed she wasn't going to throw up after all. Holding on to the counter to balance herself, she carefully searched the jumbled memories of the past few hours: the bar-hopping, the dancing, the flirting, the recreational drug use . . . That was her, wasn't it? In the restroom of Forrest and Sean's bar? With those old classmates, taking pills, and yeah, snorting coke or something? She grimaced. She'd really told herself she was going to get it together after the class reunion meeting that was such a mind-numbing clusterfuck. Those people . . . the ones she'd gone to high school with . . . She'd thought they'd all surpassed her in life, but it turned out they were just as messed up and clueless as she was. At least most of them were. There were a few standouts. The ones she'd always known would do well, although Josie Roker was sure one crazy bitch. The way she went on about Nick, like they were an item? What about that husband of hers? But she wasn't as nuts as Egan Fogherty. There was something seriously wrong with that guy. He'd been weird all through high school. Cute, but weird. But Josie . . . she acted all pure, but the way she was around Nick said she wanted to screw his brains out. That last bit was from Killian Keenan, who'd used something a little more explicit than "screw" in his description. But then, Killian always had something kind of mean to say when he wasn't standing by, silently intimidating. What did Miami see in him? Was it just that they'd been together since high school? Well, okay, he'd held up well and still had a hard body, amazing guns. When he stood back and surveyed the room, Diana's eyes invariably traveled to his upper arms, which could really get her juices going. But maybe that was what it was with Miami—Mia Miller, who'd been nicknamed Miami, a combination of her first name and the beginning of her last—maybe it was all about sex. Well, Diana could admit that she'd made some serious mistakes when it came to sex herself. But at least she didn't act like a *virgin* like Josie.

Diana rinsed out her mouth with water from the tap, then made a face. She was pretty sure she'd made it back to her apartment tonight by the grace of God. She struggled to remember how she'd gotten home and gave it up; it made her head hurt. She'd taken Uber to the first bar where she'd met her friends, so she hadn't driven herself back home.

Her hand touched the doorjamb for a moment as she oriented herself, then she left the bathroom, stepping across the carpet to her bed, smelling the scents of lavender and grapefruit from the incense sticks in the vial on her nightstand. Slipping beneath the covers, she snuggled down with a grateful sigh.

She buried her face into the pillow as her head began to

ache again. She stretched her arms out . . . and encountered another body in the bed.

Diana froze. Heart racing, she lifted her head, her eyes searching through the dimness. There was a sliver of bluish illumination glimmering through the gap in the curtain over the sliding glass door that led to her bedroom deck, the closest exterior streetlight shining in. Leaning forward, she saw the back of a man's head. *A man.* She slid back carefully, one hand reaching for the light switch. She hesitated before she flicked it on, her galloping fear beginning to slow. This wasn't the first time she'd brought a guy home and then forgotten about him. That kid she'd brought home last summer, a couple of years below her in high school, Jimmy.

She leaned over her bedmate. Noticed the way his dark hair waved around his ear. Oh, Christ! Holy Mother of God. It was *Nick Radnor.* Josie's Nick. Well, not really hers. She *was* married. But the object of her desire and, well, Diana's, too! He was the one classmate of theirs who'd made it *big.* Something in the tech field. Lots and lots of money. Diana nearly forgot her jumping stomach and aching head. A smile spread across her face. Well, well, well . . . Things were looking up. She recalled dimly that she'd run into him somewhere earlier in the night . . . Had he been with Miami? Or . . . Forrest or Sean, at their bar? Josie had been there . . . but they weren't together. . . . Nick stayed away from her because she was married . . . although everyone kind of thought they were having a secret affair . . . but he was here now. In her bed. How had that happened?

Diana had remained with the high school gang. None of them had ever really separated, those who had stayed in Edwards Bay. They hung out at the same bars with the same friends. God. It didn't bear thinking about. She'd met up with Nick at the third bar . . . wasn't it? They'd all gone to The Whistle Stop first, and the Thai place. Kerry had been there, too. Nick's sister . . . stepsister . . . really. She didn't know Kerry all that well because she wasn't a classmate, hadn't gone to high school with them, but she'd been around tonight, hadn't she? Jesus. It was tough to remember. Felt like a dream.

But *Nick*!

Oh, Lord, she'd scored big tonight. He was *the guy* from high school. And he was divorced from Marcia now, too, though honestly, even if he was still married, Diana wouldn't have much minded. Josie could play her virgin games all she wanted. Diana could admit her morals were fluid when it came to sex. But Nick and Marcia *were* divorced. Miami had told Diana that Nick and Marcia barely spoke to each other anymore. Marcia had moved back to Edwards Bay, and when Nick visited from Palo Alto, he didn't come anywhere near her. Of course, Miami wasn't exactly trustworthy when it came to rumors, but who cared anyway? Good times were few and far between these days, and Diana was ready to make the most of this opportunity. She was eager to climb atop him and make love like rabbits. Oh, man. What a notch on her belt. She couldn't wait to tell Miami and Josie all about tonight!

She leaned over him and whispered in Nick's ear, "Fancy meeting you in a place like this."

Slipping a leg over him, she turned him on his back, climbed astride his naked body.

His eyes were open.

And his tongue lolled out of his mouth.

And his skin was . . . cool . . . cold.

For half a beat, she didn't breathe.

"Nick . . . ?" she whispered, terror running through her veins.

Oh, no . . . no . . . no . . . *no*!

Diana scrambled away from him, her mouth open on

a silent scream. Her insides shriveled. He was *dead*. A corpse. A cold, naked body *in her bed*.

She staggered backward, slamming into the wall. A thin, keening wail rose from her soul, an almost inhuman sound. She stumbled back into the bathroom, slamming her shoulder against the jamb in her haste. The jolt of pain stopped the wailing.

Leaning over the toilet, she puked her guts out.

Then she lay on the cool floor tiles and shook all over. There was a pounding on her door. *Bang, bang, bang.* Alan, her neighbor, shaking the doorknob.

"Diana! You in there? You okay?"

He'd heard her shrieking through the paper-thin walls.

She continued to shiver. Didn't answer. Stared with horror through the bathroom door to the side of the bed and the dead man she knew lay on top of it.

"Diana!"

She wanted to call to Alan, tell him she was fine. She didn't want him here. She was freaked out and sick and needed to think . . . to remember . . . to consider.

What happened?

Did you cause this somehow?

The shock of pure terror morphed to a new kind of fear. The coke . . . and other things . . . behind the Blarney Stone . . . they'd all been there. . . . She remembered the toe of her boot getting caught in the gap of the deck floorboard. A small screened back porch for employees only, but Forrest and Sean owned the place and they allowed them to be back there.

"Diana?"

His voice was softer now, unsure. She kept quiet, though her heart was beating so loudly in her ears it sounded like thunder.

She heard his footsteps head back to his apartment.

You're going to have to move.

But what to do now?

Gathering up all her courage, she crawled from the bathroom to the chair at the far side of the room. Don't look, she told herself. Don't look. *Don't look.*

But her head swiveled and she peeked over the top of the bed to see Nick Radnor's dead body. With a squeak of horror, she slipped her purse from the chair, spilling the contents onto the rug. The strip of light through the balcony curtains landed directly on the tiny pill canister attached to her keys.

She grabbed up her cell phone, hugging it tightly. Who could she call? What should she do?

What time was it?

Three a.m.

Shit.

She felt like she was going to throw up again and drew several deep breaths, exhaling slowly. Okay . . . okay . . . who?

With shaking fingers, she scrolled through her call list. One of the guys? Maybe Randy? He was a good friend to Nick, wasn't he?

But thinking of Randy Starr of Starrwood Homes brought her back to Kerry Monaghan, Nick Radnor's stepsister, who worked for Randy. Or was it a half sister? No . . . definitely step . . . she was pretty sure.

You should call one of your friends to help you, not Kerry. What friends? she asked herself hollowly.

She crouched on all fours for ten seconds, listening to her own breathing, then scrolled to Kerry Monaghan's name and pressed the Call button.

Bzzzz . . . bzzzz . . . bzzzz . . .

Kerry's cell phone nearly vibrated itself off her nightstand.

She squinched up her face and tried to block it out. What time was it?

She had on an eye mask. Something she never did, but she'd definitely had a buzz going after her night out with Nick's friends and, determined not to face any kind of residual hangover, she'd downed two aspirin, drunk half a glass of water, and, upon spying the mask in the drawer where she kept the aspirin, grabbed up the black silky scrap of cloth and snapped it over her head . . . whereupon she lay in bed thinking over her life instead of immediately falling asleep, worrying that somewhere, somehow, she'd made an unalterable mistake because nothing was turning out quite the way she'd hoped, and it felt like days were passing by quickly, slipping away like melting snowpack, running down a cliffside, falling into oblivion.

It had seemed she'd lain awake most of the night, so the rattle and buzz of her cell phone as it walked itself along the top of her nightstand surprised her awake and kind of pissed her off, too. Who was calling at this time? Nobody she wanted to talk to.

Pulling her pillow over her head, she reached out a hand and blindly searched for her phone, just catching it before it threw itself over the lip of the nightstand, determined to switch it off, her finger hovering over the button.

But . . . what if it's important? her good angel asked, an unwanted guest appearing in her head.

It's not, her bad angel assured her. *Get some sleep. Tomorrow's a long day.*

She was to meet Jerry, her stepdad, here at the motel at ten a.m. to go over what he wanted done. The Sand Drift was his motel, a row of small cottages that had seen better days but were now under renovation. She'd taken on the job as Jerry's temporary manager while holding down her real job at Starrwood Homes, owned by Randy Starr, another of

Nick's classmates. Her job had started out in Seattle, but Randy had moved her to Edwards Bay when his longtime manager had retired. She hadn't been thrilled about the idea, but at least Nick came back to his hometown from time to time, so here she was.

Bzzzz . . . Bzzzz . . .

What if it was Nick? There was no rational reason why it would be, but she threw off the pillow anyway, slid the mask to her forehead, and examined the phone's lit-up screen.

Nope. Not a number she recognized.

A prank call. Just what she needed. The battery icon was only half-full, though it had been charging for hours. Something wrong there.

She set down the phone and snapped the mask back over her eyes.

Well, what if it's Jerry? her good angel worried.

Her finger hesitated over the Off button.

It's not! her bad angel shouted. *GO TO SLEEP!*

But . . . but . . .

Bzzzz . . . Bzzzz. . . .

"Oh, hell," she growled in frustration, clicking the button. Jerry had suffered a minor heart attack last year, and it had slowed him down in a way that worried her. If this was about Jerry, she would feel really bad if she refused the call.

And she was awake now anyway. "Hello?"

"Kerry?" a quavering female voice asked.

She didn't recognize the caller and her hand sank. She should have listened to her bad angel and refused to answer. "Yes?" she asked with an edge.

"Hi, it's Diana. Diana Conger, and I'm . . . I'm . . . We were together tonight with the A-Team? And I saw you, and we were . . . we were with Nick. . . ." Her voice sank to a mewl.

Diana Conger was one of Nick's old classmates. Yes, she'd been with the A-Team tonight, a dumb name, in Kerry's biased opinion, for the group of friends from Nick's high school that still hung out together. Kerry knew them, more like "of them," as they were really just acquaintances of hers because she'd attended high school in Seattle after her mother and Nick's father broke up. She really hadn't even wanted to go out with them tonight, though she liked Josie pretty well, but Nick had been insistent. *So, okay*, she'd thought. And then she'd realized, somewhere in the evening, that Nick wasn't all that excited about hanging out with them either. Or at least it had appeared that way. Nick had seemed pretty determined to make her his wingman. She could never say no to Nick anyway, and she'd thought, *fine*. So, she'd gone, and truthfully had had a pretty decent time.

"So, Diana, it's three in the morning," Kerry said, as Diana's voice had petered out on a small gasp, as if she couldn't quite catch her breath.

"Kerry . . ."

"Yes?" She was trying not to sound impatient. When Diana didn't immediately respond, a whisper of fear traveled over her skin. "You okay?"

"No . . ."

"What's wrong?" Even as she asked, Kerry wondered why she was the one getting this call. Diana could have called Josie, or Miami, or Taryn, or one of the guys, Randy, her boss, or . . . well, maybe not that Egan something or other . . . Fogherty . . . Egan Fogherty, who was a little too friendly, intense, and always invading her personal space, kind of like a stalker. Or the guys who owned the bar, Sean and Forrest, and Killian, who they all called Lady-Killerian, mostly because that's how he pretty much thought of himself . . . or maybe even Nick. Anybody but Kerry, who was the outsider. They'd all made sure they had one another's cell numbers tonight. Maybe it had been a mistake to hand hers out to Diana.

Diana started making choking sounds.

"Diana . . . you're scaring me . . ."

"Oh, God, Kerry. Oh my God . . ." she whispered tearfully.

Kerry sat up in bed.

"It's Nick . . . it's Nick . . ." Diana said something else, but she was burbling, barely making sense.

"What about Nick?" she asked carefully, frozen except for her pounding heart.

"He's here . . . in my bed." Her voice grew small. "Kerry, I think he's . . . dead!"

Kerry exhaled, alarmed and angry. "That isn't funny! Is Nick really there? If he is, put him on the phone."

"He's dead, Kerry!" she cried hysterically.

"Stop it! Stop crying!"

"I don't know what to do!"

The phone was slick in Kerry's hand. This wasn't real. "If he's hurt . . . or something . . . call 9-1-1."

"They'll come? Even if he's dead?" Diana asked on a hopeful hiccup.

Jesus. Was there even a chance she was telling the truth? "Diana, don't screw with me."

"I'm not, Kerry, I'm not." Her hiccupping had turned to a constant low and tearful *uh-uh-uh-uh*.

"Then call 9-1-1."

"Okay . . . okay. . . ."

This had to be a sick joke. "How did Nick . . . get hurt?" she tried.

"I don't know. I just woke up and he was . . . I didn't know he was . . . I mean, I thought he was alive, but he's not breathing . . . he's not . . . *anything.*"

Kerry switched on the light and threw back the covers. "I'm coming over there. What's your address?"

Diana mumbled it, but Kerry managed to hear her, just. She knew enough about Edwards Bay to recognize the general area. "The Bayside Apartments, number two-one-one," she repeated aloud, to burn it into her memory. If this really was the truth, if it really was . . .

"Hurry."

"*Call 9-1-1!*"

Kerry was already out of bed. She was terrified. If this was some kind of game at her expense . . .

But that would be the best scenario, wouldn't it?

Yes.

She ripped off the oversize T-shirt she wore at night. Nick had been perfectly fine when she saw him at that last bar, the one owned by Sean and Forrest, The Blarney Stone. They'd wrapped their evening up there, all crowded around a table in the back that was separated from the main bar by a railed wall. Kerry remembered looking through those rails and seeing Nick standing near the bar, head bent to something Killian was saying to him. Diana had been hovering to one side. Or had that been Taryn? Maybe Josie? They all had that kind of dishwater blond hair. Only Mia Miller, who called herself Miami, had darker hair, but then, she maybe dyed it.

But Nick had been perfectly fine!

He wouldn't play these kinds of games. It wasn't in him. Maybe this was Diana and the others' cup of tea, playing horrible jokes on anyone outside their group, but it wasn't Nick's.

So, was it true?

She clamped down on her mind, keeping that unholy thought right out of her head. Grabbing up her jeans, she snagged a green T-shirt out of her drawer and got dressed. Keys in hand, she looked at herself in the mirror by her apartment's front door, finger-combed her hair, her pulse racing, light and fast. It wasn't true. It wasn't.

So, why are you going?

She determinedly headed for her small Mazda wagon, which was parked on the street that ran in front of The Sand Drift's fourteen units. Normally, she parked in the back lot, by the rear door to her manager's cottage, but there had been so many construction vehicles and potholes that she'd pulled up on the street. Jerry had been so happy that she was on-site to supervise that he'd offered her free rent, but she'd insisted on paying him a ridiculously low amount, something, otherwise it felt too much like a gift.

Drawing a breath, she took a moment to assess herself. Was she okay to drive? She'd taken Uber to the first bar and then bummed her way around with Nick's friends before Ubering home as well. She felt stone-cold sober now, wide awake and filled with icy control. Still, it wouldn't do to get a DUI, especially if this all turned out to be some kind of vile prank.

You don't believe that, though, do you? Diana's not that good of an actress. Nick's hurt, or something.

Kerry shivered. If this was some kind of elaborate trick by Diana or Nick's friends or somebody, she was going to be pissed off and angry at them like they'd never known. And if by some weird chance, Nick was in on it, she didn't know what she'd do. Lay into him, that was for sure, and all his friends. Even Randy Starr. He might be her boss, but he was a son of a bitch on a good day. Maybe the others were just as bad. Maybe she shouldn't have let Randy coerce her into the Edwards Bay job, and maybe she shouldn't have accepted Jerry's largess.

Jerry. Swirling in the back of her head was the notion to call him, to let him know what kind of sick game his son's friends were playing. But as she drove through the dark streets, pavements shining beneath the streetlights in dark pools from the fitful rain that had beset them all evening, she silently shook her head. She wouldn't worry him over something that could turn out to be a hoax.

But if it wasn't a hoax . . . ?

She set her jaw and drove.

It took less than fifteen minutes to arrive at Diana's apartment and, as Kerry rounded the last corner, she got a distinct shock upon seeing the flashing red, white, and blue lights of a police car and an ambulance.

Diana had listened to her and called 911. She wouldn't take a joke that far . . .

Kerry's mouth went dry.

She threw the car into park and jogged toward the apartment, quivers running through her thigh muscles, spasms, the shock of belief taking a physical toll. She had to grab the wrought-iron rail along the front walkway as she headed toward the outside stairs to the second floor, where she assumed 211 would be.

There was a small crowd outside the door of an apartment on the far end. As if in a dream, Kerry stumbled toward it, legs trembling, fear clutching at her heart, robbing her of strength.

A policeman in the Edwards Bay force uniform she thought she recognized glanced at her. It wasn't Cole, whom she'd heard had made it to the town's police chief; the officer's name tag read Youngston. "Hey," he said, trying to hold her back, but she brushed past him. He tried to reach out a hand to stop her, and she yanked her elbow in and turned around to glare at him. He was about her age with a sour look on his face, and for a moment they silently dueled, eye to eye, but then he didn't try to physically stop her again.

And then she saw Nick. His body being lifted off the bed and onto a gurney.

He wasn't moving.

"Nick," she whispered, a soft cry.

"Kerry!"

Kerry turned blankly as Diana shrieked out her name and ran toward her. Her robe parted down the center, revealing she was naked underneath as she threw herself on Kerry. Kerry stumbled a bit under her weight, then held on, aware that Diana was quaking from head to toe. The two women staggered as a man about their age with brown, curly hair and a face that was all sharp planes and ridges, caught them and steadied them. Kerry couldn't speak. Couldn't think. Her burning eyes kept returning to Nick's inert body.

"I need to see Nick," she said, barely able to hear her own voice above the roar inside her own head.

"Ma'am." The officer, Youngston, got between her and Nick, trying to herd her back toward the door, even as the other man managed to pull Diana away from her.

"Get out of my way," she said through her teeth.

"You can't go there," Youngston said, but Kerry was already around him, shaking off his hand when he tried to hold her.

She stared down at her stepbrother before Youngston angrily put himself between her and Nick's body.

"You need to leave now," he ordered.

"What happened?" Kerry asked. "What happened?" Nick didn't look natural. Something was wrong. That wasn't natural. He wasn't natural.

Youngston seemed to want to grab her by her arm and steer her back outside, but he just remained a wall between her and Nick. "Who are you?" he asked.

"I'm . . . Nick's sister."

The other man introduced himself. "I'm Alan Jenkins. Next door. How did you find out?"

"What?" Kerry asked, dazed.

"I called her," Diana cried, her voice muffled against his shoulder. "She told me to call 9-1-1."

The officer relaxed a bit. "I'm sorry, ma'am, but I need all of you to step outside."

Jenkins repeated, "You're his sister?"

"Stepsister. Kerry Monaghan." Her voice sounded funny, faraway. "What happened?" she asked again.

"I don't know," Diana wailed.

"Is he going to be all right?" Kerry asked. The surf in her ears rose.

"Ma'am, he's dead," Youngston said.

The surf turned into a typhoon, a loud, swirling ocean inside her head. She felt someone grab her and leaned into them. "That can't be."

Diana was wailing. Or someone was. Kerry was blind with disbelief and shock.

The man holding her asked, his voice rumbling beneath her ear, which lay on his chest, "What do you want me to do?"

Alan somebody. The neighbor. He'd released Diana to grab her. Diana was keening wildly.

Officer Youngston moved toward Diana. "Ma'am. Stop!" His harsh manner had the right effect, and she stopped wailing, but she was shaking from head to toe, looked about to collapse. Youngston grabbed Diana by the arm and led her to a chair. To Alan, he barked, "Get her outta here."

Kerry, who'd been lost in a fog, came back to the present. "No. I need to see him."

There were two ambulance attendants who'd worked together to settle Nick on the gurney.

"Is he dead, Ben?" Diana cried, now clinging to the officer's hand. "Is he really dead?"

Ben? Kerry wondered as she pulled away from Alan to stagger toward the ambulance attendants. She reached a hand out to the body under the sheet.

"Don't touch him," Youngston snapped, but Kerry ignored him.

She swept back the sheet and laid her hand on Nick's arm.

Cold.

Dead.

She saw black pinpoints of light.

"Breathe," one of the ambulance attendants ordered.

"She's going down," the other one said.

Someone caught her. She fell on him hard and inhaled on a gasp. He steadied her, and she stumbled away from him. The back of her knees connected with the bed and she sank down on it.

"Get off there!" Youngston ordered. "We haven't processed the scene!"

"Scene?" Kerry repeated. Crime scene?

She saw Youngston shoot a sideways glance toward Diana, who was rocking back and forth in the chair, oblivious to the fact that the robe was wide open. Alan came toward her and tugged the lapels together, a kind gesture that brought tears to Kerry's eyes, her nose burning.

She couldn't have gotten up off the bed if she'd had to. Youngston regarded her angrily for a moment, then let her be.

She was still sitting there when the coroner's van arrived and they took Nick's body away. The ambulance attendants got in their van and left. Officer Youngston tried to talk to Kerry, but she couldn't answer him. Nick was gone. Gone.

More people came. Other apartment dwellers, roused by the commotion. It was a sleepwalker's nightmare. At some point Alan helped Diana get up and find some clothes. She headed into the bathroom and reappeared in a pair of holey jeans and a sweater that dipped over one shoulder. Her makeup was smeared and her nose ran and she just stared straight ahead, as if she'd been emptied of all thoughts and feelings. Youngston was joined by a female officer who tried to help clear the area and talk to Kerry, but she had nothing to say. She wanted away from them. From their worried or concerned looks, from their impatience, from the whole scene. With Nick gone, she wanted to go home.

The female officer asked for her name, address, and cell number, and she gave it to her in a monotone. She heard the woman mention Cole's name and surfaced enough to realize there was a chance Cole might actually come. He was the police chief, she'd heard. And he was a friend of Nick's, so yeah, he was probably on his way. Cole, her almost fiancé. Another reason she hadn't wanted to come back to Edwards Bay. She'd yearned for Cole for years after he'd broken off their engagement. His rejection had sent her spinning into the arms of another man and a short-lived marriage she never wanted to think about again.

All that passed through her mind in a flash, barely penetrating her horror, grief, and disbelief. But she didn't want to see Cole, so she turned for the door. Diana, seeing Kerry was getting ready to leave, came out of her stupor to latch onto her again. Kerry had to practically peel the woman's fingers away.

She drove herself home. It wasn't far, but the trip back was a complete blank the next day. She walked into the kitchen of her cottage and looked around the space, feeling out of time and space. Nick was dead. Her stepbrother was dead. She reached for her cell phone and saw that it, too, was dead. Dead like Nick. She plugged it in. The screen lit up. Five thirty a.m. Jerry was an early riser. Maybe not this early, but she needed to call him. Or maybe Youngston had called him. Probably he had. That was protocol, wasn't it?

She saw there was a missed call from him.

He knew.

All the stuffing went out of her. She leaned her back against the wall and slowly slid to the floor, dropping the last inches hard onto her butt. She sat there for a moment, staring into space; then she put her hands over her face and silently wept.

Chapter Two

Josie looked at herself in the mirror, pulling back the edges of her eyes, making the teeny, tiny crow's feet disappear. Better. More like high school. Everyone told her she looked the same as in high school, but she knew they were lying. It was all so fake, the frozen smiles and cold hugs, the oh-I'm-so-jealous. You're-so-cute! lines. Lies, lies, lies. They were either shining her on or green with envy. Either way, it was bullshit.

"Bullshit," she said to her reflection, examining the flecks of green in her blue eyes. Actually, there was a tiny dot of brown in her right eye. A mistake. An imperfection Taryn had told her was a beauty mark, but Taryn was full of shit, too. Half the time she simpered in the range of a good-looking guy, the other half she professed herself to be a champion of women's rights, like she'd started the #MeToo movement all by herself or something. More bullshit. And then some of the time she acted like a dyke, which was just that, an act.

But then, Taryn wasn't half as bad as Diana, who would screw anything and anyone for drugs or alcohol or just because she could, and didn't make any claims about sexual orientation because she just didn't care. Okay, Diana tended to circle around the hottest guys, but unlike Taryn, who only really seemed to like the cute ones, Diana seemed to gravitate to power. Like Killian Keenan, who was really an asshole of the first order and had really disgusted Josie more than a few times. The way he captured you in his glare? In high school it had made her stomach clench, and it had been all she could do to smile through gathering tears, but as the years had passed, she'd kind of gotten over it. He was still a prick of the first order, no question, even though Miami stuck with him through thick and thin for reasons Josie couldn't fathom. He couldn't be that good in bed. No man was. Case in point, her own husband, Kent Roker, who was determined to make her life hell and was.

Josie shut her mind down. No use going down that road now, getting herself all worked up over Kent's faults.

And the only good guy she knew was Nick Radnor.

She brushed on some mascara with a shaking hand, recalling their last makeout session with a smile. Oh, she shouldn't want him like she did. She was half in love with him, maybe fully in love with him. He was her own Achilles' heel.

She exhaled heavily and shook her head, letting her light brown, shoulder-length hair fall back into its layers. Purposely, she pulled her thoughts away from Nick. She was growing too obsessive.

Achilles' heel . . .

Was that the right use of the term? Sometimes she screwed up references she thought made her sound smart, but when she messed them up everyone laughed at her, and it jabbed her to her core. She was certainly smart enough, no matter what they thought. Maybe not Taryn smart. That girl could really lock things into that brain of hers. Taryn had some kind of science research training but was currently working at her parents' grocery store, one of those organic places that charged an arm and a leg, so she wasn't any better off than any of them really. Josie could admit that her smarts were more in the social realm. She knew how to work people, in a good way, not like Killian did. She prided herself on understanding what they wanted and could figure out how to give it to them. That was her secret gift.

Now she sighed and grimaced at herself, examining her teeth, considered maybe using another round of whitening. Nothing showed age more than yellowing teeth.

Her thoughts circled back to Miami, supposedly Josie's closest friend. They had been in high school, but they hardly spoke anymore. Miami hadn't been able to afford college and Josie had gone to Western Washington for a while until she met Kent. Miami was now a waitress/hostess at The Pier, the hotel on the Kingston side of the bay, a ferry ride away by water. It had previously been named By the Beautiful Sea, though it wasn't on the sea, it was on the bay, which Taryn, who loved to point out everything and anything that wasn't exactly perfect, made a point about over and over again until the hotel's ownership and name changed. Like Josie's eye. Taryn was the one who'd told her that Faye Dunaway died in the movie *Chinatown* from an eye imperfection. Or no, wait . . . she had an eye imperfection and then was shot through the back of her head and the bullet passed through that eye. Taryn had explained, "It's a reference to Oedipus, who blinded himself upon learning he'd married his own mother. Faye Dunaway's character had sex with her own father and was blinded for it."

Taryn watched a lot of old movies and talked about them with nauseating knowledge, like they were all supposed to find her brilliant and fascinating. She used her cinematic knowledge to hang out with the guys in their class and have something to talk about. It was also her come-on: *Let's go to my place and I'll show you my etchings,* or, in this case,

old movie collection. Sometimes it worked, sometimes it
didn't. Most of the guys found her intensity tiring.

Diana, of course, wasn't nearly so coy. She just tagged
after anybody who might want to get high and have sex.

But back to Miami . . .

Josie grimaced, thinking how good Miami had looked
the last time she'd seen her. Age wasn't working against
her the way it should. She was almost more beautiful now,
with that tanned skin and that long, dark hair. It just *shone*.
Or was that *shined*? Either way, Miami's hair was remarkable. Like a commercial for some new, fantastic shampoo,
it moved like silk.

But then . . . Miami was Killian's woman and he was her
man, and never was there a more dysfunctional love/hate
relationship. They'd been together since they were nine, apparently. One of those sick relationships that began when
they were kids and couldn't ever get over itself. Miami swore
she was going to quit him, and Killian had kicked her to the
curb more times than you could count, but they were still
together. Like maggots on dead flesh, Taryn said. You could
separate them, but they just kept coming back together.

"Josie?"

Josie whipped around, dropping her tube of lipstick,
shocked out of her reverie by her husband's voice suddenly
calling from the kitchen. Her heart thumped hard. He was
supposed to have gone to Sea-Tac airport and a flight to
Phoenix. What was he still doing at home?

"What are you doing here?" she called back, starting
to feel angry. Had he meant to scare her?

"Your phone's ringing."

She couldn't hear it. She'd turned down the ringer so it
wouldn't alert Kent every time it went off, and she hadn't
turned it back up yet. She purposely exhaled all the air from

her lungs, pushing away her anger. "Who is it?" she asked, knowing he'd undoubtedly already looked at the screen.

"Miami."

Huh. Were her ears burning? "I'll be right there."

Why was Miami calling this early? It was barely six thirty. Josie was only up because she'd partied too hearty the night before and needed to release the poisons or they would fester inside her and add to the aging in a way she just couldn't afford. But Miami never got up until she had to, no matter what she'd been doing, and Josie just didn't believe she had to be at work yet.

"What are you doing still home?" she asked Kent as she cruised into the kitchen.

"It went to voice mail," he said. "I forgot my glasses." He held up his reading glasses he'd apparently taken off when he was having breakfast.

"You could have answered it," Josie said, sweeping up the cell phone.

"Since when?" He smiled, but it wasn't a nice smile. It was that I-got-you smile he pulled out more and more often these days.

"Since whenever. I don't have any secrets from you."

Now why had she said that? It made her sound like yes, she did indeed have secrets, which was the absolute truth.

Luckily, Kent didn't press her. "I gotta go," he said, heading for the back door of their rambling ranch. She watched him leave, his shoulders tight in his suit from his obsessive working out. She liked that about him, the way he kept his body strong and taut. But there were other problems. She waited to hear the automatic garage door close behind him before she turned back to her phone.

It rang in her hand before she could speed dial. Miami again.

Josie clicked on and said lightly, "Two calls before seven a.m.?"

"Nick Radnor's dead!" Miami burst out. "He went home with Diana and died at her place!"

Josie's mouth dropped open, but she was robbed of speech. Her brain stalled and she wondered if she was in a dream. Miami didn't just say that. "What?" She couldn't get her voice above a whisper.

"Drugs . . . it was drugs . . . no one's saying it, but with Diana . . ."

The blood drained from Josie's head. She grabbed the edge of the counter with one hand. "What are you saying?"

"It was drugs. An overdose."

"No."

"He died in her bed," Miami choked out. She sounded like her teeth were chattering. "I heard from Killian, who talked to Diana. She called him from the police station. Guess she was arrested for supplying the drugs. Oh, shit. I don't know. *I don't know!*"

"What? What do you mean?"

"I don't know how it happened, but Nick's *gone*, Jose. That's what Killian said."

"He's lying. Putting you on." Her fury returned in an instant. "That *bastard.*"

"No, no! He was telling the truth. Nick's gone. He's dead."

"Stop saying that."

"I don't know how she got him to take the stuff. He never took drugs. He never did. We all knew he never took drugs. He was so *good.* He was . . . well, you know, better than any of us."

"What?" she asked faintly. She sat down hard in one of the dining chairs, nearly missing the edge and falling to the floor.

"Nick never felt right about everything from high school . . . he was talking about it . . . about Lisette . . . we all heard him . . . and I think . . ."

"What are you saying?"

"I don't know. *I don't know.* He went home with Diana and she had drugs and—"

"He didn't kill himself," Josie declared furiously.

"He should've been with you!" Miami shot back in a shaking voice. "Then he'd still be alive!"

"He's not dead!"

"He told Taryn he was going to make things right."

"Make what right?" But she knew, she knew . . . "Lisette's death was a suicide. Nick would never . . . deliberately hurt himself! *If that's what you're saying, you're wrong!*" Josie was practically shouting.

"Well, why was he with Diana?"

Josie suddenly bent forward, putting her head between her knees. She felt like she might pass out. Diana was easy . . . Diana was a drug abuser . . .

"He wouldn't be with Diana."

"I know, but he was."

"It's not true," she said determinedly.

"Oh, Jose . . ."

She mumbled something that sounded like, "I'm sorry," and the line went dead.

Nick, Josie thought, feeling herself almost float away from the moment. Nick. *Oh, Nick.*

He was the successful one of their group. The only one who'd really made it. The only one who'd left Edwards Bay and gone on to make a killing in Silicon Valley. She'd secretly had a crush on him forever, and she'd finally made it. She'd been thinking day and night how and when to divorce Kent . . . for Nick. They'd all had crushes on him at one time, and Taryn counted him as her best friend, but really, how close friends could guys and girls ever be? It was a myth. A fallacy. Josie just knew Taryn had wanted to get his pants off, too, but he'd ended up with *Diana and now he was DEAD*.

"I don't believe it," Josie said succinctly.

In a silent rage, she called Miami back and was almost surprised when her friend answered the phone with a squeaking, "I'm so sorry. I don't want it to be true either."

"Killian's lying. It's not true."

"Killian wouldn't make up a lie like this."

"Killian would do a lot of things."

"Oh, Jose. Not this . . ."

"I don't care what you say, Nick didn't purposely overdose himself!" she shouted. "And he wouldn't be with Diana! Something's off. Something's really wrong."

"Killian said . . ."

"What? What the *hell* did your boyfriend say?"

"That maybe it was Diana's fault. Too much at once, you know, because Nick wasn't a user."

"She overdosed him? That's what Killian thinks?"

"I'm just repeating what he said."

"Killian's an asshole, Miami. *An asshole.*"

Josie suddenly wanted off the phone. This wasn't happening. This wasn't happening. This wasn't the ending for her and Nick.

Miami said with more control, "Killian told me Diana called Kerry when . . . when she realized Nick was dead, I guess. Kerry was there when they took Nick's body away."

The vision of that was too much for Josie.

"Killian's telling the truth," Miami added a bit coolly as Josie muttered a goodbye, then scurried back to the bathroom, examining her face in the mirror again, gratified and almost surprised that there were no new lines. She still resembled the slim, athletic beauty of her youth, only slightly tattered. She wished she were that girl again. Wished all the intervening years hadn't happened. Wished everything was good again, like it had been before that last year of high school.

Briefly her thoughts turned to Lisette's suicide. Nick's long-ago girlfriend.

Nick wasn't to blame for that. None of us were.

Josie stared at the brown dot in her eye, the imperfection, but she saw Nick Radnor in her mind, the way he'd looked last night. Handsome as the devil. Lean and successful. Dark shirt, dark pants, dark eyes. She'd been thinking about another makeout session, planning for it, wishing all the rest of her old classmates would just disappear.

She'd tried to catch Nick's eye all night, but he'd scarcely looked at her, keeping his cool, keeping their affair under wraps, though most of their friends had already guessed. The only smiles he'd scared up all evening were for his stepsister, Kerry, as if she were the only one who afforded him joy. He sat beside her everywhere they went, keeping her close. Josie had been half-jealous, wondering what was going on. It wasn't sexual, as far as she could tell. Kerry and Nick, though they weren't blood-related, had never seemed to have any interest in each other that way. And last night she'd been oblivious to Nick's . . . possessiveness? Was that the word? More like *neediness,* now that she thought about it, but Nick wasn't a needy kind of guy. Still last night, it was true, that he'd seemed isolated from the rest of them, only interested in engaging with his stepsister, though Kerry had been somewhat remote like always, not really ever fitting in with the gang. But then Kerry had left them and Josie had been forced to head back because Kent was starting to text her and she knew she wasn't going to be able to get away with Nick, who'd barely caught her eye all evening and then . . . *how had he ended up with Diana?*

"Oh, Nick," she whispered brokenly, overcome with grief as the truth finally penetrated, gained acceptance. She leaned over the sink, panting for air, nose burning, heat suffusing her face. Tears gathered in her eyes, ran down her nose, dripped into the white lavatory. She gulped and cried for long minutes, trying to get hold of herself.

It took a long, long time, and when she finally looked up at her reflection again, her blotchy, red face was anything but pretty. She looked older, desiccated. That was the word, wasn't it? To be dried out and used up.

She was going to have to pull herself together and face the day. Mostly she wanted to go to bed and draw the covers over her head, but she already knew it was likely the friends would be gathering to grieve together over Nick's death.

Nick's death.

A hot stab of fury ran through her.

"This wasn't supposed to happen!" she screamed.

Diana was to blame. Somehow, someway, she'd picked up on Nick's neediness, and after Kerry left she'd maybe offered him a ride home or something and he'd ended up at her place and *died*.

This was Diana's fault.

Josie strode to her bedroom and slid back one of the mirrored closet doors, stripping off her workout gear. She wasn't going to the gym after all; she was going out. Somewhere. Doing something.

And she was going to divorce Kent. Right away. No more waiting. She didn't love him. She never had. She'd loved his success and his family name. The Rokers owned a bank, for God's sake, and she'd been the perfect Josie, fresh and beautiful and everyone's dream wife. All his business associates envied him; she'd made sure of it. She'd blocked out everything and moved forward into her new life, determined to remake herself. She'd been popular in high school. She could tell the guys in their group still felt the same way about her. The cute girl next door. Not as sexy as Miami. Not as desperate as Diana, or as Taryn had been then. Not as lovely as Lisette, who'd been outright beautiful and virginal, at least in spirit, because Lisette's stepfather's sexual abuse had been the reason she'd killed herself.

But Lisette was dead and now . . . now Nick was, too. . . .

She gulped back another tidal wave of sobs. Josie suddenly, fervently, wanted to forget the life she'd carved out for herself and circle back to her high school days . . . start a new life . . . with Nick.

She buried her face in her hands. This was Diana's fault. Diana's . . .

Chapter Three

Kerry stood outside the owner's unit and the motel's front office, looking up at The Sand Drift's blistered sign. The cottages were located on the north side of Edwards Bay, a briny finger of Puget Sound that dipped down from where that enormous body of water gathered in northern Washington State. She could see the bay and the ferry dock from where she stood.

She was having trouble getting into her car. It was eight o'clock and she'd spoken to Jerry, who'd told her he was going to the hospital morgue to view Nick's body. The police had shown up at his home and given him the news before Kerry had to make the decision about telling him, and he'd called her first, even before Nick's ex-wife, Marcia, who was raising the child she'd had from a previous relationship in Edwards Bay.

Jerry had rasped, "Meet me there, Kerry. Please."

"Of course."

But here she stood, trying to get her arms around the fact that Nick was gone forever. If she didn't leave soon, she would be late, but what did late matter? Nothing mattered.

She stared up at the line of white and gray clouds on the western horizon. Something ominous about them.

Slowly the whine of the tile saw behind her penetrated

her consciousness, and she didn't have to turn around to know that the workers were renovating the whole of units three through seven. Jerry had already done most of the work himself on one, two, eight, nine, and ten, but he'd grown tired and had health problems, so he'd put Kerry in place as manager and hired an outside contracting company to complete the job, one of the ones Starrwood Homes used as well.

None of that mattered anymore.

Not a healthy attitude, but then, what did health matter anymore either?

She drew a breath, forcing herself to put one foot in front of the other as she walked toward her Mazda. Her inertia and fatalism weren't going to help Jerry. She needed to keep moving forward. She became aware that she was probably underdressed in jeans, sneakers, and a workout T-shirt that said Over It.

She winced and did an about-face back to her unit, stripped off the T-shirt and changed into a plain blue one. How she'd even dreamed she would work out she couldn't imagine now, and why that T-shirt? She'd grabbed it up this morning and thrown it over her head, barely aware of what she was doing. She was numb, dull, unaware, yet sometimes suddenly seized with a clarity sharp enough to cut. What the hell had she been thinking? She'd wanted to run. Run away. And she'd dressed accordingly, thoughtlessly, ready to race away from Edwards Bay as fast as she could.

But there was no way to run from reality, so in the end she'd sat down heavily at the small kitchen table and stared at the salt and pepper shakers for several hours, moving them around, spilling grains onto the Formica tabletop. By the time she surfaced, headed out, then woke up to her clothes and hurriedly changed them, she knew she would be late.

But by the time she got to the hospital it was only nine minutes after eight. Nothing in Edwards Bay was far from anything else. At least that was a plus in this case.

Jerry was waiting for her outside reception, elbows on his knees, chin in his hands, his gaze on the floor. Kerry's first glimpse of him was his gray head with tinges of white near his ears. He'd suffered a cardiac "event" in the middle of the previous year, and that was when he'd stopped renting out the cottages, deciding to renovate them and put the motel on the market, determining it was time for a change.

He seemed to sense her arrival because he looked up and regarded her silently. Kerry's heart clutched; he'd proverbially aged overnight. The same could probably be said for her. She felt at least a decade older.

"Jerry," she said, and felt the tears threaten some more. She swallowed hard, determined not to break down, almost pathologically desperate to be her stepfather's strength. He'd been more like a father to her than her own father— much, much more—and his divorce from her mother hadn't changed that. Even when she'd been packed up and moved to Seattle, she'd stayed close to both Nick and Jerry. Even through her marriage to Vaughn. Especially through her marriage to Vaughn. Her relationship with her mother had maybe suffered a bit because of it, but Karen Radnor had moved on to a new husband, a retired professor from the University of Washington, who was smart, loved to travel and take Karen with him, and was a bit too pretentious for Kerry's taste.

Ergo, Kerry had drifted back to Edwards Bay and the family she was closest to; now down to one: Jerry.

He struggled to get up, but Kerry sank into the attached chair beside him, clasping his hand. "Let's take a minute."

"No. I have to do this. I have to see . . . to know."

She was chilled. Was he up to the task? Reluctantly, she said, "Okay."

On his second attempt he managed to get to his feet on his own, but his walk was little more than a shuffle. They took the elevator down to the lowest floor and walked beneath a series of overhead lights that gleamed in diffused spots along the gray linoleum-tiled floor. The morgue was designated by white letters carved into a black-plastic sign above double doors at the end of the corridor. Jerry pushed through with Kerry behind him. They stood side by side, and she remembered all the times he would clasp her around the shoulders and say, "It's Jerry and Kerry time!" then grab her hand and take her on an "adventure," whether it be out for ice cream, to an amusement park, to the nearby stables to ride the ponies, or just into the kitchen to whip up their favorites, Rice Krispies Treats for her, oatmeal cookies with walnuts and chocolate chips (no raisins) for him.

And Nick would always say, "What about me?" to which Kerry would cry, "You have to come with us! Come on! Come on!" and the three of them would leave Kerry's mother, who was always looking for time to herself anyway, and head out to whatever Jerry had planned.

Those adventures had dwindled as Nick became less interested and Karen and Jerry's marriage had fallen apart, but even after Kerry and her mom moved to Seattle, Jerry had taken the occasional trip across the water to pick up his stepdaughter and take her out. By this time Nick was in high school and interested in other pursuits, specifically sports and girls, and Kerry saw less of him. But they kept in touch sporadically over the years, and he'd really reconnected with her during this last year, which in turn had reconnected Kerry with Jerry.

Now, she could see his right hand was trembling and she reached for it again.

An attendant in blue scrubs came through a door to one side of the room. Spying them, she walked over and asked their names. As they answered, Kerry felt a brief waft of air as one of the double doors she'd just walked through opened again. She started to turn around and froze as she caught a glimpse of the newcomer. Cole Sheffield. Police chief of the Edwards Bay Police Department.

"Cole," Jerry said in a tortured voice.

Cole immediately went to him and clasped the hand that Jerry had dropped from Kerry's grip. He put his other arm around Jerry's shoulders, holding him steady. Cole's face was grim and tight, as if he were physically holding all his emotions in check, which he probably was; Nick had been one of his good friends as well. Cole had followed his brother into the military, had been through two tours in Afghanistan, and had eventually taken a job with the Edwards Bay PD when he'd gotten out. His brother, Aaron, along with two other American soldiers, were killed when his Jeep ran over an IED, exploding on impact.

The last time Kerry had seen Cole was at Aaron's funeral. He'd looked gaunt then, haunted. Now his physique was lean and strong, his dark hair trimmed, his gaze steady and strong. Now they were together at Nick's death. She had a broken marriage behind her, whereas he looked like he'd prospered. Maybe there was a Mrs. Sheffield she didn't know about. It didn't matter. Nothing mattered except that Nick was gone . . . gone . . .

As if sensing her thoughts had touched on him, Cole's eyes met hers. He acknowledged her with a nod and a faint movement of his lips that could be considered a smile of recognition, she supposed. Another time it might have bothered her deeply. Now there was no room to dwell on old hurt.

She stood by while Cole talked with Jerry, and then, soon enough, Jerry was being led inside a glass room with curtains stretched across the windows. No one asked Kerry to be a part of the viewing and she remained where she was.

Fifteen minutes later Jerry and Cole returned. Jerry's face was white, his eyes glassy. Kerry immediately moved to him for support and he slipped an arm over her shoulders, leaning on her, his body shaking.

"It was Nick," he rasped. "It was Nick."

"I'll drive you home?" Kerry asked, her heart thundering. She looked around for some kind of sign from either Jerry or Cole about what came next.

"Thank you, sweet girl," Jerry said, a catch in his voice.

Cole cleared his voice and said, "Do you mind if we talk later, Kerry?"

She was so surprised to hear her name on his lips, it took half a beat to answer him. "Okay."

"Ben Youngston said you came to Diana Conger's apartment last night," he said, as if having to explain himself. "Could you come by the station later? I'd like to hear what happened."

Her heart felt cold. "All right. After I take Jerry back."

"I've got a few things to take care of myself, but I'll be back at the station by eleven."

"Okay," she said.

She drove Jerry's white Cadillac to his house with care. It was a vintage car that broke down regularly, each time lovingly put back together by Marty, the mechanic, who was of Jerry's era and shared his passion for old vehicles. "Pain-in-the-ass pieces of junk," as Nick had cheerfully described them.

Jerry didn't say anything on the ride to his home, and Kerry let silence fill the space. She had no words either.

But when she pulled into the asphalt drive he insisted she come inside his house. She wanted nothing more than to go home and away from a day that had seemed to grow too bright with a flat, unforgiving light, but she couldn't just leave him. Dutifully, she followed him inside his daylight basement house, circa 1960, perched on a hill with a fabulous view of the bay. Its windows were the original aluminum and were starting to separate from their casing, and the plastered walls looked like they could use a deep cleaning as they were streaked and dull, probably as a result of the wood fireplace Jerry still used. "One of these days I'm fixing the place up," Jerry had said for years, even while he'd still been married to Kerry's mother. He'd probably been saying that while his first wife was still alive, though breast cancer had taken her away when Nick was still in the primary grades.

"Come on in here. I want to show you something," Jerry said as he unlocked the front door and headed down the hall in the direction of his home office.

Kerry reluctantly obeyed, afraid they might be up for a retrospective on Nick's life through the photo albums he kept there. Her heart was already breaking. She just didn't think she was ready. Her head was beating with a dull ache from spent tears, a sleepless night, and the overall shock.

But he didn't go for the albums. Instead he sank into his desk chair, which creaked and groaned under his weight, and then pulled out the bottom drawer of the gray file cabinet tucked in the corner. After searching around for a few minutes, he tossed a file onto the desk. "My will," he said. "I want you to keep a copy of it. When I die contact Macdonald, Kemp, and Crane on Fourth. They'll help you. Now that Nick's gone, you're my personal representative and heir. I always wanted you to have the cottages. Thought I had to sell 'em, but I don't think I will now. They're yours."

Kerry started breathing hard, stunned. "Don't talk like that. I'm not your real daughter."

"Don't ever say you're not my real daughter."

"Jerry . . ."

"Don't cry," he said brokenly, and then they both did.

She tried to talk him out of his decision, but in the end Kerry took the file and drove back to the cottages, parking in the back lot and letting herself into her unit through the rear door, distantly aware that the tile cutter had knocked off for a while, glad for the quietude.

She tossed Jerry's will on the counter and planted herself facedown on the couch and shut her mind down. Sleep, blessed sleep. That's what she needed. But her mind was buzzing. Too many thoughts crowding inside her brain. None that she could latch on to. She knew she'd never get to sleep.

Bang. Bang. Bang.

Kerry sat up with a jerk and a catapulting heart. On her feet before her brain could catch up.

Someone at the door.

She must've gone down hard, she realized, even while she'd been certain she couldn't. Her brain caught up slowly as she walked to the door and opened it to the length of the chain lock. Nick's ex, Marcia, stood on the other side.

"Marcia. Just a minute," Kerry said, shutting the door and sliding back the chain. She then reopened the door and let her in.

Marcia's hair was mussed and her makeup looked hastily applied, but it couldn't disguise her extraordinary beauty. She was a redhead and had been for at least the past few years, but as a teenager, when she'd been crowned Miss Seashell, she'd been a light brunette. "It was the gray hairs that did it," Nick had told Kerry, though he and Marcia had ceased to be a couple years before, so maybe that had only been a theory on his part. Either way, today Marcia's red hair was nothing like its normally perfect coif.

"Don't you ever answer your phone?" Marcia said.

She'd lost weight and was rail thin, the change emphasizing her sharp features and hawkish nose. She'd never been classically beautiful, but she'd always had an appealing warmth that had drawn people to her. That warmth was presumably what got Nick to propose, though their marriage had lasted an even shorter time than hers and Vaughn's. She and Nick had laughed about it once, deciding they were both bad at marriage . . . maybe bad at love.

Marcia's warmth seemed to be sorely lacking now. Her lips were compressed into a thin line. Her hands were fisted. She seemed to have an iron grip on herself, but Marcia had always been mercurial, so Kerry wasn't sure how long it would hold.

"I turned it off when I went to the morgue," Kerry said, looking around vaguely for her purse. There was the will, she realized, not wanting Marcia to see it.

"Were you sleeping?" she accused in a high voice. "Nick's dead and you're sleeping?"

Kerry saw her purse was on the counter by the sink, below the open shelves that held her plates, glasses, mugs, and one glass vase. Ah, yes, she'd dropped it there when she'd poured herself a glass of water to combat her dry throat. Residual effects of her bar-hopping with Nick's friends . . . and intermittent weeping.

"The morgue," Marcia said, as if she'd just heard Kerry's words.

"I met Jerry there."

Marcia's knees trembled and she helped herself to one of Kerry's two kitchen chairs. "Oh, God."

Kerry walked past her to grab up her purse by its shoulder

strap. She slipped a hand inside and pulled out her phone. Checking it, she drew a breath when she saw the list of missed calls. Practically all of Nick's friends had tried to contact her, including Randy, her boss. Marcia. A number she didn't recognize was from San Jose. One of Nick's Silicon Valley associates?

"How'd you know about Nick? Did the police contact you?" Marcia asked.

"Actually, it was Diana Conger."

"The *murderer?*"

"Well . . ." Kerry demurred. The file was just left of Marcia's hand. Kerry purposely kept her eyes away from it, even while she longed to whisk it out of sight.

"That's what she is. A murderer. She murdered my husband."

Ex-husband.

"Tell me what happened," she ordered.

Kerry closed her eyes, swallowed, then told Marcia about Diana's early morning call, the trip to her apartment, the discovery that Nick was truly dead.

Marcia's face drained of what little color it possessed. "The police called me this morning. You must've already been with Jerry at the morgue by then. I tried to call him. He's not answering either."

Kerry could see the file out of the corner of her eye. She didn't want to think about it, didn't want to have it be any part of their conversation. She was overloaded with thinking about Nick, and Marcia undoubtedly was, too.

But Marcia seemed to pick up on how hard Kerry was ignoring the file. Her eyes moved to it. "What?" she asked.

Kerry watched almost in slow motion as Marcia's hand moved toward the file.

"Have you told Audra?" she asked Nick's ex.

"No. For God's sake, I'm not a monster!"

"Well, okay, but I don't have to tell you that you're going to have to tell her soon, before someone else does."

"You mean like you?"

"Or Jerry."

In a kind of daze, Kerry watched Marcia flip open the file. She should have been irked at the presumptuousness, but it was too late for that as Marcia pulled the document in front of her.

"That's Jerry's will," Kerry said, wanting to rip it from her hands.

"Jerry's will?" Marcia looked up, aghast. "Are you kidding? Do you have Nick's, too?"

In a distant part of her mind, Kerry recognized that Marcia was coping with Nick's death with surprising aplomb. Maybe that was the result of a contentious divorce. Nick had wanted their split to be amicable, and with a prenup in place, he'd blithely assumed it was all settled. But Marcia had had none of that. She'd fought him tooth and nail, and he'd eventually given her more than what was in the contract, according to Jerry, in whom Nick had confided. The split had been hard on Audra, who'd been only four at the time and had no discernible relationship with her biological father, a college affair that hadn't lasted till graduation—again, information from Jerry; Nick was closemouthed about his relationships. Not so Marcia, who was full of angry outbursts, ones Kerry ignored. Kerry didn't know exactly what the division of assets had entailed, but Marcia had the house in Edwards Bay that he and Marcia had built, with a view that rivaled Jerry's.

"No. Jerry gave me his this morning." She reached out for the file, but Marcia was already opening it, one hand holding the pages flat to the counter. Kerry felt a burst of adrenaline as she let her arm fall to her side. She could already imagine the scene if Marcia came to the distribution of assets.

Marcia turned some pages and inhaled sharply. *There it is,* thought Kerry. "Jerry made Nick his personal representative and you second?" she said with bitter anger.

"Jerry's alive," Kerry reminded her. "It's Nick who's gone."

That caught her up for a moment. Stopped her from paging further through the document.

"What do you want, Marcia? Why are you here?" Kerry asked. She was tired of Nick's ex already.

"I'm here because of Nick! I want to know what happened. An overdose? That's a lie. Nick didn't use drugs. We all know that. And if that's really the cause . . . if that's what . . . happened to him—" For the first time she was struggling with words to describe her ex-husband's death. "Then it's Diana Conger's fault. She's the one responsible for his death. Nick said she was a user. I don't know her that well, but it's common knowledge, isn't it? She sleeps around and she's a drug addict."

"Well . . ."

Marcia glared at her. "Whose side are you on?"

"I'm just trying to get through today, Marcia."

"What was he doing with her?" she demanded belligerently, tears standing in her eyes.

"I don't know."

"Nick didn't use drugs," she said again. "A beer or two and maybe a scotch now and then. That was it. He was a careful guy. He never let down his guard."

In that she was right, at least for the grown-up Nick. Kerry could remember him as being a carefree kid, but that had dissipated as he'd gotten into high school and adulthood.

Her attention was drawn to Marcia's pale pink fingertips as they nervously plucked at a corner of the file. Given enough time, Marcia would read on, and Kerry wasn't sure she had the energy to try to explain Jerry's decisions regarding his will. Marcia was impulsive and canny about sensing when you didn't want her prying further, which she then always did.

"I hope she rots in that jail cell!" Marcia declared suddenly, vehemently.

"Diana's in jail?"

"Well, she killed him, Kerry. Of course she's in jail!"

"For possession?"

"She *killed* him! That's why."

Kerry knew it was way too early for that conclusion to have been reached. If Diana was being held in jail, it was likely for a different crime.

"She must've been taken in after I left . . ." Kerry murmured, running the scene at Diana's apartment through her mind again. The police officer on the scene had most likely made that decision. *Ben*, Diana had said. She'd known him. And Cole had mentioned Officer Ben Youngston.

"I hope she doesn't get out on some technicality," Marcia said. "That's how these things go way too often."

"We don't know that Nick's death was anything but a terrible accident."

"Oh, yes, we do, and so do the police. When someone dies of an overdose whoever they're with is tested, and if they're a user, they get arrested, thank God. It's time people take responsibility. And believe me, I'm going to be there on Diana's day in court to make sure she gets what's coming to her."

"Was it Officer Youngston who took Diana to jail?"

"How would I know? You're the one who was at the morgue . . . with Jerry," she reminded her.

"At the hospital, not the police station."

She shrugged and turned back to the file, lazily flipping a page.

"Do you mind?" Kerry asked coolly.

"Why do you have Jerry's will?"

"I told you. He gave it to me."

"Yeah, but why now? Because Nick's gone?"

"I guess."

Kerry so wanted to tell her to put down the will, but she felt too raw for the argument that was bound to occur. Nick had married Marcia for a lot of reasons, like the fact she was beautiful, capable, and smart. And once upon a time she'd been more full of joy than the emotional cripple she'd since become. In one of their few moments of confidence, Marcia had told Kerry it was all Nick's fault that things had fallen apart, that he was the one whose attitude had nose-dived. She wasn't completely wrong; Kerry, only seeing her stepbrother sporadically, had noticed the decline in his happiness over the years as well. But whereas Marcia blamed it on Nick, Kerry had sort of felt it was Marcia's fault. She'd been this engaging, energized person while she and Nick were dating, but that had dissipated pretty fast after the wedding. Maybe it had all been an act to snag a husband, and once they were married her true self emerged. Maybe the A-Team knew more; they'd gone to school with her.

Marcia flipped to the asset page, and Kerry held her breath. It took her a couple of long moments, then she expelled in horror: "You're Jerry's heir after Nick?"

"As I said, Jerry just gave it to me, and I—"

Marcia cut in, "You're not even his real daughter!"

That brought a surge of heat to her cheeks. "I didn't ask for it, Marcia, okay? He just handed it to me. This morning. I think he was feeling vulnerable and wanted me to have it. It's been set up this way for years."

She was on her feet. "Well, I'm sure as hell going to talk to him about that, you can be sure."

You do that.

Now tears rained down Marcia's face. "Nick's gone and all you can think about is *money*!"

"Are you kidding me?" Kerry demanded. "All I want is

Nick back. Here. Right now. Right here. Alive and well, and I don't give a goddamn, flying fu—"

She cut herself off, an image of Nick waggling his finger in front of her face, saying, "Ah, ah, ah," whenever her blue streak of swearing entered the "danger zone." The thought of her stepbrother squeezed her heart. It was too much. She sank onto the couch and buried her face in her hands. Unlike Marcia, she was cried out. She just sat there, chest heaving.

Several moments later she heard Marcia get to her feet and walk toward the door, hesitating. "Maybe I should leave," she said stiffly.

Kerry nodded.

Another pause, as if Marcia wanted to say something further, but Kerry kept her hands at her face, willing Nick's ex to leave. A moment later she did just that. Kerry heard the door slam behind her.

Immediately, she jumped up, twisted the deadlock, and pulled the chain across. Then she sank down on the couch again, only to leap back up, swearing anew as she glanced at the clock in the kitchen. Grabbing her purse, she headed to the back door, then did a quick about-face to stop at the mirror in the front entry alcove. She needed makeup. And a hair comb. And the hours of lost sleep before she saw Cole.

She wasn't going to get any of them.

Slamming the door behind her, she headed out the door to the police station and Cole Sheffield.

Chapter Four

The sound of sobbing from one of the three jail cells inside the Edwards Bay police station could be heard throughout the building as Cole used his key fob to enter the back door and then strode down the hallway toward the central room that held a number of desks and computer monitors. Ben Youngston was talking with Charlene "Charlie" Paige, flirting actually, and that made Cole, already tense over Nick Radnor's overdose and death, nearly lose his cool.

"Release Diana Conger," Cole told Youngston. He hadn't known she'd been arrested until he was at the morgue with Nick's father. That information had been kept from him deliberately, while Youngston handled the case. Only around seven, when he'd been shaving, had his cell phone buzzed and he'd been alerted to Nick Radnor's death. Hours later . . . hours when he'd been sleeping with no one calling . . . hours when decisions had been made that wouldn't have been had he been alerted.

This was the insubordination he dealt with. Nothing overt. His officers just seemed to have a general feeling that Cole wasn't the right man for the job of chief of police, that he hadn't deserved it, and they therefore didn't have to abide by the rules as tightly as they might.

Ben slowly straightened from where he'd been slouched against the counter. He was wearing his uniform, which had already seen some rough use; Cole could see the stain on the side of his shirt.

"You need to change," Cole said, knowing Youngston kept another uniform in his locker. Charlie did, too.

A flash of resentment crossed Youngston's face. He and Cole were close in age and had both graduated from Edwards Bay High, but Cole had recently taken the job as chief of police, which didn't sit well with his fellow alum.

"Conger likely killed him," Youngston said. "She's definitely on drugs. Puked up some on me. I gave her a Breathalyzer, and she was over the limit. Need to test her for other drugs."

"Let her go."

Cole's order brought Charlie's sharp green eyes darting his way. She glanced at Ben, then back to Cole. She was also an Edwards Bay grad, a number of years younger than both Ben and Cole. Though Edwards Bay High was small, Cole hadn't really known Ben by much, other than his name, and Charlie had been a complete stranger when Cole took over as chief.

The tips of Ben Youngston's ears grew red. Cole could just imagine the kind of comments that were running across the screen of the officer's mind. Cole had finished college in law enforcement and gone on to Seattle PD. When the job of chief of police came up in the sleepy town where they'd both grown up, Cole had landed the job ahead of both Ben and Charlie, to both of their chagrin. They'd felt they'd been overlooked. They both seemed to feel the fact that they'd stuck around should supersede Cole's years of experience with a much larger police department. He'd left; they'd stayed. Experience didn't matter. Loyalty did. So when old Art Beckham finally retired they'd expected one of them to be appointed chief. The Edwards Bay mayor had had other ideas, and Cole had won the job.

Youngston opened his mouth to protest, but Cole cut him off. "She wasn't driving. You don't know that any crime was committed. She could sue the department for wrongful arrest."

"She came willingly!"

Cole didn't respond, but his hard expression said he didn't believe that.

Youngston nodded a brisk assent and stalked down the parallel hall to the one Cole had just entered and toward the jail cells. Charlie didn't lift her gaze as she returned to one of the central desks, pulling out the chair with a little more gusto than necessary. Cole waited until Youngston returned with a dark-haired, disheveled woman who wore a pair of tight jeans and a sweatshirt and sandals. At least Youngston hadn't taken her shoes before she was locked in the holding cell, Cole thought. Ben handed Diana Conger her belongings: a small purse, a wallet, and keys.

Cole had only learned of her incarceration when he was at the morgue with Nick's father and Kerry Monaghan, as he'd gone straight there upon being belatedly alerted to the tragedy. His officers hadn't exactly gone against protocol. Not a lot of serious crime happened in Edwards Bay and there was a certain amount of leeway and general expectation that nothing seriously bad happened here. At least that was the sense Cole got when he'd taken over. But Nick Radnor was someone they all knew, or at least knew of. He was one of Edwards Bay's golden sons, having left for Silicon Valley and made it in the tech world. His ex-wife, Marcia, another Edwards Bay High graduate, had returned home after the divorce with all sorts of stories about Nick's success, though she'd apparently received only a stipend of his apparently enormous wealth because of the prenup in place.

And Nick had been coming back more recently, followed by rumors that he'd sold out, burned out, or dropped out, though his residence was still listed as Palo Alto.

Cole hadn't paid a ton of attention to what was up with Nick. He was, after all, Kerry's stepbrother, and Cole had made a point to distance himself from both of them rather than stir up old memories. Now, however, he needed to know everything.

"I'll drive you home," Cole told Diana.

"I'll drive her," Ben put in quickly, somewhat alarmed. He might not like Cole being his boss, but neither did he want to have any reason for Cole to upbraid him on his duty. He was that guy.

"Thank you," Diana said, looking gratefully at Cole.

She was a mess. Her face was splotchy and wet and her nose was running.

Charlie spoke up. "I'm going to be driving by Diana's place, so let me do it. I'm taking Mrs. Wrong's keys to her." Hearing herself, she flushed and amended, "Mrs. Wright's."

One of Edwards Bay's colorful inhabitants, Cecily Wright was intermittently dotty, with occasionally erratic driving. Her son, Adam, took her keys away from her on a regular basis and even went so far as to have her license revoked. But Cecily marched right back down and passed the drivers' test again. She even had herself checked out by her doctor. She could be so remarkably "on" that it was difficult to ascribe her behavior to dementia, so now they were in a period where Adam took the keys from her and dropped them at the station. He wanted somebody to take responsibility for her other than himself. When Cecily couldn't find her keys she would call Adam, and he would say he didn't know where they were. Next, she would call the police and either Uber or Lyft her way down to pick them up, or the officers would take them back to her.

The officers joked that she was Mrs. Wrong, or sometimes Mrs. Wrong Way. Since her license had been reinstated, she hadn't had an infraction, but they all knew she was an accident waiting to happen.

Diana gave Charlie a long look. Charlie was young, slim, and seemed to believe people would think she was tough and capable if she put a hard lock on her personality. The look Charlie sent back said not to test her.

"Hand me Mrs. Wright's keys," Cole said. "I'll be back in an hour."

"I'll be heading out unless you want to pay overtime," Ben said sulkily.

Cole shook his head. Their budget didn't stretch that far, and Ben was the officer who'd been on call and therefore had shown up at Diana Conger's apartment.

Charlie handed over a set of keys attached to a matted, fuzzy yellow puff with a happy face on it. He then walked ahead of Diana to the back door, holding it open for her, so that she stepped into the gray, overcast day ahead of him.

She was silent in his Jeep, then said, "Thank you" as she climbed out in front of her apartment building.

He walked her up the stairs to her door, waiting until she'd unlocked it and let herself inside. Once across her threshold, she said tearfully, "I would never hurt Nick or anybody."

Cole thought about his initial talk with the coroner before he'd met with Jerry Radnor and Kerry at the morgue. "There's a needle mark on the man's right arm," the gruff, older man had said. Cole had filed that away, wondering if they were all wrong about Nick, that he was a user. That didn't jibe with what he'd heard, but sometimes what was heard and what was the truth were two very different things.

"You take care," he told Diana.

"We were just having fun." She gazed at him earnestly. "There will be an autopsy."

She'd willingly allowed the Breathalyzer, but that meant nothing because she hadn't been operating a vehicle, so Cole wasn't certain what Ben was trying to prove.

Now she hesitated, looked concerned.

"Was there something you wanted to say?" he asked.

"Nick wasn't . . . this wasn't . . . he was just so unhappy, y'know? I wanted him to feel better. He wanted to feel better."

"What did you do?" Cole asked carefully, sensing some kind of confession forthcoming.

"Nothing. Nothing!" She backed off right away. "We were just at the Blarney Stone and he was talking to me and I could tell he was really miserable. I think that's why we . . . ended up together at my place . . . for companionship."

She sounded like she was making it up as she went along, testing it out. Cole waited, but she just shrugged, shook her head, and said, "That's all I remember."

Cole nodded at her as she closed her door, then he retraced his steps to the police-issue Jeep. He next drove to Cecily Wright's rambling old white house on the crest of the main hill that faced the Sound. It was very close to Gerald Radnor's address. In fact, a number of the homes along this ridge were the ones the parents of some of Nick's classmates, the ones he'd met with the night before, still lived in. Cole, being a few years older, only knew of them. He could remember the football fathers forming a club of sorts and cheering on their sons. It had been a loose group that spent a lot of time bragging, according to Cole's own father, who'd moved to Arizona after first Cole's mother's death from surgical complications and then Cole's brother's death while on active duty in Afghanistan. His father had since married and divorced one woman and was now dating another one.

Cole knew, as probably his father did as well, that we all made peace with unthinkable tragedy in our own way.

Mrs. Wright was just coming down her front steps, a flight of concrete stairs cut into the mounded grassy slope that led to her wraparound porch. An Uber driver was waiting for her. Cole pulled up behind the driver's Prius, got out, and said to the henna-haired woman in the flowing blue caftan coming toward him, "Mrs. Wright, I have your keys."

"What?" She stopped, holding fast to the metal rail that ran down one side of the steps.

"I have your car keys. I'm Cole Sheffield from the police department."

"You the new chief?"

"Semi-new," he said. They'd met several times, though this was the first time he'd been the one to bring back her keys.

"Someone keeps stealing my keys. I think it's my son."

He held up the yellow fuzz ball. "Let me bring them to you."

"You can go away!" she called to the Uber driver, waving one arm at him.

Cole walked to the driver's window. The man rolled it down and gazed at Cole with a frown. "What's going on?"

"I brought Mrs. Wright her keys, which is why she called for Uber."

"She doesn't need the ride?"

"Not anymore."

"Cole Sheffield," the man said in sudden recognition.

It took Cole a moment longer to recognize the bearded man behind the wheel. "Lawrence Caufield?"

"Sure thing. I heard you were back. Hey, God. Is it true what I heard? Nick Radnor overdosed last night?"

The heavy stone pressing down on Cole's own chest over Nick's death, a weight he'd managed to ignore somewhat while he'd been dealing with Diana, Ben, Charlie, and Mrs. Wright, suddenly felt heavier.

"Chief! Chief!" Cecily motioned from her perch on the steps, clearly wanting him to come to her with the keys.

"Heard he died at Diana Conger's apartment. Is that true?" Lawrence asked.

"I've got to deliver these," Cole said, pulling away from the driver's window.

"She's going to have to pay for the cancellation, you know. She called me here."

"Okay."

He left the Prius and took the stairs two at a time until he reached the older woman, who was about halfway down the twenty-some steps and stopped at a small landing. Cecily turned around and headed back up the steps, surprisingly spry, and Cole had no choice but to follow. At her front door, she stopped and turned around to accept the fuzzy ball that held her keys. "He's trying to make it out that I'm losing it," she said in a whisper, as if afraid someone might hear them. "He wants my money. Thinks it's his already. He's gaslighting me, Chief. Thought you should know."

"You mean Adam?"

Cecily waved a dismissive hand. "Conrad was a son of a bitch. Doesn't hurt my feelings. Everyone said so. Wanted Adam to be on the team, but Adam liked tennis."

Cole tried to make sense of her non sequitur but gave up. There were too many more pressing issues. "You be careful out on the road," he told her, heading down the steep steps.

"But Conrad wanted Adam to be one of those guys!" she called after him. "When Adam joined with 'em, look what happened. Now our son wants our money before I even follow Conrad into the grave. I should never have married him. I'm gonna change my plot. I'll be damned if I lie next to that man for eternity!"

Cole parked his Jeep in the back lot and headed for the rear door again. The Edwards Bay Police Station was a squat, red-brick building that spread over a tableland at a point about two thirds of the way up the hill that rose from the Sound. It was composed of a reception area, six offices jutting off an open central area with a number of desks arranged back to back, three jail cells, a records room, two unisex bathrooms, and a kind of break room that housed one vending machine, a half dozen lockers, two rectangular collapsible tables surrounded by varying chairs and stools, an undercounter refrigerator, and a microwave. There was a Boyd's coffee maker on the scarred counter and a cupboard filled with coffee-making paraphernalia, paper towels, paper plates, and paper cups.

Cole headed directly to the break room and poured himself some coffee into a paper cup. He took a sip, smelling the scent of the hot cardboard. He'd learned never to reheat his paper cup in the microwave; invariably the glue reacted to the increased temperature and tainted the smell and flavor of the coffee. He reminded himself to bring a mug from home, just as he had nearly every day since he was hired at the Edwards Bay PD.

Charlie strode into the break room moments later, sliding him a look. He couldn't tell yet whether she disliked him because he'd "usurped" his job as chief or if there was a deeper reason. One of the other officers, Nathan Spano, had floated the idea to Cole that Charlie actually liked him and was playing the long game. If that was the case, she was wasting her time. Since his brother's death he had been incapable of feeling anything that remotely fell into the romance range. He'd felt a pang of regret upon seeing Kerry earlier, sure, but the end of that relationship had been best for both of them. He'd long ago recognized he wasn't husband material. He liked being alone. She deserved someone who could commit fully, and that wasn't him.

"Any decaf?" Charlie asked, moving past him to check the coffee supplies. Cole tested his coffee for heat. Hot. No smell of glue. "It's leaded in the pot."

"I guess it's still early enough to have caffeine." She grimaced. "Although I lost count at three cups."

He left her pouring herself a cup and headed to his office. They were all on edge about Nick's death. Drug overdoses, all too common elsewhere, weren't the usual in Edwards Bay. Car and home accidents were the norm. And illnesses, and age. An occasional fight that escalated too far. They'd had a few suicides, more in recent years, which was concerning, but mostly Edwards Bay's crime was on a smaller scale. But maybe they'd all lulled themselves into believing they were impervious. Edwards Bay was a sleepy, beautiful town, nowhere close to Seattle in size and problems, the big city versus the waterfront village. Still, Edwards Bay had grown much larger over the last few years, changing while its residents weren't looking. The motels on the waterfront had morphed into sprawling resorts. The homes were growing bigger, taller, and more expensive. Restaurants and cafés had taken over the local variety and used furniture stores. While still in Seattle, Cole had heard that Edwards Bay had become *trendy* and in the summer months, which they were just embarking upon, the trickle of tourists could grow into a rushing river.

It was June 3, still cool and blustery, but come July and August the town, which always ballooned with people, would likely fill to bursting. This seemed to somehow surprise Cole's friends and classmates who'd never left. They constantly marveled with some alarm at the changes. The generation above Cole's was even worse. He knew of a group of men who met with some regularity, their main function seeming to be talking about the good old days. Funny. Cole still remembered this group as being vaguely overaggressive parents at the high school, especially the fathers of the boys who'd championed their own children above anyone else's. His own father had groused about them, saying they thought their shit didn't stink, though Richard Sheffield's lost invitation to their group might have been because he was an ornery son of a bitch who couldn't get along with anyone.

Cecily Wright's comments had reminded Cole of some of those dads. Conrad Wright may have been in that group of football dads, even if Adam had played tennis. Adam was really their grandson; his parents had lost custody because of their drug abuse, and Cecily and Conrad had adopted him, and Conrad had joined with the younger dads, cheering on their sons. Cole made a mental note to ask Adam about his father next time he brought Cecily's keys by the station.

Cole hadn't been part of the football cult either; he'd played baseball and basketball. For a time after his brother's death, Cole had careened out of control, drinking too much, quitting the force, quitting Kerry. But then he'd thrown himself back into the job, and it had saved him. He'd excelled at the academy and had won a good job with Seattle PD before taking his leave. When he'd returned, he'd worked his way up in record time. He'd planned to be the best officer of the law they'd ever had and had certainly been one of the best. The only criticism he'd received was from one of his first captains, who'd warned him not to be too dispassionate. "Try to find something you care about" had been his advice.

Well, he sure as hell cared about what had happened to Nick Radnor.

Rigor mortis was just coming on by the time Gerald Radnor had seen him this morning. Maybe that timing had been a mistake. It was far too early for the coroner to declare cause of death, but the preliminary evidence suggested drug overdose. Cole was waiting for the final word on that. He'd known Nick Radnor more as an acquaintance than a friend, as he had been a few years younger, but everything he did know and had heard about Nick said he was no addict.

Still, people changed, times changed, life changed. There was evidence of a needle mark, although the coroner had mentioned only one. Hard to say what the real story was. Maybe Diana was Nick's dealer.

He tried fitting that on and had trouble making it work. He needed to know more about Nick, and that was why he'd asked Kerry to come in.

Or maybe you just want to see her again.

He shook his head at the thought. Nope. He wished her well. He just needed information on her stepbrother.

He glanced at the clock. Ten minutes past eleven. Kerry was late, as ever. One of the quirks he remembered about her. A bit flustered, generally in a sunny mood, she'd always been an unaffected, beautiful girl whose presence drew people to her. He'd wanted her, that was true. Had gone out of his way to have her. Would have killed anyone who got in his way to that end.

But he'd let her go. She wasn't right for him; no one was. He'd told her the same after his brother died. Broke off their relationship. She'd been taken aback. Hurt and stunned but dry-eyed. He'd said something stupid about him not being marriage material, and the wounded and angry look she'd given him had called him a liar. He'd told her he wanted her to be free to find someone else.

She'd called bullshit on his "false nobility" and then walked away. Her words had stung, maybe because there was a truth in them he wanted desperately to deny. But he'd made the choice—one made when he was swirling in the depths of emotions he normally could control. He'd thought about her over the years, telling himself he'd done the right thing, sometimes wondering what exactly that was. He'd definitely felt scorched when she'd married less than a year after their split, but it reaffirmed that he'd made the right decision. When he heard she'd divorced, he made a point of pushing that thought to the very back of his mind. The time for the two of them had passed. She'd probably found someone else by now. Maybe someone better suited for her.

He heard the buzzer that allowed visitors through the locked door behind the reception desk and into the squad room. A moment later Kerry pushed through, pale as the moon in a camel-colored turtleneck, jeans, and ankle boots. Her light brown hair was held back at her nape with a dull gold clip. Her eyes were solemn, her mouth held in a tight line, which was how her whole body looked: tight. She was holding herself together with an effort.

"Hi, Cole," she said.

"Why don't you come to my office?" he invited, leading the way to the room that faced west, where he could watch the sunset. The station had a partial view of the water. Once upon a time it had undoubtedly been a clear view, but development had added second floors to some of the houses below and now there was obstruction, and a fight in city hall that had gone on for years about maximum roof heights.

He sat behind a utilitarian desk that had probably been there since the station's inception. Kerry sat primly on a chair opposite him.

"Any news on Nick?" she asked. "I mean . . . about cause of death. Something more than rumor?"

Her voice was husky, raw from tears, he thought. He wanted to reach out and comfort her but held back showing any emotion. "Not yet." He almost told her about the needle mark, but without more information it would be just fueling the rumor mill. Maybe it was from something perfectly legit. He toyed with the idea of asking if Nick was a diabetic, or took intravenous medication, but the words stayed unspoken. He needed the autopsy report before he let out anything about Nick Radnor's death.

"I wanted to ask you about—" he began.

"Is Diana Conger in jail?" she questioned at the same time.

They both paused and Kerry inclined her head, indicating he should go first.

"She was released about an hour ago. One of our officers brought her in, but she was released," he repeated lamely. Youngston had been too hasty. He was a bit of a cowboy on a good day, taking charge and making decisions outside of the agreed protocol. Cole had learned that Ben had pretty much always been this way to a degree, but his near insubordination had ramped up since Cole had "waltzed off with the job" . . . Youngston's words. "There was no reason to arrest her."

"No reason?"

"Cause of death hasn't been determined yet."

Kerry flicked him a look, then nodded slowly. Her purse was on her lap, her hands tightly gripping the strap as if it were the reins of a running horse.

Cole soldiered on, "I understand you were with Nick last night, along with a number of his friends, before he ended up at Ms. Conger's apartment."

"That's right."

"Can you give me a rundown of the evening: where you were, what you did, who you saw, that kind of thing?"

She released the strap and reached into her purse, withdrawing her cell phone. Cole wondered if she was one of those people who couldn't move without the security of their phone.

"They've been calling me and I haven't called them back," she explained, looking at the screen. He caught enough of a glimpse of her phone to see the list of missed calls. "Marcia, Nick's ex-wife, caught me at home this morning. She wasn't there last night, but a lot of his friends were. Killian and Josie and Randy . . . Miami . . . and Sean and Forrest . . . Diana, obviously . . . Egan Fogherty. Taryn. It was kind of a loose group, some catching up with us later, some there at the beginning. When I left Nick, it was only Diana and Josie and Egan with him, I think. Do you know them?"

"By name, maybe." Edwards Bay was small, but not that small. "How was Nick?"

"He was fine. He was glad I was here. I moved from Seattle, too, not too long ago," she added, then flushed a bit. "Did you know Nick's father, Jerry? I mean, before today?"

"We've met a few times."

"He had a heart attack last year, so I came to help out. We're renovating The Sand Drift. I've been staying there. Nick was happy about it, because he lives—lived"—she swallowed— "in Palo Alto, although last night he was talking about moving back to Edwards Bay. His daughter's here."

"But his business was still in Palo Alto."

"Yes, of course. It was probably just talk. Nick outgrew Edwards Bay years ago. His business was global, so he didn't really fit here anymore. That sounds snobby. I didn't mean it that way. Oh."

"What?" he asked.

She looked concerned. "His business partner. He doesn't know yet."

"We'll contact him," Cole assured her. "You know his name?"

"Chad . . . something. I can't think of it right now. I don't know why. I know it so well." She shook her head. "He and Nick were good friends, have been for a long time, and then they . . . started this business. . . ." She stopped and her eyes filled with tears. Cole reached around to the credenza behind him, as old and heavy and beastly a piece as the desk, and grabbed the tissue box, then came around the desk to hand it to her. She shrank back a bit from him as she plucked a couple of tissues. "Sorry."

He moved away from her. "No need to be."

"But Chad . . ."

"I'll get in touch with him."

"Thank you." She held the tissue to her eyes, trying to pull herself together. She dropped her hands and looked down at the dampened tissue. "Is this Diana's fault?"

"We don't have all the evidence yet."

"But you think it is. You think Diana and Nick were doing drugs and he was accidentally overdosed."

"Kerry, I just don't know." She flinched. Maybe because he'd used her first name? "That's one scenario."

She dragged in a long breath. "Diana was drinking a lot, but she always does. She was all over him last night, but she's that way. I hope it's not her fault, but I'm mad at her." She looked at him through the tops of her eyes, as if expecting him to scold her.

He settled back into his chair. He was far too tense himself. "Was Nick drinking last night?"

"He had one or two beers, maybe three? We had a pitcher at Blarney Stone, Sean and Forrest's place. Nick was drinking along with the rest of us, but it wasn't anything I noticed. I had a glass of white wine, and so did Miami. Josie had a martini, I think. The guys were drinking beer. That was pretty early on."

"What about Diana?"

"Wine. Taryn had soda water, I think. Might have had vodka in it, or gin. And Killian's drink was whiskey. He tried to get us all to take shots. I didn't, but Diana did. She's . . ."

"She's what?" Cole asked when she trailed off.

"A party girl. She's kind of always been that way, from what they say."

"They, the other friends?"

"The ones who went to high school with him. From what I know, Diana's tried a few things. Randy called her a 'dabbler.' Randy Starr," she added for clarification. "He and his wife popped in at the Blarney Stone. I don't remember either one of them drinking. Oh, wait . . . Angie had a Coke with a cherry, maybe rum and Coke? I don't know. Angie's Randy's wife."

"Who else was with you?"

"Different people throughout the night. We didn't see Sean and Forrest till we arrived at their bar. The Blarney Stone was last."

"Were you with them all night?"

"I was late to the first place, Thai Me Up."

Cole nodded. The only Thai restaurant in Edwards Bay. "I know it."

"Then we went to Gianella's, but the bar was really

crowded, with customers waiting to be seated. So we walked across the street to The Whistle Stop and stayed there till the Blarney Stone."

The Whistle Stop was close to the water and practically on the train tracks for the commuter train into Seattle. Gianella's was an Italian restaurant with great food and a snootier attitude than most of the places apart from the one at the Bristol Hotel. Cole could see why they hadn't stayed in Gianella's quiet bar long.

"But Diana mostly drinks," said Kerry, continuing. "Nick was just a social drinker and he didn't do drugs. Ever."

Cole looked at her. "You sure?"

"Yes, I'm sure. Why? What are you saying?" She sat up straighter.

"Nothing. But he's been gone awhile from Edwards Bay. So have you."

"And?"

"People change."

"Not Nick . . . and not me."

Cole let that go and asked instead, "How close are you to him?"

"Close," she stated flatly.

"He's been down in Palo Alto and you said you just moved back. When's the last time you saw him?"

"Last night," she declared, clearly not liking the direction he was taking the conversation.

Cole nodded tolerantly. "And before that?"

"I've seen him a lot recently. He's been in Edwards Bay."

"Okay."

"You're trying to put this on Nick," she accused.

"No."

"Yes," she insisted.

"I'm trying to get a feel for Nick. I want to know what happened to him. I know you do, too."

That brought silence, then fresh tears filled her eyes. She blinked them away and crossed her arms. "Marcia came back here after the divorce, so Nick came back a lot because of Audra. I've seen him a lot . . . quite a bit. And I *know* him. This is just so wrong."

"Who's closest to him? Knows him the best?" Cole asked.

"Not Marcia," she said definitely, as if that were the question he'd asked.

"You?"

Kerry hesitated a moment. "Maybe in some ways."

"The business partner?"

"Maybe."

"Was he seeing anyone?"

"Romantically? Well, it wasn't Diana."

He could have pointed out that Nick had ended up in her bed, but he left it for the moment. She'd been there last night. She undoubtedly already knew. "They weren't an item, then."

"God, no. He hardly noticed her. He wasn't looking for that. He wanted companionship. He wanted me to be there, and no, it wasn't like that with me either," she said swiftly, reacting to something she'd expected to see in Cole's face or demeanor maybe. "Nick hung out with Taryn a lot, but she pushed that because Nick was cute and she gravitates to looks, even though she's all about #MeToo these days, if that makes any sense. She says she was abused when she was younger but that she trusted Nick, and maybe that's true, but she's . . . in to whatever's popular." She made a face. "Anyway, they weren't together like that. If Nick liked anyone it was Josie, but she's married, and maybe Miami, but she's with Killian and has been since grade school. But the bottom line is, Nick never changed. He was still a great guy. A smart guy. A really, really *good guy.* And it's unfair that he's gone, and he was with Diana, and if she did something, anything, that led to his death . . ." She left the threat unfinished, swallowing.

Cole said, "Would you like some water?"

"Do you need anything else from me?" Her voice wavered.

There were a lot of questions he still wanted to ask. About what the night before had been like from top to bottom. About Nick's state of mind. About his relationship with his family and friends.

But Kerry was running on empty and the answers weren't critical until he got the full autopsy report.

"No. Thanks. But I'd like to talk more later."

She nodded.

"Are you okay to drive?" he asked when she got up from the chair and seemed a bit unsteady.

"I'm fine. I live just down the hill. I'm at The Sand Drift. Jerry's motel. My stepfather."

"I know it."

"I'm the manager. I'm renovating it with Jerry. Nick was going to help, when he was in town, but . . ." She was lost for a moment, maybe overwhelmed by her loss, but before he could say anything she lifted a hand, as if to ward him off, then with a mumbled, "I think I need to go," she made her way past Charlie's desk and out of the station.

Jesus. Damn. Hell. Shit.

Kerry drove the few blocks to her cottage, silently swearing. Did Cole think it was her fault somehow that Nick was dead? The way he'd stared at her had made her want to scream her innocence . . . and then check her hair, her face, her whole self. It was hellish. Terrible. Unfair.

She didn't want him back. She hadn't wanted him back for years. He'd moved on and so had she. He'd said they weren't right for each other. He was correct.

Still . . . she'd expected . . . something. But there wasn't a word about their relationship, not a syllable. Not that she would want that. Good God, no. But she'd expected something. A trick of the eye, the lips, some miniature signal that they'd been something to each other once.

But nothing.

And Cole Sheffield didn't matter anyway. Only Nick . . .

Her cell phone rang as she was pulling into the lot behind the cottages. She'd turned on the ringer as soon as she'd left the police station and now was sorry she had. She paid no attention to it as she walked through the cool June day, a strong breeze blowing off the water and sending its muddy, briny scent wafting up the hillside. She felt incredibly weary and didn't want to talk to anyone.

Her cell stopped ringing, then immediately started up again. Sighing, she pulled out the phone to look at it as she reached her back door. Hers was the only cottage that had both a front and back door. The rest of them just faced the front, and unless the occupants parked on the street, they had to circumvent the building to get to their door.

She looked down at the cell's screen. Josie Roker. She almost answered but stopped herself. She didn't think she could handle anyone else's emotions right now, and Josie was the kind who wanted to bond together, probably cry together, talk over every aspect of everything, given the chance. Kerry hesitated. Did she want that? A part of her yearned to be with people who cared about Nick. The ringing was about to end when she pushed the button. "Hey, Josie. You there?"

"Yes, yes. You know it's me?"

"I inputted your number last night, remember?"

"Oh . . . oh, yeah . . . oh, Kerry . . . Are you okay? I'm not okay. I'm so, so sorry about Nick." Her words were quick and squeezed, as if they'd barely made it through her throat.

"Me too. It's terrible." Her words were quick and short. If she had to say more, she'd break down.

"It is. Terrible. Really terrible. Everyone's upset. Miami called this morning and I talked to her, and then I called everybody and . . ."

Kerry zoned out as she unlocked the back door. She actually dropped the arm that held the cell as she pushed open the door and let herself inside. Her head ached and she wanted to sleep for a year.

When she lifted the phone to her ear again, there was silence. "Josie?"

"Oh, I thought you hung up on me."

"No. I'm just . . . trying to get through the day."

"Did you hear what I said about the Blarney Stone?"

"Uh . . ."

"We're meeting there tonight. Around six. We want you to come."

"We?"

"The gang . . . the usual suspects . . . most of us from last night."

"Thanks, Josie, but—"

"Please, Kerry. Please. Come on. You're our sanity in this insaneness."

"I barely know you," she blurted out, too raw to say anything but the unvarnished truth.

"But you knew Nick. We all loved him." Her voice was thick with unshed tears. "We need you."

"Will Diana be there?"

"God, no. I hope not. I didn't call her." Josie was hard.

Kerry didn't want to go. Really, really didn't want to go. But she thought of Nick, what he would have wanted, what he had wanted. He'd wanted family. And friends. He'd said as much last night. Had it really been less than twenty-four hours? Twelve hours? He'd been trying to tell her something, she realized belatedly. He'd felt guilty for . . . leaving? She'd had a few too many drinks herself to remember exactly what he'd been saying. Maybe someone else remembered.

"Come on, Kerry. Please."

"I'll try."

"Six o'clock. Come. Okay?"

"I'll try," she repeated, then hung up before Josie could pressure her further.

Chapter Five

The Blarney Stone was one third of an older brick building only three blocks off the waterfront. It was on the western end of Edwards Bay and had been faced with rough-cut basalt, its uneven, gray exterior and wrought-iron grilled windows giving the otherwise nondescript one-story building a faint old-world charm.

Forrest Borland, six-feet, twenty pounds overweight, his reddish-brown hair disappearing from the top of his head—to which he'd added a close-cut beard, kind of tit for tat—stomped up the back stairs through the exterior alcove and inside, past the storeroom door to his right, the kitchen entrance to his left, to the interior of the bar. There was an ornately designed walnut Irish bar running down the left side of the room, the barstools crowded by a smattering of scarred wooden chairs grouped on either side of several load-bearing posts. A dartboard was hung at one end of the room, a fireplace stood at the other. Sean had wanted to make the fireplace coal-burning instead of wood, in keeping with pubs he'd visited in Great Britain, but Forrest had put his thirteen-and-a-half-sized foot down. Authenticity wasn't important in his mind. Making a profit was, and most of the regulars who came into the bar wanted only a drink, some snacks off their bar food menu, and a hookup.

As he entered, Sean was standing behind the bar, still as a statue, staring toward the front windows with their wrought-iron, curlicuey design—again, Sean's idea—focused on something beyond, or possibly nothing at all.

Forrest seriously thought about giving his business partner a slap or two to wake him up. Sure, Nick Radnor's death was a shock and a tragedy, but they had a bar to run. And even before Diana caused Nick's overdose, Sean had been acting weird.

"What the fuck, buddy," Forrest greeted him. It was how he always greeted him.

Sean nodded back. He was an inch or two taller than Forrest and wasn't carrying the extra weight. He was also holding on to his hair, a dark brown mop that perpetually needed cutting. Half the time Forrest wanted to buy him out, the other half he wanted to get in deeper with him, knowing Sean was the reason women came in the door. He drew them in with a half smile and a distracted air, which was all bullshit. Forrest had to be more direct when it came to the female persuasion, which sometimes worked, oftentimes didn't. He'd apparently been a little too friendly a time or two, trying to get a woman's attention, and had been reviled and threatened with lawsuits. Why? He'd just been chatty. Maybe an unsolicited hug here and there. No harm, no foul. He thought everybody was *insane* with all their worry about what was okay and what wasn't in the meet-and-greet world. Luckily, lubed up with a little alcohol, most of the women could ease up on that shit.

Sean, however, didn't seem to have any of these problems. He was cool, man. Women went fucking crazy over that untouchable kind of stuff.

Forrest lightly rubbed his stomach, checking for fat. Maybe he should cut back on the french fries and burgers. Tonight the gang was coming by to have an impromptu goodbye to Nick Radnor. Josie and Miami would both be here, and Forrest still got a boner thinking about both of them. Taryn, not so much. Diana . . . well, he'd successfully hit that a time or two, so yeah, he'd do her again, but he didn't feel the same way about her.

Briefly he thought about Randy's wife, Angie. Cute enough, but a clinging bitch if there ever was one. Kerry, now . . . she had something, too. Same kind of cool, touch-me-not thing Sean had. She seemed single, but he didn't know that much about her. He made a mental note to check out what she was all about. Maybe she wasn't as touch-me-not as she appeared.

For some reason his mind wandered back to high school and another cool girl. Lisette Benetton. Beautiful. Great breasts and long legs. His dick stirred and he had to shake himself back to the present. Lisette wasn't with them anymore. Long gone. Turned to bones and ash by now. And even when alive she'd only been interested in Nick.

Nick . . .

Jesus, it was weird that he was gone. Really gone. Dead and gone. His ex-wife, Marcia, was a looker. Forrest let his mind travel around Marcia Radnor. Another one who'd only had eyes for Nick, but that relationship had ended in divorce, though it hadn't been her idea. She'd been in the bar a few times, and Forrest had talked to her some. She was the restless kind, always watching the door, maybe still looking for Nick.

Well, she was going to be waiting an eternity now. He'd joined the hereafter with his first girlfriend.

Maybe Marcia would need some consoling . . . maybe Kerry would, too. He wondered idly if she and Nick had ever gotten it on. Stepsiblings. Kerry was as hot as Josie, but then, neither of them stirred him up as much as Miami. Long dark, glossy hair and that smooth, tanned skin. She was probably part-Hispanic, something like that. Somebody had said Hawaiian. Maybe. She looked it. She came in occasionally and sat at the bar, talking to Sean about Killian, her longtime lover. Killian was crazy, so no one messed with Miami. She seemed to like talking to Sean. He was everybody's buddy. The bartender who listened, and dys-fuck-tional relationships were his specialty.

Sometimes, though, it seemed like Miami would look around and catch Forrest's eye with questions in hers. Maybe she was tired of the kind of bullshit Killian was always blabbing; maybe when she was under Killian she had dreams of other guys. Maybe she imagined Forrest above her, sliding in and out. He had a big dick and everyone knew it. Maybe she was just waiting for the chance to be with him, on the sly, behind Killian's back. Maybe he could get her on the bar's back porch, in the alcove, which wrapped around the side of the bar and was hidden from the store next door by a fence on their side, a hedge of arborvitae on theirs. The high school kids still tried to hang out there—he'd done it himself when he was a kid, long before he'd ever known he would buy this place—because it was perfect for some grab-and-go sex if you were willing to get some splinters in your bare ass as you were standing up, gripped onto some fair lass and running her up and down your flagpole.

His thoughts turned his semiflaccid dick into a woody of impressive magnitude, one that started to immediately fade away when he considered how long, how very, very long, it had been since that particular scenario had happened.

"You think we should really open today?" Sean asked.

"Shit yeah. What are you talking about?"

"I'm just not sure I'm ready for business."

"You want to delay, put a goddamn sign on the door that

says, 'Sorry, the management's not feeling up to opening today. Go to The Whistle Stop.'" Forrest purposely mentioned their biggest competitor on the bar scene. He fucking hated Billy J. Kramer, the owner.

"When Siobhan gets here, I might leave," Sean said. Siobhan was their best waitress and sometime relief bartender, the only one they currently had; they'd had serious turnover in the past few months. There was that bitch who slapped Forrest's hand off her arm when he'd tried to squeeze by her behind the bar. She now worked for Kramer at The Whistle Stop. Probably gave him good head, too. Forrest had caught her with a guy in the alcove doing just that.

"Don't think you can close tonight, pal. The gang's all coming here tonight," Forrest pointed out.

"They were here last night and look what happened."

"They were all over the place and ended up here. You wanna blame someone, blame Diana."

Sean shook his head. "We were all drinking, hanging out." He rarely seriously imbibed and had last night. Now he was trying to grow a conscience.

"We were working, and they stumbled around town and ended up here," Forrest reminded him. "We were their fucking last stop and they expect a fucking discount from us. Always."

"You didn't give it to them last night," said Sean.

"I didn't give it to Egan or Randy . . . or Killian."

Sean turned to lift an eyebrow at him, which Forrest did not approve of. So, okay, he tended to comp Killian. The man was a beast. He'd been a beast on the football team, he'd been a beast in school. Hell, his old man was a beast, probably the whole goddamn family. You didn't fuck with the Keenans.

"You gave it to Nick," said Sean.

"Nick's money, bro. You don't mess with money."

"Nick's dead," Sean said.

"Jesus Christ, man. Stop acting like you're going to throw yourself on his grave. You didn't like him. Just like you don't like Killian."

Now Sean turned to him, his mouth hard. It was the most emotion Forrest had seen from his old buddy in a long time, and it gave him a moment of pause. "I don't like the way Killian treats Mia," Sean snapped. "I liked Nick just fine."

Sean was the only one who wouldn't call Mia Miller "Miami." Forrest almost snickered. Maybe it was his way of "honoring" one of the hottest girls from high school, but Miami liked being called Miami, and that was a fact Sean didn't seem to get.

But as long as Sean brought the women in, fine. Forrest was willing to keep working with him. And he was a pretty decent manager, too, always on top of the ordering, which left Forrest to handle the finances and bottom line. They were a pretty decent team, all things considered. They weren't getting rich, but their heads were above water and the tourist season had just begun.

"Fine. Killian's an asshole. We agree on that," Forrest said with a shrug.

"Who are we comping tonight?" Sean gazed over at him, hard.

"Nobody. Well, the girls maybe. Not Diana, but then, Miami said she's not invited."

"You talked to Mia?"

"Yeah, bro. I talked to *Miami*. She was pretty broken up, too. Josie organized this thing, even invited Egan . . . and Killian, of course."

"Fine."

A couple came through the front door, looking around. The bar's afternoon crowd hadn't really gotten going yet;

there were only a few tables occupied by a few guys. No women. Things would pick up around four and go on till one o'clock. Their night manager was a guy who generally closed, although two nights a week it was either Forrest or Sean left to do the deed.

The man of the couple came up to the bar and ordered from Sean, who scribbled on a scratch pad and walked back to the saloon doors that led to the kitchen. Forrest moved behind the bar in case anyone else needed help, but the customers were satisfied for the moment. His gaze traveled to the big table on one side of the dartboard. That was where everyone had sat last night. Nick had been in the middle, with Taryn hovering possessively on his right. She'd been spending lots of time with him; in friendship, Josie had said, though she'd lifted her brows to Forrest with the unspoken message of *Oh, sure*, though Forrest knew Nick wasn't interested in her in that way. That was just Josie being possessive. She wanted Nick in her pants, that was clear.

Weird that Nick had ended up with Diana.

Forrest picked out a toothpick from the box on the counter and stuck it in his mouth, chewing on it. Better than smoking. Or drinking.

Nick Radnor was dead. Hard to believe.

Mr. Success. Lots of money, lots of accolades. In Forrest's mind, Nick had just gotten lucky. Hooking up with some guys in Silicon Valley, starting their own company, making bank hand over fist. He'd heard Nick's partner was the main man, the driving force. Everyone said so. Nick was just the hitchhiker, but right place, right time . . .

Nick Radnor hadn't been that great a guy.

Forrest felt bad that he'd died, him being a classmate and all, but he wasn't all that devastated about the loss, not the way the girls were. Not the way Sean seemed to be. The truth was, Nick's death didn't really affect Forrest one way or another. One less guy he needed to comp.

Bad things happened. That was a fact.

Kerry swam up from a dark and nightmare-plagued sleep.

Bang, bang, bang!

Someone was pounding on her front door. Once again she looked at the clock, unsure what time it was. Three p.m. She'd forced herself to eat half an apple, stripped off her clothes, and taken to bed after turning off her phone. Remembering she'd tossed the cell on the bed, she reached for it blindly, still shaking off the dregs of a dream that seemed to have been her walking down a corridor with a lot of doors, hands reaching for her from behind those doors.

Bang, bang, bang!

Jesus. She scrambled from her bed, threw on a cream, quilted robe, cinched it at the waist, and walked with trepidation to the front door.

"Kerry? You in there?"

It was Randy Starr, her boss.

Immediately she wanted to sag down and forget answering the door. She'd texted him she wouldn't be in, then had ignored his calls, along with a number of others. That had been a mistake. She should at least have texted them back to say she would call later or something.

"*Kerry?*" he shouted through the panels.

"I'm coming. I'm here. Wait." She slid back the chain and opened the door.

Randy was about five ten, stocky, with a thick neck and reddish skin, the result of spending most of his time outdoors. He'd inherited Starrwood Homes from his father and spent a lot of time on job sites, although Kerry had never seen him practice any skills other than directing his subs.

Randall Starr Sr., his father, had worked concrete in his day as he built his construction business, but Randy hadn't taken up the trade. Now every job at Starrwood Homes was handled by the subcontractors.

Randy let himself inside, running his hands through his hair, messing up the thinning strands in a way he never usually touched them. "You okay? I called you, but you didn't answer. Thought you were playing hooky at first." His smile was thin.

"No, sorry. Thought I texted you I wouldn't be in." She plucked up her phone from the counter.

"Doesn't matter. God, it's weird, right?"

"Written but not sent," she realized, looking down at her phone. She hadn't had the energy to even give him an excuse.

He waved that away. "Just can't believe Nick's really gone."

"Me neither." Kerry attempted a smile. Her stomach hurt, though she still didn't feel hunger.

"Killian called me. It made the news. 'Suspicious death.'"

"Is that what they're saying?"

"Yeah. Overdose."

"For sure?"

"I don't know. Probably."

"I mean, they couldn't possibly have done the autopsy yet."

"Maybe it's just conjecture, I don't know. But that's what it looks like."

Kerry nodded. "Where's Angie?" she asked after a moment. Randy's wife was never far behind her mate. She seemed to have a sixth sense when he was talking to other women.

"Holding down the fort, because you're not there."

Kerry had only been working a few months for the home office of Starrwood Homes in Edwards Bay. The small firm had spread to satellite offices in Seattle, Bellevue, and Olympia, with varying degrees of success as only the Seattle office was still open, but since Kerry had moved to Edwards Bay, its management was in a free fall that Randy seemed paralyzed to stop. Or maybe it was because his father had been against the expansion into other cities and had been somewhat gleefully "right" after recognizing the other offices had failed. Randall Sr. had always believed he knew best, according to Randy, who'd swallowed the bitter pill of failure with equanimity, although Kerry, who'd been called upon now and again by Randy to help out with his dad, who now lived in assisted living, suspected resentment burned deep in Randy's soul. Such were the duties of office manager at Starrwood Homes: keeping Randall Sr. and Randy in their own corners and happy enough with each other while making sure the business kept humming along.

"Do you need me to come in?" Kerry asked.

"Today?" He looked surprised. "Nah. Take tomorrow off, too. We'll muddle through."

Tomorrow was Saturday. They'd all met for drinks and dinner last night because Nick was due back in Palo Alto today.

"Who's cutting tile?" he asked against a sudden shriek of the saw.

"Jerry's doing renovations." Kerry didn't elaborate; it was a tender subject. Jerry hadn't employed Starrwood Homes, who specialized more in new construction rather than renovation.

"Is that Emilio out there?" he asked shortly.

They'd been standing at the door, and now Kerry moved the few steps it took to enter the kitchen, a small U-shape. There wasn't much in the way of décor; she'd always considered the cottage temporary. Her mind couldn't grasp that Jerry was bequeathing the place to her.

"It's Emilio," he answered himself. "He's supposed to be doing a job for us, but he put it off, obviously for this." He looked at Kerry as if she were a turncoat.

"I don't think this is the time to take it up with Jerry."

"Of course not. I'm just saying, schedules should be met."

There was a loaf of bread on the counter. She pulled out the toaster and added two slices. "You want some?" she asked.

"No, no. Go ahead. Are you going to Blarney Stone tonight?"

"I told Josie I'd try, but I don't know."

"Killian said Nick's friends are meeting there. I feel like I should go."

Randy's cell phone buzzed in his pocket. He pulled it out and read the incoming text. He made a sound of annoyance. "Angie. I'd better go."

Kerry buttered her toast, then took a bite as she walked to the door to draw the chain behind him. She then picked up her cell with her free hand and examined the list of missed calls and the smattering of texts that had come in. Nick's mother might be gone, but her own mother was alive and well and might have missed the news.

You should call her.

Kerry thought about Nick, whom her mother had pitted her against without maybe even knowing it. Whereas Kerry adored him, Karen had seen Nick as an adversary.

Kerry picked up the phone, figuring better to get it over with, and called her mother, who had always wanted to move to a sunny climate and had gotten her wish when she'd married her latest husband, a native of Phoenix.

* * *

"Isn't Kerry coming?" Miami asked Josie when they were seated at the only large, community table in Sean and Forrest's bar. Her long hair was loose and thick, dark brown, and she'd stuck a tropical flower, a hibiscus, behind one ear.

"I told her to." Josie had tried to ignore the pink flower but now pointed to it. "What's with that?"

Miami's hand fluttered upward and her lips quivered. "Nick always said I looked Hawaiian. I just saw a bouquet at Flowers by Nadine, and I went in and bought it."

A little flame of jealousy ignited in Josie's breast. She knew this was pure Miami, but it bugged her.

Nick wasn't yours, she reminded herself, which in turn reminded her of Diana's possessiveness of him the night before, which pissed her off. Her eyes slid toward Taryn, whose hair was chin-length and curly and mousy brown. Well, it was almost the same shade as Kerry's, really, but Kerry's was glossier, longer, and just better. Taryn could be a knockout if she knew the first thing about putting some money into her looks where it mattered, but the truth was, she always looked sort of half-assed. Like she'd gotten tired of taking care of herself partway through putting on her makeup, fixing her hair, getting dressed. She did have great tits, though, and they were real.

Josie did a quick rundown of her own appearance, glad for the skinny jeans and blue cotton shirt with the big pockets over her breasts, the thin gold hoops with their blue gems in just the right shade that peeked out from beneath her own light brown, blond-streaked hair. She'd kept the makeup down, as she always did, fostering the "natural" look she tried so hard to achieve. That was her cornerstone. Josie Kenney Roker, the fresh-faced, natural beauty girl next door. It sure had snagged her Kent and she'd gone with him eagerly enough, though, yes, now she felt a whole lot different.

She glanced back at Miami. She *did* look Hawaiian. In fact, that long, dark, shining hair could be in a commercial for some shampoo made with coconut oil and the scents of mango and hibiscus. Except her parents had been born and raised in Washington State just like the rest of them, and they currently lived in a rented house across the sound in Kingston.

Taryn turned her gray eyes Josie's way. "If Diana shows up, I'm not responsible for my actions."

"I'm there with you, girl." Josie forced herself to sound friendly, even though Taryn annoyed her because she'd had Nick's ear the past six months, ever since Christmas. Nick had apparently decided it was time to get out of Palo Alto and return to Edwards Bay and had been in the process of looking for a house. Taryn had taken it upon herself to be his personal real estate agent, even though her real job was in private practice as a nutrition adviser, though Killian had indicated she'd lost most of her clients some time ago for accusing every male coworker of sexual misconduct. Well, maybe *every* male coworker was a stretch, but it sure seemed like she went out of her way to antagonize people, men and women. Josie didn't want to minimize anyone's experience, but she had a niggling suspicion Taryn embellished her trauma, latching onto #MeToo like some kind of badge of honor, which really pissed Josie off. Sexual abuse wasn't an issue to be crying wolf over.

And then Diana . . .

Josie was sure as hell glad she wasn't going to be here tonight. Diana was voluptuous and . . . just really ripe . . . and guys went for that, but she was sloppy, too. And a drunk. And a drug user, apparently, to get Nick involved. Josie could just kill her for taking him from them.

She had to take in a couple of long, careful breaths, remembering that Nick was dead, exhaling slowly. It was too unreal. She half-believed it was a lie, that Nick would push through the door to the bar any second.

She blinked, willing it to happen. Her breath caught when the door opened, but it was just Sean Blevins, coming back inside the bar. He wore dark jeans and a black hoodie and his hair was slightly mussed, adding a boyish twist to his otherwise grim appearance. Sean was good-looking, but he'd never done it for Josie, though he did share that aloofness Nick had. She remembered fantasizing about Nick in high school. She'd wanted him, but he'd been with Lisette . . . so she'd settled. . . .

As Sean came back their way, Josie's thoughts flashed to her husband. She'd escaped to Kent. He'd made her feel special for a time, and she'd needed to feel special. But now, in truth, she'd be far less anguished if it was Kent's body laid out on that slab instead of Nick's.

Your marriage died a long time ago. You need to get through the death throes.

Or was it *throes*? She needed to look that one up. Seemed like it should be throws because she wanted to throw the remains of her marriage away, but she was pretty sure that was wrong.

"If Diana shows up, none of us are responsible for our actions," Killian drawled.

Josie squinted an eye at their "fearless leader." He was seated near Miami, but not really sitting by her. Kind of behind her. Miami didn't seem to notice he was alive, which was a lie. It was difficult to tell whether they loved or hated each other. A thin line.

"Where's Kent tonight?" Killian asked Josie with a slight smile.

She shrugged. He knew too much about her relationship

with her husband, which also pissed her off, and he loved, loved, loved to twist the knife, just a little, then follow up his meanness with "you know I'm just kidding," which, in fact, she knew he wasn't. He was tall, dark, and handsome, just a hint of gray at his temples, with a hard, lean build, although she thought he might run to fat if he didn't keep up his obsessive workouts. She'd had a high school crush on him—a small one, but that had died long ago. Not like her feelings for Nick, which had only improved with age.

The door opened and Josie braced herself again, half-expecting Diana, but instead it was Egan Fogherty. She let out the breath she'd held in a kind of disgusted sigh. Egan was the hanger-on of their group, the guy everyone just tolerated. He wore jeans, a long army green jacket, and a black T-shirt and a baseball cap that said "Boaters Are Better." He was a ferry boat captain, or an assistant—lieutenant maybe? Josie didn't quite know, and how he'd gotten the job here in town was anyone's guess. Seemed like it might be a plum assignment, but then, what did she know? She'd asked him once about it, but Egan was squirrelly and weird and stood too close, undressing her with his eyes. Miami thought he was flat-out creepy. Josie agreed. Surprisingly, Taryn put up with him.

"He just needs medication," she'd said.

"Don't we all?" Killian had drawled.

"No, I'm serious. He just hasn't figured it out yet."

Killian smiled that rare killer smile. "How? I've told him enough times."

"He's bipolar, if you ask me." Taryn was positive. She was always positive. "I've talked to him about it, but he's not there yet."

"Taryn Whitcomb always knows best." Killian's smile widened, but there was no humor in it.

Josie ran that little scene through her head as Egan

approached. She hoped he wouldn't sit by her, but sure enough, he squeezed in a chair, breathing heavily, smelling of peppermint. He was always popping Altoids. Maybe to cover up any scent of booze? She'd never known him to drink too much, but maybe she wasn't paying close enough attention.

"Is Kerry coming?" Egan asked her.

Well, good. He'd apparently put Kerry, not her, at the top of his stalker list tonight. Praise be for small favors. "I told her to," Josie said, repeating what she'd told Miami as she leaned as far away from him as she could. Maybe she'd made a mistake, organizing this event. Last night had been bad enough, especially with Egan. He'd tried to grab all the attention for himself, though everyone ignored him because he was such an ass. All eyes had been on Nick, seeking out a crumb of his approval. That damn Taryn. She'd hovered close and eyed the rest of them like she would battle them one by one if they tried to get too close.

And Diana . . . taking Nick home with her? Josie tried to remember how that had happened and couldn't. Maybe she would ask Taryn about it, but right now Taryn was sitting across from her, white-faced, crushed, and miserable, the effects of Nick's death very evident on her face. She'd gained a higher level of popularity as Nick's confidante, and now she was back in the pits, though she was clearly hurting.

"Is this a wake?" Miami asked.

"No, babe," Killian said with extreme patience. "We're just Nick's closest friends getting together."

Sean was perched on a chair at the end of the table, his eyes looking around the bar even while he joined them. "They'll have a memorial service, I'd bet."

The door opened, and Josie looked over to see Randy

Starr and his unlikable wife, Angie, enter. Angie was clamped onto his arm as if expecting him to run off.

I would if I had to be married to that.

Sean got up and Randy took his seat, forcing Angie to grab a chair from a nearby table and try to squeeze it between Randy and Miami. Forrest moseyed over, turned a chair around and straddled it backward, clearly not as worried about running the bar as his partner.

There followed a discussion of the events of the night before, a recap of where they'd all gone, who'd been at which bar. No one could quite remember who'd been with whom by the end of the night, so they all gave their account. Miami and Killian had left after the last stop at the Blarney Stone, each to their own car. Taryn had reluctantly split from Nick as soon as they got there because she'd had an early appointment. Egan hadn't even made it to Blarney Stone, peeling off at The Whistle Stop, the bar before, saying he'd just needed to turn in early. Randy and Angie had left about the same time he did, while Diana had hung on to Nick till the bitter end, following him to the Blarney Stone. Sean and Forrest were at the Blarney Stone when the rest of them arrived. Josie left about the same time as Kerry. They'd walked out together, and Kerry had driven Josie home. They'd been talking a little about Nick. Josie had wanted to pry anything she could get from his stepsister, but Kerry said she hadn't really talked to him that much since he'd returned and Kerry had moved to Edwards Bay.

It had made Josie wonder, momentarily, if Kerry might be moving in on Nick, but she'd shaken herself out of it. No. Then she'd gone on to make all kinds of plans to see Nick again in her head.

That memory was sharp enough to slice. Josie's chest hurt. There would be no seeing Nick again.

Everyone suddenly turned to look at her, and she realized

the cry building inside her must have broken through. She scolded herself not to break down. Sternly reprimanded herself, while her nose burned and her eyes watered. Where was Kerry? It looked like she wasn't going to show, which burned Josie. She wanted to be friends with her, her last link to Nick. She could really use a friend and Kerry was the best choice. Miami was too remote . . . and Taryn was too opinionated and easily bruised, and Diana was a wreck. And forget Randy's wife, Angie, who was no one any of them wanted to befriend. Ditto Nick's ex, Marcia, who luckily was as disinterested in Nick's high school friends as they were in her, although she'd popped in at their first stop, Thai Me Up, where they'd had dinner, to have a few tense words with Nick. That had been a bust, too; Miami had barely touched any food, and the others had gone cheap, worrying about the bill. Josie was pretty sure Miami was dieting, hanging on to her killer bod. It had made her think she might need another purge; it was getting harder for her, too.

Now, Josie could see Miami was looking down, blinking back a few silent tears, while Killian stared at the back of her head.

Unable to stand it any longer, Josie suddenly demanded, "What the hell are we doing here?" All conversation ceased. All eyes turned to her.

"Honoring Nick?" Taryn said, slightly accusingly.

"You're the one who spearheaded this thing," Randy reminded her.

"Yeah, you were the one who called the A-Team together," Killian reminded her, always the one to point fingers.

"It just feels wrong, that's all. Like playacting," said Josie.

"That's not true," said Miami.

"Poor Josie. Won't be able to get Nick in bed anymore." Killian's teeth gleamed.

"Stop it." Miami's mouth quivered.

Josie glared ice at Killian. He'd always been a bully. She wanted to give him a piece of her mind, but it never paid to get on Killian's bad side, so she forced herself to settle for a tight smile and turned away from his evil grin.

Forget everything else, she thought, anger stabbing through her grief. *It might be Diana's fault, but it should have been Killian who died last night.*

Chapter Six

Doctor: *Tell me about Nick.*

Patient: *What do you want to know?*

Doctor: *Anything you want to tell me. You were friends.*

Patient: *Well . . . yes.*

Doctor: *Was there a problem? Something that precipitated his death? An incident or event that . . . threatened you?*

Patient: *There you go again, Brain Digger.*

Doctor: *What did you mean by "The devil always gets his due"?*

Patient: *Pretty self-explanatory, isn't it? What goes around comes around. As ye reap, so shall ye sow, you gotta pay the piper . . . etcetera, etcetera, etcetera.*

Doctor: *What does it have to do with Nick Radnor?*

Patient: *Maybe nothing. Maybe something.*

Doctor: *You were responsible for his death.*

Patient: *Oh, come on. Nick did it to himself.*

Doctor: *That's not what you said.*

Patient: *That's exactly what I said. Nick wanted to be the good guy, right to the end, but it was a lie. He set this up. The tumblers were falling into place. No one had to push him. He chose a path and it ended in his death.*

Doctor: *That's not entirely true.*

Patient: *You're going to say that I helped him, but we all did. You can't pin this just on me.*

Doctor: *Are you recanting your confession?*

Patient: *Man, you don't listen. I never said this was my fault. It's Nick's and Nick's alone. You want to know how Nick died? He killed himself. That's what he did. He killed himself.*

Doctor: *With your help.*

Patient: *With a little help from his friends. And Doc, we're all sorry he's gone. All of us. But Nick was not a good guy.*

Seven days after Nick's death.

Diana wrote the words on the calendar she had thumb-tacked to the wall next to her stove. She hadn't used the calendar much. Scribbled down a few important dates. It was a gift from her mom, with rural pictures of covered bridges. June's bridge was of weathered gray boards with a thatch roof over a rickety span that looked like it wouldn't bear the weight of a smart car. She'd barely looked at it till last week. Now she'd marked each square since Nick's death with a number, denoting the time since she'd discovered Nick Radnor in her bed.

Dropping the pen onto the counter, Diana rambled around her apartment in her bathrobe, sick at heart, sick to her stomach, sick. She'd tried calling Taryn, and Josie, even Miami multiple times, but their cell phones had gone silent. None of them were available, probably never would be again. She'd resorted to the guys, starting with Egan first because even though he was odd, he'd always been decent to her. She'd even made the mistake of sleeping with him once when they were both really high, which she could barely remember, though he'd acted like they were in some kind of relationship afterward, and she'd had to ease out of that one. No easy task. She'd found herself sleeping with him again, just kind of to keep things okay between them. That time he'd been the one to say it had to be the last time; he just wanted to be friends. Little shit wanted control, apparently. Fine. *Go ahead*, she'd thought. *Whatever lets you sleep at night.*

Egan had answered his phone, but he'd said what she'd suspected, chilling her to the bone. "No one wants to talk to you. In fact, they'd be happy if you didn't come to the memorial service. They think you killed him."

"I didn't!" she gasped. "I didn't!"

"Well . . ." And he'd hung up.

She'd gingerly tried to call Randy after that, and when Angie barred the way, she'd phoned Sean, who hadn't answered. She hadn't bothered with Forrest or Killian. There was only so much abuse one person could take.

She'd finally gotten up the courage to call Kerry, who had answered, even if she sounded like she was reluctant to talk. Or maybe she was just sad. Kerry said she and Nick's father had set up the memorial service for this coming Friday. Diana had tried to get together with her before the service, but Kerry had demurred. She'd understood then that Egan was right: everyone blamed her.

Not wanting to break the fragile connection she had with Nick's sister, she'd thanked Kerry, hung up, and then returned to her bed, weeping hot tears into her pillow.

After long days of barely getting out of bed, she'd roused herself enough for a trip to the store for some vodka. She'd been aware how Mel, who ran the place at the corner and knew her, had been alarmed by her blotchy face. She'd almost screamed at him, *I didn't kill him!* but had left silently with the bottle in a brown paper bag, her head low.

So now she was sipping vodka on the rocks, the end of the bottle and feeling a little better. She'd sworn off alcohol and pills after Nick's death and managed to abstain until today. She'd been nearly insane with grief and worry when she'd been hauled down to the police station and thrown in that holding cell. She'd hardly eaten anything all week. Just crackers. Tea. Some stale peanuts shoved to the back of a shelf. She was actually finishing that jar now, with her vodka.

As she sipped, she felt herself relax a bit, nourished by the warmth flooding her veins. This was better. Much better. She should never have tried to give up everything cold turkey. It hadn't done her one bit of good.

She let her mind travel back to that last night with Nick, a worn groove that left her miserable and scared. But she'd started recalling little moments, however hazy: her fingers on his hand, the way he turned and smiled at her, the icy glare from Josie, the look of amusement from Killian.

She'd been so excited that Nick was showing her attention, excited enough to ignore the stares and disapproval from the others. She could remember thinking things were going remarkably well. . . .

But something was wrong with that picture.

The whole view of that evening kind of slipped away. Blurred. Only seen when droplets of memory ran down the fogged screen and allowed her a glimpse of truth. But . . . she had some pieces, little shards of recall that cut through here and there, and what they told her was, there had been someone in the background that night. Someone who'd helped Nick and her back to her apartment. That wasn't just wishful thinking on her part. She could almost *feel* that someone had been there. A ghost.

They had been taking pills . . . she'd lied about that to the cops . . . kind of forgotten it actually. But Nick had been sort of down, she'd thought, earlier in the evening, and she'd suggested something to take the edge off. She didn't remember them at her apartment, but she had a mental snapshot of Nick in her kitchen and the bottle of OxyContin on the counter. Her secret, emergency stash. She'd told him about it.

I know everyone thinks I do drugs all the time, but I don't. Too hard to get the stuff. Too expensive. Just once in a while.

That's what she'd told him, wasn't it? Something like that. And it was mostly true. She didn't really buy for herself, but if she was with people and they were handing them out, or someone at a party wasn't tending their pills maybe as diligently as they should . . .

Of course, that bottle was missing, and Diana was damned sure she hadn't thrown it away or misplaced it.

Maybe the police had it.

The vodka kept on doing its trick and Diana let her tensions melt away. She'd taken off the week from the candy store—her aunt's business—where she was the manager. Her aunt had been calling every day. Aunt Eileen tried to be nice, but she was desperate. It was summer and she needed help, and Diana was her mainstay. Hah. Aunt Eileen was in serious trouble if she was counting on her. Diana never wanted to go back.

She took another sip, tried to push her memory of Nick being in her apartment, struggled to recall some details. The whole thing felt kind of fake. Like a false memory. But there was something there. He'd certainly been in her bed. She could almost remember kissing him . . . him kissing her . . .

She strained, but the memory danced away. She sighed. She'd been here before. Forgetting whole blocks of time to have a sudden memory bloom into consciousness in full color. Good and bad. Like her astride Egan in his pickup truck, the damn gearshift knob digging into her ass, his hands on her hips, hers around his throat . . . and him moaning and groaning while she squeezed. . . .

She shook herself back to the present, enjoying the feeling of things getting a little softer, warmer.

She had a bright, sudden memory of Nick's blue eyes staring into hers. Her heart galumphed. She'd kissed him. Leaned right in and laid one on his lips. She could almost feel it.

Lightly, she ran her index finger over her lips, remembering.

The image faded . . . maybe it was a lie. A wish. Or maybe it was the truth.

And there was the feeling of that other presence hovering around.

She tipped back her glass. The ice had barely melted, but the vodka was gone. She refilled her drink and sat in the chair by her back window. Her view wasn't much. An empty field with some trash, and then the back fences of several houses.

Eventually she would remember everything, she was convinced of it. Eventually she would know what happened that night, enough to put the pieces together. To date there had been no announcement about what had killed him. The police were apparently still working on that, or they just weren't telling yet. But if it came down to a drug overdose, she wasn't going to take the blame. Nick had looked at that bottle of pills. She hadn't shoved them down his throat. Maybe it wasn't even drugs that killed him, she thought hopefully, though that was a burst of enthusiasm that quickly died.

But she was determined to prove Nick's death wasn't her fault.

Something tugged at her consciousness and she tore her gaze from the window to look around the room and through the hallway. Had someone been in her little utility room off the kitchen? A figure? Was that just her imagination?

No . . . it was real. A person. An uninvited guest, spying on her and Nick.

But who?

Diana struggled to remember as she drained her second glass. Oh! she thought suddenly. She would go see Nina, the hypnotist! She'd never used her. She was more of an acquaintance than a friend, but she could help! With Nina's help, she would remember. She would. And when she did she was going to call Kerry.

Thursday morning Kerry awoke able to get out of bed without wallowing in pure grief. The hurt was there, a rock inside her chest, but she sensed she was going to be able to join the living again, something that had been in serious doubt. Over the last few days she'd managed to help make the arrangements for Nick's memorial service, though the real work had been done by Marcia, who'd appointed herself to spearhead the event. With the help of Nick's high school friends as well, Marcia had secured The Pier for the venue, the hotel where she worked across the sound from Edwards Bay in Kingston near the ferry terminal, a place Nick had liked while growing up.

Kerry had also learned that her mother and Terrence were in Athens on a tour, so there was no worry that Karen would jump on a plane back to Seattle to meet her daughter in Edwards Bay and muscle in on the arrangements, though it wasn't beyond her to change her mind and arrive at any moment, such was her mother's way. It would be best for Jerry if Karen stayed in Europe through the memorial service, though saying as much would probably only ensure she would return to cause havoc, so Kerry had kept her mouth firmly shut.

Kerry had blown off the previous Friday's get-together with Nick's classmates. Josie had called on Saturday, telling her she hadn't missed anything, waving off Kerry's apology. "It wasn't all that much," she'd said, which was big, considering she'd been the one who'd seemed to be in charge of getting the friends together. She went on to say that Kerry was the one who'd been missed, by her, which was nice to hear. Josie was really making an effort at friendship. Kerry just wasn't sure if there was an agenda at work that she couldn't see yet, or if Josie was sincere.

Picking up her cell phone, Kerry texted Randy, saying she would be coming to work today. He'd been more than understanding when she'd called to ask for some extra time off. Luckily, she hadn't gotten Angie on the phone, who was never as obliging as her husband.

She took a shower, dressed in gray slacks and a black top, clipped her hair into a ponytail at her nape, ate a plain yogurt with raspberries and strawberries she'd added on top, and was just slipping on a pair of black flats when she heard Jerry's rattletrap truck pull into the parking lot behind her cottage. She peered through the blinds on the back door's window and watched as he took one of the empty slots between her door and the tiler's vehicle. The wet saw was already shrieking away as Jerry slammed out of his truck and hobbled her way. She didn't remember him having such difficulty walking before. When he came up the two steps, Kerry opened the door for him, though they could do little more than nod at each other over the noise until she'd shut the door behind him.

Two days earlier Jerry had asked her to meet him at The Bank of Edwards Bay, where he'd added her name to his checking accounts. She'd balked at first, but he'd insisted, saying, "Nick's gone. I need someone on my accounts with me. This way you'll be able to move money to pay for the remodel."

But now, as she watched him approach, it wasn't just the

change in his gait. He'd aged mightily since Nick's death. She'd noticed it when they were at the morgue together and at the bank, but if anything, his physical appearance had deteriorated since then. He coughed several times after greeting her with a hug and accepting a cup of black coffee.

"Got any cream?" he asked.

"Sure."

Kerry poured a dollop into his cup and replenished her own, adding cream to it as well. She watched the clouds form inside the dark liquid and decided she would be a little late today as well. Randy would understand. He wasn't the strictest of bosses at the best of times, and these were not the best of times.

"Just wanted to stop by to see how you were," said Jerry.

"Doing better, sort of. How're you?"

He wagged his head slowly from side to side. He gestured to her clothes. "You going to work?"

"Yeah."

"Good. I also came by to see how the work was progressing around here. Tired of sitting around and thinking too much."

They both listened to the screech of the tiler's wet saw in the silence that followed. She thought about talking to Jerry about his will again. Explain that she was uncomfortable with it. But she let the silence stand, unable to know quite how to approach it. The space between them was filled with the enormity of Nick's death; everything else felt superfluous.

"The autopsy results should be ready today," Jerry finally said.

The autopsy had been done earlier in the week, but there'd been no word about it from Cole or the police department as yet. The general feeling was that Nick had died of an overdose, and that, despite no history of drug abuse, he'd chosen to go with Diana and take a deep dive into oblivion, too deep a dive. Everyone wanted to blame Diana, herself included, but it didn't seem plausible that she could force him into something he didn't want to do.

"Cole said he'd call when the results came in. I'm sure he'll call you first."

"I'd rather just talk to you."

"It's better to hear it from the horse's mouth."

He made a face but said, "Okay."

The thought of talking to Cole made Kerry feel weary. Everything felt surreal, and he was just an added piece she didn't need.

Jerry's hand started shaking so badly, he sloshed hot coffee onto it. The burn caused him to gasp and he lost control of the cup, which crashed to the floor and broke.

"You okay?" Kerry asked anxiously.

"Shit," he said at the same time.

She quickly set her own cup on the counter and took a step toward him, but he waved her violently away. "I'm fine. Let me clean up. It's hell getting old."

"I've got it."

She grabbed several paper towels from the spool hung beneath her counter and bent down to the spreading brown coffee and broken shards. Jerry stumbled a bit, and she said, "Please, sit down. Jerry. Please."

He staggered to one of her kitchen chairs and sank into it, head in his hands. "I'm sorry, Kerry."

"I've already got it mostly cleaned up."

"I'm complaining about old age and Nick'll never get older," he choked out.

She gathered up the broken cup, feeling a pang when she realized it was one she'd purchased in San Francisco when she was on a rare visit to see Nick, then dumped the lot into the trash, mopping up the rest of the spill with paper towels. There might be a few shards left for the broom, but she would wait for that till after Jerry left.

"Sorry about my language," he said, ever the gentleman.

She had to think back to what he'd said. Hell. She snorted. "You should hear what comes out of my mouth when I get going."

He rubbed a hand over his chest, and Kerry regarded him with concern.

"Maybe you should go to the doctor, just have yourself checked out."

"He'll tell me I have heart disease and I need to take it easy." It was Jerry's turn to snort. "My son just died. I'll take it easy when I meet him in heaven. Oh, don't bother," he added, seeing she was about to pour him a new cup. "I'm not going to stay long. I didn't even want coffee. Just accepted it to be polite."

"You sure?"

He nodded, letting his eyes close. His face was lined with pain. She could feel her anxiety ratchet up. Jerry looked as if he could collapse into a heap at the least provocation.

"I was kind of hoping to walk the property with you. Wanted to check out the motel, the improvements. Share it with you." His voice quavered and he held up his hand to stop Kerry from interjecting. "I'm not up to it. You can see that."

"Maybe after the memorial service. Next week," she said.

"After we meet Nick's lawyer."

"Right." The lawyer for Nick's estate had called them both, and Marcia, and asked for a meeting. It was scheduled for the following Monday.

Jerry shook his head and his watery blue eyes met hers. "What are we going to do, Kerry?"

She took his hands in hers. "We're going to get through this. It'll slowly get better."

He eyed her ironically. "You really think so?"

"Yes. Because this is too hard."

He held on to her hands as he got back to his feet, then he pulled her into a hug. "I'll see you tomorrow," he said as he headed back out.

Twenty minutes later, at her desk at Starrwood Homes, Kerry got a call on her cell phone from a number with a local area code she didn't recognize.

"Hello," she answered.

"Hi, Kerry, it's Cole" came the familiar voice, shooting a thrill through her veins.

"Oh. Hi."

"I called Jerry, but he's not answering his phone. I wanted to go over the autopsy results."

"I just saw him. His phone may be off; he's kind of sketchy about keeping it on all the time."

"I'd like to meet both of you to go over it," he said.

"He asked me to get the information from you and tell him about it later. I told him it was better straight from the horse's mouth."

"I agree," said Cole. A pause. "Any way we can all meet sometime today or tomorrow?"

He sounded so serious. Something was up. Maybe something she didn't want to know, she thought with dread. "I'll pick him up and we'll come down to the station in a few. If Jerry can't make it, I'll let you know." Angie walked by Kerry's desk at that moment, her steps slowing as she unabashedly eavesdropped.

"Call me on my cell," Cole said and gave her the number.

Angie gave her a hard look as Kerry reached for her purse. "You barely got here and you're leaving?"

"I'm picking up Jerry and going to the police station to discuss the autopsy results."

She looked somewhat taken aback by that news.

"I should be back fairly soon," Kerry told her and pushed past her, feeling a certain amount of satisfaction at her discomfiture.

"There's someone who wants to see you in the breakfast room," Toni told Miami as soon as she walked up to the reception desk of The Pier, ready to lock her purse in one of the small office lockers allowed for the staff.

Miami had worked at the waterfront hotel for about a year, and that was how she'd wrangled the use of one of the rooms for Nick's memorial service. Management had wanted to charge an arm and a leg, but she'd negotiated an employee discount, and if they weren't happy about it, too bad.

"Who?" Miami asked as she clipped on her name tag, which simply read "Mia." The powers that be wouldn't let her put Miami on her tag—too familiar, too confusing— which made no sense, but she'd gone with her real name rather than fight it.

"I don't know. Some older guy." Toni was about forty-five, with a boyish figure from all the massive running she did, half marathons and marathons, and she seemed to have zero interest in anything outside her next running event. Miami found it both refreshing and somewhat frightening. That kind of dedication to anything was outside her world.

Miami drew a breath, worrying who might be waiting for her. She also had a job in the hotel's bar, and on occasion she was routed to the spa, where she worked the reception desk there as well and kept the massage rooms supplied with oils and towels and any other paraphernalia the customers might want. She'd been propositioned a time or two by male customers, and once by a woman, who'd seemed to believe she might be ready for something a little different. At first she'd wondered if she had a reputation she didn't know anything about, though Killian had assured her he was the "soul of discretion" when it came to all things Miami.

"All parts of you are mine now," he'd said on that long-ago occasion when she'd been shocked to learn the truth about what he thought of her, what they all thought of her. But Killian had said he would protect her, and he had ever since. When he made love to her now, it was without some of the possessive power he'd shown when he would place her on the bed, on her back, spread her legs, and lower himself over her, making sure both of them could see his dick sliding around on her before he pushed inside, working her open before slamming into her over and over again in a way that would do the trick, making her arch and scream and rake her nails down his back.

Long, long ago . . .

It embarrassed her now. He'd called her a wildcat at the time, and she'd reveled in it. She'd teased him and made love to him, and sometimes pretended to break up with him, a game he'd enjoyed because the leash was always pretty tight, though sometimes he seemed deep down angry, and she had to work extra hard to remind him they were just playing. Occasionally, he wanted her to play up to other guys, make it seem she was available, only to shut them down. He told her it gave him a hard-on to watch her flirt with other men, and she did it for him, trying to enjoy the game as much as he did. Afterward he would "make love" to her in ways she really didn't appreciate but he did. She put up with it because mostly it was good with him and he was her man. He loved her and she loved him. She never questioned that. It was just the way it was, and also maybe what she deserved. Those high school days might be far behind, but they were fresh in her mind.

Except now . . . she wasn't quite so sure she and Killian

were good for each other anymore. Something had subtly shifted between them.

Miami turned toward the breakfast room with trepidation. The Pier offered complimentary meals with certain plans, and the breakfast room doubled as an early morning and lunchtime café, along with afternoon cookies and coffee and soft drinks.

"I won't leave till you get back," Toni promised, and they both glanced at the clock. Toni was due for her early morning break, but she wasn't a stickler about it. Miami nodded to her and headed from reception to the breakfast room. She could look right across it and through the windows on the far side to see the bay beyond. It was a half-hour ferry ride to get to work from Edwards Bay to Kingston every day, sometimes an annoyance but oftentimes a joy in which Miami could just sit back and commune with her thoughts, thoughts that had been in turmoil the last few months. She seriously needed to make a change and that terrified her.

Glancing around the room, her gaze landed on a familiar face. Her heart clutched. Oh. No.

"Mr. Keenan?" she greeted Killian's father as she walked toward him, her steps ever slowing the nearer she became. In gray slacks and a white shirt, his silver hair groomed and cut short, his tanned skin evidence of a lot of time on a golf course, Carroll Keenan was the epitome of the successful businessman.

"Now, you know it's Carroll, Mia mi," he greeted her as he always did, standing up to give her a hug. She just let it happen, trying to force herself to put her arms back around him, unable to do so.

He let her go and held out a chair for her at the two-person table.

He always pronounced her name as if it were two words, Mia and me. He also told her to think of him as her own father, which was impossible. Miami still lived with her parents or, more accurately, had moved back with them after some personal issues that were still being resolved.

And there was no way she could ever think of Carroll Keenan in the same way she did her own father, Michael Miller.

She sat down gingerly, aware that others were looking at her. She wanted to cover her name pin with her hand but refrained, sitting across from Carroll as if an iron poker were up her back.

"I'm very sorry about your friend. The one who was a coder, is that the proper term?"

"Thank you. Nick was into tech . . . I'm not exactly sure how. I think Killian knows more about it than I do."

"Made a fortune, though, right? Terrible loss."

The Keenans owned a Jeep dealership that had lost ground during the last recession, but they'd put their money into real estate, buying up everything they could, squeaking through the bad times to profit wildly in the next boom. Now the dealership was doing well again, and the family had several apartment buildings, and commercial buildings as well. Carroll Keenan was known to crow about his successes, as did his son, whereas Miami's parents worked steady jobs with long hours, both of them at local grocery markets. Michael and Margarita Miller made a living, but sometimes money was tight. Miami paid them rent and they, in turn, helped her when they could.

"I don't know much about what Nick did," Miami reiterated.

"Of course, of course. You were good friends with him in high school, and that's been a while."

She nodded.

"Did you talk about those days with Nick?" he asked lightly.

"High school? No, not really. I mean, some, I guess . . ." Her throat felt hot. Nick had always been a gentleman to her. He'd been horrified when Lisette died. Devastated. She knew he blamed her suicide on himself, even though he never said so, even though it wasn't true.

"Killian always wanted me to meet Nick. He thought it would be good for the company. Too late now," he mused. "A real shame."

Miami waited for the true purpose of his visit to emerge. Beneath the table she clenched her sweating hands. She could guess what it was. He'd thought she was damaged goods, nowhere near good enough for his only son. Of course he would never say so directly to her.

"I know we've had some differences in the past," he said now, warming up to the real reason he'd sought her out.

Like when he'd told Killian in no uncertain terms that he couldn't marry that "used-up, hot little whore"? Well, she wasn't meant to overhear, of course, but she had, and those words had seared into her brain . . . even after what they'd all done.

Miami hoped all he could see was her poker face. Did he know? All of it?

"But I've come to see things with more clarity over time, as has Killian's mother."

Faye Keenan had never had any say in her husband's or her son's affairs. She was even less effective in dealing with either of them than Miami was.

But Carroll blew her away with his next words. "Are you and Killian planning a wedding?"

She felt the blood drain from her face. "Um . . . no . . ." she said faintly.

"It's no secret I've always felt that both you and Killian should broaden your horizons, meet other people, find out there's a bigger world beyond Edwards Bay. I know you've both dated some, but I thought it would be best for you if you actually moved somewhere far away. You knew that."

"Yes." How far is far away? Miami had wondered. Did

the next state count? Oregon or Idaho? California maybe? Or maybe across the Pacific? How about Japan or Taiwan, or better yet some country with a dictatorship that named you an enemy of the state and jailed you? Would that be remote enough?

Carroll leaned forward, folding his hands on the table. His blue eyes stared into her brown ones. "Well, I was wrong."

"What?"

"I was wrong to get in the way. Faye feels the same way."

Was this some kind of game? Some kind of trap? She stayed silent, waiting for the next shoe to drop.

"I've always liked you Mia mi. You know that, don't you? I just wanted to avoid a teen romance that ended in a messy divorce. You understand?"

"Ye . . . es."

"Can you forgive an old man his mistakes?" He leaned back and spread his hands, smiling that same smile that Killian gave. A salesman's smile. The kind that said, *Would I lie to you?* while they were crossing their fingers behind their backs.

She glanced at the clock above Carroll's head. "Uh-oh, I've already used up my break time. I need to get back."

"That's not really an answer," he said, the edges of his smile turning grimmer.

"I'd better go."

His hand shot across the table, holding her firm as she tried to push back her chair. "I'm making you an offer," he said softly. "A good one."

An offer.

She slowly and carefully twisted her arm free, got up from the table fast, and forced herself to walk out, though she wanted to hurry. Carroll Keenan's change of heart was a lie. He still didn't like her. No matter what he said, he didn't want his son's half-Mexican girlfriend to become his wife. Whatever his reasons for suddenly condoning their union, you could be sure they benefitted him in some way, but not her. Maybe not even Killian.

She thought of texting Killian and asking what the hell was going on, but it was a fleeting idea. Killian's relationship with his father was fraught as well, and he would be unlikely to be honest with her either. But Carroll Keenan would never elevate her to wife status without some serious impetus. Something that would compel him to go against his true feelings, because in his eyes she would always be that used-up, hot little whore.

Chapter Seven

Cole held open the door to his office to let Jerry Radnor and Kerry inside. Jerry practically shuffled his way to a chair and wiped a hand over his face in preparation. Cole took the seat behind his desk while Kerry perched on the chair next to Jerry.

"What's wrong?" Jerry asked.

"How are you both doing?" Cole responded, working to bring their nerves down.

"Not great," Kerry said.

"How do you think?" Jerry demanded. Then, hearing himself, he waved the air. "Nick's solicitor called. He's in Palo Alto. He wants to have a reading of the will next Monday with me, Kerry, and Marcia." He shook his head. "I'm not going anywhere."

"I believe he's coming here to meet with us," Kerry said. She was watching Jerry closely, clearly concerned for his well-being.

"They're putting my boy in the ground tomorrow." Jerry's mouth worked and he had to expel a slow breath. "That's what I know."

Kerry said, "We'll figure it out."

Cole nodded. "I meant to remind you, Nick's belongings are downstairs in Property, his wallet and clothes. You can check with Ben Youngston or Officer Paige to pick them up."

Jerry expelled a sharp breath, the thought seeming to hit him like a hammer. Leftover flotsam and jetsam from a life cut short. Cole thought about what he was about to say and knew Jerry was going to be hit even harder. Looking down at the open file on his desk, he drew a breath. Never easy to talk to grieving family members. "It's as we suspected; Nick died of a drug overdose."

There was a moment of pregnant silence. Kerry threw a look at Jerry, then gazed at Cole. "I know we keep saying it, but Nick wasn't a user. Or he hadn't been."

Jerry was shaking his head, as if that could stop whatever Cole was about to say.

Now for the really hard part. "Nick was administered a lethal dose of heroin through a hypodermic needle into the jugular vein." At their two blank looks, he pointed to his neck.

"I know where the jugular is," Kerry said a bit testily. "I just don't . . . that's not . . . usual."

"Cole, you're just plain wrong," Jerry snarled. "That's not my boy. He would never do that. There's a mistake somewhere."

"We found one needle mark. No others . . . so it could have been a onetime event," said Cole. He tried not to sound skeptical. He, too, would have said Nick was the last person that he knew who would use drugs, but there was other evidence as well that he hadn't gotten to yet.

"You're saying Nick died of an injection . . . in his neck?" Kerry's eyes flashed with repressed anger.

"He apparently took an opiate orally as well," said Cole.

"Nick didn't do drugs!" Jerry declared stubbornly, his florid face thunderous.

"What does it mean?" asked Kerry. She was blinking, absorbing the horror of his words.

"It's a lie!" Jerry glared at her.

Cole's chest was tight. He folded his hands on the desk. He understood what they felt. He felt it, too. This was Nick they were talking about. "If he . . . self-injected . . . he was very accurate. He hit a vein. The neck is arguably the most dangerous injection site. There are tendons and arteries clumped near the veins. If a mistake is made, say into an artery, the drug goes directly to the brain, which can cause serious damage. A stroke or even death. I know," he added, when Kerry was about to protest. "He died anyway. Of an overdose, which may have just been a miscalculation."

"What's the difference?" Kerry asked after a charged moment.

"You think it was an accident," Jerry said.

Kerry's eyes were boring into Cole's. He could tell she wanted to somehow blame him for Nick's death. Grieving family members and friends had blamed him plenty of times before, so he told himself it shouldn't matter. But it did. He didn't want to be the ogre in Kerry Monaghan's eyes.

"I just wanted to lay out the facts," Cole said.

"I don't understand. You don't think it's suicide, though," Kerry said.

"It depends on his intent."

"Maybe he and that Diana were . . . experimenting and it went wrong . . . ?" She looked up at him.

Jerry's face was drained of color. "She's the one you should be arresting. Diana Conger. How come she's not here, behind bars?"

"We're bringing her in to question her again."

"Too little, too late," Jerry ground out.

Cole held back from telling them that Youngston had thoroughly gone over Diana's premises and found no sign of drugs or drug paraphernalia. Diana had either cleaned up surprisingly well, or she and Nick had their party elsewhere. It was Cole's opinion they'd tried a few pills before the syringe, and Diana, who'd seemed to hold nothing back when she was brought in, had admitted to taking a few pills but wouldn't say the same of Nick.

"He was drinking beer," she'd said through tears, over and over again, according to Youngston and Charlie. "We were having fun."

"He didn't kill himself, accidentally or otherwise," Kerry stated firmly now. "If someone shot him up, it was without his consent."

"*She* killed him," Jerry said firmly.

Kerry looked pale, almost as pale as Jerry. "Maybe she didn't mean to kill him, but—"

"Doesn't matter. She killed him." Jerry was positive.

"He wouldn't have done it himself." Kerry stared at Cole, as if for corroboration. "That's just not something he would have done."

Cole said, "If the two of them were experimenting—say it was Nick's first time—it's unlikely they would have chosen the jugular vein. It's just not the way it's done. Too dangerous. Nick would have known all that, and so would Diana."

"So where does that leave us?" asked Kerry.

"How come you let her go?" Jerry demanded. "How come she's out there, not here, *in jail*?"

"The investigation's just begun," Cole said.

"It wasn't suicide," Jerry hissed.

"What do you think happened?" Kerry asked Cole.

"I don't want to conjecture."

"Oh, come on. Conjecture away," she told him, jaw tight. "Do you think they were experimenting? And Diana went too far, say? Maybe she was too messed up to do it right? Is that what happened?"

"We've spoken to Diana several times. She's coming in for a full interview later today. She denies giving Nick any drugs."

"Well, it wasn't suicide," Kerry said again, echoing Jerry.

"It's not like Lisette," Jerry said tautly.

Both Kerry and Cole looked at him, and the older man seemed to catch himself. "A friend of Nick's used pills to kill herself," he muttered.

Cole didn't like to offer up possibilities. Too many times grieving people latched on to a theory, declaring it fact. But he also didn't want to appear like he was keeping things from them, so he broke his own rule and gave them his true thoughts. "I think either Nick's death was caused by extreme recklessness or he was deliberately killed by someone who stuck that needle in his neck, not caring whether they hit a vein, an artery, or anything else. Whatever the case, Nick died as a result, and I plan to investigate as if it's a homicide until I learn differently."

Kerry felt light-headed and nauseated. She could barely register Cole's words. In her mind's eye she could see Diana pressing a syringe into Nick's neck.

She went for the jugular.

"Shoulda never let her out," Jerry said again, but he was losing steam. He got to his feet with an effort, swayed a bit, then headed for the door before Kerry could even get up to help him. Kerry scrambled from her chair, apparently unable to look at Cole.

It was hard for Cole to take. He'd known Jerry some, back when he and Nick were friends, during those high school years. They'd been a few grades apart, but they'd been acquainted through sports and other friends.

"I'm really sorry," he said as Kerry headed toward his

office door. He almost added, *I know what it's like to lose a brother*, but decided to keep himself out of it.

She hesitated, her fingers holding on to the doorjamb for a brief moment. Past her, Cole could see Jerry crossing the squad room, oblivious to the officers at their desks, although they collectively turned to watch him as he headed jerkily toward the front exit.

Kerry wanted to make some kind of snappy comeback, but all she could think of was that Nick was gone. He hadn't signed up for active duty like Cole's brother. All Nick had done was visit his hometown. He didn't deserve this in any way. Neither had Cole's brother, but joining any arm of the military came with the prospect of danger. Nick had just come back to Edwards Bay to be with friends and family.

And he'd died.

By mistake. Or someone had killed him. Murdered him. A homicide. It didn't matter to her whether it was by accident or design. She wanted whoever had done it to be brought to justice, and if the police couldn't do it, she was going to do it herself.

"Kerry," Cole said.

She was two steps into the squad room, but this time she glanced back at his tone.

"I'm going to find out the truth," he said grimly.

Kerry gave him a brief nod, then, ducking her head, she determinedly headed after Jerry, catching up with him outside the station under the cool, somewhat threatening skies of a June day.

So am I, she thought.

She drove Jerry back to his house. He was silent most of the way, but his mouth was working as she drew up to the curb, as if the words were there, but he couldn't or wouldn't spit them out.

"You okay?" she asked, walking him to his front door.

"It wasn't suicide," he said. "Nick was a good son. He would never hurt himself or anyone else. He made mistakes, sure, but he was always careful, especially after . . . he grew into an adult. He used his money for good causes. Drove his ex crazy with how much he donated, but Marcia . . ." He dolefully shook his head. "Never shoulda married her. Pretended she was pregnant, you know."

Kerry let that wash over her. For years she'd heard the rumor that Marcia had played that game to snare Nick, though he had never said as much. He'd protected himself with a prenup in any case, but what did it really matter now? Nick was gone and it felt petty to even think these thoughts.

But Jerry wasn't holding back. "Then Marcia did get pregnant and miscarried. And then Nick was done. He'd made a mistake in marrying her. Someone once called her the prettiest girl in three counties, but she never had the temperament to match. What she wanted was a blood heir and a way to tap into Nick's money. Didn't happen for her."

Miss Seashell. Marcia's crown . . .

"But Nick always loved Audra," Kerry said.

"Marcia wanted him to adopt her. He might've, if he'd lived." His mouth worked and he climbed out of the car. "Who knows where he left things. When that lawyer finally talks to you, I guess we'll know."

"To *us*. He wants to talk to you, too."

At the front door Jerry wouldn't let her help him any further. "I'm fine," he said curtly, letting himself into the house.

"You sure?"

"Yes, ma'am. I'm just going to sit myself down and relax. Nothing more for you to do today."

"Okay."

As he was closing the door, she almost asked if he felt

there was even the teensiest possibility Nick had committed suicide. She didn't believe it, and Jerry had said he didn't want to believe it, but the way he'd brought up Lisette clearly said her death, at her own hand, was on his mind.

The door shut firmly before she could ask, which was probably just as well; Jerry had looked all in.

She drove back to Starrwood Homes, her tired mind buzzing with what she'd learned at the meeting with Cole. The jugular vein. It seemed so . . . vicious. Could Diana Conger, maybe with Nick's blessing, have plunged a hypodermic needle into his neck? She couldn't quite put that picture together.

She felt weary all over from worrying and wondering. Somewhere she felt like she'd forgotten something, but for the moment she couldn't recall what it was.

"When's Conger coming back? You want me to pick her up?" Ben asked Cole, the words shooting out of his mouth like darts.

"She's coming in on her own."

"Shoulda never let her out."

Cole was getting pretty sick of people telling him that. Youngston had made up his mind about Diana the night of Nick's death. Cole said again, and he swore to himself it would be the last time, "She's cooperating fully. We don't have enough evidence to charge her in Nick Radnor's death."

"She oughta be in a cell."

Charlie looked up from her desk. She seemed about to put her own two cents in. Regarding her steadily, Cole asked, "Something on your mind, Officer Paige?"

Paige was smarter and more careful than Ben, apparently, because she hesitated a moment before saying, "Just got a call from Heather Drury. Justin's run off again. She wanted us to know."

"We'll look in all the usual places." Justin Drury was a chronic teen runaway and his mother, Heather, called in his disappearances as a matter of course. She'd grown weary of her middle son's inability to stay in school and abide by any social rules. His constant truancy had become a fact of life. He had a tendency to hang out with some of the known town miscreants down by the waterfront.

"I'm gathering that information for you," she added, and Cole nodded at her as he went back to his desk. She was getting him the phone numbers and addresses of Nick Radnor's family, friends, and business associates. He planned to make a few phone calls to get a feel for Nick Radnor, maybe pull a thread or two that might lead to unraveling some unobvious truth.

Fifteen minutes later Diana Conger walked into the squad room, appearing a helluva lot better than when he'd seen her the previous week. She had a tousled look about her that seemed to be part of who she was. Something a little messy that declared she wasn't interested in total perfection. Cole came out to meet her and, spying him, Diana hurried forward, tripping a little bit on wedge heels.

Was she high? he wondered. There was something a little off there.

"Hi, Chief," she said, her voice friendly.

Charlie looked over the top of her computer monitor. Cole ignored her as he led Diana to his office. She wasn't a suspect . . . yet . . . and there was no need for an interrogation room, no matter what Youngston wanted.

"I've been thinking," she said before Cole could even ask her a question. "I think Nick maybe did take some pills. Maybe at . . . the Blarney Stone? He might have . . . dabbled."

This was far more than she'd admitted the last time she'd been at the station. He'd spoken to her once more over the last few days, but she'd still been insisting she couldn't remember a thing. "Did you dabble?" he asked, purposely using her word.

"I'd been at the bars all night with our friends."

"Is that a yes?"

She looked at him directly but couldn't help blinking a bit, a tell. "I was drinking. I didn't . . . I don't . . . usually . . . mix things. It's very dangerous."

No kidding.

"So that's a no."

She ran a hand through her hair, tousling it further. "It's all a little hazy, like I said. I was messed up. We'd been bar-hopping. Everybody was feeling it. Even Kerry." She slid him a sideways look.

Cole's pulse jumped. So. They knew about him and Kerry. Of course, Kerry had probably told them. He'd been foolish to think she would keep their relationship to herself. Not that any of it mattered now.

"Tell me about the barhopping," he said.

Diana dutifully related much the same story as Kerry had. Where they'd gone, who'd been at each place, what they'd had to drink, although Diana wasn't nearly as clear as Kerry had been. He let her ramble on until she wound down, then he said, "Nick was given heroin straight to the jugular." He gestured to where the needle mark had been. "I don't think he gave it to himself. Too dangerous. Not what he was about. If he was going to dabble, like you said, he would have taken pills."

Diana's mouth had slowly dropped open. Either she was

a good actress or she was completely taken by surprise. He considered, but it was too early to make that distinction. "No," was what she finally said.

"Yes. He had several drugs in his system, but it appears it was the shot of heroin that killed him."

"I don't believe you!"

"I'm sorry. It's the truth."

She seemed completely taken aback, horrified even. He tried to read whether this was an act, but he couldn't make himself believe that. Diana was too open a person, who enjoyed socializing and had no serious line that couldn't be crossed when it came to "dabbling" in sex, alcohol, and drugs. If she was responsible for the hypodermic and Nick Radnor's death, she was doing a masterful job of masking her guilt. He just couldn't believe she had that in her. But then, some of the best criminals were the ones who appeared the most innocent.

Her eyes glimmered with sudden tears she didn't bother to wipe away. "Nick was the cool guy, you know? Too cool for any of us. We always knew he would leave Edwards Bay and do something fabulous, and he did. Marcia chased after him and she got him. For a while. But we all knew it wouldn't last."

"Who are 'we'?"

"All of us. The A-Team. We all were in the same class. Well, you know. You went there, too."

"I didn't know many people in your class," said Cole.

"But you knew Nick . . . right?"

Cole nodded.

"And Killian . . . and Forrest and Sean?"

"Not really. This isn't about me, Diana."

"I know. It's just that . . ." She shrugged, lightly wiping the tear tracks from her cheeks. "It's like we've all been together

forever. Nick left, but he came back. And now Kerry's part
of our group. And there are others, too. Egan and Miami
and Josie and Taryn and . . . oh, some of the other guys we
don't see as much . . . but we're all still here. Marcia was a
couple of years younger." She trailed off, and her eyes slid
to the side, though she didn't move her head. "Ben was in
our class."

Cole looked through his office window, following her
gaze to where he could see the back of Ben Youngston's
head as he hunt-and-pecked his way through the computer
keyboard writing up an incident report. Youngston wasn't
half as good as Paige was on paperwork. He, and some of
the other officers, had a tendency to try to wheedle Charlie
into helping them, but she was a hard-ass.

"Can you remember anything? Anything at all that
might explain how and when Nick was injected?"

"No." Her answer was immediate.

"You were with him at the end of the evening. At the last
bar. The Blarney Stone."

"I was sitting by him, that's all."

"But you left together."

"I just remember sitting there and Josie was glaring at
me from across the table. She thinks she owns him. Taryn
was mad, too. She was on Nick's other side."

Cole gazed at the distraught woman. Diana looked about
ready to break out in more tears. "Nick was giving you his
full attention."

"I guess so."

"Did that start at the Blarney Stone or earlier?"

"I don't know. Maybe . . . maybe at The Whistle Stop?
He was looking at me, and I said something funny and he
laughed."

"What did you say?"

"God, I can't remember . . ." She screwed up her face and closed her eyes. "No, it was Josie who said something about her husband . . . Kent. It was about him being gone for a few weeks, and Killian said, 'Maybe you'll finally get some good sex,' and looked at Nick, and I said, 'Nick's practically perfect in every way,' you know, like Mary Poppins, and Nick laughed. Kerry did, too, I think. She said I was going to give him a big head, and then the guys kind of went off on that. . . ." She threw an apologetic look at Cole. "You know, saying 'big head' and joking around."

He nodded. Could easily visualize the scene.

"Taryn cut them off. She's . . . well, she has her reasons, but she's kind of a buzzkill. Told them they were all a bunch of pervs or something. They ignored her. They always do."

"She was Nick's good friend," said Cole.

"Hmm." She shrugged. "She was always with him. Nothing sexual, I don't think. You can kinda tell. Taryn sort of latches on to guys. She's big into the women's movement, which is great, but she can really go off on a rant, sometimes at the worst time, and it makes everyone uncomfortable. You know what I mean?"

Cole nodded.

"She said some guy at work came at her and it really scared her. Nick was really nice to her about it. Okay, this is mean to say, but I think she kind of played on that? To keep his attention? She always says what great friends they are . . . were . . . but . . ." She caught herself, swallowing hard. "Anyway, when I found him in my bed . . . I was thinking that, well, I was just so happy. I was glad he saw me differently than Taryn, or at least that's what I thought at first . . . until I realized he was gone."

Sensing she was ready to cry some more, he asked

quickly, to divert her, "Did the guys in your group feel the same way about Nick as the women apparently did?"

She sniffed. "How do you mean?"

"Let me ask you this: Did all the women feel the way you do? That Nick was a . . . good guy?"

"Oh, sure. Miami doesn't say much, but she can't with Killian right there. Killian can't handle hearing anyone's better than he is. Kerry looks at him like a brother; I mean, he is her stepbrother, but they both act like a real brother and sister. She thinks he's a good guy. And then Josie sure does. She's in to him. Was in to him." She darted a quick glance his way. "She acted like they were sleeping together. It's kind of a known thing, but I don't know. Maybe."

"You don't think she and Nick were an item."

"Nick . . ." She gazed out the windows of his office to the squad room. "Until he was with me . . . I didn't think he was really with anybody. He was too sad."

"Sad?"

She tossed up her hands. "I don't know. Disinterested? Like other things on his mind?"

"What did the men in your group think about Nick?"

"Oh, they're all jealous of his success. I mean, come on. They give him shit all the time, but you can see how they feel. *Gave* him shit," she corrected herself. "Just like guys do. But I think . . . I mean, they know he was a good guy. Forrest said something to him about showing them all up or something. This was all earlier or other times, not by the time we got to the Blarney Stone, or even much at The Whistle Stop."

Cole nodded, then switched gears. "Do you have any need for a syringe?"

"No. Didn't you search my apartment?" she asked, lifting her chin.

"We didn't find anything."

"Well, then, I guess you know I don't have syringes lying around. I'm not that kind, Chief."

Cole asked her a few more questions about Nick and her fellow A-Teamers, but she was apparently tapped out. As much as everyone seemed to be in a hurry to throw the book at her, apart from some reckless choices Diana had made, Cole didn't have the evidence to charge her with Nick's death. And truthfully, she didn't fit the profile. Maybe she was a consummate actress and she was playing a real number on him, but at this point he just didn't believe. And there was still a question whether Nick's death was even murder. Cole was going to keep an open mind, but he couldn't visualize Nick Radnor plunging a needle into his own neck.

Kerry's cell phone rang as she was trying to get her mind on the work in front of her on her desk. Seeing it was Marcia, she almost let the call go to voice mail, but that would only delay the inevitable. "Hi, Marcia," she answered.

"I hear you were at the station with Jerry, talking to Cole."

Her tone was accusatory. Kerry wondered who her spy was and asked, "How'd you know?"

"What did you talk about?" she demanded.

"Nick. His death. How it happened."

Her own tone was cold and Marcia drew in a breath, sounding a bit taken aback. "Is he going to talk to all of us?"

"Cole? I don't know, maybe. Who told you we were at the station?" The penny dropped before the words were out of her mouth. "Ben Youngston."

"Does Cole think it was an accident? You know Nick didn't use drugs."

"Ask Ben. I don't want to talk about it."

"I should have been with you and Jerry. Audra and I are Nick's family, too."

"Marcia, I've got to go."

"Was it really a hypodermic needle to the jugular?" she asked, her voice rising to a horror-filled squeak.

Kerry's throat tightened. If Cole was trying to keep that information under wraps, it was too late. "Goodbye, Marcia," she said and clicked off.

A moment later her phone rang again. For a second she wondered if Marcia was calling back, but then she saw it was Diana Conger's number. She almost turned off the phone, but instead she girded her loins and answered. "Hi, Diana."

"Kerry, can I talk to you?"

Diana's voice wavered. *No,* Kerry almost said. She didn't want anything to do with her and realized she'd sided with the other members of their group against her. Maybe that was unfair, but Nick had died by drug overdose while he was with Diana and that was enough for Kerry.

At her hesitation, Diana said, "I know you don't want to talk to me, but I just got back from the police station. Did you know Nick died of a heroin overdose? From an injection?"

So Cole had told her. Maybe it wasn't Ben Youngston telling tales out of turn after all. Maybe she was the only one who wanted to keep the terrible truth out of the headlines. "Cole told us what the cause was."

"Well, I didn't do it. I would never do that. You've got to believe me. And let everyone know, please. I would never hurt Nick, and I don't do that kind of thing anyway!"

"Okay." Kerry just wanted off the phone. She could hear the *tap-tap-tap* of Angie's heels as she headed her way, probably called by the siren song of Kerry's trilling cell.

"Would Nick do that? To himself, I mean?" she asked.
"No."

"I don't think so either. I've been thinking about that night. It just feels like there's something more . . . someone more . . . I'm scared. In fact . . . I feel like I'm being watched."

"You think someone was watching you that night?" Kerry asked.

"Does that sound paranoid?"

Yes.

Diana started to cry. "Kerry, you've got to believe me. I didn't do it! I couldn't do that. And with a hypodermic needle? Never! I loved Nick like all of us did. I just kinda wanted to be with him, that's all. It's not my fault."

Angie slowed by the wide, open door to Kerry's office, more of an anteroom down the hall from Randy's. Kerry glanced her way, then back to the pages at her desk. "I have to go."

"You're going to be at the memorial service tomorrow?" Diana asked.

"Of course."

"I'll talk to you there. I'm remembering a little bit, you know. I really am. It's coming back in bits and pieces. And I'm seeing someone tonight who's going to help me. I'm going to remember who did this. I think maybe someone came in after Nick and I . . . after he, maybe, took some pills? And that's how they . . . that's how it happened?"

"Someone else at your apartment?" Kerry didn't mean to sound dubious, but she couldn't help the disbelief that crept into her tone.

"I don't know . . . maybe . . ." she said defensively.

"Okay."

"I'm serious, Kerry. I'm really serious."

"You didn't tell Cole?"

"No . . . not yet . . . I'm, I'm trying to remember." As if finally catching on to Kerry's skepticism, she said, "I'll think on it. I'll see you tomorrow."

Kerry replaced the phone, fully aware that Angie was standing in the aperture, unabashedly eavesdropping. She sent Angie a what-gives? look, but Angie just regarded her stonily, arms folded around her chest, before meandering off.

Chapter Eight

Kerry shimmied into the little black dress she'd decided would work for Nick's memorial service. Marcia had gone across the bay to The Pier early and was making sure everything was just right. Unlike Kerry, who'd practically shut down at Nick's death, Marcia had become energized, ready and eager to put the service together. Marcia had almost lorded it over her up till Kerry's meeting with the police. Since then: crickets. Marcia apparently didn't want to talk to her anymore.

Fine. Kerry had rustled up some photographs, as had Jerry, and given them to Marcia, and she had done the rest. Nothing more to do. Kerry was both grateful and a little pissed off about it. Marcia had this uncanny ability to swoop in, take control, push you aside, then make sure you felt guilty about it.

Eyeing herself critically in the bathroom mirror, Kerry made a face. She was going to have to go deep with the makeup to take care of her washed-out face.

She slathered on the mascara, then leaned back to examine her handiwork. Too thick? she asked herself, then thought of Mia Miller's long lashes and smooth, caramel skin, and added another swipe or two. Her own hazel eyes looked back at her as she thought about Nick, Jerry, Diana, and Cole—especially Cole, who'd been polite and professional, just like he should be.

She grimaced. So why was that a problem? Why did she feel like banging her fists against the wall and primal screaming?

Get a grip.

She inhaled and exhaled several times. Her emotions were out of control. And the effort to hold them in while she was at work and dealing with Angie, who she'd really like to throw something at, was taking its toll, too. And when Randy had called upon her earlier this week to take something over to his father at his assisted living facility, she'd asked him to send Angie, which had raised his ire.

"Angie and my dad don't get along that well," he'd snapped. "Just the way it is. And I've got phone calls I can't miss. If you won't do it, I'll do it after work."

"What do you want me to take?" Kerry had asked. Easier to capitulate than fight.

"Some papers he needs to sign."

As it was work-related, Kerry had started feeling a bit embarrassed. Randy had been great to her since Nick's death. It was Angie she was rebelling against, so she'd said, "I'll go on my lunch break," and the frown on his forehead had cleared immediately.

She'd taken the papers to the Callaway Center, a one-story, rambling brick building on a parcel of land about two miles out of town that looked like a motel and was named after its founder, Anne Callaway. Kerry walked into the facility and said Randall Starr Jr. had come to see his father, and she was given his room number and a dismissive wave. Not a whole lot of serious ID checking. She knocked on the door and was surprised by Randall Starr Sr.'s spryness as he opened the door with a flourish and ushered her inside. "Randy said you'd be by. Great to see one of you kids again," he greeted her enthusiastically. "I remember you from high school."

She hadn't attended Edwards Bay High and started to correct him, but he swept on. "Were you in on it? Or was it a secret?" He cocked his head and his eyes glittered like a bird's.

"What do you mean?" she asked, unfolding the document Randy had given her and laying it on the table next to his BarcaLounger.

Rather than taking the cue and climbing back in his seat, he leaned into her, smelling her hair. She put him in his midfifties, but he'd been in a car accident that had "rattled his brain," according to Randy, and his demeanor and conversation reflected that of someone much older. Early onset dementia was the diagnosis, although he seemed sharp in other ways.

His fingers reached for her elbow and he held on tightly for support as they headed back to his chair. Once settled, he leaned his head back, gray hair against the cushion, dark brown eyes staring upward into hers, a smile playing on his lips. "You're pretty, but that little *chiquita*, she was something else. Pretty, pretty, pretty. Got around some, too, didn't she?"

Kerry had carefully pulled away from his grip and tried to direct him to the papers. "Randy said you need to sign these?"

"You're not that pageant girl, are you? Miss Seahorse?"

"Miss Seashell. No."

"She was pretty, too. Got herself knocked up right outta high school, Randy said. Married the guy that just OD'd."

"Uh . . . yeesss . . ."

"You going to the funeral?"

"Memorial service." He clearly didn't know she was

Nick's stepsister and she didn't want to encourage him, so she just said, "I plan to."

"I wanted to go, but Randy said no. My friends'll be there . . . Bart and Millard . . . and . . . Bart . . ." He trailed off. "You didn't mind, did ya? The boys and their hijinks."

"Umm . . . what hijinks?"

"Ah." He nodded knowingly. "Don't talk." He put a finger to his lips. "Shhh."

She started to think he believed she was Josie, or maybe Taryn, so she came clean. "I didn't go to Edwards Bay High. I'm Nick's stepsister." She moved the papers closer to his hand.

"You're pretty anxious to get on with it, aren't ya?"

"Randy's expecting me back at work, so yes."

He hmphed out a huge sigh but reached for the papers.

At that moment there was a knock on his door and a head popped around the corner: a middle-aged woman with silvery-blond hair. "Knock, knock," she said as she entered.

"The love of my life," Randall Sr. told Kerry with more than a trace of irony.

"Well, who's this?" Mrs. Starr asked. Her eyes were all over Kerry, as if checking for flaws.

"What's your name, doll?" Randall Sr. turned his gaze from his wife to Kerry.

"Kerry Monaghan."

"Works for Randy. Brought me some papers." He held up the sheaf, as if for corroboration. "This is Bette . . . my better half."

"You work with Angie?" Bette asked politely, but Kerry sensed an undercurrent in there somewhere.

"And Randy," her husband put in before Kerry could answer. "Angie works for our son." The way he said it made it seem like this was well-worn territory.

"Angie runs that office." The polite smile stayed in place on Bette's face, as if it were screwed on.

"Yes, well, I'd better get back," Kerry told them. She'd handed Randall Sr. a pen, but he paid no attention to it. There was an awkward tension Kerry could have done without since Bette's arrival. She was doing Randy a favor and somehow had stepped in a pile of dung. There was something possessive about Bette. Was there something about the Starr men that made their wives feel they had to intervene whenever they were faced with other females? Kerry could have told them she had no interest in either of them. It irked her that she even had to deal with this.

Randall Sr. finally signed the papers, his hand shaking a bit as he looped out his signature. He handed the papers back to Kerry, who made good her escape.

Now, back at the office, she wondered if she'd made a serious mistake in transferring to the Edwards Bay office. The main Seattle office had been closing down. Too much competition from huge conglomerates building homes. But there was a satellite office on the eastern edge of Seattle. Maybe she should have gone there. She hadn't chosen that location because Randy had asked her to move to Edwards Bay and she'd known she'd be in a position to see more of Nick.

And Cole.

She blew her bangs out of her eyes. She was a little fascinated with him, she could admit that, but so what? They'd dated . . . very seriously . . . and there was always a bit of a fascination with someone who dumped you. But Cole was off-limits. She knew that. And besides, she wasn't looking for a relationship right now. It was unlikely she would ever get married again after the first one hadn't gone so well.

Thinking of Vaughn, she wondered if he knew about Nick's death. They'd been friendly enough during Kerry's marriage, though she sensed they'd mostly been acting for her benefit. The two men were very different. Not so much in looks but in attitude. Vaughn envied anyone with money, though he tried to hide it behind a superfriendly exterior. He had a sharp wit that had captured Kerry's attention and her heart, at least for a little while, until she'd realized she'd married a sham. A half-formed personality that could put on a good show, one he just hadn't been able to sustain.

It would be big of her to call him and tell him about Nick. She considered it a moment, seesawing over actually picking up the phone and talking to her ex. Oh, bullshit. Who was she kidding? She didn't care what Vaughn knew about Nick or didn't know. Someone else could tell him. Vaughn wasn't her responsibility and she didn't owe him anything. She could still remember the cold, cutting criticisms he'd delivered to her on the way out the door that final time, just after they'd visited Nick in Palo Alto:

"You embarrassed me in front of your brother," he'd accused.

"What are you talking about?" she'd flung back, shocked and angry.

"You kept changing the subject," Vaughn declared. "You clearly didn't want me to talk to him or Worster. You were laughing your ass off about . . . I don't even know. What were you trying to prove?"

Chad Worster. Nick's partner. Kerry hadn't been able to come up with his name when she'd first spoken to Cole, but she'd remembered it later. She'd called the station and spoken to the woman officer, Paige, the only one in the department as far as she could tell. Paige had said she would relay the message and Kerry had been relieved she didn't have to talk to Cole.

"I wasn't trying to prove anything!" she'd declared. "I was talking to my brother and his business partner . . .

friend. I didn't know you were trying to talk business. What kind of business? You're in commercial real estate in Seattle."

"Jesus Christ! If I could land Nick as an account, the sky's the limit!"

"But he's not interested in leaving Palo Alto. He said that."

"Why the fuck does he come back here all the time, then? Huh? Tell me that."

"To see his family! Jerry . . . and me . . . and some high school friends."

"You just don't see the big picture, Kerry. I don't know if you're living in your own world or if you're really that dense."

"Maybe a little of both," she'd answered through her teeth. She'd then walked to the door and held it open for him. Their relationship had been a cold war until that last visit to Palo Alto, and had then exploded into that final fiery battle. Vaughn's fists clenched, and there was a charged moment between them before he stalked out. He'd called her once to test the waters between them with a half-hearted apology. When Kerry didn't thaw, he started dating one of the office staff at his firm.

The last Kerry had heard was that this coworker was pregnant . . . although the child might not be Vaughn's. Echoes of Nick and Marcia's romance . . .

Their divorce had been as amicable as it could be, mostly because Kerry wanted nothing from him. Nothing. And that was pretty much what was left. Any money Vaughn had earned from partnering with agents to make sales had been used to further his profile. He'd wined and dined potential buyers and managed to spend most of what he made. Kerry had worked for Randy, which had been a small-time operation opposed to Vaughn's high-flying deals, most of which never materialized, stolen by other agents, he griped, or maybe the would-be clients had sudden changes of heart. Vaughn never seemed to be the guy to land a real seller. His good looks and charm and cleverness only went so far, it seemed. Or maybe his cutthroat ways had boomeranged. Kerry never knew. She just knew she wanted out, and so she ended up with her job and the rest of the lease on their apartment. As soon as the divorce was finalized and there were only a few months left on the lease, she started looking for a less expensive place to live. About that time Randy started making noises about her moving to Edwards Bay. When the lease finally did run out on her Seattle apartment, she accepted the new position and moved, signing a one-year lease on a small efficiency apartment only a few blocks over from Diana's. That lease had recently ended and she'd chosen to move to The Sand Drift. If Vaughn knew anything about where she currently lived and what she was doing, she had no idea. They'd cut off communication, and it was probably a relief to both of them; it certainly was to Kerry.

The piece that Kerry had been forced to face, the one that still made her cringe, was that her marriage had been a sham. She hadn't loved Vaughn. She'd used him as a substitute for Cole. Though her romantic relationship with Cole had been short-lived—it could be measured in days, weeks, and months rather than years—its emotional power still resonated. At the time she'd acted as if she'd taken the breakup in stride, but nothing could be farther from the truth. Cole probably thought she hadn't cared all that much. She hoped he did. She *really* hoped he did. Because she didn't want him knowing how much he'd devastated her. It wasn't his fault she'd run to the next man she'd had any kind of spark with at all. That was all on her. But Cole was the reason. The hurt that followed their breakup had propelled her into reckless decision-making, and now she was bound and determined not to fall into that trap ever again.

"Be smart," she told her reflection, examining her makeup carefully, searching for flaws before she headed out the door, aware that Cole would undoubtedly be at the memorial service.

It was a little after four when Cole made it to the ferry dock. He parked his car on the Edwards Bay side and walked along the planked pier. A stiff breeze was blowing cold, riffling the green water, cutting through his sport coat. Typical June weather. Summer hadn't really started yet.

He could see a group who'd also left their cars on the Edwards Bay side already waiting. Probably more of the memorial service crowd for Nick Radnor; the service was at The Pier, a restaurant only a few blocks from the ferry dock on the Kingston side. He recognized Killian Keenan, the tallest and most impressively built. He knew from the short bios he'd gotten on Nick's friends that Keenan was a gym rat, obsessively so, and his physique—the broad shoulders, wide chest, and arms that seemed to stick out from his body—was testament to that.

He wasn't certain who the thin, nervous guy was, but he wore a baseball cap that read Washington State Ferries, so that might mean he was Egan Fogherty, who was employed by the ferry system and was working his way up to captain. Privately, Cole thought he'd worry if Fogherty were the man at the helm. Egan didn't seem to have the shoulders to take on the responsibility.

There were two women he recognized from photographs Charlie had compiled of Nick's Edwards Bay friends. One was Mia Miller. Beautiful. Brown-eyed, olive-skinned, with lustrous dark hair that brushed her shoulders. She had a slim build and a healthy pair of breasts that were encased in a black velvet, long-sleeved shirt atop a cream-colored midcalf length suede skirt, and black boots. Sexy without trying, looking almost too touchable. The other woman was attractive but didn't hold a candle to Miller. She had blondish hair and pale blue eyes. She had a couple of extra pounds on her, but her body was hard, as if she were an exercise fiend; maybe to take off those extra pounds? She had a faint smile on her face as she tried to ignore whatever Fogherty was saying to her. Fogherty made her give a quick smile that momentarily lit up her face before she clamped down on it again and turned away from him. Her expression grew sober once more, sadder and stonier. Taryn Whitcomb. Her eyes kept drifting back to Keenan, and Cole wondered what she was thinking.

There was no sign of Kerry. She might have taken an earlier ferry. It was unlikely anyone from Edwards Bay would drive all the way around this finger of the sound; it would take miles longer.

Another woman—Josie Roker, Cole decided—came hurrying toward the group. She had long, light brown hair and a pert smile and wore a black skirt and a blue blouse. Her makeup was either minimal or artfully designed to appear so. "The tomboy," Cole recalled Ben Youngston's description when he'd asked about Nick and Kerry's friends, although Josie's attractiveness was in an overall freshness that seemed to come from within. She was accompanied by another man. Her husband, Kent Roker, Cole guessed, whose silver-winged hair was smoothed back from his head and gray suit looked expensive. Josie hurried ahead of him, either in her eagerness to join the others or just to get away. Cole couldn't tell for certain, but he seemed to be deliberately plodding behind her, maybe from dread, maybe from a need to be passive-aggressive; this was obviously Josie's show, not his.

Others arrived. The two bar owners, Sean Blevins and Forrest Borland, and a number of older people joined the flow toward the ferry. One of the older gents slapped Killian's father, Carroll Keenan, who Cole knew by sight, on the shoulder as the group moved forward. The slapper seemed to be a good friend, though the senior Keenan paid him little or no attention. Keenan's gaze appeared zeroed in on Mia Miller, who was sidling away to ostensibly stare across the water as she lagged behind. Killian Keenan apparently realized she wasn't by his side and stopped to turn and stare at her. The weight of his gaze seemed to bring Miller back to the present. She lifted her chin to Killian and then walked toward him. He put his arm around her shoulders in a proprietary manner.

Cole waited till the last moment, watching the ebb and flow of mourners heading toward the ferry until he recognized he would literally miss the boat if he didn't get moving.

At that moment a vehicle pulled into the lot with a screech of brakes. A Mazda. He glanced over and saw Kerry slam out of her car and hurry, half-running, toward the dock, about thirty feet in front of him. He smiled to himself. True to form, she was almost late.

As if feeling his eyes on her, she turned her head while still hurrying forward. He was walking fast himself and nearly caught her by the time she realized it was him.

"Cole," she said, slowing to allow him to reach her.

"Hi, Kerry."

"Are you here as a friend or an officer of the law?" She said it lightly, but he could tell she really wanted an answer.

"A little of both."

They reached the ferry and walked up the gangway

together. She said, "I remembered Nick's partner's name. Chad Worster. I called and gave it to Officer Paige."

"I got it."

"Of course." She flashed a smile. "You probably know a lot about everyone now."

"Some," he admitted.

She was wearing a black dress that hit her knees. Bare legs in black pumps cut out at the toe, where he could see a few of the rose-colored toenails. Her calves were trim and tapered to really nice ankles. He felt a stirring of interest and had to drag his mind back to what she was saying.

"—wanted him to come with me, but he was driving from Tacoma, so he's meeting me at The Pier."

"Jerry?" Cole asked.

She nodded. "Since Nick's death he's concentrated on the remodel of the motel even more than he was already."

"It's good he has a project."

"Yes. If he didn't . . ." She trailed off.

Cars were loading onto the ferry's lower deck, and they skirted the boarding area as they made their way toward the metal stairs to the enclosed upper deck. The smell of diesel competed with the brine and dankness coming off the water. A flock of seagulls passed by, squawking, as he and Kerry entered the main salon, where the mourners had gathered. A young couple with a child were eyeing the group askance and moving their belongings toward the front of the room, away from the crowd, apparently trying to get as far from them as possible without heading outside or to the enclosed top deck. Another single woman was heading toward the stairs, probably for the same reason. Kerry walked toward the group and Cole ambled forward more slowly. He wanted to stay a bit apart to observe them. He planned on interviewing them in the near future. Someone had stabbed Nick Radnor with a hypodermic before he'd ended up in Diana's bed. Maybe Diana. That was certainly what it looked like. Or maybe there was another explanation.

Adam Wright spied him and left the group, ducking into one of the seats to allow Kerry to pass as she walked down the aisle toward the group. He stepped back out and greeted Cole with a handshake.

"Thanks for bringing Mom's keys back again," he said.

"Not a problem."

"I know it's not your job, but I appreciate it. How do other people do it? Take the keys away? Every time I hide them, she finds them. It's just easier to bring them to the police station and let you guys handle it," he said somewhat apologetically. "I keep thinking she'll forget. She forgets a lot of stuff, but not that. She's a danger on the road."

As if suddenly remembering where he was, Adam came out of himself and his problems. "Shame about Radnor. Overdosing. Just doesn't seem like him."

"No. It doesn't."

"What do you think happened?" Adam asked. "He just suddenly went off the deep end? Decided fuck it all and made a mistake?"

Adam didn't know how Nick had died yet, apparently, and Cole wasn't ready to announce it. "That's what I aim to find out."

"You don't think it was an accident?"

Cole looked over at Kerry, surrounded by the group of Nick's friends. She was hanging on to a tremulous smile with an effort. Her naked grief had his thoughts turning to his own brother, Aaron, and the pain, anger, and confusion he'd felt at his death. It had taken years for him to feel normal again. Longer to find pleasure in his own life. He glanced toward Kerry, understanding what she was going through. He wanted to help, but he'd pushed her away, hard, when she'd tried to do the same for him.

He reminded himself: *Now is not the time to try to rekindle anything.*

Kerry was extremely conscious of Cole standing a number of feet behind her. Of course he'd be the one person she ran into as she raced to make the ferry. It had been a phone call from Jerry that had made her forget the time. Jerry had complained about a tightness in his chest and she'd spent a good twenty minutes trying to convince him to go to an emergency room. He might have done it had he been in Edwards Bay, but he was in Tacoma. He'd assured her he was feeling better by the time he'd gotten off the phone, but Kerry had only been partially appeased. She was anxious to see him at The Pier. See how he looked. Judge how he felt. She would take him to the ER herself if necessary and to hell with the memorial service. She couldn't lose both Nick and Jerry.

Randy sidled over to her. Angie was in a conversation with a man who looked to be in his fifties or sixties. She shot a worried glance at Randy, but she was rooted to the spot by the silver-haired man with the commanding manner.

"So it was suicide?" he whispered in her ear.

She turned to him and they walked a few steps away from the others. She could just see Cole speaking to another man, though Killian was in her sight line, and whenever he shifted position, he became a wall. "Where'd you hear that?" she asked. "It wasn't suicide."

"Stabbing yourself in the neck? What a way to become a user."

"That isn't how it went."

"Well, that's what I heard."

"From who? Officer Youngston?" Kerry glanced over the ferry. She'd seen Ben Youngston earlier, but he'd found Marcia and followed after her. Kerry thought they'd headed for the upper deck.

"I don't know. Everybody was talking about it. It was either suicide or murder, right? I mean, Nick was a smart guy. He didn't make those kinds of mistakes. Nick was too smart to do that. Nobody does that unless they want to die."

"Nick didn't kill himself."

"So Diana killed him?"

Kerry recalled Cole's words about the difficulties of a neophyte hitting the jugular vein just right. "I have trouble believing that. I just . . . wish he was here."

Randy nodded. "Nick was pretty down this time. Didn't seem like himself. You felt it, too, didn't you?"

Yes, she had. They all had. Nick had been in a funk. "That doesn't mean he wanted to kill himself, if that's where you're going."

"No, I'm just talking." He sighed and looked over at Angie, who glared pointedly at him. She couldn't seem to escape the conversation she was having, or maybe she didn't really want to, but she didn't like her husband with Kerry. Randy shrugged at her. His body was going to seed a little bit. A high school linebacker on the football team, he'd once been a formidable-looking guy, though by all accounts he'd always been a nice one. Now he had the beginnings of a belly and a softness around his jawline.

"Maybe we didn't know Nick as well as we thought we did. He was down in Silicon Valley a long time. Whatever he came back here for, it wasn't just to connect with old friends. I think he was looking for something."

"Like what?"

"Somebody to love?" He gave a derisive laugh, his gaze traveling to Josie. "Did he say anything to you?"

"No."

"Well, he said something to Ange."

"Ange" was still glaring their way. It irked Kerry, and she realized she was feeling anxious and a bit angry with all the talk about Nick. Not the emotion she wanted to feel at her brother's memorial service. With an effort she tamped down her emotions. She didn't like what Randy was saying about Nick, but maybe that was her problem more than his.

Angie finally broke free with a smile and a goodbye to the older man whose eyes followed her as she worked her way down the ferry aisle to where Kerry and Randy were standing. "What are you two getting so cozy about?" she asked as she reached a hand up to rub her husband's back. Her gaze was on Kerry.

"We're not getting cozy," Randy snapped. He signaled Forrest Borland and Sean Blevins and tried to squeeze past Kerry and his wife.

"Where are you going now?" Angie demanded.

"I'll be back."

Angie's lips were a straight line, as if she were holding herself back with an effort.

Kerry said, "Randy said Nick talked to you about . . . why he was back in Edwards Bay more and more?"

"That's not exactly what I said," Randy muttered.

Angie said, "Oh. It was about that girl from high school. He felt bad about the way he treated her."

"Which girl?" Kerry asked.

Randy said, "Nick dated a lot of girls. It was high school. We all did."

Angie's face reddened a bit at her husband's abrupt tone. "I thought, from the way he talked, it was about that girl who killed herself."

"Lisette's suicide wasn't his fault. It was that stepfather of hers," Randy stated flatly. This time he did push past them to join his friends.

Angie swept in a breath. "You don't think he's here, do you? Her stepfather?"

"Would he be?" asked Kerry, taken aback.

"I don't know. He never went to jail for what he did. Oh, Lord. He wouldn't come, would he? I mean, those other old men are here. . . ." She swept her gaze around the ferry, zeroing in on a table where a small group of older men, some with wives, some single, were crowded together. "He could be one of them." Her voice quavered.

Kerry glanced around Angie at the group of older men, then at members of the A-Team who had also drifted to a large, nearby booth among a row of identical large booths that marched down the center of the ferry. Others from their group were leaning over the back of the next booth, hoping to be part of the crowd. Egan Fogherty was one of those who'd apparently been relegated to the lesser table. He tried to stick his head between Killian and Miami and was elbowed back by Killian for his efforts.

Kerry suddenly felt weary. It was all so much work to be their friend. Was that what Nick had felt? If so, why had he upped his visits back to Edwards Bay? Was he, as she'd heard implied, tired of his life in Silicon Valley and ready to make a change? Or did it have something to do with Lisette Benetton's suicide?

The ferry was chugging across the water and nearing the Kingston side. Kerry was glad she would be able to put some space between herself and the other mourners. It was all a little claustrophobic, especially with the negative vibes coming off Angie, who'd gone silent beside her, her gaze burning into the back of Randy's head. He had made it to the main booth.

"Were charges ever brought against Lisette Benetton's stepfather?" Kerry asked.

"I don't know," she said nervously. "I didn't go to school here. Just like you. But Randy said he got off scot-free. Just another pervert they allowed to keep roaming around."

Egan Fogherty moved out of his booth and started heading toward the snack bar. He had to first pass Cole, who'd been joined by Ben Youngston, and then Kerry and Angie. One look at him and Angie was gone. She hurried the other way to circle around toward the A-Team.

"Hey," Egan greeted Kerry.

Kerry felt Cole's eyes on her and looked up to meet his gaze. Her attention was yanked back by the hard feel of Egan's hand on her arm. She immediately wanted to pull back, but she waited, not wanting to offend. "Hello," she greeted him.

"You look lonely. Are you a lonely lady?"

"I'm a grieving sister," she said, keeping her voice neutral.

He lifted his hands. "Of course, of course, of course. Nick was a great guy. A great guy. Well, as much as any of us are. But what happens in Edwards Bay stays in Edwards Bay, right? High school and all. You were in Seattle, right? Your parents divorced?"

"My mother and Nick's father split up."

"That's right. You were stepbrother and -sister. Yeah, that's right." His grin was impish and sly. "Never got into each other's bedroom?"

"No."

"Not even just once?"

"No." Kerry's voice was ice.

"Nick was pretty much at the top of his game in those days. All the girls wanted him, so it was easy. Top of the charts, if you know what I mean."

"Fogherty, leave her alone!" Killian's voice boomed out.

Kerry realized the A-Team seemed to be regarding her en masse. Josie slid out of the booth and made her way over as Egan began protesting that he was just having a conversation. "They're so afraid I'm going to give something away," he whispered to Kerry in an aside as Josie glared at him.

"Stop being creepy, Egan. Jesus." She shook her head and rolled her eyes at him as he sauntered back to the group, sneaking into the spot she'd vacated. "Don't listen to him," she advised. "He's got some serious issues. Being bipolar isn't even the worst of it."

"He's bipolar?"

"Well, that's what he says, and I'm sure it's true. But he can make you feel uncomfortable. Doesn't really have the right boundaries."

As if hearing her, Egan suddenly shouted, "This is a fucking wake, right? Don't we all need some drinks? To celebrate Nick's life? Isn't that what he'd want?"

Forrest Borland said, "Here, here."

Sean Blevins added, "First round on the Blarney Stone," to which a cheer went up.

Forrest seconded the idea, but the hard look he gave his business partner said he resented the gesture.

And then the ferry's engines altered and their progress slowed. They were approaching the Kingston dock.

Chapter Nine

The A-Team and some of the older guys had taken turns telling stories about Nick as they crossed the water. Most of the guys had had something to say, and a few of the older generation as well. Carroll Keenan said he'd always known Nick would make good. Some guys just had it. Forrest told a funny story about trying to make it with a girl named Kim who'd only wanted to be with Nick and had finally followed Nick home and crawled through his bedroom window. Someone else asked where Kim was now, and Sean Blevins said she'd moved away. The last they'd heard, she was married and had four kids. Egan had once tried to console another girl Nick had dumped, to no avail. Killian argued that Nick hadn't dumped her; he just hadn't been all that interested. Josie threw Killian a dark look and said Nick had been generous with helping her and others with their math homework. Miami said he'd always been a sweet guy. The guys looked at one another and guffawed.

Taryn Whitcomb listened to these tales with a sour face. She'd never been all that good at hiding her emotions and tonight was the worst. Nick had been her best friend and now he was gone. She'd wanted to tell some tale about him, but she was angry and upset and the rest of them had *no right* acting like they knew him so well when she'd been the one

he'd turned to. She wanted to burst out with the fact that
Nick had been reliving Lisette Benetton's suicide these past
few months, lamenting his part in it. Lisette had been the
girl Nick hadn't been interested in. The one Egan thought
he'd dumped. The truth was, Nick hadn't cared about her
all that much. She'd been another cute girl with problems
who'd fallen for the high-school heartthrob, just like every
other girl in school. Taryn, too, had suffered a secret crush
on Nick. He'd just been that good. If he'd crooked his finger
at her, she would have slept with him, too. She was pretty
sure the rest of them all had.

She still couldn't get over the fact he'd left with Diana!
That was so out of character. What had he been thinking?
Diana wasn't good enough for him in any way. But boy, had
it tweaked Josie, who practically threw herself at Nick at
every opportunity. She sure had that night. Nick had even
told Taryn he wished Josie would lay off some, but of course
she hadn't.

So now Taryn was alone, just like always. Ever since
she'd ratted out her handsy boss at Jefferson Motors, she'd
been the girl no one wanted to be around. The other sales-
men avoided her, as if it were somehow her fault. She
hadn't done anything to encourage him. And he'd done it
for *years*. Putting a hand here, rubbing against her there.
One time actually pulling out his penis to show her how
hard it was. Like that was going to make her fall all over
herself with wanting him. The other women in the office
just looked the other way when he harassed them, but Taryn
had resented it. And then the #MeToo movement started
and finally, *finally*, it was okay to speak up about Dan's
sexual peccadilloes. *There's a word for you, Josie!* And
she'd spoken up long and loud. The boss had apologized
and been sent to sensitivity classes, and that was about it.
He'd returned, angry and cold, and everyone else acted like

she was Typhoid Mary. She knew they all wanted her to quit, but she sure as hell wasn't going to. She worked in the finance department and was damn good at her job, and they could all go fuck themselves as far as she was concerned.

But Nick . . . he'd *listened.* "I'm sorry," he'd said sincerely. "I've done such stupid things myself. I don't even want to think about it."

"Not you," Taryn had insisted. "Never you."

He'd looked at her then in a way that had made her heart gallop. "I was as shitty as all of them. You know."

"As shitty as Killian? You don't even come close."

Killian had always been a bully. A true asshole. He sneered at her that she worked at Jefferson Motors, even though their sales kicked his daddy's company's ass more often than not. The girls had flocked around him in high school, but he'd been as bad then or worse, and he hadn't improved much with age. Miami was like a lemming; she would follow him to her death.

Taryn's gaze shifted to Kerry Monaghan, Nick's stepsister. Nick was particularly fond of her, and Taryn had wondered briefly if it was something more than just brotherly love. But it didn't appear to be. He'd told her that Kerry had been with Cole Sheffield, the police chief, but the relationship had broken up at the time of Cole's brother's death, and Kerry had ended up in a rebound marriage. Nick's marriage had been a mistake, too. He didn't talk about it much, but it was common lore that Marcia had lied about being pregnant, then had claimed a miscarriage. Maybe that was the truth, maybe it wasn't, but it didn't matter anyway; Nick had gotten out of the matrimonial chains pretty fast. Miss Seashell had gotten a house out of the deal—a pretty nice one—but word had it that she'd done her damnedest to hang on to Nick and considered the house a consolation prize.

But Nick wouldn't say anything bad about Marcia. He just didn't talk about her.

Why, oh, why, was he the one of all of them who'd had to die? As each day passed, Taryn felt worse and worse. She couldn't imagine never seeing Nick again. Never.

As the ferry churned up to the dock, one of the older men—Sean Blevins's dad—suddenly broke into a story about Nick and a cheerleader from another school and shenanigans at the fifty yard line after a football game. "She was one . . . healthy . . . girl," he said, pushing out his chest.

"Jesus, Dad," Sean whispered fiercely. "That wasn't Nick."

"Oh, no?" he asked, lifting a brow. A couple of the older guys snickered. One of them's wife squinted her eyes at him.

You get 'em, girl, Taryn thought. Smack that old fart around.

She saw Miami's eyes shift to Killian, who was smiling faintly. Then Miami looked down at the floor, and for just a second, Taryn saw her mouth drew into a hard line. Well, well, well. Maybe the beautiful little mouse had more of a spine than she'd shown thus far.

Taryn realized Sean had noticed Miami's small rebellion as well. She could tell he was embarrassed about his dad's creepy attitude. Taryn warmed to Sean. It was old dudes like Sean's dad, and younger guys like Killian, who treated women like dirt.

She was sick of it, and maybe Miami was, too. Kerry was still looking at Sean's dad as if he were poison, as were Josie and Cole Sheffield and just about everyone else. Forrest broke the uncomfortable moment by announcing they were docking, and Taryn walked over Sean's way. He was one good-looking dude and he'd shown more backbone than she would have expected.

* * *

The Pier was a gray clapboard building with white shutters and a double black door at the entrance. A cupola was perched atop the graying roof shingles and fitted with a weathered brass bell, an equally weathered brass weather vane in the shape of a seahorse at its crest. The parking lot was filled with SUVs, sedans, and pickup trucks, and several of the cars aboard the ferry pulled off and drove directly to it.

Kerry walked with Josie toward the wide-open doors. People were already milling around inside, a hostess directing them to the room at the back. Josie was telling her who all the older men and women were, the relationships to Nick's friends, and what the whole awkward conversation with Sean's father, Millard Blevins, had been about.

"Those old guys ogled all the high school girls. There was a group of them. Football dads. They still thought they had it. Like we thought they were hot. C'mon . . ." She choked back a short laugh. "Sean's dad was the worst."

"What about Killian's?"

"He had a little more class. Kept his tongue from hanging out when we walked by. I used to swing my hips, just to be saucy. Miami jabbed me so hard with her elbow, I had a bruise for a month."

"She didn't like that?"

"She didn't like any of it. But she went along with it."

"What do you mean?" asked Kerry.

"Oh, you know. Stupid girl stuff. We should've known better." Josie looked toward the bar at the end of the room as they entered and asked, "Who's that?"

A good-looking man with light brown hair, graying at the temples, a mocking expression on his face, who'd been leaning on the bar straightened as they entered. He headed toward them as if he'd been waiting for the sight of them.

Kerry stilled. "My ex-husband," she said in a controlled voice.

Cole tried to hang back and let all the mourners enter before him, but Carroll Keenan stayed back with him. "Think I'll have a cigar first," the older man said. "You're the cop, aren't you? The chief of police? I'm Carroll Keenan," he added before Cole could respond. He held out his hand and Cole shook it. "You knew Nick Radnor?"

"Yes," said Cole.

"You think it was suicide?"

"That's one theory."

"And another's murder?"

Cole nodded.

"What have you got on that?"

"Nothing I'm at liberty to say," Cole responded, his tone friendly. No, it wasn't suicide, and no, it wasn't an accident. Though he had no proof, Cole could feel that someone had killed Nick Radnor. He'd been interviewing Nick's friends and family over the past week, just doing a general workup of where they'd been, who they'd seen, what they thought about Nick, and he cataloged the information, letting it lie for the moment. After the memorial service, after seeing everyone he'd interviewed again, he would go over the information, see what jumped out at him.

"Radnor was one of those tech guys. Too much computer work. Too many violent video games. Gives a slanted perspective," Keenan said, pulling out a cigar and rubbing it a bit with his fingers.

Cole didn't remark on that. Keenan was fishing.

"Heard he died from a needle to the neck. That true?"

"Yes," Cole said, then he headed inside.

"Hi, Kerry," Vaughn said, dropping an arm over her shoulders and pulling her in for a hug.

Kerry was stiff and silent. Over Vaughn's shoulder she watched Josie's brows climb toward her hairline. In the past she might have hugged Vaughn back, just to stop the awkwardness, but today she remained a hard pole. His demonstrative move had surprised her, though it shouldn't have. Vaughn was always on stage for everyone else.

Easing herself out of his embrace, she stepped away, mad at herself all over again for ever getting involved with him.

"I'm so sorry about Nick. I know how much you loved him," he said earnestly.

Bullshit. Utter bullshit. Politely, she said, "Thank you. Excuse me."

Kerry brushed past him, fighting the burn of tears. She'd been holding it together throughout so far, but Vaughn's words, knowing how insincere he was about nearly everything, infuriated her. She wanted to blame him for everything. Unfair, but it made her feel better. Bastard. Goddamn, self-serving ass.

She almost ran into Chad Worster, who quickly stepped out of her way as she started blindly past him. She stopped and gave him a weak smile. "Sorry. Hi, Chad."

"It's all right. No problem. It's plain awful, isn't it?"

"That's exactly what it is."

She wanted to warm to him, but Chad and Nick had had their problems. A falling-out over the business that had led to its dissolution. Though everyone had made out very well, from what she'd heard—Nick had never related firsthand knowledge—the two friends had turned into frenemies . . . again, as rumor had it.

"It's just so hard to believe," he said.

That rang true to Kerry, who nodded jerkily. Chad was lanky, like Nick. His dark hair was longish and he wore a collarless black shirt under a gray sport coat, a pair of pressed denim jeans, and cowboy boots. He was the least dressed-up person in the room. Maybe Silicon Valley had had its influence on him, or maybe this was his own personal style.

Josie had kept by Kerry's side, after she'd run from Vaughn. She said now to Chad, "You're Nick's business partner?"

"Used to be. Nick sold the company to me a while ago." He gave Kerry a small smile. "Heard you were the main beneficiary."

"Me? No. I really doubt that."

"You don't know?" He was surprised.

"We're meeting with Nick's lawyer next week."

"You and Jerry?"

"Yes."

"A reading of the will, huh." He glanced around until his gaze fell on Nick's ex.

Kerry nodded. She and Jerry had each gotten a letter from the local law firm with whom Nick had entrusted his will. He'd apparently drawn up the document in California, then had it tweaked by Barnes & Barnes, Attorneys at Law, here in Edwards Bay.

"Don't expect Marcia to be named. Maybe Audra. But Marcia really burned her bridges with Nick."

Josie's neck craned and she half-turned so she could have Marcia in her sights. "Didn't they have a prenup?"

"That's the rumor," said Chad.

"What'd she do?" Josie asked, her gaze hard on Marcia, her brow furrowed.

"Marcia's a pretty self-centered bitch." Chad smiled. "She made his life a living hell. He put up with it as long as he could because of Audra, but in the end he had to run for his life. And yes, she was pregnant. She got Nick to sleep with her. Was the kid his? We'll never know. He married her and she miscarried. End of story."

Something about his tone led Kerry to believe he was holding something back. She almost asked, "What?" but stopped the question from passing her lips. She didn't want to gossip about Nick like that. It felt cheap and disrespectful.

Not so Josie. "If you know something, say it," she demanded.

"Nick didn't drink a lot, but one night he was wasted and angry. He'd seen some medical records he wasn't supposed to, apparently. Marcia miscarried before the wedding and didn't tell him."

Josie stared at Chad a long moment, then tears filled her blue eyes. "He would have married her anyway if she'd been honest. That's just how he was."

"Honey, that's bullshit," he said, not unkindly. "Let me buy you a drink and I'll tell you about Nick. He was a great guy and he wasn't. You come, too," he said to Kerry with a wink.

Kerry was still processing what he'd said about Nick. "No. I'm part of this event. I've got to help Marcia. Thanks."

"One drink?" Chad proposed. "Just one?"

"No, thanks."

She moved away from him, unaware she'd been holding her breath until it came out in a rush. She was blindly furious.

"What's wrong?" Egan Fogherty was suddenly at her elbow.

"Nothing," she said coldly.

They'd all gathered in the large room that overlooked the water. Sunlight was streaking through the clouds, bouncing on the gray water in glittering diamonds. Rows of chairs had been lined up facing a dais, which was flanked by two huge sprays of white flowers, chiefly lilies, baby's breath, and orchids. Marcia's choice.

As if she'd heard her name invoked, Marcia suddenly walked up to the podium. Looking around, she spied Kerry and motioned her forward. Kerry took several steps toward her and away from Egan, her eyes searching for Jerry. They weren't going to start anything without Nick's father.

She was a little surprised to see he was already there, propped up against the bar on the far end of the room, the opposite end from which Chad was leading Josie. Jerry was leaning over the counter, in a conversation with Millard Blevins, Sean's father. As Kerry headed that way, she saw Cole approach to Blevins's right. Blevins didn't notice, just kept right on talking to Jerry. As Kerry neared, she realized the conversation was about football, specifically Edwards Bay High football, and the poor team shaping up for next fall.

". . . Conway kid's got an arm but can't get close to his wide receivers. Last year's interceptions damn near cost as many points as they made all season. And there's nothing coming up. You look around here, at our kids, and they aren't even getting married or having sons. We're in a dearth, man. A dearth."

Jerry's eyes appeared glazed over. Kerry put a hand on his arm as Cole garnered Blevins's attention, changing the topic to college football and the University of Washington's chances of taking the Pac-12 North this season. Catching Cole's eye, Kerry gave him a faint smile of thanks. Blevins, however, tried to turn back to Jerry and expound some more on Edwards Bay. Jerry picked up his beer in a shaking hand and moved away with Kerry.

"Marcia's getting ready with the slideshow," Kerry told him.

"I didn't want to give her those pictures. I don't want to see 'em."

"I understand." She was pretty sure she'd feel shaky seeing the tribute as well. "Do you want to say anything?"

"No. Are you going to?" he asked her.

They'd already gone over this, but clearly Jerry hadn't heard her answer. "Yes," she said.

"Then can you speak for the both of us? I don't feel like I can do it."

In truth, Jerry was pale and sweating a bit. He'd hardly touched the beer and, as if realizing it was in his hand, he walked back to the bar and set it down. When he returned to Kerry, he said, "I'm going to sit down back here."

"There's a spot for you up front."

He shook his head.

Everyone began taking seats. Kerry had put her purse down on a chair near the front and, as she headed toward Marcia, who was impatiently waiting, she heard her cell phone ring. Embarrassed, she grabbed it up and switched it off, not before noting it was Diana calling. Diana? She had to know the memorial service was going on, didn't she?

Kerry turned off the ringer and headed up the two steps to stand by Marcia as she started the slideshow. Marcia narrated each picture, talking about Nick as if he were the love of her life, almost as if they were still married. Beside her, Kerry felt idiotic and superfluous and embarrassed. Nick would have hated it.

I'm sorry, she silently said to him, letting Marcia's words turn into an indistinct hum in her ears. *I should've known she'd do something like this, but I forgot.*

She could almost hear Nick making fun of Marcia's syrupy tone. If he were still alive, he would probably find it funny. He loved the absurd and ironic. It kept her from becoming too maudlin.

Did you take your own life, Nick? Did you?

She almost waited for an answer, but of course there was none. Still, it crystallized in her mind that he hadn't. Not from suicide, not from an accident. Someone had killed him. The two questions were, was it deliberate? And who did it?

"Kerry?" Marcia ended her tribute to Nick with tears in her eyes. Kerry could hear sniffling all around. Tissues were clutched in the hands of every woman along her row. She was glad she'd paid faint attention to Marcia's words so she could stay in control of her emotions.

"Nick was my brother and he was deeply loved by his father and me," she started in. "Nick's father, Jerry, asked me to speak for both him and me. We all have stories about Nick. Great guy, great friend, great athlete, great success—"

"Great husband," Marcia broke in, leaning toward the microphone, bravely fighting off tears.

Kerry had stepped back when Marcia swooped in. Now she looked over the crowd to see Josie roll her eyes. Marcia seemed reluctant to cede the mic back to Kerry, but she finally stepped back. Kerry continued. "Nick was the big brother I always looked up to. He helped me with math. He knew numbers. Boy, did he know numbers."

The crowd murmured its agreement, and a voice from the back yelled, "He knew how to make dollars and cents, that's for sure!"

A ripple of amusement followed, or was it envy?

Deciding she was veering into territory she didn't want to explore, she returned to memories of her childhood, telling several anecdotes from growing up as Nick's little sister. Just as she was winding up, the same voice, one of the older dads, said, "He could make points, that's for damn sure!"

"Thank you. And don't be shy about the buffet," Kerry said. The hair of the man who'd spoken was nearly white. He was being pulled away by Carroll Keenan, who was whispering fast and hard in his ear. Killian was there, too, looking more amused than his father, who was clearly irked with the guy who'd yelled out.

"Does anyone else have anything they want to say?" Marcia asked, practically grabbing the mic out of Kerry's hand.

Several people moved in the direction of the podium, while almost everyone else rose from their seats and worked their way to the back of the room near the bar, where a buffet table was set up along with a smattering of bistro tables.

"Who was that?" Kerry asked Josie and Miami, inclining her head toward the white-haired heckler as she joined them near the bar. Kent Roker stood a length of the bar away from his wife, as if he didn't want to bother her while she was with her friends. Or maybe he didn't feel like socializing.

"Bart Borland. Forrest's dad. He's an asshole," said Josie.

"Not as much as some," murmured Miami.

Kerry looked at her. She wasn't one to offer her opinion freely. "Who do you mean?"

"I mean all of them." Miami had her back to the bar and all of the A-Team dads, deliberately, Kerry realized. "All those old guys. They deserve what they're getting."

Kerry was about to ask her what they were getting when Diana suddenly stumbled into the room on four-inch heels.

Diana's black dress was skintight and short enough to raise eyebrows. A pink tulle scarf was draped over her shoulders and she wore clanking brass bracelets and matching hoop earrings. She threw a glance around and then, spying Kerry, lurched forward. Kerry realized it was more than just teetering ankles making her so wobbly.

Great.

Kerry looked around for Cole, hoping he would intervene here as well. It bothered her a little how much she wanted to depend on him. Maybe it was because he was the law. She hoped that was the reason. She didn't like believing she just wanted to be around him, which was entirely possible, but if that was the case, she had to get over it. She'd been congratulating herself on how much he was in her past, but maybe he wasn't as far back as she wanted to think.

She steered Diana to one side, away from Miami and Josie. Diana gripped her arm like a lifeline. "Kerry. I called you a few minutes ago, but you didn't answer."

"I was about to speak. I couldn't answer."

"I'm sorry. I've been thinking about Nick." Tears welled and she gulped in air. "And that night. He was so nice to me. I'm just kind of remembering little pieces, you know?"

Kerry saw people's heads turn to look at them . . . well, mostly at Diana.

Diana went on, "Something reminds you of things you forgot. You know, after you've been really drunk and you can't remember? But something triggers your memory. You know what I mean?"

Kerry guided her back toward the entry, away from all those curious faces. She pulled her through the open doorway toward the entry. The reception desk was across an expanse of gray tile that looked like weathered boards, but Kerry headed for the pair of chairs near a gas fireplace that was hissing softly, orange flames leaping around ceramic driftwood logs. "Are you drunk now?" she asked Diana.

"Because there's a whole room of people who are here to remember Nick and they might not understand."

"I'm sorry. I'm so sorry." She hiccupped out a sob. "But there was someone there. I saw him. I know I did. There was someone there."

"Where?"

"In my apartment. They had to be there. Because I didn't kill Nick!"

"Diana, you can't just make stuff up."

"I'm not! I'm not! I'm telling the truth. I can kind of remember. Well, I couldn't, but I went to a hypnotist and it's coming back. I saw him, Kerry. Behind Nick! I don't know who he is. He was waiting, though. It's all blurry, but I saw his shadow . . . his or hers . . . it seemed more like a him. He must've brought the hypodermic with him. I don't know why! But he killed Nick. He must've!"

"Shhh," Kerry said. Diana's voice had risen to a tight, loud shriek.

"You've gotta believe me!"

"Did you tell this to Cole . . . the police?"

"They think *I* did it. They think *I killed Nick.* I would never hurt him! Never. I loved him." She started to cry noisily. "We all did!"

"You didn't remember before, but now you do . . . with the help of hypnosis?"

She bobbed her head. "Yes! It just started coming back and I remembered he was there. I'm not making this up. Nina put me under and I saw the door to my deck was open and the curtains were blowing, so I closed the door. . . ." She turned, as if visualizing the scene. "I was going to bed and I wasn't thinking about Nick or anything. I just was going to bed. But I looked up and I saw them."

"Them?"

"Nick and him. He was behind Nick. I saw the shadow.

I think . . . maybe . . . I think he surprised Nick and . . . then he killed him."

"Isn't your deck on the second floor?"

"There are back stairs to it. And they were out there, Kerry. I remember. Somebody killed him!"

"You should tell this to Cole. Or Ben Youngston. He's here, too."

"No! Not Ben. And I don't want to talk to anybody but you. You're Nick's sister. You should tell Cole. And his dad. Let his dad know I didn't hurt Nick. I did . . . I . . . did give him a pill at the Blarney Stone. That's all he wanted. Just one, or maybe two. I don't know. But that's all."

"Nick asked for drugs?"

"He was sad, Kerry. He wanted it all to go away for a while."

Kerry could feel a headache building. From inside the room where the service was taking place she could hear a man's voice speaking through the microphone. Chad Worster.

"Oh. And he wanted to fix things. That's what he said."

"What things?"

"I think he was . . ." She looked down, her brows drawn into a line, concentrating hard. "Working himself up to something. He said . . ."

"He said?" she prompted

"I can't remember. But it'll come back to me. I know it will. I'll go see Nina again." She looked at Kerry with horror-filled eyes. "You think that's why they killed him?"

Kerry felt a cold wave wash over her. She didn't know what to believe. Looking down at Diana's messy hair, the body-hugging dress, the black heels, she urged, "Diana, you need to go home. Did you come over on the ferry?" She nodded. "You need to turn around and go right back."

"No. I have to stay. I didn't hurt Nick. They need to know I didn't hurt him."

"But if someone was there, like you say, then—"

"They were there!"

"—you should be careful. You know? Be careful."

Diana just shook her head. "I need them to know I didn't hurt Nick. You can tell Cole." She staggered away from Kerry and back toward the other room. Kerry drew a careful breath, then hurried after her, catching up just in time to see Diana nearly barrel into Angie, who was half-leaning into the reception room, eavesdropping. Diana grabbed onto the open doorframe to steady herself, and Angie pretended to just be walking into the other room.

"How much have you had to drink?" Angie asked Diana.

"You were listening," Diana accused, then lurched away from her.

Kerry and Angie exchanged a glance, then Kerry followed Diana. She was a train wreck. And if there was the slightest chance she was telling the truth . . . Angie had overheard. She glanced back to see Angie had given up her charade of having some business in the reception area and was trailing after her and Diana.

Ooof!

Kerry suddenly slammed into a wall of flesh. "Oh! Sorry," she murmured as strong male arms steadied her.

Killian Keenan.

Chapter Ten

Killian let go of Kerry without looking at her, practically setting her aside. His glare was reserved for Diana, who'd stopped short on her teetering escape toward the bar when Kerry had run into Killian.

"What are you doing here?" he demanded.

Diana flushed. "I just . . . Nick was my friend, too."

"Get out of here," he snarled.

"Okay, okay. Stop. Shhh." Taryn pushed between Killian and Diana, her thin glare toward him just as aggressive as his was leveled on Diana. "Leave her be."

Kerry tried to say something, anything, but Killian pushed her aside, turning the full brunt of his ire from Diana to Taryn. "You were supposed to be Nick's friend and you're defending *her*."

"Not the place, Killian," Taryn warned. "Don't be a jerk."

"Better than being a whiny bitch," he leveled back at her.

Taryn ignored him, turned to Kerry. "I have something to say, but Marcia's guarding the microphone like it's her lost virginity."

"Just tell her you want to talk," Kerry advised, wary of Killian, whose size and anger were daunting. Her heartbeat was running fast and she glanced over at Cole, who was talking to some of the older men near the bar.

Egan Fogherty was currently at the mic, mumbling something about Nick. When he looked up to see Taryn approaching, he stopped in midsentence. Kerry could see the way his gaze devoured Taryn as she neared the podium; she'd been a recipient of that same predatory look. Egan wore his horniness like a second skin, a downright creepy sexual vibe. She'd felt it when they'd been barhopping and earlier tonight. Briefly, she wondered if he'd exhibited the same behavior in high school.

Marcia grabbed the mic from his hands almost before he was done and handed it to Taryn.

Diana was practically cowering behind Kerry, but, like Egan, Killian's eyes had followed Taryn.

"Taryn always thought we were all dying for her," he said, his smile cold. "No one ever liked her. Not even Nick, no matter what she says."

As he walked away, Diana said, almost apologetically, "Killian's always been kind of mean."

"Diana, I'm not kidding. I think you should go home." Kerry would have liked to leave, too, but she felt duty bound to stay. For Nick. For Jerry.

"Just stick with me and I'll be fine," Diana whispered. She clutched Kerry's arm like a lifeline.

Cole had been listening with half an ear to Millard Blevins wax rhapsodic about the good old days when his kid was in high school and the football team took regionals and, almost, state. He'd compartmentalized the man's nostalgia to one part of his brain while listening with the other part to Nick's friends and family eulogize him. Except for a few unlucky errors—"that Palance kid had no business being a safety. Little fucker would just watch as they cruised right by him into the end zone"—Blevins assured him the

Edwards Bay team would have taken state that year. A glorious time. Halcyon days. The man's obsession with high school football was mind-numbing, though he didn't seem to have the same burnished memory for anything related to his son, especially when Sean sauntered over to remind him that that they were at a memorial service and if he couldn't move on to another subject, maybe he should leave. "Mediocre on the field" was Blevins's remark as Sean left.

Cole's main reason for engaging the man had been to give Jerry Radnor a chance to move away from the windbag's monologue on the subject, but he had another motivation as well. Cecily Wright had brought up the football "dads," complaining about how her husband had wanted Adam to join the team even though Adam had only been interested in tennis. Cecily's remarks had been about her disdain for her deceased husband, but she'd also condemned the football dads as a group. Cole wanted to know as much about Nick Radnor as he could, and having the fathers of Nick's friends in one place was a way to interview them en masse.

"You were part of the 'football dads' from Nick's era?" Cole questioned Blevins.

He nodded. "EBF Dads. Edwards Bay Football. I don't think they use those initials anymore, but yeah. We started the group."

"It's still functioning?"

"On life support." He snorted. "Nobody wants their kid turning into a vegetable from getting their bell rung too many times. It's a shame really."

"Nick was on the team. Was Jerry part of EBF?"

Blevins looked over toward Jerry Radnor, who'd taken a chair and was still sitting in it, raptly listening to whoever took the mic, while most of the guests had turned their attention to the food, though maybe still with an ear toward the speaker. "Jerry was an honorary member. He didn't really fit with us that well. And Nick was kind of different, too."

"Meaning?"

"Football . . . when fall comes it's everything, you know?" He gazed at Cole hard, as if that would help him understand. "It's like religion. You either have it or you don't."

"You don't think people can like football with less commitment?"

He grinned. "Nah. You're either in or out. And Jerry was kind of out. Nick was a good player, but he had other things on his mind when he should've been concentrating. I remember Coach Bergen reaming him out at the end of the season. Coach didn't know about the Benetton girl yet. It wasn't public knowledge at that practice about what happened. Nobody knew till after. Nick just took it. Didn't seem to hear him or care. Even though Coach apologized later, Nick wasn't fazed. He was in his own little world. If he hadn't been a senior, he woulda been cut from the team."

"Wait a minute. You're saying Nick got dressed down for not having his head in the game the day he found out about Lisette Benetton's suicide?"

"Well, when you put it like that," he complained. "Nobody knew, see. Not then anyway. 'Cept maybe Nick. It was a tragedy, for sure, but nobody knew."

Cole pretended to understand, though it was an effort. It wouldn't pay to alienate Blevins while he was interviewing him. "Who were the other EBF Dads?"

"Oh, Keenan, Borland, Fogherty . . ."

"Egan Fogherty played football?"

"If you can call it that. He was smart, but no emotional control, you know what I mean? Definitely second team."

"What about Conrad Wright?"

"His kid didn't play. Adam was really his grandkid, but they adopted him, you know. His dad was a bruiser in his day, before the drugs and all took him, and Conrad wanted to relive that. We were happy to have him. He didn't complain. Just liked hanging out. RIP to both him and Nick." He lifted his beer.

Cole thought about sports and the culture it created between boys and their fathers . . . the strain of expectation, which could be good or bad, depending on the individuals. "Who was the quarterback back then?" Cole asked.

"Keenan. Always thought Killian would go on to have a college football career, maybe even more."

"He was that good?" Cole let his gaze rest lightly on Killian Keenan, who seemed to feel the weight of his stare and looked up to coldly meet his eyes. A silent challenge, maybe.

"He was that good. Got injured that spring, right before graduation. Busted an ankle that's never worked the same again, according to Carroll. No explanation how. Some people say it happened in a fight."

"A fight with . . . ?"

Blevins shrugged. "Nick, maybe. Or maybe not?" As if waking up to the fact to whom he was speaking, he asked, "What's your interest, Chief?"

"Background," he said, just as Ben Youngston hitched his chin at him, indicating he wanted a confab. Cole excused himself and headed Ben's way. Ben had been a classmate of Nick's as well, but he wasn't particularly close to his circle of friends and had spent most of the night detached from them.

Cole met up with him by the bar just as Taryn Whitcomb took the mic.

"Something?" Cole asked Ben.

"Diana Conger's here." His tone was deep with disapproval.

"I saw."

"She should be in jail."

Cole was slow to anger as a rule, but Ben was really

pushing him. He could feel his scalp tingle with the effort to control his emotions. "That's why you called me over?"

Ben started to say something, then thought better of it.

From the podium, Tara announced loudly, "Nick Radnor and I became close friends over this past year."

Cole broke eye contact with Ben, pulling himself back from his anger as Taryn glanced over the group in such a commanding way that all the twos and threes of people holding their plates and chatting with one another fell silent and looked to her. "We'd always known each other, but it wasn't until recently that we found we were of like minds about a lot of different issues. Nick was not only good at making money, he was even better at giving it away to worthy causes. He was a philanthropist, and we worked together at the Brighter Day Center, which, as many of you know, is a place the homeless can find help and recapture their dignity. I've been involved with the center for years, particularly in helping displaced women who've come to this stage in their lives because of physical abuse, often-times at the hands of their husbands or partners. Nick shared that involvement. And, though I understand his will hasn't been released yet, I already know what a big part of it is: aid for the homeless at Brighter Day Center. Nick left nearly his entire fortune to Brighter Day. It truly is a brighter day for the homeless in Edwards Bay!"

Her voice rose into a crescendo and people stood frozen for a moment, then looked around at the other mourners, as if deciding how to act. One person began to clap slowly, and a few others joined in. Cole's anger with Ben was set aside as he considered Taryn's fervent announcement. To date none of them—Kerry, Jerry, and Marcia included—had been briefed on Nick's estate, yet she knew this?

He glanced at Kerry, who was in turn looking with concern at Jerry, who was just sitting in his chair, staring at Taryn. Kerry moved toward her stepfather, excusing herself away from Diana, who seemed to want to cling to her, and a brown-haired man in a charcoal sport coat who Cole had noticed watching Kerry's group. He'd wondered if the man had his eye on Kerry or someone else but now saw he was also making his way toward Jerry.

Taryn was going on about Nick's goodness, but the crowd's attention had shifted toward Kerry, Jerry, and Marcia to see how they would react to her words about Brighter Day. Marcia was still standing near the podium. She took a couple of steps toward Taryn, her hands outstretched as if to grab the mic from her hand, or stop her, or maybe even attack her. As if realizing everyone was watching, she dropped her arms, but her face had paled.

"And so honoring Nick today is a wonderful gesture, but not half as wonderful as his own gesture to the people suffering in our community every day!"

Taryn held on to the mic tautly and looked like she wanted to say more. Marcia, however, couldn't take it. She muscled Taryn aside and yanked the mic from her fingers.

"Anyone else?" Marcia asked. "Well, then, let's all eat. *Mangia, mangia!*" Her smile was brilliant and fake and she stalked away with the mic in hand, as if fearing Taryn would take it back from her again.

"What is that, French?" Cole overheard Josie ask as he left Youngston and made his way toward Jerry and Kerry.

Miami, following behind Josie, said, "Would Nick really leave all his money to Brighter Day?"

Josie threw a hard glance to where Taryn was still near the podium, speaking with a small group of mourners who'd come up to talk to her. "I doubt it. Taryn would. She's obsessive that way. But Nick?" She shook her head.

As Cole approached, the man in the charcoal jacket put his arm around Kerry's shoulders, but her attention was fully on Jerry. Cole's heart chilled. A lover? Relationship?

He'd been thinking Kerry was free; arrogantly so, he saw now. But this man was clearly staking a claim.

Kerry leaned over Jerry, who was pale and sweating profusely. "Jerry," she said, trying to hide the concern in her voice.

"I'm fine." He raised a hand to wave her off, but she saw it was trembling.

"Do you want some water? Let me get you some water."

At that moment she felt an arm drop onto her shoulder and she glanced back to see it was Vaughn. Immediately, she turned her attention back to Jerry.

"I'll get the water," Miami said from behind her.

"You all right, babe?" Vaughn asked Kerry.

"Perfectly fine," Kerry said with an edge, sliding from beneath his embrace, wondering what the hell was going on with him. He'd walked out on her years before and good riddance.

Jerry said to her, "I think I'm going to leave."

"Okay. I'll go with you. Oh, you have your car," Kerry said, thinking fast. "I'll drive."

"I can drive," Vaughn offered.

"No, no, I'm fine," said Jerry, waving them off.

"Jerry, I'm not letting you leave here without me," said Kerry. "That's not the way it works with us."

"You haven't even had anything from the buffet yet," he protested.

"I'm not hungry."

"What about all the guests?" He gazed around blankly.

"It's fine. Most of the speeches are over. They're at the buffet. Marcia can take it from here."

Vaughn said, "Do either of you need a drink?"

"Yes," Kerry said firmly. Anything to get rid of him. "Glass of white wine?"

"You want to join me . . . ?" Vaughn inclined his head toward the bar.

"Would you mind bringing me one?" Not that she planned on drinking it.

Vaughn hesitated, clearly minding very much. For some reason he wanted to hang by her. Several awkward moments passed before he headed stiffly to the bar.

"Do you believe what she said?" Jerry asked Kerry softly, in the moment when they were finally out of earshot of everyone else.

Kerry leaned in closer. "Who? Taryn?"

"You think Nick left all his money to that shelter?"

"I don't know, Jerry. She acted like she knew what she was talking about."

"Maybe he did. I guess we'll know soon. He was in a bad way, you know." Tears filled his faded blue eyes.

"Nick?" Kerry asked.

"He was really sorry for Lisette . . . and other things."

Kerry's heart lurched uncomfortably. "Lisette's death wasn't his fault."

"He never got over it."

"But it wasn't his fault," she argued again. It felt like the ground was continually shifting beneath her feet when it came to Nick.

"Atonement," said Jerry, so softly she could scarcely hear him.

"What?"

"Here you go," Miami said brightly, coming up on Kerry's right and holding out a glass of water.

Kerry straightened as Jerry accepted the drink. She wanted to grill him on what he meant, but he'd turned his attention to Miami, maybe deliberately shutting her out.

"Thank you." His voice quavered a bit as he gave her a smile.

"You're welcome. Anything else?" she asked him.

Jerry focused on Miami for a long moment, as if memorizing what she looked like. He opened his mouth to say something to her, but no words came out.

"Jerry," Kerry said, alarmed anew.

"I'm okay, I'm okay," Jerry assured her. "You stay and finish up. I'll be fine."

Miami, her brow furrowed with worry, said, "How about I get you a plate of food?"

"I think we're leaving—" Kerry began.

"That would be great." Jerry overrode her, and Miami headed back to the buffet table.

"Jerry, I'm ready to go," Kerry told him. "Marcia's got this handled. I—"

"You're *leaving*?" Marcia gasped, coming up to the two of them. "Kerry, you can't leave. Who's going to clean up? I can't do this all by myself!"

"Jerry isn't feeling well. He wants to go, and—"

"No, no," Jerry interrupted her, holding up a hand. "Stop arguing. I can wait."

"You shouldn't have to. I'll take you."

"No, I've changed my mind. I want to do this right for Nick. I just felt claustrophobic for a minute, but it's passed."

"Are you sure?" Kerry questioned, eyeing him closely.

"Yes."

Miami returned with a small plate, which she handed to him. Some color had returned to his face as he looked at the shrimp, mushroom caps, carrot sticks, celery, and tiny tomatoes with ranch dressing. His hand wasn't shaking as much and he seemed to come to life in Miami's company.

"Okay," Kerry said dubiously.

"So you're going to stay?" Marcia snapped at Kerry. Her gaze was on Jerry, a glower as she watched Miami cater to him.

"Looks like it." Kerry shot a glance in Cole's direction as she headed to the back of the room . . . or at least where he'd been. He was no longer there. She saw Josie standing near Kent, but there was a strange awkwardness between them. A marriage in free fall, she thought.

Vaughn returned with her wine. Kerry thanked him and he said, "I know you're crazy busy with this whole thing, but I want to talk to you."

"You're right. I am crazy busy."

"Maybe you could carve out a little time for me."

She glanced at Jerry and Miami, then took a gulp of wine. She left Vaughn to squeeze through several people, trying to avoid talking to him, but he kept right behind her, following so closely he was practically stepping on her heels. "I've been thinking about us a lot lately," he said. "Thinking about things, you know. How the wheels came off the bus."

Good God. This? Now? She'd had some hurt feelings at the time of their breakup, regret over the decisions she'd made, but she'd never been sorry they'd divorced.

"Not now, Vaughn."

"Later, then? I could stop by your place. You still at the apartment?"

"No."

"Where are you?"

She stopped short and turned to face him, shoving the wineglass in his hand. "Thank you for the wine. I don't have time for you right now."

He looked at the glass. "You don't want the rest of it?"

"I don't even know what you're doing here," she told him in exasperation.

"I'm here because of Nick. Because of you." He blinked. "Of course I am."

"Okay."

"You don't have to take that tone."

"Pay your respects to Jerry. Have some food. Leave me be."

"Well, thanks, Kerry. It's great to see you, too."

She'd headed blindly toward the buffet table. Momentarily lost, she snatched up a small plate and began loading it with vegetables. Vaughn slid in behind her in line.

"I feel bad for you, and for Jerry. It's terrible," Vaughn said, picking up a plate.

"Thanks. I appreciate it."

"Hey, I'm just trying to be friendly."

She had to bite back a dozen mean comments. Had to remind herself that Nick's death wasn't his fault. Had to remind herself that just because Vaughn was a master at making himself the victim, there was no reason to become a raving maniac.

And then, suddenly, Cole was across the table from her.

"How's Jerry?" he asked her.

Kerry looked at him, her chest filling with emotion. Now she wanted to cry? She wanted to scream with frustration. "He says he's okay, but I don't know. Miami got him some food, but before that he said he wanted to leave."

"Who are you again?" Vaughn interrupted, eyeing Cole.

"Cole Sheffield. The Edwards Bay chief of police," Kerry answered before Cole could, knowing full well Vaughn wouldn't have forgotten the name of the man Kerry had been so in love with.

Vaughn stuck out his hand. "Vaughn Campfer. Kerry's husband."

"Ex-husband," Kerry corrected as he and Cole shook hands. "Don't do this, Vaughn. I don't have the energy for your games."

"Games?" He looked affronted.

She walked away.

Chapter Eleven

Diana watched Kerry stalk from the buffet table back to her stepfather, holding a plate that she dropped on an empty bistro table on the way. She looked upset. Well, it was upsetting. She was upset, too.

Was Kerry right? Should she leave? She looked around at her friends and could feel the bad juju they were all leveling at her.

But it's not my fault!

They'd been coming over to her one by one. Some were nice. Some weren't. She'd told Kerry about the other person she'd seen at her apartment. It was sort of a lie. She didn't really remember. It was more of an impression, one aided by hypnosis, but she was pretty sure it was true. And she needed something to get them off her case anyway. Besides, it was almost the truth and that was what counted.

She'd told Josie Roker about the other person in the room, and then she told Sean Blevins, who really was a cutie but now looked so dolefully unhappy. Nick's death was bearing down on him, too. And she told Miami, and Killian was right there, hovering behind her like always, and she told Marcia, who was really nasty and screamed at her that she was a whore, to which Forrest said she wasn't a whore because she hadn't gotten paid. He followed that up with "but Nick maybe paid her for being his dealer . . ." which pissed Diana off but made Egan laugh. Man, she was sorry she'd slept with him. She almost made a crack about him hardly being able to get it up, but that was too mean, and no matter what they thought of her, she wasn't mean.

And then one of the dads had tried to get in on the conversation with her. Maybe Forrest's dad? She'd gotten out of that fast. Those old men were creepy and a little too touchy-feely. Maybe worse now than in high school.

Randy had tried to talk to her, and he was kind of nice, but Angie was right there, of course, hanging on his arm. She asked about the hypnotist, picked up from her eavesdropping, no doubt, and Diana just knew she'd spread that bit of gossip throughout the party. When Randy patted her on the shoulder and asked if she needed a ride home, Diana could've cried. She shook her head and looked at Angie, who was staring at her so hard it was amazing her laser gaze didn't burn right through her. Some things never changed.

At one point that guy who was hanging around Kerry, Vaughn something, had asked her if he could buy her a drink and, well . . . she'd popped a couple of pills before the service. Just a couple. No one could really make it through this without help. As it was all she wanted to do was bawl about Nick. So she'd taken the drink and talked to him briefly. She could tell by the way he'd looked at her, he was interested, but then he'd given her an apologetic smile and followed Kerry to the buffet table, though it was pretty clear she wasn't interested in him. Had he upset her? He'd followed Kerry from the buffet table back to a place a few steps away from Nick's dad, who wasn't looking so hot. He was one of the nicer old farts. Miami had brought him a plate, but she was back with Killian near the bar now. Marcia had been there, too, but she'd gone off in a huff with

Ben Youngston and they were talking in a corner, though Marcia kept looking over at Nick's dad and Kerry.

Josie and Kent had gotten into a fight. One of those hissing-through-your-teeth-at-each-other-hoping-others-won't-hear fights.

As she was watching, Nick's dad suddenly wrenched up to his feet, dropping his half-empty plate with a clatter as he jerkily moved away from the group and toward the small hallway alcove that led to the restrooms.

Kerry followed after him, as did Cole, who came from another direction. Vaughn took a few steps their way and then held.

Well . . . he was fair game, wasn't he? Diana thought, walking up to him. "Hey," she said.

Vaughn flicked her a look, glanced back in the direction in which Kerry had gone, then turned to Diana. "Want another?" he asked, gesturing to her empty glass.

"Sure. You having one?"

"Might as well."

They went to the bar together, and as Vaughn ordered her a glass of wine and himself a Maker's Mark, she asked, "Is Mr. Radnor okay?"

"I'd give that a big no." He knocked back his drink when he got it. Diana sipped hers. She felt better hanging with Vaughn. No judgment.

"You're drinking," Taryn's voice rang out.

Diana looked behind her to see Taryn staring at her, her lips a line of disapproval. "Just one glass," Diana said airily, although it did sound like the last word came out "glash," to which Taryn lifted her brows in a *see?* gesture.

Diana determined right then and there that she couldn't stand Taryn. She was the judgmental one. Sure, it was Taryn who'd first introduced Diana to Nick, who hadn't immediately remembered her from high school, which hurt a little, but Taryn was just so unlikable sometimes. Diana even wondered if she was really as into the women's movement as much as she professed. Sometimes it felt like Taryn glommed onto things in order to be cool.

Diana immediately felt bad for her thoughts. Just because she didn't like Taryn didn't mean she had to diminish what she'd suffered.

"I don't know what happened at your place." Taryn's voice was ice. "But Nick died there."

"It's not my fault," she said for about the hundredth time, her voice warbling.

"Then whose is it? Maybe everybody else will let you get away with it, but I won't. Nick was my best friend. You took his life."

"I did not!" Diana cried.

"Harsh," Vaughn observed.

Taryn threw him a cool look.

"I just can't remember what happened," Diana moaned. "I'm sorry. I'm so sorry. But maybe somebody else came inside from the back deck. I told Kerry. And everybody. It's not my fault if none of you believe me."

Vaughn gave her a penetrating look. "It was your place? That's where Nick died?"

Diana shriveled inside. The way he was looking at her was the way everyone had looked at her. She felt tears building, burning behind her eyes. The pills and wine were roiling her emotions, fueling her own rage and hurt over losing Nick. "Excuse me," she said, stumbling away from them.

Josie watched Diana weave around people, aware she was way past her limit already. Josie, too, was drinking more than she wanted. She was sick about Nick. Sick. Could scarcely speak without her throat closing up.

And she was annoyed with Kent, who'd hinted he knew she was having an affair. He hadn't mentioned Nick's name, but she knew he was fishing. If he knew the truth, if any of them did, it would be laughable.

"I'm going to head home now," Kent clipped out. He was eyeing the hallway where Kerry and Cole had disappeared, following Nick's father.

Kerry had caught Kent's eye, which was also laughable. Kent was too straitlaced and repressed to go after another woman, although sometimes Josie wished he would. But The Bank of Edwards Bay, his family's bank, had some strict behavioral rules that Kent would never defy. Unless Josie started divorce proceedings he wouldn't leave her. And if she started the proceedings, she'd be screwed out of the comfortable life she'd made for herself.

Maybe she should just stay with Kent. Nick was gone anyway. A bleak future looked to be in the cards no matter what.

"You can take Uber or catch a ride with one of your friends," Kent said in that superior tone of his that drove her insane. *Supercilious*, that was the word. "I'm flying to New York tomorrow."

Josie watched him leave, then conjured up an image of Nick and her in her shower, his hands on her hips, hers on his chest to drift lower and lower still until they wrapped around his huge shaft and she guided him to her. He had to bend down and pick her up, and their slippery hands and bodies created laughter and desire until she set her on him, thrusting deep to her core.

A sexual thrill zinged through her and she forced herself to walk toward the buffet table and act normally. God. She could damn near have an orgasm in front of the whole room if she wasn't careful.

Killian Keenan ate the three olives off the toothpick, swallowing them after two quick bites, before he poured the martini down his throat. He rarely drank anything stronger than a beer, but Nick Radnor's death was a special occasion. He allowed the tight rein he kept on himself to ease a bit.

He could feel his father's eyes on him and looked up resentfully, but dear old dad was in a deep conversation with Millard Blevins. Knowing Blevins it was about football. Killian automatically rotated his ankle, the one that had ruined his football career. Though surgery was long over and the thing barely bothered him in daily life, he could imagine the sound of fine bones crushing against each other like potato chips. Someone had given him that image and it was a curse he could never forget it.

"Another?" the bartender asked.

Killian looked at the guy. He was pretty sure they were of an equal age and he'd met him across a high school field somewhere, but he couldn't place him. Maybe not. Everyone started to look like an old enemy in time.

"You sold me my 2017 Explorer," the bartender said, interpreting Killian's lack of recognition correctly.

"Ah, yeah. I did." Killian scared up a smile, though he now remembered how the asshole had hemmed and hawed and brought his girlfriend, who wore enough makeup to scare a transvestite. "Sure, give me another." He slid his empty glass toward the guy.

Killian was working at his dad's Ford dealership, which was no joke. He'd thought the old man might move him into management, but so far he was stuck in sales. Not that he didn't do all right for himself. Except for this dithering idiot making his martini, most of his sales were pretty damn quick. He had the gift of gab and he knew his shit. If you didn't buy a car from him, Killian figured there was something wrong with you, not him.

Fresh martini in hand, he turned his back on the bar and leaned against it, observing the crowd. He'd always disliked funerals and memorial services, made excuses never to go. But this one was different. All his friends were here. Like old times . . . even to the now gray-haired dads who'd once ruled over the team as if they were gods.

The old fuckers.

His eyes found Miami and his gaze followed her around. She was being all caring and sweet to Nick's dad, which was so her. He didn't get what she saw in old people. She said it was because she'd been close to her grandparents, but Killian didn't buy it. They'd been gone for years.

He wondered if she was just trying to get in Jerry Radnor's good graces, looking for maybe a chunk of the inheritance when he passed on. Maybe some of Nick's would be mixed in there, too. It wasn't a bad plan, if that was what she was doing. He could almost applaud her for it. Except she'd grown a bit distant lately.

His gaze returned to his father, who'd told him he'd had a talk with Miami. For reasons still unknown, the old man suddenly wanted him to be with her . . . after years of saying she was "that Mexican whore." Miami's mom was Cuban, but that was too fine a point for the old man. At least he had stopped calling Miami a whore, and then, recently, he'd come fully around, saying he would bless their union if Killian and Miami finally wed. He wanted a grandson. Killian wanted a child, too, for that matter. He'd never really thought about marriage until recently, to Miami or anyone else. He'd just known he was never going to let

Miami go. She was his. Forever. But his thoughts had changed around a bit with his father's blessing.

He thought about calling Coach Rawlings again. Edwards Bay High's current football coach had agreed to have Killian work as an assistant coach this coming fall, like he did last year, but he'd been impossible to get hold of lately. There'd been that small incident last year; not even really an incident, just a horsing-around moment, when he'd grabbed the Palance kid around the neck after the kid had snapped a towel at him and nailed his balls just as he was getting out of the shower. He'd wanted to rip the little fucker's head off, but he'd just scared him. The kid had, of course, whined to his parents, who in turn had whined to Coach Rawlings. Killian had been upbraided and it had not set well, but he'd swallowed his anger at the time. He'd taken it out on Miami a bit. He could admit that. But he'd said he was sorry for shoving her up against the refrigerator. She'd just been standing there and he'd tried to get around her, that was all.

Anyway, Coach Rawlings had had to keep him away from the team for a couple of weeks, but he'd been with him through the first playoffs . . . where they'd sucked, but some of the better players were returning.

He pulled out his cell phone. Thought about texting. Nah. The coach was old school. He phoned his number, and when he got the recording he put a smile on his face and left a message, asking him to call him. As soon as he clicked off, the smile fell off. He could smile with the best of them to make a sale. People liked to see it and could hear it on the phone.

Diana headed past him and he stuck out a hand and steadied her, holding her until she was right on her heels again. "Thanks," she said, not looking at him.

"Sure thing, murderer."

"For God's sake, Killian," she said tiredly.

"Just kidding. I know you didn't do it." She slowly, hopefully, looked up at him. He added, "On purpose."

Zing! Gotcha, bitch.

"It was somebody else," she insisted. "I told you."

"Oh, don't cry."

"Fuck you."

His dick stirred. There was some real heat to her words. Very un-Diana. The angry glance she sent his way reminded him of the time they'd ended up in her bed together. She was hot. Like Miami used to be.

"You've always been jealous of Nick. He was successful and you . . ." She lifted her shoulders.

He was shocked that Diana—*Diana*—felt she could backtalk him. "Watch yourself. Remember the chart?" he said coldly.

Diana glared at him. Actually glared. "You can't scare me with that."

"Because you're such a slut no one cares?"

She shook her head. "You've always been a bad guy."

"Want me to come over tonight and prove different? I can be really good, and you, above all else, know."

"What would Miami say?"

Her words irked him. Not for her meaning. Because Miami would probably say nothing. Because it was Diana saying it and she was *nothing*.

He suddenly wanted to take Miami, throw her down on the floor, and make love to her like the old days. Hard. Quick. Both of them crazed with desire. He threw Diana a scathing look, then went to find Miami. He liked the way Miami, his woman, looked, the smooth contour of the dress over her hips and butt. Coming up behind her, he wrapped his arms around her waist even though she jumped a foot when he came up behind her.

"Oh, it's you," she said.

"Who else would it be?" He pressed his mouth into the back of her neck, his body up behind her so she could feel how hard he was.

She didn't move.

"I think we'd better take care of this right now," he whispered against the shell of her ear.

"I can't leave yet."

"Yes, you can."

"Not yet, Killian. I just need a little more time."

Bitch! He released her in disgust, stalking back to the bar. If anyone saw his erection, too fucking bad. But then he thought of Nick, shot full of embalming fluid—or no, probably more likely turned to ash. He'd been cremated, hadn't he?

His hard-on disappeared as if doused in ice water.

And then he felt someone's eyes on him.

He slowly looked around and his gaze landed on Marcia Radnor, head bent, listening to something Ben Youngston was saying. It was Youngston who was looking at him. Jesus. Ben took his job with the police department way too seriously. He'd graduated with the rest of them but now acted like he was too good for them. In Killian's mind he'd always been a weasel and a suck-up. But no, Ben wasn't looking at him. He was just staring straight ahead but tuned in to Marcia. Killian could tell Ben was feeling about Marcia the same way he was feeling about Miami. Horny. Ready to make a scene, if necessary, to have his woman.

But did Marcia feel the same? By the look of things, Killian would say no.

Sean Blevins sidled up to Killian, which was unusual because Sean wasn't one to start a conversation. Too busy being cool. It amused Killian, the way the girls fed off Sean's shtick. Nothing special about him, though.

Now Sean inclined his head toward Cole Sheffield, Edwards Bay's own police chief as he, Kerry, and Jerry Radnor returned to the main room. "Cole was a friend of Nick's," he reminded Killian.

"Yeah?"

"I just don't want any problems."

"Maybe you should gag your old man."

Sean grimaced, a crack in his studied exterior.

"None of us did anything wrong," Killian reminded him. "Nick's death's not on us."

"I know that."

"Yeah? You look like a frightened mouse. Diana killed him. Lucky for us, huh?"

"What's that supposed to mean?" Sean was trying to sound blasé, but he never took his eyes off Cole.

"Stop worrying." Killian leaned in, a cold grin on his face. "Your reputation is safe with me."

A sudden movement in his peripheral vision. Killian glanced across the room. Jerry Radnor, trying to retake his chair, suddenly stumbled forward and toppled over. Cole leaped to catch him a half second too late and Nick's father crashed to the ground and lay still.

Chapter Twelve

Doctor: *What happened when Diana Conger showed up at Nick Radnor's memorial service?*

Patient: *You want to hear it for the fiftieth time? No one wanted her there. She's the reason Nick died. She gave him some pills and he went home with her.*

Doctor: *But she didn't kill him.*

Patient: *No, she didn't kill him.*

Doctor: *You were at her apartment that night.*

Patient (heavy sigh): *I've said so, haven't I?*

Doctor: *And you brought the hypodermic needle with you?*

Patient: *Yes.*

Doctor: *And you used it on Nick.*

Patient: *Again, yes.*

Doctor: *So how does it follow that Diana Conger is the reason Nick died?*

Patient: *She exposed him . . . she was about to, anyway. Nick always acted like he was better than anybody, and we all kind of believed it. Let him get away with it. But it finally caught up to him. We finally reached the tipping point.*

Doctor: *Who's "we"?*

Patient: *Anybody who got to know him well. All of us.* Murder on the Orient Express, *Doc. We all wanted to see him go, so we took him down.*

Doctor: *That doesn't follow with the facts.*

Patient: *Okay, fine. Ya got me. I did it. Only me. But I'm not wrong. We all knew Nick was as much to blame as anyone. No one gets a pass just because they suddenly sprout a conscience.*

Doctor: *What do you mean?*

Patient: *There you go, game playing again. You know as well as I do.*

Doctor: *I know Nick was facing a crisis of conscience. You said he was being "too honest," I believe.*

Patient: *If I said that, I was joking. Honest? Nick wasn't honest. He was a hypocrite. He was killed for a lot of reasons. Honesty wasn't one of them.*

Doctor: *This is an about-face from what you've said about him for years.*

Patient: *Yeah, well, things change.*

Doctor: *What did he do that changed your mind?*

Patient: *He broke ranks.*

Doctor: *And you killed him for that?*

Patient: *Don't sound so skeptical, Doc.*

Doctor: *I think there might be a deeper reason you're not facing.*

Patient: *Think what you want, I killed him for a lot of reasons. He wasn't who he claimed to be.*

Jerry crashed forward into several women, then hit the ground with a thunk.

Kerry leaped to save him half a second too late and her stepfather lay still on the ground, his folding chair toppling over behind him. Gasps and cries all around her. People stumbling away. Scared.

"Jerry," she whispered fearfully.

His eyes were flickering. Cole was suddenly at her side, bending down to him.

"He's breathing," Cole said. He whipped out his phone. "I'll call 9-1-1."

Jerry groaned. "No . . ." His face was gray as he struggled feebly to sit up. "Help me . . ."

Kerry held on to him, easing him to a sitting position. "You okay? I think Cole should still call 9-1-"

"No." He was adamant.

"Take it easy," said Cole.

"No ambulance." His face began pinkening up. "Help me to the chair," he mumbled, clearly embarrassed.

Cole righted the seat and Jerry plunked himself heavily into it.

"You need a doctor," said Kerry.

"You can drive me," he told her.

"An ambulance would—"

"*No!*" He tried to get to his feet, but Cole put a hand on his shoulder, holding him in place.

"I can drive you," Cole said. "I'll take you to the hospital."

"Okay . . ." Jerry capitulated, breathing hard. "In Edwards Bay."

"It would be closer to go to one on this side," Kerry started to argue, but Jerry cut her off.

"I want to go to Griffin Park Hospital. Call Doc Stevens. My cardiologist." Jerry clambered to his feet and reached one hand to his back pocket, the other to Cole's arm for support.

"Jerry—" Kerry began.

"I'm a stubborn old man, honey," he said, wheezing a bit as he pulled out his wallet. He fished inside for a business card. "I'll go. But I'll go my way. Cole can drive my car."

Kerry was ready to keep arguing, but Cole said, "Where's your vehicle?"

"He needs an ambulance," she said. "I can be stubborn, too."

"It's out thataway . . ." Jerry ignored her, gesturing to the side of the restaurant, where the east parking lot was.

Cole looked at Kerry and she lifted her hands and dropped them.

"You okay to move?" Cole asked Jerry, carefully turning to aim them both toward the direction of the door they'd used to enter from the lobby.

"Yep."

"I'm going, too," Kerry told him.

"No, honey. Stay. Finish up here. Sorry I caused a problem. Do it for Nick."

"Jerry, I'm coming with you," she said tersely. "Don't think I'm not."

"You're leaving?" Marcia, who'd come rushing over, narrowed her gaze at Kerry. "You can't leave! If you're leaving, I'm coming, too!"

"No!" Jerry and Kerry chorused.

Miami stepped forward, interjecting herself between Marcia and Kerry. "Marcia, Josie and I will stay and help clean up."

Josie, who'd been talking to Chad, swung her head around in surprise but didn't argue.

"No. I need to be with Jerry, too," Marcia insisted.

Ben Youngston put in, "I'll stay and help you, too."

"I don't need help," Marcia snapped, which was patently untrue. Hearing herself, she pressed her lips together in a line of protest. Her gaze traveled from Kerry to Jerry, who was already working his way out of the room with Cole's help. Turning back to Kerry, she flapped a hand angrily at the three of them.

Kerry easily caught up with Cole and Jerry as they were slowly making their way toward reception. She felt everyone's eyes on them and looked up to catch sight of Carroll Keenan's grim face as she hurried by.

"If you get Jerry's keys, I'll go find his car," said Kerry.

"I've got 'em," said Cole, holding out the set and dropping them into her outstretched palm.

"I'll bring the car over and follow you and Jerry in yours."

"Good."

She hurried to find Jerry's Volvo, then drove it to where Cole was just helping Jerry into the passenger seat of his Jeep, ignoring the older man's chatter that he was really just fine.

Kerry almost reminded him that Jerry'd had a cardiac event not so long ago but kept her mouth closed. He knew.

It took about forty-five minutes to make it back to Edwards Bay and beneath the portico outside the ER of Griffin Park Hospital, Jerry still trying to deny that he needed any help. Cole wisely ignored him and caught the attention of an orderly, who brought out a wheelchair, which Jerry sank into heavily.

It took about thirty minutes to get Jerry settled into the bed of a private room and hooked up to a cardiac monitor. The physicians on staff made him comfortable while they alerted Dr. Stevens that he was in the hospital. Marcia called Kerry three times, ostensibly to check on Jerry but also to complain that Kerry had left her high and dry.

"You can go back," Jerry told her from the bed. "I'm fine."

"They're still checking you out," she argued. The doctors had agreed it might be another cardiac event, which could mean anything, apparently; no one could tell her the degree of severity.

"Cole's here," Jerry said.

Indeed, Cole was still at the hospital, although he was currently in the hall, speaking on his cell phone. Kerry had heard enough to understand he'd been first talking to Ben Youngston and currently was with Officer Paige at the station.

"I'm just worried about you, that's all," Kerry said, while Jerry fiddled with the controls of the bed to lift his shoulders. He'd already managed to turn on the television.

"I feel stupid being here. I'm okay. It's just been . . . hard." He struggled to hold on to his emotions.

She reached forward and squeezed his hand.

Nodding, he cleared his throat and said, "Go help Marcia or we'll never hear the end of it."

"I don't want you to be alone."

"Nothing more you can do here, honey. I'm just going to watch TV and go to sleep. If they make me stay here tomorrow, you can come back for dinner. Soup and Jell-O."

"Okay."

She walked by Cole on the way out and signaled that she was leaving. He held up a finger, wrapping up his call.

"You going back to The Pier?" he asked.

"I think so. Marcia made it abundantly clear what she thought about me leaving."

"Need a ride back?"

"Mind if we take Jerry's car to his house? Then I could use a lift to The Sand Drift and my car."

"Okay. I'll say goodbye to Jerry and meet you outside."

The light was fading as Kerry walked across the parking lot, climbed into the Volvo, and drove up the hill to Jerry's driveway. She parked alongside the house, then sat in the car for a few minutes, watching the leaves on an old oak in his front yard quiver in a stiff breeze. She'd hardly let herself think about anything but getting Jerry safe, but now she reviewed every moment of the memorial service and this past, terrible week. It felt like an ongoing nightmare. She was lucky Cole was around to help pull her out of it.

Within minutes Cole's Jeep pulled in behind her. Locking the Volvo, she signaled that she was putting Jerry's car keys inside his house. She unlocked the front door with her key, then dropped Jerry's into a clear glass ashtray on a console table in the entry hall before heading back to Cole.

It felt strange to climb in beside him, a distant déjà vu memory plaguing her as she clicked on her seat belt and shut the door. Before she could say more than, "My car's at The Sand Drift," her cell phone buzzed. She glanced at the screen and inwardly sighed. "Marcia."

He nodded as she answered. "I'm on my way," she told Nick's ex.

"Don't bother. Everyone's gone and I've put things right." Her tone was frosty.

"Miami and Josie helped you?" Kerry asked. "And Ben Youngston?"

"Well, yes, but there was a lot to do. I would have liked to have gone with you, you know. Jerry's important to me."

"So you don't want me to come," Kerry reiterated.

"It's all taken care of."

Kerry took her at her word. "Okay," she said, pretending to ignore Marcia's passive-aggressive pique. "I'll see you Monday at Jerry's." Nick's lawyer, Gil Barnes, from Barnes & Barnes, Attorneys at Law, had agreed to meet them there at Jerry's request. No one had foreseen a scenario in which Jerry might not be there.

Marcia said, "Taryn has got to be lying about Nick's commitment to the homeless. I've never known him to have a particular interest in them, or any other charity."

"I'm sure we'll find out on Monday." She could feel Cole listening, even though his attention was on the road.

"Come on, Kerry. You know she was lying, or at least

exaggerating. Why are we having this reading anyway? Why can't we just get copies of the will?"

"This is what Nick wanted, apparently," Kerry stated shortly. "I know as much as you do. Jerry's health is the main issue right now."

"Which I was left out of. Well, okay. We'll see what Monday brings. And you're welcome for the cleanup." She clicked off.

Kerry did the same, her temper smoldering. Marcia always made things all about her. Even with Jerry in the hospital and Nick gone. She wanted to gnash her teeth and scream. Instead she just glowered.

"You okay?" Cole asked her.

"Nope. Not sure I ever will be again."

"Miss Seashell . . ."

"Yeah. Her."

He slid her a sideways look. "Seems she hasn't evolved a lot since high school."

"You got that right." She drew a breath. "Did you know her back then?"

"Of her. I was out of school when she went through, but her looks were legendary."

Kerry made a strangled sound, even though it was true.

They pulled up in front of The Sand Drift. Rain had begun to fall, a mist coalescing on the windshield as Cole parked and turned off the ignition. They sat in silence for a moment, Kerry's fingers on the door handle. She didn't want to leave just yet. "I heard tonight that Marcia was pregnant when she went after Nick, but then lost the baby and didn't tell him until after the wedding."

"Who told you that?"

"Chad, his business partner. Chad Worster. There was a question whether the baby was even Nick's, but I figure it was, because Nick stuck with her, even after he knew the timing. We're meeting with Nick's lawyer on Monday for the reading of the will. Hopefully Jerry's up to it."

Cole absorbed that, then said, "Taryn Whitcomb seemed convinced Nick had left all his money to the Brighter Day homeless shelter."

"Who knows? Maybe she's right. But it was a strange announcement to make at the memorial service."

"Yeah," Cole agreed, his hands resting lightly on the steering wheel.

"Have you gotten anywhere on finding out what happened? Who killed him?"

"I've been interviewing some of Nick's friends, saw some more tonight."

This was more than he'd offered up so far. "And?"

"Just background information so far."

"Did Diana talk to you?" Kerry asked. "She asked me to, but everything just got crazy."

"No. I never talked to her."

"She said she's remembering there was another person in her apartment the night Nick died." She related Diana's comments about the hypnotist named Nina, and a sense that this other person in the apartment had actually killed Nick. She finished with, "Maybe she's remembering, or maybe she's covering her own . . ."

"Ass?"

"I was going to say that, but I stopped myself." She chuckled, then felt herself blush, glad it was dark inside the Jeep.

"How credible do you think she is?" he asked.

"Diana? Oh, I don't know. She's hurting over it all and she's not exactly reliable, so . . . It made me nervous for her, though. If she's remembering something real, and that person is out there . . . maybe even at the memorial service . . . I told her she should go home."

"That was good advice."

"If she'd taken it, but she didn't."

"If someone else was there, why would they use a syringe?" he mused.

"I don't know," said Kerry.

"Was it a 'party' that went wrong? Diana says finding Nick at her place was a surprise, but she vaguely remembers hanging out with him earlier. She might not have remembered someone else joining them."

"I don't know what to think," she said truthfully. "I heard some things tonight, about Nick, about him not being as good a guy as everyone says. I know he was a good guy," she added quickly, "but people are envious, jealous, I don't know." She paused, then added, "But I do know that recently Nick's outlook changed."

"In what way?" Cole asked.

Atonement.

The word Jerry had used swam into her mind.

What had Nick been thinking these past few weeks, maybe months? Others had alluded to his change of mood as well. Maybe she should ask Josie about it. Josie had some kind of relationship with Nick that his friends seemed to understand. Was it an affair? Kerry couldn't see Nick getting involved with a married woman, but then, what did she really know about her stepbrother? Maybe not as much as she'd thought.

She finally opened the door and let herself out into the rain. "Thanks for everything."

"Keep me informed on Jerry."

"Will do."

She ran toward her front door, digging inside her purse for the key, dodging raindrops.

* * *

Cole watched her go. He'd wanted to ask her dozens of other questions, some about Nick, some about his friends, a couple of big ones about her ex-husband. He'd been happy to note she seemed less than thrilled to see Vaughn.

He drove back toward the ferry station, thinking there might be a few of the A-Team or others still straggling back to Edwards Bay. The memorial service had wrapped, but he suspected some of Nick's friends had probably moved to The Pier's bar. They were a barhopping group, after all. He wanted to see how things had shaken down if he could.

Sinking down in his seat, he pulled a cowboy hat from the back footwell, dropping it low over his eyes. He wanted a little protection to keep from being recognized immediately if and when the A-Team, or anyone else from the memorial service, disembarked.

Come Monday, he was going to dig deeper into the backgrounds of all Nick's friends and families. Something was rotten, something that had tentacles that reached back into the past. Whether it had anything to do with the current day and Nick's death was hard to say. But he could feel it within this group. A secret of some sort that seemed to fill the space surrounding Nick's friends with uneasiness.

"Football," he said aloud.

The rain slid off the portico roof outside the front doors of The Pier while Marcia Radnor tapped her foot angrily against the concrete. Not everyone had left as she'd told Kerry. Some of the A-Team had migrated to The Pier's restaurant and bar as the event room for the memorial service was closing down.

Not that she'd been invited to join them. Kerry would have been, if she were here, and she wasn't even an Edwards Bay High graduate. Sometimes Marcia just wanted to strangle Kerry. Nick had always doted on his little stepsister in a way that had driven her insane, like fingernails scraping on a blackboard. It was a screech in her ears anytime she heard her name. Kerry, Kerry, *Kerry*. And, of course, Kerry had shared Nick's weird sense of humor. She could still hear the way they made each other laugh. Nick clearly enjoyed being with Kerry. Not romantically, but like that best buddy that steals your husband whenever he's around and leaves you standing by yourself, which is almost worse because everybody acts like you should stop being a bitch and just take it.

Marcia fumed for a few moments, glaring at the rain, then headed back inside to the restroom. She examined herself in the mirror. Her blue eyes glared back at her through darkened lashes. Her makeup still looked flawless. Her brows were defined. Her lipstick needed a refresher, though, so she quickly applied a pink gloss.

She opened her eyes wide and stretched her mouth, then looked at herself again. Could Miss Seashell still be lurking behind a decade-plus of age? She smiled to herself. That had been a real highlight. Crowned her freshman year in high school. Oh, she'd acted like it was a dumb award, but that crown had meant she was the prettiest, most beautiful girl around. Miami might have given her a run for her money, but she was too quiet and careful. Josie was a clear third, and no one else in Marcia's own class had even come close. She'd put everything she had into winning and she had. Too bad they'd discontinued the event. Someone had complained it was sexist, and so another great tradition had bitten the dust. No more sitting on the back of a convertible in the July Fourth parade . . . no more presiding over the Autumn Crab Feed . . . or the Valentine Sweethearts Ball. Nothing.

The all-year reign of Miss Seashell was a victim of "changing times," someone had said.

She sighed, and then her thoughts turned back to Nick. He'd noticed her right away, that's for sure, but he'd played it cool. She was only a freshman and he was a senior, and though some of the other senior boys had tried to pick off the freshman girls, like weird Egan Fogherty and make-me-vomit-in-my-mouth Forrest Borland, Nick was always aloof and unavailable.

But she knew, oh, she knew he wanted her. She'd tried to capitalize on his interest, but every ploy, every happen-stance meeting, every extra-long eye hold, only seemed to push him farther away.

And then . . . there was Lisette Benetton. She wasn't even half as pretty as Josie, Miami, or her, but Nick had fallen for her . . . apparently. There was something going on with that whole crowd. Marcia had been sick with jealousy over Lisette. Worse than how she felt about Nick with Kerry, much worse. She'd fretted and stewed and finally decided she needed to put out to land him. And she wanted to be with him anyway, so sex was an easy answer.

But it had taken most of that whole freshman year to find a way to be with him. Meanwhile, she'd had the at-tention of all the boys, and the envy of all the girls, after winning the Miss Seashell crown. What a coup! She'd half-expected Nick to finally make his move, but he didn't. It was fall. And football. And all that shit. Shortly before Lisette overdosed, Marcia had run into Nick and some of his friends hanging around Coffee Time, a local coffee shop whose main décor was a clock on the wall made into a silvery coffee cup shape that had curled metal lines of "steam" emanating from its brim, those steam lines tick-tocking back and forth with the seconds. The place, long gone now, had served a late-night menu of half-price bakery items that all the kids bought, especially the slices of French bread, which could be dipped in oil and vinegar.

Nick was with Killian, Forrest, Sean, and Randy, all of them dipping the bread and scarfing it up. Egan was at a booth behind them, trying to lean over them and pretend he was part of their group even though he clearly wasn't. In those days Sean was too skinny to be as cool as he'd later turned out to be, and Forrest wasn't quite so fat. Randy had been in as great shape as Nick, and Killian looked more or less the same as he did now: big, silent, assessing. But it was Nick with his lean, dark good looks and disarming smile who was the hero of that group. And Marcia was determined to have him.

The guys were talking about something up close and personal as Marcia walked in. Something that closed off abruptly when she crossed the threshold. Because she was a female? Or because she wasn't in their senior class? Or something else?

It was Killian who said lazily, "Well, if it isn't royalty. The queen herself, dropping in to check on us peons."

Marcia had initially wanted to shrink inside her skin, but instead she said boldly, "Off with their heads!"

The guys laughed or grinned and Nick lifted an appreciative eyebrow. Only Killian seemed irked by her show of bravado. Egan slipped over her way and tried to engage her, but all her radar was on Nick. He caught up with her as she was ordering a latte, and they bantered a bit about her Miss Seashell crown and some about the upcoming football game with one of the school's archrivals.

"Coming to the game?" he asked, to which she chirped happily, "Wouldn't miss it."

Only she did miss it.

Her parents had already made plans to head to Spokane, hours away, for a family reunion, and Marcia was forced to go. She didn't even have a sibling to complain to about these yahoo relatives who lived in a rural area outside the city. She chafed through the weekend, sulking and counting the minutes.

Back in Edwards Bay, which felt like a *metropolis* compared to that backwoods area outside of Spokane, she put a plan in motion to be with Nick. She had a heck of a time of it, especially with Nick interested in Lisette Benetton. Then Lisette committed suicide and her stepfather was arrested. Marcia thought that would be the end of that chapter, at least where Nick was concerned, but instead it was like all the guys fell off the planet. There were no more senior-class parties, no more fun. That was football season, and it took the rest of the year for things to even out. Finally, just before graduation, there was a seniors-only party that Marcia and a few friends managed to crash. She hooked up with Nick in a back bedroom of Randy Starr's parents' house while Mr. and Mrs. Starr were on some wine tour— after they'd made Randy promise he would only have a few friends over and there would be *no drinking*, and Randy had adhered to the "few friends" part—and she drank just enough to claim she'd been too drunk to think clearly, if somehow her reputation got completely trashed and it came out that she took Nick to bed. He, too, had been drinking, though not as much as the other guys. He and Marcia made out for a time until she wondered if she was going to have to yank his clothes off. She hadn't gone all the way yet, though she'd experimented with some boys outside their school, just to see what it was all about. Messy. Kind of disgusting. But she was bound and determined to get Nick in bed, so she figured she'd just have to get used to it.

And it worked. Her eagerness finally won out and they had sex. Marcia thought it was fine. Not the big deal everyone said, but all right. She could do it again. She *would* do it again, in fact, given the chance with Nick. But she never got another chance. Nick was nice enough to make certain she was sober when her friend's mom picked her up, which she was, stone-cold sober and plotting how to see him again, but he didn't make any plans with her. She'd had a little niggle of worry but figured she was overreacting.

But . . it never happened again. Graduation was just weeks away, and Nick and his friends were completely preoccupied with it. Nick did say "Hi" to her in the halls and gave her his big smile, but it was clear that would be as far as it went. She was seized by the terrible feeling he regretted making love to a freshman, because that's what it was: making love, for her at least. And Nick Radnor soared from being a cute guy she wanted to be with to the Love of Her Life. Period.

Marcia was crushed by Nick's rejection. All the other guys wanted her. All she had to do was crook her finger and they followed after her, tongues hanging out, but not Nick. It was disheartening really, especially when Nick graduated and left Edwards Bay entirely. Some said it was because of Lisette. Well, maybe. It was sad what had happened to her, but she did it to herself. It was no one's fault but her own.

It took five more years and a trip to Palo Alto before Marcia saw Nick again. She learned his address. She followed him on Facebook, though he rarely posted. For a guy in the tech industry, he seemed to have no use for social media, but she'd wheedled his address out of Forrest, who wanted a little nookie payback, which grossed her out. She deigned to give him a kiss before sliding away and eluding him for fucking weeks afterward.

She went straight to Nick's condo and pretended she was in town on business and thought she'd look him up. He answered the door and was totally surprised to see her.

Unfortunately, he'd had a woman over that night. Marcia had seen past Nick to her crossed legs as she sat in a chair in a room at the back of the house. That vision was burned in her brain. Those crossed legs in front of windows that looked over a panoramic city vista. Nick was happy to see her, however. "You've got to come in," he invited, opening the door wide.

"Oh, no. I can't. I've got a meeting. But maybe later this week? While I'm still in town?" She was damned if she would share him with that woman, whoever she was!

"Sure. Give me your number."

She asked for his as well, even though she had it from Forrest. She pretended she knew his address from something she'd seen online rather than admit she'd all but stalked him. He wanted to know who, what, and where his personal information was out there, but she said she couldn't remember. Or maybe someone told her? She made out that it was a long time in the past and she'd just written it down.

He let it go, though she could see he filed the information away. She should have paid more attention, because she learned that was Nick's superpower, the filing and retrieving of information that could come back and bite you in the ass if you weren't on your toes. And she hadn't been. On her toes. Not enough to keep the marriage going.

He did remember to call her, though it took several days during which Marcia paced her hotel room, paid for dearly with her limited funds, but she had needed to strike the right chord. No freeway motel for her while she was visiting Palo Alto. A nice business hotel with a nice restaurant and bar. They agreed to meet at her hotel for a drink. She hoped he was paying as she'd looked at the cost of drinks and practically choked.

As it turned out, he did pay. Easily and without much

fuss. She'd practiced her "sort of" lies enough that she almost believed them herself: that she'd just left a job with one of the premier banks in Seattle—actually, she'd been phased out, a nice term for we-don't-want-you-anymore, though they gave her glowing references—that she'd been approached by the Bank of Edwards Bay—more like she'd camped out on their doorstep and practically begged for a job, one that hadn't materialized—and that she'd been out of the relationship with Audra's father for more than a year, when in reality she'd gone back to Craig several times because she was stone broke, though his wealthy family had cut him loose years earlier, a fact he'd hidden from her and which she only found out after she was pregnant. She didn't know then that Nick was cataloging the information. He didn't check up on her until much later, after the marriage, because, as he confessed to her later, he wanted to believe her. He wanted to believe in something.

Well, okay. She was happy to be that something. The woman at his condo that day? A business associate. And even if she was something more, Marcia never ran into her again.

And then she found out she was pregnant with Nick's baby. Hurray! She hurried to tell him. He was surprised but happy. Fantastic! But he wanted confirmation, so they made an appointment at his clinic and his doctor, who confirmed the diagnosis and referred her to a local gynecologist. They were both thrilled. Nick questioned how she became pregnant when she was supposedly on the pill. Well, the pill is only 99 percent effective, she reminded him. That 1 percent was still out there, to which Nick casually pointed out that 1 percent was likely caused by human error.

Well . . . yes. She never told him that she'd quit taking the pill from the moment she first visited him, though he might have suspected. That was Nick. But they were having such a good time! Marcia had really worked on being the fun girlfriend, the one game to do anything, the one who didn't let things bring her down, the one who could handle whatever life threw at her.

Maybe he wondered why the job with The Bank of Edwards Bay fizzled out. Maybe he knew half of what she said or did was bullshit, put on for his benefit. Maybe he didn't care. Maybe he just wanted to be married and have a baby like she did. Her miscarriage scared her to the bone. She couldn't tell him. Not while everything was going her way. She would just get pregnant again, as soon as possible. That way she would be pregnant by the time he learned the truth and all would be well.

That was the plan when they decided to elope. Just got in his car and drove to Vegas . . . after signing a prenup that really hurt her feelings. Still, she believed it would all work out in the end. She told him she loved him, over and over again, and he said the words back to her, though only when she said them first. She convinced herself he would grow to depend on her, find he couldn't live without her, really, really love her. She would make sure of it.

Nick traded in his condo for a palatial home they lived in happily for a couple of months, and then she told him about the miscarriage. Nick wanted to meet with her doctor, but she was so bereft and sick with disappointment—an Oscar-winning performance fueled by the fear he would leave her—that he seemed to let it go. She wanted to get pregnant right away again, but it didn't happen. Her doctor told her to relax and it would likely happen for her, because she'd conceived twice already.

Nick seemed to take the news in stride, but it was never the same for them. After the miscarriage, Nick and Marcia as a couple were over. Even his love for Audra—because he did love her, that was a fact—couldn't keep them together. Nick was gone. Checked out. No longer hers.

She was devastated at the loss of their closeness, but Nick seemed blasé. In fact, it was his commi ci, comme ça attitude that had made her lose her temper in the first place, and once she lost it, she couldn't seem to find it again. It was out there, flying free, hitting everyone with zingers and sneak attacks. Her change of attitude, the dropping of her congenial facade, was the end for them. Nick filed for divorce and Marcia was cut out of his life.

End of story. Except now Gil Barnes, Nick's lawyer, had asked her to be at the reading of the will. She could scarcely stand to wait. If Kerry and Jerry had their druthers, she'd be left out in the cold, she was sure of that, but she wasn't having any of it.

Would Nick really leave you anything? The fucker took back the ring, remember?

In the mirror, her mouth quivered. It took a few moments, but then she tightened her lips into a hard smile. Actually, she'd thrown the ring at him. Just hurled it across the travertine entryway and watched it glance off his forehead and skitter across the polished stone. A foolish move she now wished she could undo. Where was it anyway? Had he sold it? Pawned it? Given it to some undeserving California blond bitch?

Or had he left it for Kerry? God. That would be the limit.

Or Taryn? Or *Diana*?

Grinding her teeth together, Marcia snatched up her clutch purse and headed to the bar. To hell if the A-Team—God, how she hated that name!—hadn't invited her. It was a free world, wasn't it? She was going to join the party whether they liked it or not.

When she walked into the bar they were in a huddle at

one of the tables, but that cretin, Egan Fogherty, upon spying her, strolled over, a man on the hunt. He wasn't all that bad-looking. He was just weird. And unlikable.

She walked past both Egan and the rest of them and took a stool at one end of the bar.

Egan was persistent and slid onto the stool beside her. "Can I buy you a drink?" His voice held a promise of more to come.

Oh, brother. Marcia turned to the bartender. "A Bombay Sapphire martini, straight up, three olives."

"Whoa. A woman who knows what she wants." Egan leered as the bartender went to make her order.

"That's me," she agreed, not looking at him.

"And what is it that 'me' wants?"

She wasn't going to answer at first, but then she said what she really felt. "Nick. I want Nick back."

"Well, yeah, sure . . ."

More pointedly. "And if I can't have him, I don't want anyone."

He shrugged that off, apparently used to bald rejection. "Oh, who knows? Maybe you could use a stand-in. Just to get over him."

"I don't think so."

He ignored the icy chill in her tone. "How's Miss Seashell doing anyway?"

She refused to answer that one as the bartender slid her martini across the bar, its surface shimmering with teensy ice chips. She took a swallow. This was an occasion that called for something more than her usual single glass of white wine.

"You know I'm moving up to captain," Egan said. "Been working my way up."

Goody for you. "Break out the brass band."

"Soon to be a captain on the very ferry you came over on."

"I'll have to remember that." She tried to close him off, but he was a spigot that just kept gushing.

"My uncle was in the coast guard. Just retired. Our whole family's been on the water. In fact . . ."

There followed a mind-numbing recount of every fucking member of his family and a few friends, along with a list of their accomplishments. Marcia turned around on her swivel seat to keep an eye on the rest of the A-Teamers, who had split into twos and threes. Josie was in an animated conversation with Chad, Nick's ex-partner. Chad and Nick's "amicable" split had looked like a cold annulment from where Marcia sat; she'd thought Nick had gotten the lion's share of the business in the end, though she didn't know for certain. Chad had held on to a portion of the company and then sold out to another tech business who'd swallowed up his idea, according to him. Marcia and Nick had been apart by that time, but she thought Chad had done all right. She gave him a considering look. He wasn't nearly as good-looking as Nick, and he didn't have his savoir faire either. That didn't appear to be stopping Josie, whose husband had vamoosed from the service a while ago. In Marcia's biased opinion, Josie looked like she wanted to lay down on the table and spread her legs for him. Was that how it had been with Nick? Though everyone assumed Nick and Josie were an item, Marcia knew her ex well enough to sense that maybe that wasn't so. They could have had a one- or two-night stand, she supposed, but Josie was married, and maybe that didn't mean anything to her, but it would have to Nick. Marcia eyed closely the girl next door who seemed to want to cheat on her husband.

Well, Chad's single, so good luck, girl.

Egan had switched subjects. ". . . none of their wives showed up, but then, they weren't in to the high school football scene. Those old guys just can't let it go, though, huh? Glory days and all that. They sure liked the high school girls back then."

Marcia said, "All old guys like looking at high school girls."

"These guys were more than looking."

"Leering, then."

"They were kinda handsy back in the day," Egan revealed carefully. "You must know about that."

Well, yes, she could remember jabbing one old lech in the rib cage when his hands slid around a little too much when he went in to hug Miss Seashell. "If I was one of their wives, I wouldn't show up either," she said.

"Wonder if any of them knew."

"That they were horny for teenage girls? Of course they did." Marcia snorted.

"Well, and the rest of it." Egan had ordered a beer, and when he was served, he dragged the sweating glass toward himself across the bar, leaving a wet trail.

"Okay, I know you want me to ask, so I will. The rest of what?" Marcia was growing really tired of Egan and they'd been talking, what? Ten minutes? Felt like an eternity.

He gave her an assessing look, then, glancing around, he and Killian made eye contact. Something seemed to pass between them and they both looked toward Miami, who was at the other end of the bar, ordering a glass of wine.

As if believing Egan had extended him an invitation, Killian moseyed over, putting himself between Egan and Miami, who hadn't even seemed to notice he was there . . . or maybe she was pretending.

"What are you two talking about?" Killian asked.

"The horny geezers here tonight," Marcia said, knocking back the rest of her drink.

"My old man one of those 'horny geezers'?" Killian's smile was indulgent.

"Guess so," Marcia said. "Egan was saying how much they wanted to get into the high school girls' pants."

"I was saying they were into football," Egan denied hotly.

"And that their wives aren't here because they didn't want to see their men's tongues hanging out over all your A-Team ladies." Marcia waved a hand in the direction of their table.

Taryn, who'd been hovering around, moved within earshot. "You talking about the dads? They're even more disgusting now than they were then."

"My dad isn't disgusting." Killian still wore the smile, but it was fixed in place.

Marcia waved a hand at him. "It was just an observation." Jesus, these people were intense. She slid off her stool.

And just at that moment Angie Starr threw her drink in another woman's face and shrieked, "Leave my husband alone!"

Chapter Thirteen

Kerry sat at her kitchen table, dunking a tea bag systematically in and out of her cup of hot water. She'd made herself a peanut butter sandwich on wheat bread, which she'd cut into quarters. She was nibbling on the second quarter but pushed the rest of the food away. She'd filled up a plate at the memorial service, but then had been too upset, annoyed, and busy to eat anything. Now she was too tired and fretful to finish the sandwich.

It was too early to go to bed. She tried television, switching through channels, then reading a novel, but she couldn't keep her mind on it, so she tossed the book aside and paced from the bedroom to the kitchen.

Maybe she should go back to the hospital.

No, Jerry needed his rest.

Maybe she should check the motel? Take a walk?

But it was raining and dark.

She thought back on her conversation with Cole. She had the deflated feeling that Cole had just been being polite to her. He seemed to give her more attention than some of the others, but it was because she was Nick's sister and close to Jerry rather than because they'd once been in love.

Well, at least she'd been in love. Maybe he'd never felt quite the same way, but she'd had stars in her eyes from the start. And if she was honest with herself, she felt a little bit of it still. That jolt of her pulse when she saw him. The prickle of heightened awareness when she heard his voice.

"Oh, stop," she muttered, washing off her plate and putting it in the dishwasher.

Why was it that Cole had to be the one for her? Honestly, it was a real pisser. She'd love to feel that way about someone else, anyone else. Her attraction to Vaughn hadn't even come close to scaling the same heights; she could admit that now. Half of her attraction to him had been because she'd felt *something*. Call it lust. Or maybe just a yearning for what she'd had with Cole. Either way, she'd let herself be taken away by it, and she'd paid the price in a very unhappy marriage.

Shivering, Kerry reached for her jacket. She was still in her dress, but she slipped on the pair of black clogs she kept by the door to wear when she was walking the grounds, and stepped outside.

There was a light on in the unit farthest from the office, number twelve. Not the first time the workers had forgotten to hit the switch when they finished. She'd left the master key in her unit, so she turned around and returned to the office reception area, which was an adjunct to her apartment, currently open to her rooms during renovation because the outside door to the office had been boarded shut. Hurrying back inside her apartment, she slipped into the reception area and the safe with the electronic code that held all the keys. She punched in the number, and the safe's door whirred open. Grabbing the master key from the small tray inside, she headed back through the misting rain to number twelve. She peered in the window first and saw the place was empty.

Sighing, she let herself in and flipped the switch, sending the room into darkness. She locked the door on the way out, then checked all the other units. Two other doors were unlocked. Damn. She was going to have to talk to the workmen.

Bending her head against the light rain, she had a sudden feeling of impending doom. She looked up. Her lungs felt compressed, starved for air. She quickly gulped some in. It felt like she was suffocating.

Jesus.

Back inside her apartment, she hurriedly threw the dead bolt and pulled the chain on both the front and back doors. Then she returned to the office and replaced the master key in the safe, listening to it whir shut. Her heart was pounding like she'd run a marathon. Taking in several deep breaths, she sat down on one of the kitchen chairs and put her head between her knees.

She didn't have to ask herself what it was all about. Nick had been murdered. Stabbed in the neck. Purposely overdosed. No chance it was suicide.

When she finally sat up again, she felt only slightly better.

She tossed out the cold tea and reached for the bottle of pinot gris cooling in the refrigerator. She was nervous and scared.

She wished she wasn't alone.

She took a glass of wine to bed, determined to try reading or watching TV again. She needed to find a way to force herself to relax.

Fifteen minutes later she switched off the television and turned out the lights, unable to concentrate. It was all just noise. She stared up at the ceiling.

Maybe you can call Cole?

Turning over, she punched her pillow into submission and buried her face in it. No. She wasn't going to call Cole.

Her cell phone blurped her tone for a received text message.

She snatched it out of her purse only to realize the message was from Vaughn.

Can I see you tomorrow? There are some things we really need to talk about.

She clicked off and then powered her phone down even while she plugged it in to charge.

Josie checked the time on her phone, wondering if she was going to be in trouble with Kent for lingering so long at the service. She had the blues, a low-grade depression that had rolled in after the mind-numbing grief had loosened its grip a little. That grief was still there, just more under control. Not that her eyes didn't still tear up and her chest quiver whenever she thought about her loss; she just wasn't going to let it consume her. Yet, *how could Nick be gone*? It wasn't fair. It didn't feel right. Her Nick. No matter what Taryn, or Diana, or even Kerry thought.

"Who's that?" Chad Worster asked her, nodding toward Angie Starr, who'd been dragged away by Randy from a woman she'd thrown a drink on.

"Oh, she's married to Randy Starr."

"The guy hanging on to her?"

Randy had a hard grip on Angie's arm. "Angie's the jealous type."

"Never would have guessed," Chad drawled. "Who was her victim?"

The woman wiping off her blue blouse and black skirt and throwing furious glares at Angie was actually someone

Josie recognized. "Sheryl Reyes. She works at the bank with my husband."

"Your husband?"

Josie debated how much to say. She liked Chad. He reminded her of Nick somewhat. Kind of looked like him . . . if you squinted and tried real hard to overlook the fact that his eyes were a little too close together and he was slightly pigeon-chested. "He was here earlier but had to leave."

"Nick never mentioned you were married."

"Nick talked about me?" Josie tried to keep her tone neutral, though she came alive at the thought.

"Yeah. You and Miami and some others. Taryn."

"Ah." Of course. "Taryn acts like they were besties, but I always thought it was all in her mind."

Catching her tone, Chad said, "I think she might be disappointed about Nick's involvement in any homeless shelter. He donated money all the time, but moderately. I just don't see it."

Josie watched Ben Youngston edge out Egan Fogherty at the bar and move in on Marcia, who appeared to be on the verge of getting really sloshed. Her gaze slid past them to the doorway where a newcomer, Diana, shook off a few raindrops. She'd been outside for a while, it appeared. Doing drugs?

Josie stated flatly, "I thought she went home."

Chad looked around, focused on Diana. "Her?"

"Nick's killer."

Chad's brows lifted. At the same moment Diana glanced at Josie, before her eyes slid away. She took a few tentative steps into the room and stopped.

"It was her apartment where Nick . . . ?" Chad asked.

"Yes."

"You think she injected him?"

"To hear her tell it, she was just drunk and high and somebody came in and took Nick out." Josie kept her eyes on Diana who, after assessing the room, apparently decided she wasn't wanted and headed back outside.

"She says someone else was there?"

"That's the latest story."

"You don't believe her?"

"I don't know. It's possible, I suppose."

Chad asked, "How well did you know Nick?"

"Well."

He turned dark eyes on her, eyes very different from Nick's blue ones, but eyes that somehow carried the same message, one that made Josie catch her breath a little. Chad said, "Nick and I worked very closely together, until we didn't. Change of philosophies. He sold out and quit the business and I kept on for a while before I sold out, too. But we stayed friends . . . We didn't always get along, but we understood each other."

Josie sensed this was going somewhere, but she wasn't really listening. Her mind had moved on to other places. She was concentrating on Chad's right hand, holding his drink. It looked . . . masculine. She imagined it traveling slowly up her arm to cup her chin, forcing her gaze to meet his.

The noise level in the room had increased with the consumption of alcohol and Josie had to lean in closer to hear Chad, whose lips just brushed her ear.

"I just don't remember him talking about you," he finished.

Well, shit. Josie felt a searing jolt of disappointment. She pulled back from him. She'd wanted to kiss him. Feel that hand, both hands, caress her breasts and drag her to him, but now . . .

"I've heard from your friends that you and Nick were seeing each other. Nick never told me."

"Taryn was his friend. Just ask her," said Josie. She looked around for the bartender, who was busy pouring Marcia another martini. A few more and she'd be on her ass.

"But you're the one linked to Nick . . . romantically."

Josie caught the bartender's eye and lifted a finger for another glass of pinot gris. Miami and Kerry's drink. She would have preferred a vodka martini, but she didn't want to wait. The wine was at hand. "Thought you said you and Nick weren't close anymore."

"We still kept in contact."

"Well, I am married," Josie admitted, "if you can call it that. Kent and I are having a few problems. Who said that about Nick and me?"

"The big guy leaving with your friend Miami."

Killian.

Josie turned to watch Miami and Killian as they headed toward the door together. Killian held the door and touched the small of her back, but Miami tightened up and shifted away.

That relationship was doomed. Doomed. But then, it had been for fifteen years and it was still going.

Diana was just reaching for the door handle again when, through the glass door panes, she saw Killian and Miami heading her way. She'd locked eyes with Josie as she'd started to enter and had felt naked and exposed, so she'd melted back outside. A stiff breeze had whipped up and sent bursts of misty rain slapping at her, so she'd wrapped her pink shawl around her neck and hugged herself, wishing she'd brought a coat and wondering if she should just go home. They didn't want her at the memorial service and they didn't want her at their impromptu party afterward.

She knew what they thought of her, and it was so hypocritical. They'd all been part of the A-Team in high school, too, only they didn't call it that then. Then it was the Dream Team. Egan had once said they were all wet-dreaming about the girls. That was close enough to the truth to cut like a knife.

She'd decided to charge inside again and to hell with them all when Killian and Miami started heading toward the door. Now she moved away quickly, scurrying into the parking lot between two huge SUVs. The wind snatched at her hair and she huddled against the nearest vehicle, away from its grabbing fingers.

". . . get out of this place," Killian was saying as they came through the door. "Go somewhere south, warm. Maybe Mexico. I wanna make love like it's our last day on earth."

"I have to work," Miami said.

"Fuck work. We'll get married and you can stay home and make me dinners like you do those old people you take care of."

"Those old people are members of my family. My great-aunt and -uncle."

To Diana's consternation, they were walking right to the vehicle she was hiding behind. In a moment they would see her, so she boldly hurried forward, head bent against the rain, nearly running straight into them, her intention.

"Diana!" Miami said in surprise.

She stopped short, skidding a little on the wet sidewalk. "Oh, hi. Sorry. Are you guys leaving?"

"Yeah. Away from you," said Killian.

"Shhh. Stop that," Miami said, then turned back to Diana. "Are you really going to a hypnotist?"

"Um . . . yeah . . ." Maybe she shouldn't have been so forthcoming about Nina, although it had been Angie's big mouth that had blown that bit of gossip around the room.

"So there was someone else in your apartment? Cool," Killian said. "I hope you told Cole Sheffield."

"I've talked to Cole a couple of times," she said.

"If he doesn't know what a liar you are, I'll have to tell him," Killian said.

"Killian," Miami moaned as Diana yanked open the door and walked into the bar, this time with authority. To hell with him. What a one-note act. She was the bad girl and he was the bad boy who loved to tease, torture, and laugh.

Her mind was still on Killian and her blood was pumping hot as she looked around at the people who had stayed on. They sent her oblique looks, as if worried she might actually engage them in conversation. She started feeling insecure again. Maybe this had been a bad idea. She glanced at Josie, but her head was bent to listen to something Nick's friend, Chad, was saying.

Should she get herself a drink?

Vaughn got up from a table and started heading her way, smiling. "So you didn't leave?"

"No, I . . . no." She smiled back at him. And then her eyes started watering.

"Okay. Let's get you a drink." He tucked a hand under her elbow and guided her toward the bar.

"Thank you," she said gratefully.

Cole sat in his truck for nearly two hours. Sean's father, Millard Blevins, and Bart Borland, along with Borland's wife, a slim, silent wraith of a woman who was the man's second wife, all disembarked as a group, along with some others he'd said a few words to at the memorial service, including Adam Wright and Lawrence Caulfield, the Uber driver who'd shown up to drive Cecily Wright to pick up her car keys before Cole brought them to her and was a classmate of Nick's as well. They got in their vehicles and left as the ferry chugged back over to the Kingston side. When it returned, it deposited Egan Fogherty, Marcia Radnor, and Ben Youngston. Cole had a bad moment when he wondered if he was going to have to explain himself to Ben, who might recognize his Jeep. He didn't want to have to say that he'd rather look for a possible murderer among Nick's friends, family, and acquaintances than return to his empty house.

But Ben's attention was taken up by Marcia. It was almost comical, the way he wanted to swat Egan away from her, but Fogherty wasn't the kind of guy who took a hint.

He watched the boat go back and return one more time. At ten thirty, the ferry would be coming back on its last trip. After that, it was the long way around the water, and a lot of people had left their cars in Edwards Bay, so it was Uber, Lyft, a taxi, or rides with friends who'd taken their cars aboard the ferry for anyone homeward bound at that time.

Rain splattered his windshield in fits and starts as he waited. It finally started to clear, but in its place was a shuddering breeze that would sometimes turn to a slap of wind that jiggled his vehicle.

As the ferry docked for the last time, he saw lines of people walking toward the parking area, while headlights from the disembarking cars bounced up and down as they clattered ashore before heading up the hill into town. A last straggle of pedestrians found their parked vehicles.

He recognized none of them.

A lot of Nick's friends were still on the Kingston side. Likely at the bar. Or maybe deciding to stay over, he thought, as he switched on his ignition. The Pier was, after all, a hotel.

Midnight . . . maybe one o'clock. Or two?

Diana moved around her apartment in the dark, stumbling into the metal post at the foot of her bed, slamming her toe.

"Ow," she said as pain registered sluggishly in her brain. She half-giggled. Probably would hurt like hell tomorrow.

Tomorrow . . .

Tomorrow she had a *date*.

She unbuckled her open-toed pump and rubbed the throbbing digit, then saw that she'd actually sliced it a little. Blood.

"Oh, shit . . ." She lurched toward her bathroom and looked at herself in the mirror. "Oh, *shit*." She looked scary. Her eye makeup had run a little and her lipstick was gone. How could he have asked her on a date when she looked like this?

Was he playing with her?

She stood still a moment, really thinking that over, though it was tough because her mind wanted to wander in about ten directions at once. She shouldn't have had that last drink. What was it? Someone had put it in her hand . . . Vaughn? No . . . Egan? . . . or that tall blond guy whose name she never got, the one who drove her home. Vaughn had been there, but . . . he'd melted away, hadn't he?

God. She looked a mess. Pulling out a drawer, she found another tube of lipstick and was applying a new coat when she remembered she just needed to go to bed.

She hobbled back to the bedroom to take her second shoe off and undress. She'd sleep naked. Who cared?

She'd just gotten the second heel unbuckled—what a bitch. Teensy little metal tongue and holes in a really thin belt that wrapped around her heel. Had to practically be a contortionist to manage it—when she heard the light knocking on her bedroom slider.

The curtain was drawn and she couldn't see who it was. Her heart clutched, but then her nighttime visitor called out, "Diana. Let me in."

Huh, she thought, and walked barefoot toward the door. Blood. Shit. She'd forgotten to bandage the toe. Blood on her bedroom carpet. Shit. What did you use to get that out? Salt, right? Baking soda? Something to wick it up? Hadn't her aunt said that?

Or was that for spilled wine?

She threw back the curtain and unlocked the door. "What are you doing here?"

No answer.

Diana blinked, but suddenly she was grabbed by both arms and thrust back across the room, stumbling over her own feet.

"What? What?" she cried.

And then she was slammed up against the wall and her pink scarf was tightened around her neck. Too tight! She clawed at the material, gasping for air, screeching, but no sound was coming except for a high whistling from her collapsing trachea. She tried to cry out, to struggle, but she was mute and weak. She stared upward, gurgling, her fingers weakly clawing at the fabric.

"Why? Why?" she tried to cry to her assailant, whose whole attention was on cutting off her air.

And then everything faded into oblivion.

Kerry was awakened by a three a.m. phone call. Once again she had her eye mask on, and once again she resisted answering. But then she thought, *Jerry.* Her hand blindly searched for her cell, and when she found it, she ripped off the mask and stared at the screen. Diana. Again.

She almost didn't answer, but then she clicked on. "Yes?" she demanded, letting her pique sound in her voice.

She heard breathing but no response. "Diana?" she said. "Diana?"

The hairs lifted on the back of her arms.

And then the phone clicked off.

Chapter Fourteen

Cole was in the break room, lost in thought, about ten a.m. on Saturday, when the call came in. He'd just pulled a bottle of water out of the refrigerator as rapid footsteps approached.

"Chief?" Charlie asked as she entered.

"Yeah?" He tipped up the bottle and took a long drink.

"Spano took a 9-1-1 to Diana Conger's apartment. He's there now. She's dead. Looks like she was strangled. One of the neighbors called it in."

Cole sputtered a little, water down the wrong pipe. He shook his head in disbelief. "What? Conger?"

"Looks like a homicide. ME's on the way."

"*What?*"

He was shocked. That immediate feeling of disbelief he encountered every time someone from his personal life faced sudden death overtaking him for a second. Officer Spano worked most weekends because Youngston had made it clear he never wanted to, and Spano didn't object, so Cole had let the understood rotation stay as it was. Charlie's schedule was every other weekend, while Cole tended to use weekends to get work done that hadn't been completed during the week.

"Tell Spano I'm on my way," he said.

"I also have other news . . ." She was extremely sober.

"What?"

"Body of a young, white male was discovered in the bay. It's Justin Drury. Looks like an overdose."

Cole shook his head, his chest tight. Heather Drury's runaway son was dead? "Does Heather know yet?"

"No. We heard right before the call about Conger. I can go tell her."

"She'll need to identify the body. Wait for me. I'll go with you. I just want to check with Spano first."

"Of course."

"And who's Diana Conger's next of kin?"

"I'll check on it while you're at her apartment," Charlie said.

Cole strode out to his Jeep, processing the information. Diana Conger had been strangled and Justin Drury had overdosed. And Nick Radnor had been killed a little over a week ago. A lot of sudden and suspicious deaths in a short period of time for a town that normally had one, maybe two, a year.

He took the stairs two at a time to the second floor of Diana's apartment building. Officer Nathan Spano, short, compact, with a black mustache and a stony attitude that seemed far too grim for his twentysomething years, greeted Cole at the door. He was looking a little gray-faced. He'd been hired at the department a few short months before Cole and had limited experience.

The ME and forensic crew had arrived and were examining the body. Diana was crumpled at the base of a wall, still in the black dress she'd worn to the service, her shoes haphazardly tossed around the room. The marks on her neck told the story of how she'd died.

Seeing Cole, the ME, Miles de la Fuente, said, "She was

strangled with something wrapped around her neck. We haven't located it yet."

"A pink scarf," Cole said.

De la Fuente looked at him hard.

"She was wearing it at the memorial service." He had a sharp memory of Diana entering the event room and everyone turning to stare at her. "If you don't find it, I'm guessing it was the weapon and the killer took it with them. People had cell phones and were taking pictures at the service. Bound to be one of Diana. I'll get Officer Paige on it."

De la Fuente grunted his assent.

"Is her cell phone here?" Cole asked.

"Yep," one of the techs answered. "But no purse or keys."

"Okay. Let me know if you get anything off the phone."

"Her car's parked downstairs in her slot."

Cole glanced down at the body, currently being examined by the forensics team.

His stomach felt like lead. To Spano, he asked, "Who's the neighbor who called it in?"

"The same one on the scene at Radnor's death. Alan Jenkins."

"How'd he seem when you got here?"

"Freaked out, man. Really freaked out."

"Okay."

He would have Youngston or Paige interview Jenkins later. Spano, Cole had learned, was an excellent note taker but not as good at interviewing. Paige was the best, but Cole knew he was already stretching the young officer too thin. Youngston was okay with men, but a little too forceful with women. He had a tendency to intimidate them, which made it hard to educe information.

He gave a last, lingering look at Diana, memorizing her and what the killer had done to her. It steeled his resolve to find out who had done this and bring them to justice. And though the methodology was different, he'd bet whoever had killed her had killed Nick Radnor the week before.

Twenty minutes later he was back at the station. "You ready?" he asked Paige, who shook her head and took another trip to the bathroom to redo the small ponytail she kept her hair in nearly all the time. "Now," she said when she returned. "Diana Conger has a brother living in Maine, and an aunt who owns The Candy Woman here in town, where she was working."

"That's right," Cole said. Charlie had not only gotten Cole some names of people who knew Nick Radnor, she'd also worked up short histories and pertinent information about Nick Radnor's friends and family, and Diana, by virtue of her apartment being the site of Nick's death, had already been a target of Charlie's investigations. "You have the brother's number?"

"Yes, and the aunt's. Eileen Conger. Never married and no children."

"We'll take care of that next."

After that they drove in near silence to the Drury home, an apartment in a building about a half mile from Edwards Bay city center, closer to I-5. Cole glimpsed the freeway traffic as he turned down a street that ran parallel to the interstate. Like Diana's apartment complex, it was about three stories high in an L-shape, the parking lot in front. The Drury apartment was on the first floor, and Charlie drew a deep breath before she knocked.

When Heather Drury saw the two police officers at her door, her hand flew to her mouth and her eyes filled with sudden tears.

"May we come in?" Charlie asked, but Heather had already walked backward away from them, leaving the door open.

With heavy hearts, Cole and Charlie followed her.

* * *

Kerry had gotten up at seven a.m. after a sleepless night and gone for a jog, something she rarely did since moving to Edwards Bay, but a habit she was thinking about re-employing. She'd needed to clear her head. A way to work through the grief that had loosened its grip a little, but still lay heavy on her soul.

The rain had stopped, but the clouds were heavy and gray as she ran along the front of the motel and down the hill for half a mile. She'd tried to run back up the hill and got a side stitch, so she walked the rest of the way, throwing herself onto her couch, breathing hard and sweating. As soon as she'd cooled down a bit, she took a shower, washed her hair, then toweled off and threw on her light blue, terry-cloth robe. She made herself another cup of tea and thought about the events of the past week, the same thoughts that had circled her mind from the moment she'd learned of Nick's death.

Some of the workmen showed up at eight a.m., but they didn't appear to be using the tile saw today. They were cognizant of it being the weekend and that the noise drove nearby residents to call and complain.

By eight thirty Kerry was sitting at her kitchen table with a notepad and pen, making a list of questions for herself. Her phone beeped with an incoming text, which reminded her of Diana's call in the middle of the night and caused the hair to rise on her arms in response. She had to shake off the creepy feeling and find her phone, which she'd left on her nightstand.

Can you come in today? The text was from Randy.

No, she texted back. On a weekend? The day after the memorial service? She didn't think she owed him any other explanation.

Angie's sick and I need someone at the office.
Gotta be at Starrwood Heights and man the
model home.

Angie's sick? She wondered when that had happened.
Too much alcohol at the service? She hadn't been drinking
all that much when Kerry had last seen her.

She was about to put him off. Randy would work her
seven days a week if he could. He was someone who
grabbed up people to help him whichever way he needed.
Case in point, having her drop off papers with his father.
Normally, Randy would have someone else manning the
model home—it wasn't a job he cared to do himself—but
maybe he hadn't been able to find anyone. On the other
hand, with Angie out of the office, it would be a much more
pleasant place to work.

It would help me be in two places at once today.

Okay, she wrote. Thought about a qualifier and decided
screw it. Randy knew how she felt. After I go see Jerry at
the hospital.

She gathered up the notepad and pen, grabbed her purse,
took a look at herself, and quickly brushed her hair and
clipped it at her nape. In a white shirt and jeans and black
mules, she was as dressed up as she planned to get for a
Saturday, not that Randy had serious expectations about
how she looked on the job. That was Angie's complaint.

She stopped in at the hospital and listened to Jerry
grouse for twenty minutes about how he needed to get out
of there. Deciding he must be doing better, she gave him a
quick kiss on his forehead, ignored his begging, and headed
to work.

Two hours later, seated at her desk and staring at a few

lines she'd written on her notepad—What was bothering
Nick? Why a hypodermic? Was Diana right that someone
else was there? Why did she call me last night and then
decide not to talk?—she plucked her cell phone from her
purse and quickly punched in Cole's number before she
could lose her nerve. The call went straight to voice mail,
so she clicked off, worried that he could see her number
and had chosen not to accept the call.

She sat back in her chair and was lost in thought, remembering snippets of conversation at the memorial service.
She wanted to know what was going on. Who'd killed her
brother. Diana? Or this mysterious extra person Diana had
finally remembered with the help of hypnosis? Did that
seem credible, or was it a way for Diana to wriggle out of
blame? But why a hypodermic needle to the jugular? Of all
the pieces that seemed not to fit the picture, that was the
one that stuck out. It just didn't seem like Diana.

Her cell burbled cheerfully, and she looked at the screen
to see Cole's name and number. Her heart jumped a little.
"Hi," she said, unable to keep the smile from creeping into
her voice.

"Kerry."

Now her heart really jumped at his sober tone. "What?
Did something happen?" Then, before he could answer, "Is
Jerry all right? I saw him this morning and he seemed fine."

"It's not about Jerry. It's Diana Conger." He paused a
moment, which only added to her anxiety, then said, "She
was killed last night, sometime after midnight in her apartment. It appears she was strangled. Possibly with her scarf."

"What? *What?*" Kerry went cold. All she could see was
that pink scarf draped around Diana's neck. "She called me
on her cell this morning. At about three."

"She called you?" Cole's interest sharpened. "What did
she say?"

"Nothing. The line was open. I heard breathing. And then she hung up."

There was silence on the other end of the line. She could practically hear his thinking, so that when he asked, "Are you sure it was Diana?" her flesh broke out in goose bumps because the same thought had crossed her mind:

"Oh my God," she said.

"Are you at home? Diana's aunt, Eileen Conger, just left the station. I took her to the morgue, but I'm on my way out of here and I'd like to see you."

"I'm at work. Starrwood Homes. But I think . . . I think I'm going to leave. Should I tell Randy why?" She was having trouble processing and her words were slow, disconnected from her racing brain.

"Go ahead. The news station got wind of it, so it won't be a secret for long."

"I'll see you at my place."

Once again she swept up her notepad and pen. One question leaped out at her: *Why did she call me last night and then decide not to talk?* Was it even Diana on the other end of the line? Or was she trying to say something but couldn't . . . because someone was there?

But why call me?

She didn't really like what that meant in either scenario.

"*What?*" Josie nearly shrieked into the phone. Kent had packed early and left while she was still in bed. Gone for the rest of the weekend apparently. He hadn't even waited until Monday to get the hell out.

Miami was crying a little. "Diana was strangled," she repeated. "She's dead, Jose. Taryn called. She saw it on the news."

"Oh, lord," Josie whispered. She'd been standing by the

sink, cutting up a pear, which was one of the few things that sounded good to eat this morning. Too much alcohol, not enough food. Too many emotions. Now she set the paring knife down with trembling fingers.

"I don't even want to leave the house, but I've got to show up for work at four. It's just . . . unbelievable."

"What happened? What did she do? Are they sure it wasn't suicide? That I could see. After what she did to Nick."

"Diana said she didn't hurt Nick."

"I know, I know. But . . . I thought she did it." Josie was already feeling guilty for the way she'd treated Diana. *Diana.* "What's going on?"

"I don't know."

"I didn't think there was someone else there when Nick died. If someone really killed her, it could be the same person who was there with the hypodermic needle. I just don't know if I buy it. I mean, Diana's a mess." Her throat closed over that last comment.

"Why? Why us? Why now?"

"I'm going to call Kerry," Josie determined. "She's friendly with Cole. Maybe she knows something."

"You think?" She sounded like she'd turned away from the phone.

"I don't know. But strangled . . . dead . . . ?"

"I've been thinking, you know. A lot about everything . . ."

"Miami, if you've got me on speaker, you've got to talk into the phone. You're fading out."

"You're not on speaker. I'm just . . . my hand's shaking. I can't hold the phone."

"If I learn anything from Kerry, I'll call you back. Hang in there."

"Jose, I know you were really . . . different . . . than me and Diana in high school. You weren't part of it."

Josie was scarcely listening. She was thinking of Nick. His white teeth, that great smile. And Diana. She'd been so mad at her for being with Nick! And now she was *gone*? Just like that? How come they were together? Nick and Diana had never fit. "What are you saying?" she asked, dragging her attention back.

"You said you only slept with one guy in high school."

"Well, yeah. From Bellevue. Why?"

"You thought he was the one, you know."

"Did I say that? Yeah, I said that." Josie felt weighted down. "Where is this going? I don't want this conversation. I don't care. I want to know what happened to Nick and Diana. I want to know what's happening now. That's all that matters to me."

"Okay." Miami paused to inhale hard. Josie could tell her nose was running. "I do, too. I just wondered, do you think Nick was the one, now?"

"Miami . . ." Josie could scarcely keep herself on track of their conversation.

"I know. I just . . . you always were so kind of aloof and now with Nick . . . and Kent . . ."

"Stop. What are you saying? No, just stop. You're making me want to scream. Why is Nick gone? That's what I want to know. And what's Diana got to do with it, and why did somebody kill her? Did they really . . . *really*? Is that a fact? Someone *killed her*?"

"That's what Taryn said." She sounded utterly miserable. "I'm . . . I'm going to blow off work and go to the Blarney Stone. I want to be with friends."

"Good idea," Josie said, though she wasn't really certain that was true. She was sick of the A-Team. Their small circle of friends. Sick to death.

"You coming?" Miami asked hopefully.

"Nah, I've got . . . I need to think."

"Okay," she said. "If you change your mind, come by."

Josie was glad to get off the phone. Her whole body was buzzing. Diana, dead. Nick, dead. Diana *strangled*? What the eff?

She couldn't get her brain engaged. Who would do this? Why?

She sank down on her living room couch, staring at her cell screen for a moment before putting a call in to Kerry. It went straight to voice mail. Damn. She tossed the phone onto the next cushion and it slipped down the edge. She was scrambling for it, yanking up the couch cushion, when it started ringing.

Kerry.

She snatched up the phone and looked at the number. Nope. No one she knew.

"Hello?" she asked cautiously.

There was a wait on the phone, as if they couldn't hear her, whereas she could hear background noise. "Hello?" a male voice asked.

Chad.

Immediately a sizzle ran through her, from the soles of her feet to the crown of her head. "Hi, Chad?" she asked.

"Hello there. I'm here at the hotel and I was just thinking how sorry I was that our night ended so early."

"You haven't heard about Diana?" she asked flatly.

"Huh? No." He was immediately cautious. "What?"

"Somebody killed her last night. Strangled her. It's been on the news apparently."

"No!"

"Yes."

A long pause. Josie found herself holding her breath. She'd warmed to Chad last night. She'd wanted him. Like she'd wanted Nick. Miami was right. She'd been slow to start in high school. Had made a point not to be with any of the guys in their class. But now, after years of marriage . . . it felt like a lost opportunity. She'd just been afraid back then. Of her reputation being ruined. Of the boys laughing at her.

And who the hell cared about any of it now?

"My God," Chad said, sounding shattered.

"You want to come over?" she blurted out. "Kent left today on a business trip and I was thinking of having a glass of wine or two. I just feel kind of scared and weird."

A long, long pause. "I have a flight out this afternoon . . ."

"Oh."

"But I could rebook to Sunday, or Monday maybe?"

Her heart was pounding. She was crossing the Rubicon. Wasn't that what it was? The river Julius Caesar crossed? The point of no return?

"Should I do that?" he asked.

"Yes."

"See you in an hour."

Middle of the day. Afternoon delight.

"Rubicon," she whispered, hugging herself close. She was cold inside, through and through.

Chapter Fifteen

Randy called Kerry as soon as she stepped in the door to her unit. "What the hell, Kerry? You were supposed to be at the office."

She'd left him a message on his cell when he hadn't picked up. She hadn't known how to baldly say what had happened to Diana, so she'd asked him to phone her.

But now, faced with the moment, she couldn't think of any way to palliate the information. "Randy, Diana's dead," she said, then she went on to deliver the facts as she knew them while he sputtered and gasped.

"Jesus Christ!" he declared. "Oh, God . . . oh my God . . . are you sure? Oh, God."

"Yes, I'm sure. I've got to go, Randy. I'm . . . talking to Cole. If I learn something more, I'll let you know." She'd pulled herself back from telling him Cole was coming to her place.

"Okay, yeah . . . yeah . . . you're not coming back in?"

"I'll see you Monday."

"Okay . . . okay . . ." He didn't sound all that sure.

By the time Cole arrived she'd picked up any clutter around her place and had poured herself a mango LaCroix. As soon as she saw him standing on her doorstep, she wanted to throw herself into his arms. To her horror, her eyes filled with tears and she stared at him mutely. He let himself in, drew the door shut behind him, then pulled her into his arms. She started shaking all over, her chest heaving.

"I'm sorry," she muttered against his chest. She could hear the hard beating of his heart. "I'm sorry. Just reaction. Too much. Oh, God. I'm soaking your shirt with tears."

"It's okay."

"It's not." She shook her head against him. He held her close and she leaned into him, squeezing her eyes closed. "None of it's okay."

"Do you want to sit down?"

"Sure. Yes."

He led her over to her couch and they sank down together. She felt compelled to pull away from him, but she didn't want to. She wanted to crawl into his arms and stay there forever. The urge was so strong, she could barely fight it.

Cole's arm was still draped lightly across her shoulders. "I went to see someone this morning whose son died from an overdose. I sat across from her as she wept. She said losing a son was the most devastating, worst feeling in the world. I'm sure it's true. I felt what it was like to lose my brother again. That terrible weight. The grief. I've seen other deaths, other tragedies . . . I saw Diana Conger this morning and that was . . . really difficult. But witnessing Heather's pain and loss right afterward . . ." He drew in a careful breath. "I just wanted to see you."

Kerry felt new tears form.

"It's part of the job. You have to compartmentalize. I wasn't good at it when Sam died. I'm sorry. I'm better at it now."

"You don't have to apologize. It was . . ." She was unable to go any further. She'd always imagined how it would be if she ever had a chance to talk to Cole again. To air her feelings. Tell him how much she'd loved him, how much he'd hurt her. She'd never imagined it this way . . . that she would understand.

He was waiting for her to go on, and she finally said, "It just . . . wasn't the right time for us." She managed a short laugh. "That sounds lame."

"Nah . . . I wasn't emotionally available after Sam's death. That sounds lame, too."

"Okay, we're even."

"Okay . . . I didn't want to hurt you. I know I did. I'm sorry for that. Here's another lame line: it wasn't you, it was me."

Kerry actually laughed, swiping at her tears. Cole laughed, too.

When they'd both sobered up, Cole added, "I thought maybe someday . . . when I was thinking clearly, which wasn't for a while, that we would get back together. I was arrogant. Expecting we could just pick up and go on from where we left off. But that time never came."

"I got married," Kerry said.

"That happened, too," he agreed.

"Here's the fourth lame line: it was a rebound. I never felt the same way about him that I did you."

Cole's gaze met hers. "Seriously?"

"Yes. Absolutely. It was wrong from the get-go."

"He came to the memorial service."

"I know," she said on a groan. "He wants to get together and talk. Why? We're divorced and he's never wanted to before. I have no interest in anything to do with him."

At that moment her cell phone buzzed. "I'm not going to answer it."

And his buzzed as well. He swore softly. "I'd like to say the same, but it could be work."

"Go ahead. I guess I might as well answer, too." While Cole fished his phone from his pocket, Kerry rose to her feet and grabbed hers from where it lay on the counter.

She saw it was Josie.

Cole said, "It's Officer Paige. She was with me when I gave Heather Drury the news about her son." He got to his feet, as well, as he texted her.

"I'll call Josie back later," she said, letting the cell keep ringing. "Are we . . . going to talk about this some more?"

"Yeah." Cole's expression was lighter.

"Good." She almost wanted to grin.

"One thing. Be careful. I don't know yet what happened to Diana. I don't think she killed Nick, but it's pretty clear she didn't kill herself. The newspeople are making connections between the two deaths, but we don't have any kind of motive. But someone's out there who's possibly killed twice already, two people you've been closely involved with."

A shiver went down her spine at his suddenly serious tone. She recalled feeling like she was being watched the night before. She didn't see how this had anything to do with her, but she said, "Okay."

"I gotta go, but I'll see you later."

And then Cole took her face between his palms and kissed her lightly on the lips.

A few minutes later, after the door had swung shut behind him, Kerry sank onto the couch, her body liquid.

Her door suddenly opened again and she leaped to her feet, heart pounding. Cole ducked his head back inside and said, "Lock the door behind me."

She did just that, watching through the window as he got into his Jeep and drove away.

Then she sank onto the couch once more, reliving every

moment, making certain she hadn't misinterpreted any touch or gesture, putting it into her own internal hard drive to take out and examine again and again.

Officer Charlie Paige chewed on a stale doughnut and tried to put the meeting with Heather Drury into some kind of perspective. She'd had to tell a number of families when they'd lost loved ones over the course of the two and a half years she'd been with the Edwards Bay Police Department, but none had been as wrenching as this one. Having Cole there had definitely helped. His calm, take-charge demeanor and clear empathy had helped the crying woman. In his care Heather had revealed that she was divorced and had lost touch with Justin's father. Justin himself had had no contact with the man since he was a young child.

Charlie had been tasked to find him and it hadn't been hard; he'd been in and out of jail in Idaho for minor offenses, mostly petty theft and one DUI that had ended in a scuffle with a police officer, the first time he'd actually served jailtime. She'd found a number where he could be reached, but he wasn't answering. Charlie had left a message explaining she had information about his son, Justin Drury, that she wished to convey to him directly. To her surprise, he'd called back, sounding suspicious and belligerent, and she'd given him the news of Justin's death. This was not the way it was usually done, but Charlie had determined any police officer showing up at the man's residence would not be welcome. She was right on that, as it happened, because Drury said quite succinctly, "Good thing you didn't come to my door, ma'am, because I have a shotgun for intruders."

Even half-expecting that reaction, Charlie had been surprised. "You understand what I just told you, sir?"

"Yeah, my kid OD'd. You want a medal for that?"

Well.

Charlie had thanked him, for what she didn't know, then hung up and put the distasteful call out of her mind. Or tried to. She'd been replaying those moments in the Drury household, with Heather shredding Kleenex after Kleenex, dabbing the bits to her eyes or staring down at the white globs of paper that trickled to the floor. Charlie had glanced at Cole and realized he was affected, too, though he'd disguised it well, holding himself together even while offering up empathy. She, herself, had been in a self-imposed tomb of detachment, a learned exercise, one she'd been warned to embrace in order to deal with death.

Cole had come straight from the scene of Diana Conger's homicide, which undoubtedly had added another layer onto his emotional load. She felt bad about Diana, too. Youngston had condemned the woman, blamed her for Nick Radnor's death, and privately, Charlie had kind of sided with him. Maybe it was jealousy, because Cole had seemed to defend the woman. She could admit she had a teeny thing for her boss. Very teeny. Well, moderately teeny. She admired him. She liked him . . . a lot.

And it looked like he'd been right about Diana. Someone had killed her, and unless it was retribution for killing Nick, which was a thin possibility but an unlikely one, there was some kind of conspiracy going on.

Currently Cole was meeting with Diana's aunt, Eileen Conger, at her shop, The Candy Woman. Though she'd come in to identify Diana's body, she'd called back and asked for Cole directly. She seemed to suggest she had some information that might help in the investigation.

Charlie had wanted to go with him, but he'd tasked her with following up on Justin's death, so here she was.

She finished the doughnut, washed it down with cold coffee, then chewed on the end of her Pilot pen while she pulled up the list she'd compiled earlier for Cole on her computer screen. He'd asked her to keep adding to it.

Now she glanced down at some of her notations on Nick Radnor. *Death by lethal injection.* The autopsy report had confirmed the methodology for Nick's death. The ME hadn't been able to say for certain from the evidence alone that it was homicide, but the overall supposition was that it was.

But now, Diana Conger's strangulation . . .

Most killers kept with one MO. That was a fact. But these two deaths . . .

Hmmm.

Before he'd headed to interview Diana's aunt, Cole had asked Charlie to also keep up with Heather Drury, saying, "Make sure she's okay. And if you can, get some more background on Justin."

"He runs away all the time," Charlie had answered. "And she said he's used before."

"Just talk to her. She needs it, and I'd like to know what his habits were, who he saw, especially the last few days."

"Okay."

She put in a phone call to Heather, who answered desultorily. Charlie asked her how she was doing but didn't get much back. She gently queried if Heather could supply a little more information on her son in order for them to continue the investigation, but Heather wasn't able to offer much more. Feeling more like an intruder than any kind of helper, she thanked her and said she would call again later.

She sent the computer list on Nick's case to the printer. She'd run off a copy for Cole, but now, with Diana's death as well, she wanted one for herself. Heading to the adjunct room at the back of the squad room that held the printer and its supplies, which crowded the overhead shelving in the small space, she gathered up the pages, reading off the top one:

Killian Keenan, 30, son of Carroll and Faye Keenan, no siblings. BMOC at Edwards Bay High School. Football star, defensive player, cornerback. Ankle injury senior year. Two years at local community college. Employed at Keenan Motors since leaving college. Longtime girlfriend Mia Miller, classmate from Edwards Bay High.

Cole had told her he wanted a brief synopsis of each person that showed his or her relationship to the others among Nick's friends, family, and acquaintances, especially his high school friends. She'd done what she could, but Cole had mentioned this morning that he wanted to add to the character descriptions, planning to give her information and impressions he'd gleaned at last night's memorial service. Then all hell had broken loose, so Charlie was a little bit on her own.

Egan Fogherty, 30, son of Karl and Carin Fogherty, both deceased, no siblings. Employed through Washington State Department of Transportation, Washington State Ferries. Working his way up the ladder. His uncle, Ray Fogherty, was a captain until his retirement three years ago and seems to have helped Egan get the job. Bit of an odd duck. Possible bipolar diagnosis. Part of the "A-Team," by his own admission, though only partially accepted by its other members. (See list of A-Team members below.)

Charlie wrote a note to herself on the hard copy: *Romantic liaisons?*

She was reading between the lines here, but it kinda seemed like no one wanted to be his girlfriend. None of the A-Teamers anyway.

She glanced down at the brief précis she had on the rest of Nick's classmates, stopping at a note on the bottom that Cole had asked her to add.

Lisette Benetton, deceased. Suicide victim. Nick Radnor's classmate and his last high school girlfriend. Stepfather, Durant Stipe, accused of sexual abuse, which led to Lisette's suicide. Stipe not convicted on lack of evidence.

She wrote beside that: *Stipe innocent or escaped justice?* Circling that several times, lost in thought, she hit on something else: *Was there a suicide note?*

After that she went to the break room and, realizing they were out of coffee, started making a fresh pot. While it percolated, her thoughts turned back to Heather and Justin Drury. She knew Justin from the times they'd picked him up and hauled his ass back home. He wasn't a so-called "bad" kid; he just couldn't seem to discern when he was headed for trouble and always chose the more crooked path.

Back at her desk, she wrote notes to herself on Justin. *Who were his friends? How did he spend his time?* She and Youngston had picked him up a couple of times down by the train depot, loitering around the back of The Whistle Stop. She'd caught him smoking dope twice, at which he'd said with some affront that it was legal in the state of Washington, to which she'd pointed out he was underage in any case.

She decided she would try to check in on Heather again tomorrow. Maybe stop by in person. The woman needed today, at least, to fathom the horror.

When her cell rang, she didn't recognize the local number, but it seemed familiar. "Officer Paige," she answered, even though there was a chance it was a personal call.

"Oh, hi. This is Heather Drury . . ."

Charlie straightened up in her seat. Well, okay. She'd been wrong about that. "Hi, Heather. You all right?"

"I want to help. I want to find out what happened. It just doesn't feel right. He was a dope smoker. That's all Justin did. Smoke dope. I didn't want him to. I just wanted him to go to school and graduate. But it's what he did. He didn't use hard stuff. He made fun of those guys who did. I mean, he put them down."

"Classmates of his?"

"Yeah. And Perry. Umm . . . Something Perry. God, why can't I think of his first name? Anyway, he's a guy from the streets that my son kind of liked, but Justin thought he was a doper. Something like that." She sighed. "All the trouble Justin was in, I swear if there was anything really bad it was Perry's fault. He really led Justin astray. They were . . . *frenemies.* Justin didn't trust him. He just hung with him and look what happened." The sigh had changed to a choked sob.

"You think 'Perry' was . . ." She had to tread carefully here. ". . . the person who gave Justin the drugs that killed him?"

"Ted Perry!" she said with sudden recall. "Ted Perry. Yes. I think he's definitely the guy."

"Do you know anything more about him?"

"Justin said he was homeless. That's all I know."

"Okay. We'll follow up."

"You will, won't you?" she asked suspiciously. "You're not just saying that."

"Of course not. I want to know what happened to him, too."

"Okay. Thanks."

"If you think of anything else. Or you ever just want to talk?"

"I'm going down to see my boy today. I just haven't got there yet."

The morgue. That was going to be a tough one. "How about I meet you there?"

Heather drew in a shaking breath, said something that might have been "Yes," and then, "I'll be there in half an hour," before quickly hanging up.

Charlie had quickly jotted down some notes from their call. She called across the room to the only other officer in the squad room, Dave Hoffman. "I'm meeting Heather Drury at the morgue. You know the name of that homeless shelter down off Fifth?"

"Brighter Day," he called back.

Grabbing her jacket from the back of her chair, she pulled her gun from her desk drawer and fit it into her hip holster. She had yet to use it, and it still felt cumbersome, but she'd been in a couple of situations when her hand had hovered over it, which had heightened her nerves and made her feel safer at the same time.

"I'm going to stop by there later, too."

He gave her a Boy Scout salute and she headed out.

"You seem preoccupied," Jerry said to Kerry. He was shrunken into his bed, which had alarmed her when she'd walked into his room. It made him seem diminished.

"You sure you're okay?" she asked again.

"I'm gonna be fine as soon as I get outta here. Doc Stevens came by last night. Said he'd stop in again today. Going out of his way to check on me," he grumbled.

"Isn't that a good thing?" Kerry scooted the only chair in the room closer to his bed.

"Makes me feel like an invalid."

"Try to think of it as being concerned."

"Hmph."

Jerry subsided into a scowl, but Kerry took it as a positive sign. Patients who were grumpy were often seen to be on the mend. She hadn't answered his question about being preoccupied because she knew she was and why, but she didn't want to talk about it. She'd been holding on to good feelings about Cole as hard as she could, though other thoughts kept creeping in around the edges. Diana's murder most of all. And Nick's . . . and she'd even thought about the poor mother who'd lost her child, Heather, whose loss had affected Cole so much.

And Cole's warning to be careful. The whisper of danger that she sensed, even if it was nebulous.

"Can I get you anything?" she asked.

"Yeah. Out of here. ASAP."

"As soon as Dr. Stevens says it's okay."

"It's a conspiracy," he groused. "I'll be outta here by Monday, no matter what. I'm not missing that meeting with the lawyers."

"Probably sooner. Hospitals don't hang on to patients unless they have to."

"Well, make sure they don't have to hang on to me," he stated firmly.

"I'll do what I can."

His grumpiness made her want to smile. She stayed around for a few more minutes but could see, despite his assurances to the contrary, he was growing weary.

"Jerry . . ."

He looked at her, hearing the change in her tone.

"Do you remember telling me that Nick wanted 'atonement'?"

His gaze slid away until he was staring straight ahead

at the blank TV. His chin quivered a bit, but he finally said, "Yes."

"You don't want to talk about it?"

"No . . . but it should be said. He blamed himself for her death."

"Her, as in Lisette Benetton?"

"She was fragile. Very fragile. Nick wanted the suicide to be because of her stepfather, but he knew it wasn't. Maybe we all knew, deep down." He licked his lips. "Nobody stood up and told the truth. Nick said he was going to do that."

"What was he going to say?"

"He tried to see Stipe that Memorial Day weekend before graduation, but he wasn't home. Lisette's mom was already ill. Died a few years after Lisette did. Heart trouble. Broken heart, most likely." He absently rubbed his own chest. "I told Nick at the time there was nothing to apologize for, but he disagreed. I don't know if he ever contacted Stipe, but that was only part of it. He blamed himself. Said he caused her to kill herself and wouldn't listen to anyone saying different. I thought he was over it . . . all these years . . . but this last time he came home, I don't know. Some of his friends tried to talk to him about it, but it was no good." Jerry closed his eyes and sighed.

Kerry opened her mouth to ask, "Which friends?" but Jerry looked wiped out. She could ask them herself. She got up, wished him goodbye, and leaned in and kissed him on his forehead again, then headed out.

Her phone buzzed again as she was getting in her car. Josie. A second time. It took her a while to answer and by the time she did, Josie was gone. She texted her that she was on her way home and had some time if Josie wanted to call back.

* * *

Josie aborted her call to Kerry when she heard her door-bell ring, a tinkling of bells that went on for-effing-ever. Something she'd had to have when they moved into the house and now was like fingernails scraping on a black-board. "Be right there," she called, then headed into the den with its window that faced the front door, catching a corner of it so she could see who was there.

She carefully twisted the blinds to allow herself a view. A man's back was to her.

Chad.

Well, you invited him over, didn't you? Why the trepida-tion now?

She smoothed her hands down her short skirt, worrying it was too short. She'd put it on precisely for that purpose, but now she was nervous, almost scared. It had pockets in the back where she'd slipped her cell phone, which she touched now, making sure it was there. The light blue blouse she'd chosen had delicate buttons that would be difficult to undo, if she were to, say, be taking her clothes off for any reason . . .

What the hell are you thinking?

Man, she wished Kerry would have answered her call. Kerry would have talked her out of it, if Josie had told her about inviting Chad over, which she might not have. She didn't know her that well. Expecting her to be some kind of conscience was wrong. But she knew that was what she would get from Kerry.

"Hi, there," she greeted him, hanging on the door while she looked out at him on her doorstep. He was attractive enough, in an average sort of way. Nothing like Nick really, seeing him in the light of day. What had she been thinking, inviting him over while Kent was away? He had to be fo-cused on one thing and one thing only, and he'd be right. She'd invited him over knowing full well that they might get together and let one thing lead to another and . . . well, it wasn't going to happen now. She'd come to her senses.

"Hi, yourself," he said. He slid a look toward the driveway and garage. "Your husband . . . on that trip?"

"Yes."

"Are you going to invite me in?"

She was still hanging on the door, hesitating. Did she want him to come in? She sensed she was angry at Kent for just about everything. Nothing was that big of a problem, but there were problems. Dallying with Chad would only add to them.

"I don't know," she said a bit sadly.

"I didn't take you for a prick teaser." He said it with a smile, but it got Josie.

"I'm just flagellating."

"Whoa. That sounds dirty."

"It means I haven't made up my mind." That was what the word meant, wasn't it? Sometimes she got them a little wrong.

"Uh-huh. Well, flagellate this." He grabbed her by the shoulders and pushed into her, driving them both into the entryway of her home, kicking the door shut behind him.

"Hey," Josie protested, but then his mouth was on hers and his viselike grip on her upper arms tightened even more.

She went slack, sensing to fight would do her no good. But she was panicking inside. She remembered Taryn saying how persistent her ex-boss had been, how she'd understood the power and been desperate to get the power back.

"You've got to be wilier than they are or they'll take everything from you . . ."

She tried to think of Nick, but it was no good. He went from kissing to biting her neck and ear. "Ouch," she whispered, hoping he would let up.

"You like that? You like that, bitch?"

There was an underlying trill of excitement in his tone that she found more worrisome than anything else. Oh, God. What had she done?

She let him manhandle her against the entry-hall wall for several moments, her thoughts sharp and rapid. She flinched a bit at his increasingly painful bites at her neck, mouth, and ear.

He finally surfaced, his lizard brain slowly becoming aware that she was a nonparticipant. He pulled back to look at her hard, his hands, which had briefly released their grip to cop a feel of her breast, one sliding between her legs to squeeze her hard in the crotch, one still gripped like a claw on her upper arm. There was a cold flame of desire in his eyes. Desire to hurt, maybe.

Oh, Jose. You really did it this time.

"Oh, come on," he whispered. "Bet Nick wasn't the only one. You're bored with your husband."

"Not bored."

He gave a harsh laugh. "All right. Come up with some word that describes it better. Disgusted? Turned off? Repelled? Nick said you married for money. How's that money keeping you satisfied in bed, hmmm? Not much, by the looks of things."

"I didn't marry for money." Josie's heart was heavy. He wasn't completely on target but close enough.

"Money's not all bad. I certainly wouldn't do without it." He moved in closer again, rubbing against her. "Let's move this to the bedroom."

"No."

He laughed again, his hard, marauding hand back at her upper arm, both hands squeezing tightly. She was going to have bruises. "All right, we'll do it right here. Your ass is going to hurt against that hard wall."

"I didn't sleep with Nick."

Josie kept her lips together, but her mouth was trembling uncontrollably.

"Yeah?"

"You said you wondered about it. That Nick didn't sleep with married women. Well, you were right. I flirted with him. I probably would have, no, I definitely would have slept with him, but we never got that far. I just made it up in my head. I've always just made it up in my head. Everyone kind of assumed and I let them."

Chad pulled back for a moment. "Who cares?"

"I do. I didn't sleep with Nick and I'm not going to sleep with you."

Her heart was pounding so hard, it felt like it was battering her rib cage. She knew he was calculating whether she was lying or not. She wasn't, and the truth rang like a bell to her own ears.

"Makes no difference. I'm here now. I don't give a rat's ass what you did or didn't do with Nick."

But he did . . . She could tell his passion had subsided and he was having a helluva time picking it back up.

"And now he's gone," she added. "Just like that. And Diana's gone, too."

"What?" he asked sharply.

"Guess you haven't heard. Diana's dead. Someone strangled her."

His hands lost their grip. He stared at the floor as if not being able to grapple with his thoughts. Josie's every instinct was to run. Push him aside. Race to her bedroom, or the bathroom with the lock. But she stayed frozen, poised, waiting.

"Fuck," he said, a note of worry, maybe fear, in his voice.

"I know," she said, watching him carefully.

And then her cell buzzed. It was in her back pocket and had dug into her butt cheek when Chad had pushed her to the wall. Carefully, she reached a hand back for it, but Chad didn't seem to care.

"It's Taryn," she said.

He didn't seem to hear her, just stepped back, clearly lost in his own thoughts.

She answered with a careful, "Hi," her eyes never leaving Chad.

"Have you heard?" Her voice was high and panicked. "About Diana?"

"Yeah."

"Oh. My. God!"

It was rare to hear Taryn so out of control. The one thing she always was, was in control. "I know."

"I'm . . . I'm . . . was it suicide? Over Nick?"

"I don't know." Josie's mouth was suddenly desert dry. She needed a glass of water, and maybe one of wine.

"Oh, God, Jose. What are we going to do?"

Taryn never called her Jose. Not that she could recall. They weren't that good friends. "I don't know. Can I call you back?"

"Are you getting together with anyone from the Team? Oh my God. Diana." A sharp breath. "I was so . . . hard on her."

"I can't really talk right now. Maybe Miami this afternoon . . ."

"I thought Miami was working."

"I don't know what her schedule is. I'll check."

"Are you okay? You sound strained."

"Taryn, I've gotta go," Josie said, edging away from Chad a bit.

"I'll call Miami. Okay?"

"You do that." She clicked off, tried to shove the phone into her back pocket and missed.

Chad gave up his perusal of the tile entryway floor and now lifted his eyes to look at her. "You seeing Miami today?"

"I don't know. We might get together."

He ran his hands through his hair and closed his eyes. "Man, I don't know what to think." When Josie didn't answer he reopened his eyes and regarded her with chagrin. "You didn't want to have sex, did you?"

She almost laughed, but the danger wasn't completely over. "No."

"I knew you hadn't done it with Nick." His mouth was hard.

She didn't answer that. Didn't know how to.

He turned to leave, and Josie got ready to lock the door behind him, but he stopped at the threshold. "I'm going home tomorrow. I just wanted to pay my respects and meet Nick's old friends. He always had this charmed life."

She didn't know if that was completely true, but she saw that Chad never felt quite good enough. Nick's friend, maybe . . . Nick's competitor, definitely.

As soon as he was through the door, she snapped the lock, then ran back to the bedroom, heart galloping, and peered through the blinds, willing him to go. If he came back, she didn't know what she'd do.

As soon as he drove off in his rented Audi, she threw herself on her bed, sick with relief, sick with grief. *You're pathetic*, she told herself. *Effing pathetic.* Fucking *pathetic*!

She realized his mauling had torn one button off her blouse, while another was hanging by a thread, gapping the fabric, showing the lacy bra underneath. Immediately she got up and ripped off her clothes. Then she stepped in the shower and let the hot water run over her body. Her fantasy affair with Nick had never made her feel this dirty.

Some half an hour later, when she finally ran out of hot water, she turned off the taps and toweled off.

Then she phoned Miami.

Chapter Sixteen

Cole got back to the station to find Charlie gone. He checked in with Hoffman, who said she'd left about an hour earlier, then went into his office, sat in his chair, linked his fingers behind his head, and stared at the ceiling. He'd spent a lot of time thinking about Kerry and he needed to set that aside for the moment to concentrate on Nick's and Diana's deaths. Unless the ME found something that said otherwise, they were both homicides, and in Cole's mind, based on the evidence, they were linked.

So what was that link?

He'd gone to The Candy Woman and met with Eileen Conger, Diana's dour-faced aunt. The pink-and-white-striped shop was redolent with the sweet perfume of chocolate and sugar, an almost fairylandish venue, a direct dichotomy to the stern woman who ran the establishment. He'd already met her once today, and he was hit anew by her lack of warmth, hardly the image for a purveyor of confections, but then, she'd been burdened with terrible news.

"Why?" she'd asked him earlier, after viewing Diana's body. "Why?"

He'd had no answer for her. She'd hardly changed expression before or after viewing Diana's body and all she'd said as she left was, "I'll call Martin," who was Diana's brother,

Cole knew, from Charlie's ever-growing compilation of people, facts, and impressions about Nick Radnor. Charlie would be adding the same for Diana Conger.

When he'd arrived at The Candy Woman, he'd asked a young woman behind the counter for Eileen, who appeared from the back a few moments later. She immediately shooed the girl away from the counter and then said, "I know who killed my niece. That neighbor."

"Diana's neighbor? Alan Jenkins?" Cole had asked. The bell to the shop had tinkled as other customers arrived. Eileen had given them a hard look, then called the girl out from the back to take care of them. She'd then come from behind the counter and quickly waved Cole outside and out of earshot.

"He was first on the scene at her apartment when that poor boy was killed."

Nick Radnor was hardly a boy, but Cole decided to remain quiet and let her go on, which she did.

"He was always pressuring Diana. Coming over. In her way. Diana told me all about it. He's who you should be looking at."

Cole nodded. Ben Youngston had been on scene when Nick's body was discovered. "They weren't friends?" he asked, recalling how Youngston had mentioned Diana falling into Jenkins's arms.

"Not the way you mean," she said, affronted.

"I only meant friendship. Nothing romantic," Cole clarified.

"Well, I know Diana had a reputation with men." She crossed her arms over her chest. "But she didn't ask for his attention. He was just always there. He's psychopathic. Jealous. He killed that boy out of jealousy, if you ask me, and Diana knew it, so he had to kill her, too." She fumbled over the last couple of words, sniffing against sudden tears, finally connecting to her loss.

Cole almost told her that Spano had seen Jenkins, who'd been devastated by Diana's death. Cole hadn't yet interviewed Jenkins today, but the way Spano had described his horror, loss, and bewilderment had convinced both him, and therefore Cole, that it was unlikely he was part of the crime. But he decided to keep that to himself. He had sensed that whatever he might say, Eileen Conger was armed and eager to shoot down. It was a battle that could not be won, so he wasn't going to even start.

Instead he listened to her expound on the same theme for several minutes, until the traffic into the candy shop increased enough that she was forced to help out.

"You'll arrest him?" she said as a closing salvo.

"When there's enough evidence against him," was Cole's answer.

"There will be," she decreed as she headed back inside, pasting a totally fake smile on her face as she held the door for arriving customers.

Now Cole considered if he should maybe interview Alan Jenkins again today. But Spano was pretty right on with his impressions. "If he faked it, he deserves an Oscar," Spano had said, so that was an avenue of investigation he thought he might put aside for the moment.

Don't get distracted.

He let his mind travel back to Nick's death. It was the first homicide and the possible kickoff to Diana's as well. What had happened? Why had someone felt compelled to kill him? Cole had spoken to a lot of people who knew Nick, both locally and in Silicon Valley. Most who'd seen him within the last year said he'd seemed the same as he'd always been, though a handful had said he'd been quieter, more serious. Had something happened in the last few months? Something that had caused him to start coming to Edwards Bay more often, something he was working through? Even Kerry had mentioned it, though she didn't know its cause.

He thought about the means of Nick's death and made a note to himself about the hypodermic needle. Not hard to obtain, but not something the general public had lying around as a rule. So who'd brought it to Diana's apartment that night? Diana swore she didn't have one, and there'd been none on the premises, but the ME had determined that was what the tiny puncture wound was from. And Diana, for all her documented drug use, didn't shoot up. She was strictly a pill popper. Even so, he'd asked the ME to look for evidence to the contrary in the autopsy. So far de la Fuente hadn't contacted him. Cole doubted he would.

So . . . the killer had brought the syringe with him or her.

With the intent of doping Nick? With or without his consent? Maybe Nick, whose personality had by all accounts changed, had requested the heroin shot? As a means of numbing reality or pain? That would be way outside what Cole knew personally about the man. Could he have changed that much?

Alternatively, the killer brought the syringe for himself . . . or Diana. But Diana had balked at the sight of it. She'd sworn she had nothing to do with it, but had she? And now the real killer considered her collateral damage?

His mind shifted to Diana. She'd been under the influence of something at the memorial service. She couldn't follow the simplest directions, and she couldn't remember what had happened that night in her apartment. She'd been spouting theories about a third person, something she'd picked up from seeing a hypnotist.

He picked up his phone and called Kerry, feeling a bit of something like heat in his chest near his heart. He hadn't meant to go so deep into emotions with her earlier. He wasn't one to just suddenly break down and confess his feelings. But he wasn't sorry either. Since seeing Kerry again, the hard lock he'd placed on his feelings had sprung open.

He paused, deciding to wait a bit before calling her. Had to get himself together. They'd had a breakthrough of sorts, and he didn't want to screw it up. There were other calls to make anyway.

The first was another to Durant Stipe, whose cell number Charlie had found for him. As with the first two times he'd called Lisette Benetton's stepfather, the call had gone straight to voice mail. This time Cole didn't bother leaving a message. He'd left two already. He had an address for the man, but he lived in Woodinville, on the other side of Seattle. With traffic, it would take up the rest of the afternoon if he decided to go to his residence, and there was a good chance he wouldn't be there anyway.

The second call was to Carroll Keenan. It took him a moment or two to decide on Keenan as he looked over a list of the football dads' names he'd given to Charlie, who had matched them to cell numbers. He didn't know quite what he was looking for with them, but there was something there. A kind of members-only attitude coupled with nostalgia that seemed way out of proportion to a short and long-past period in their lives. But maybe he was wrong. Maybe their sons' football glory days had a bonding mystique he could only guess at. A commonality that lasted through the years. Maybe it was a natural for conversation. It had just seemed so . . .

Cole made a face. Couldn't put his finger on it. At the memorial service those men, especially Blevins, had seemed almost disrespectful.

Putting that aside, he placed the call to Carroll Keenan, who answered with, "Keenan. Who's calling?"

"This is Chief Sheffield," Cole introduced himself, letting the man know immediately this wasn't a social call.

"Oh. Cole. What can I do for you?"

Was it his imagination or was there a thread of caution in the man's voice? "Have you heard that Diana Conger was killed in her apartment last night?"

"Killed? You mean, purposely? Murdered?"

"She was strangled. We believe it's in connection with Nick Radnor's death."

"Truly? Huh. I saw on the news that she was dead, but I thought it was accidental."

Cole had asked the media to keep the strangulation out of the public eye for a while, though he'd had little real hope that would happen. But at least in this case it had bought him some time. "We're treating it like a homicide. We believe it's connected to Nick Radnor's death."

"So she didn't kill Nick." He sounded dubious. "That's not why you're calling me, though."

"No. Actually, I wanted to ask you about Nick's last year of high school," Cole said, then launched in with, "He was on the football team with Killian. Nick was the quarterback."

"Well, yeah, but . . . you're going a long way back, son," he said, and this time his tone shifted to a kind of patriarchal wariness, a warning before Cole had even started.

"I've been trying to reach Durant Stipe without much success. He was Lisette Benetton's stepfather, the man accused of sexual assault. You all knew him, right?"

"Of him," Keenan clarified. "He had a daughter and she wasn't playing football, so I didn't know him."

"Lisette was dating Nick at the time of her suicide?"

"This might be a question for Killian. I'm a few rungs out, I'm afraid."

"It was football season. It must've made a pretty big impression on the whole team. The quarterback's, the team leader's girlfriend committing suicide."

"Well, now, Killian was as much a leader, maybe more so, than Nick Radnor ever was. Don't want to speak ill of the dead, but Nick wasn't all that strong."

"Killian was a running back?" Cole searched through his memory to all the football memories that had been pouring out of the older men as the service wound up and the liquor flowed. "He'd wanted to be quarterback."

"It was a long time ago," Keenan said.

"I was hearing some of the recaps last night," said Cole.

"Killian was a great quarterback, but they needed a running back. They needed speed. Not that quarterbacks don't need speed, too. They do. But who's gonna run that ball? You gotta have somebody with strength and speed, and Killian was the best on the team. It was the coach's decision. Coach Bergen was a friend of Jerry Radnor, you know. Not that I'm saying that made the final decision, but it had some influence. Killian was looked at hard by a lot of schools, and I mean across the country, but if he'd been quarterback, there would have been even more."

"Did I hear he played both offense and defense?" Cole asked.

"Sure did. He was their best safety, too. Couldn't do it all, though."

"But he didn't go on to college ball."

"No." He was abrupt.

"Why?"

"If you were listening last night, you already know," he said evenly. "Nick Radnor. Nobody wanted to talk about it much at the man's memorial service, but it was there. He and Killian were wrestling around, just horsing around, and this concrete post got loose and crashed down on my son's ankle. Just murdered it."

"Where was this?"

"At some graduation party they were at. Killian was devastated."

As were you, Cole thought.

"But he and Nick stayed good friends," he added quickly, as if realizing how that might sound. "It was just a lousy end to the year."

"Do you remember Diana Conger from that time?"

"No. Not really."

Again the caution. As if he were afraid to say something that might come back to bite him. "Lisette Benetton?" Cole asked.

"She was Nick's girl. Sure."

"And the others, Josie and Miami and Taryn—"

"What is this really?" he demanded. "What are you getting at?"

Cole wasn't sure exactly what he was searching for. He just knew he was making the man uncomfortable in some way.

"I think I've talked enough about this," Keenan growled. "You want answers about Nick Radnor, forget high school. Go check with those people in Silicon Valley. I've heard he screwed his partner out of millions. All Nick was to us was a mediocre football player on the same team as our kids."

He hung up.

Charlie returned while Cole was still absorbing the conversation with Keenan. She came to his door and stuck her head inside. "I went looking for the homeless kid Heather

Drury told me about who was supposedly a bad influence on Justin, maybe supplied him the drugs."

"And?"

"Not so sure that's the way it was. Justin did hang out with Ted Perry, but there were other guys at Brighter Day as well."

"Brighter Day?" Cole snapped to attention in a way that made Charlie stop talking. "Brighter Day?" Cole asked again.

"Well . . . yes," she said uncertainly.

"And?"

"And yeah, I think there could be a drug connection between Justin and Ted Perry. No one's supposed to be using who stays there, you understand, and I ruffled the feathers of the director, Jill Potts, by asking questions. But these kids are sneaking stuff in every which way, if you ask me. I don't have proof. Just something about it. Perry's over twenty-one, but I'm not sure he's entirely to blame. Heather's looking to blame him, though. But you know . . . it could be the other way around. Justin supplying Perry."

"Where was Justin getting the stuff?"

"I don't know yet."

Cole had already grabbed up his jacket and was heading for the door.

"Where are you going?" Charlie asked, stepping back to allow him to pass.

"Let's go back to Brighter Day. According to one of Nick's friends who's affiliated with it, it's where Nick Radnor gifted most of his estate."

"You want me to go, too?"

"Yep."

"You think it's connected to Nick Radnor's death?"

"If Brighter Day benefits from his death, and his death was by drugs, which apparently are being sneaked into the facility 'every which way,' it's a coincidence at the very least."

"All right. I'll grab my coat and let's go."

"Okay."

Cole headed outside, calling Kerry as he ducked his head against a fretful wind that was making the bright red roses planted outside the station's front door dance. This year, like every year, the wind was shredding the blossoms just as they were becoming lush and fragrant. He inhaled their scent, which, combined with the brine off the water, was a heady mix.

"Well, hello," Kerry answered, a bit shyly, he thought.

He felt much the same way. "I have a question for you. Do you remember the name of Diana's hypnotist?"

"It's Nina Gudner."

"Nina Gudner," he repeated, committing it to memory.

"Are you going to interview her?"

"As soon as I can, I guess."

"Can I go, too?"

He wanted to say yes. He almost did. But he said, "Well, that wouldn't really work, given the rules of my job."

"I know. I just . . ."

"If I can, I'll tell you what she says," he promised. "I'll come by the motel later? I've got another interview, and then I'll try to contact her."

"Okay. See you then."

He was smiling as he clicked off and Charlie met him at his Jeep.

Kerry clicked off and clutched her hands together in alarm. She'd just gotten off the phone with Nina Gudner herself and had likely scared the woman senseless. Oh, no. She'd just been thinking about Diana and what she'd said about the hypnotist and had decided to be proactive. If she'd gotten in the way of Cole's investigation there would be hell to pay.

And for what? The conversation had been a disaster. She'd called Nina and learned right away that she hadn't yet heard about Diana's murder. In a frightened voice, the hypnotist had cried, "I don't know anything! We had one session. One! Diana felt she'd seen someone at her apartment that night, but she couldn't describe him!"

"Him?" Kerry had repeated.

"I don't know! I don't know! Don't call me again." And she'd hung up.

She went back to her laptop, which she'd left open on her kitchen table, her nerves buzzing with anxiety. She'd been going over accounts and the construction bills that had piled up, bills that came to her address or were left on her doorstep. Jerry wasn't using Starrwood Homes as his main contractor, but he was using some of their subs, which had created its own little hell for Kerry; the competition for workers had pissed Randy off. He'd tried to keep his enmity from spilling over onto Kerry, who had worked for him long before Jerry decided to renovate. Mostly, things had gone smoothly, and with Nick's death and Jerry's hospitalization, Randy had really backed off.

But her thoughts drifted back to Nina. And Cole. And then to Diana. Strangled.

She gave a full-body shiver and tried to settle her thoughts.

A knock on her back door nearly sent her through the roof. She hurried over and saw it was Emilio, the man in charge of the tilers. "Hello, Kerree," he greeted her. "We are having some trouble with thee machine. Thee safetee guide is broken." He threw a dark look over his head to one of the other men, who was standing back, head down.

"Okay." She hadn't really noticed that the noise had stopped, but now she did.

"We will be back later. Be careful."

"Oh, I will. I've used a tiler before. Not well, but being around home construction, I . . ." Why was she even talking? He was politely waiting for her to finish, but he was clearly upset with his worker. "So you'll be knocking off . . . quitting for today?"

"Yes, queeting. Thank you."

"Oh, Emilio. I found the lights left on in some of the units, and the doors left open. Could you make sure everything's buttoned up tight?"

"Yes. Absolutely."

She closed the door behind him, hearing rapid-fire Spanish leveled at the hapless man who'd broken the machine.

Her cell rang and she saw it was Randy. Now what? Her hand hovered over the Connect button. She'd told him she would see him Monday. Whatever he wanted, she wasn't interested. But in the end she hit the button, and then kicked herself when he said, "Hey, I know I shouldn't ask, but can you come back? I'm drowning here, and with Ange out, I just can't do it."

"Randy . . ." She stopped herself.

He jumped in. "I know what you're going to say. Angie should come in. She should. But she's having a helluva time since Diana . . . and what happened at the reception. It's making her sick, really sick. I just need help."

"What happened at the reception?" Kerry asked.

"Oh, you know . . . at the end . . ."

"No, I don't know."

She waited, but he clearly didn't want to tell her if she didn't already know. "Randy," she pressed.

"She got in a fight with her friend Sheryl. She thought Sheryl was . . . coming on to me, I guess."

"And that's why she's out sick today and you need to be in two places at once and want me to come back in."

"I know. I'm a bastard. But I need help. Ange is just heartsick. She and Sheryl have been friends a long time and it's killing her. I know they'll work it out. They always do. It just might take some time."

Try to imagine how little I care. "Uh-huh."

"Just for one more hour, then done till Monday. Okay?" he pleaded.

"Sure. Fine."

Randy was a flirt, and that flirting had gotten him in trouble with his wife, and now he was relying on Kerry. Big surprise. When she'd taken the job, she'd been very clear about her "space" with him, which he seemed to generally understand, although not if it inconvenienced him.

"And I might need you to take something over to my dad," he burst out, as if he couldn't contain it any further.

"Jesus, Randy . . ."

"I know, I know."

This job . . . the boundaries were growing far too fluid. "Don't forget I did this for you," she warned.

"I won't. Scout's honor. I won't."

"Bet you never were a Scout," Kerry muttered as she clicked off.

She looked at her laptop screen, then took a moment to search for "Nina Gudner," "hypnotist," and "Washington state" and found an address in Lynnwood. Lynnwood was right up I-5 from Edwards Bay. Maybe if she went to see Nina . . . before Cole did? Except he was calling her next.

She tried calling the woman again but got no answer. She'd really spooked her and, in turn, Kerry was spooked as well. But she had to know what had happened. She had to know the truth. Yes, she'd told Cole she would be careful, but with Diana's death, her murder, on the heels of Nick's . . .

Grabbing up her purse, she headed out. She would figure out what she was going to do later. After she put in what was turning out to be the second half of a split shift at Starrwood Homes.

Josie checked her phone as she hurried through the back door of the Blarney Stone. Four ten. She was barely late, but as she entered she saw she was the only one there apart from Miami, who was seated at the bar talking to Sean. As soon as Sean saw her, he straightened and headed toward the bottles lined up on the narrow glass shelves that filled the wall behind the bar. He pulled down Grey Goose and offered Josie a small smile. "Vodka martini?"

"Yes, please."

She slid onto the stool next to Miami just as she was straightening up and inclined her head toward their favorite table, the largest one, tucked in its own corner farthest away from the dartboard.

Josie followed her, sitting down across from her. She hoped the remnants of Chad's attack didn't show. She'd covered her arms with a long-sleeved black T-shirt and had really overdone the blush to brighten up her white face.

Miami's expression was shuttered. She looked as if she were under enormous strain. "You okay?" Josie asked her.

"No. No, I'm not. Someone killed Diana . . ."

"I know," Josie said. The whole day felt surreal. As if it had happened to someone else. Maybe it had. A second personality that seemed to lie beneath Josie's good-girl, fresh-faced tomboy exterior.

"What are we going to do?"

"What can we do? I mean, throw another memorial

service?" She heard herself and tried to work up a smile, failing miserably.

"We know what this is about. We need to do something. We can't just sit by any longer."

Josie stared at her friend's drawn face. "What are you talking about?"

"You *know*, Josie."

"I don't know if I do . . ."

"The chart, Josie. The reason Lisette's dead!" she hissed.

"That's not the reason."

"Of course it is!"

Tiny ice chips felt like they were floating in Josie's veins. The mythical chart from high school. "Someone killed Nick and Diana, and it isn't because of high school."

"Everything's because of high school," she said bitterly, staring into her drink. Exactly the same drink Sean was now bringing over for Josie. Josie thanked him, and he gave Miami a worried look before he headed back to the bar. Whatever world she was lost in, it wasn't a pleasant one.

"I'm thinking of . . . telling the truth," Miami whispered, her gaze darting around the room.

"About . . . ?"

"Remember that guy you dated in high school?"

"'The love of my life,' as you reminded me?"

"No, not him. I mean at our high school."

"I dated a bunch of guys, none seriously." *And all pretty much losers,* Josie thought now, which was unfair and she knew it and didn't care.

"But there was the one who said all those things about you. About how you put out and went down on him and gave great suck."

"Jesus. What a memory. And it was all lies," Josie declared, surprised and a little repelled that Miami recalled it all so clearly. On the heels of Chad's attack, to think back to that high school asshole . . . she felt under siege, damn near paranoiac. Was that the right word? And Miami sure as hell wasn't helping. "You know none of it was true."

"But it made the chart."

Josie stated clearly, "*That guy* and I had a makeout session that didn't get all that far, and afterward he bragged about all kinds of stuff that wasn't true. He *lied* about it, and it wasn't even a good lie! At least the one about Nick on the fifty-yard line was inventive."

Miami shot Josie a look. "That wasn't a lie."

"Well, whatever. I was lied about. If I made the chart, it was on a total, effing lie."

"He just wanted to be cool. Like the football guys."

"Oh, now you're taking his side?"

"I'm just remembering, Jose."

"He wasn't cool. At all," Josie told her flatly. "At first I thought he was an okay guy. I didn't even like him that much. I just was mostly being nice. And then he said all that shit about me, and I never spoke to him again. Why are you even bringing it up?"

"Some people believed it."

"Well, great." Josie was angry. "Who gives a damn about high school anyway?"

"Some of us weren't as strong as you. That's all I'm saying." Miami's voice, already low, sounded trapped in her throat.

"What the hell, Miami? What *are* you saying?"

"I just know where this all started. And it's time I spoke up."

At that moment the back door clattered shut behind a new arrival. Josie looked up to see Killian enter, with Egan on his heels, an eager puppy hoping to be noticed. She inwardly groaned. She hadn't realized how over Lady-Killerian she was. And that went double for Egan.

Egan, as if drawn to her negative vibes, walked straight over and took the seat next to her as Killian bellied up to the bar. "I know who killed Diana," he whispered to her in a conspiratorial voice.

"Do tell," Josie said, bored. *Don't talk to him,* she warned herself. *It only encourages him.*

"Shut up, Egan," Miami flashed with sudden fury. She snatched up her drink and headed for Killian.

"What the fuck?" Surprised, Egan watched her leave.

"Okay, who killed her?" Josie asked, draining her own drink. It would be rude to get up and leave him alone at the table, wouldn't it? Should she care? Nope.

"I can't tell you because you'll tell everybody else."

"You were going to tell Miami and me. Now you won't?"

He waggled a finger at her. "I'm not going to tell either of you. But I know who it is."

"Okay, fine. Tell the police, if you're so goddamn sure."

He cocked his head. "I could maybe be persuaded. If you were to, say, meet me outside? My Camaro's parked in the back lot." He let his tongue stick out of the side of his mouth.

Josie's anger boiled over. She wanted to push him out of his chair, slap his face, pull his hair. "Not the day to test me."

"This isn't a test. I was just—"

"Being an asshole. Okay, fine. You want to go outside to your Camaro, jump in the back seat—"

"The front seat's fine."

"—and have all kinds of great sex, starting with maybe a blow job first? And then you'll tell me who killed Diana?"

He regarded her uncertainly. "Hey . . ."

"I believe that's extortion, Egan."

He held up his hands. "I was just asking."

"Is that what you proposed to Diana? The Camaro idea? We all know you had sex with her."

He eyed her cautiously but didn't speak.

"And now you're using her death for your own gain?" She was holding herself together with an effort. It felt like her head was going to explode. Through a red haze, she realized she would be far better off if she just went home.

Taryn had joined Killian and Miami at the bar. Seeing Josie, she lifted a hand in greeting. Forrest had appeared as well. Probably from the kitchen area of the bar. Everyone but Sean started moseying toward Egan and her.

Egan's hand suddenly shot across the table, clasping one of Josie's. Surprised, she automatically yanked it back, but his fingers formed a manacle. "Be careful," he said through his teeth, then abruptly released her.

Fear formed a fist in her stomach. She sat for a while, conversation rising and falling around her as the others joined their table. The shock of Diana's death, on the heels of Nick's, was the current that ran through every word, every syllable. No one noticed Josie's quietude. No one knew what she'd been through today, or that she was feeling a little out of control.

She sensed Egan's eyes on her, drifting over her, then moving away, then sliding back. She refused to meet his gaze. She waited what she considered an appropriate amount of time, then edged away from the group, murmured an excuse, and went home.

Chapter Seventeen

As soon as Kerry returned to Starrwood Homes, Randy came into her office. He looked stressed, his hair practically standing on end from where he'd run his hands through it. Kerry had barely registered that when his fingers raked through the thin strands again.

"I've gotta go," he said. "Promised my dad the latest monthly reports. Lots of expenses, damn it. The price of things . . ." He threw his hands in the air. "I'd give it to you, but he's not gonna like it."

"You want me to take him this report?"

"Yes, Kerry. That's what I need. Don't give me a hard time. I've got . . . I've got things to take care of."

She crossed her arms. She was tired of being run roughshod over. She'd told herself she enjoyed her job, and maybe she had once. But those days were long gone. "What kind of things?"

"Things," he repeated, his jaw tightening.

"It's my day off and I've been here twice. I think I deserve an explanation."

"Okay!" he practically exploded. "I'm trying to save my marriage. That explanation enough? I can't do everything. Jesus."

"What did you do?"

He gaped at her. "It isn't my fault!" But his eyes slid away. A tell.

She was growing angry. Tired of always being the one who had to pick up the pieces. "You know what, I don't even care. You and Angie . . . working with you both . . ." She shook her head.

"You're not quitting. Kerry. You're not quitting." He was aghast.

"I'll take the report to your dad and then I'm going home."

"You'll be here Monday." He said it like it was an order, but his normally ruddy cheeks had paled, his eyes pleading.

It took her a moment to respond. Part of her wanted to quit on the spot. Job burnout. But she said, "I'll be here Monday afternoon. I have a meeting with Nick's lawyer in the morning."

"Oh. His will."

"What did you do, Randy? Why did Angie throw a drink at her friend?"

Color seeped back into his face and he pulled himself together with an effort. "Nothing," he said belligerently, then he strode out of her office and came back with a thick file, which he slapped in her hands. "And this is really your fault, you know. The extra expenses."

Kerry couldn't believe his gall. "You don't want me to quit, but you don't want to pay me? Is that what you're saying?"

"You're stealing all our subs! That's what I mean! The delays cost money. And now I've got to explain it to my dad, but first I've gotta talk to Ange. Explain how sorry I am. Beg for forgiveness. Jesus Christ!" He strode out of her office and out of the building, slamming the door behind him.

Kerry drove to the Callaway Center, seething. She was going to quit. Period. She would find some other job. Jerry would be thrilled if she oversaw the renovations at The Sand Drift full time, and with his current incapacitation, she really needed to. And where did Randy get off playing the victim when clearly whatever had happened between him and his wife was his fault?

Randall Sr. called to her to come in when she arrived. He was once again seated in his BarcaLounger. He'd grabbed the handle on the side and was pulling himself to an upright position as she entered.

"Hello, Mr. Starr," she greeted him. "I'm Kerry from the office. Randy asked me to bring by the monthly report for May."

"'Bout time," he grumbled, reaching for it. His gaze slid over her, and he smiled.

"You're one of Randy's girls."

"I work for him." *Although not for much longer.*

He waggled a finger at her and winked. "You're one of his high school friends."

Kerry started to disabuse him, then stopped herself. He clearly thought she was Josie or Miami or Taryn, maybe Diana. "That's right," she said, remembering the somewhat lecherous way he'd acted last time she'd dropped off papers to him.

"Top of the chart, huh?"

"Is that what Randy told you?"

"He said that Mexican girl was the top. And Miss Sunshine."

She'd corrected him last time that the title was Miss Seashell, but this time she let it go. There was an inherent sleaziness in his tone.

"You must be right up there, though. What's your name again?" he asked.

"Kerry."

"My boy collected quite a few points, but so did that Lady-Killerian." He snickered, sounding like the epitome of the dirty old man.

"How many points?" Kerry asked.

"Oh, four apiece, for sure. That was the top. You know that."

"Ah, yes."

"You look like a four-pointer." His gaze slid over her body, and Kerry felt icked out by the leer. He squinted at her, maybe feeling her revulsion. "You shinin' me on, girl?"

"Nope. Just delivering that report." Time to go.

A crafty look had come into his eyes. "You're trying to get me to say something I shouldn't."

"I don't know what that would be." She gave him a quick smile to reassure him, then pulled out her phone. "I'd better get back to work."

"No, you don't. Sit on down." He gestured to a folding chair leaning against the wall. "Pull that out."

"Much as I would like to, someone should really be at the office. Randy's not there and neither's Angie."

"Where are they?"

"I don't really know. I just know where I should be."

She made a beeline for the door, ignoring him as he called, "Hey, come back here."

She was definitely quitting. Definitely. There was too much misogyny going on at Starrwood Homes.

She drove back to the office and hung around for another half hour. Two Realtors showed up at different times looking for Randy, and Kerry gave them his cell number.

She was way over her one-hour limit by the time she closed up shop at five.

On the way home her phone buzzed, and she looked down with a bit of trepidation, expecting it to be Randy complaining that she'd knocked off early. She was pleasantly surprised to see it was Cole.

"Hi, there," she greeted him.

"Sorry it took so long to call," Cole said. From the background noise she could tell he was in his Jeep.

"No problem. I've been at work." She told him about Randy asking her to cover for him. She almost blurted out about her call to Nina but caught herself in time. She might have to tell him that face-to-face.

Cole said, "Charlie—Officer Paige—and I went to the Brighter Day homeless shelter. We were looking for Ted Perry, a known dealer of sorts."

"Brighter Day? The shelter Taryn said Nick was involved with?"

"The same. I wanted to see the operation."

"And?"

"The director didn't know Nick, but she had praise for Taryn. Said she's been a great campaigner for the center. We didn't talk long. She was careful about giving up Perry, who wasn't there. He's twenty-one, in and out of the center. Doesn't like the rules. He might be the drug connection for a fifteen-year-old whose body was found in the bay. Maybe there's something there for the investigation into Nick's death. Paige is going to follow up."

"Okay. Thanks." There was an awkward silence between them, then Kerry asked, "Are you . . . still stopping by later?"

"Could I take you to dinner tonight?"

"Sure."

"Do you like Thai?"

"Why, yes, I do."

"Great. I'll be by around six thirty." She could hear the smile in his voice and was smiling herself when she clicked off.

Kerry had changed into a pair of light blue denim jeans and a white blouse and coral sandals by the time Cole showed up. She opened the door and he was standing there. He wore blue jeans, a black shirt, and cowboy boots, a distant observation as she felt a trill of anxiety, knowing she was going to have to tell him about her call to Nina Gudner.

"Hi," she greeted him with a strangled voice. She cleared her throat.

He peered at her. "You okay?"

"Oh, yeah. Fine." She grabbed her purse, slinging the strap over her shoulder, and followed him out to his Jeep.

Thai Me Up was near the bay, a small space with good food and a jumping bar scene. The dining area was squeezed in on the back side and the décor was basically red walls with a narrow shelf at head height filled with Buddhas and Hindu deities of every shape and size made of metal, ceramic, and wood. The aroma was the draw, and on a Saturday night they were lucky to get a table at all—the restaurant didn't take reservations—but somehow they managed to time it right to be seated near the bank of windows that looked down the street toward the water or up the street to the hub of town. Pedestrians, ignoring the fitful rain, were hurrying between the bars, restaurants, and shops.

Kerry had collected herself on the short drive over, but her conversation had been distracted, almost monosyllabic. Once they were seated, Cole said, "What is it?"

"What do you mean?"

He lifted a brow.

"I . . ." She trailed off.

"'I wish I hadn't chosen Thai food'? 'I don't know the difference between pad Thai and pad me fung'? 'I . . . made a mistake coming out with you'?"

She smiled. "No."

"What's going on?" he asked, smiling back, but there was something in his tone that was as serious as a heart attack.

"Okay. I did something that maybe I shouldn't have."

"Sounds dire."

She drew a breath and plunged in. "I called Nina Gudner. You said you were going to call her, but I called her myself."

"Okay."

He'd gone very still and she couldn't tell what he was thinking. Nothing good, she suspected. "I told her about Diana. She didn't know. I think I scared her. She said Diana thought there was someone in the room, but she didn't know him."

"Him."

"Well, no. I said the same thing, but Nina said she didn't really know. She wanted me to know that she didn't know anything. Period. She got off the phone fast."

"You should have waited for me."

"Yes." She nodded.

Cole pulled out his cell and punched in a number. When there was no answer, he swore softly, then left a terse message on someone's voice mail: "Call me." He then clicked off and placed a second call. "I know you just got off duty. Youngston's not picking up. I need a team to go to Nina Gudner. You have the address. There may be . . . issues. Move her to a safe place." He listened for a moment or two, then said sharply, "Bring her to the station, then, and we'll figure out where to stash her. Just do it. I'll meet you there."

"I'm sorry," Kerry said, horrified, when he clicked off.

"What about your motel?" he asked. "Any rooms available?"

"Uh, no. All the rooms are in disarray. No furniture."

"Scratch that. I'll put her up at a different motel. I've got two unexplained deaths in a week. I don't want another."

"I'm very sorry. I'm . . . I never meant to put her in jeopardy."

Cole was looking at her in a way that made her feel small. She couldn't breathe. She had a flashback to their breakup. Except at that time he hadn't looked at her at all. She'd been invisible beneath the weight of his grief.

"I'm not going to say it," he finally said.

"Say what?"

"Oh, hell. I am going to say it. I warned you to be careful. There's a killer out there." He was already up from his chair. They hadn't had time to order and the waiter stopped in dismay as he saw they were leaving.

"Is something the matter?" he asked.

Cole said to Kerry, "Stay here."

"No, I'm going with you."

He'd been looking ahead, and now his head whipped around. He was in lawman mode. Compartmentalizing her.

"I'm going with you," she repeated with more grit than she'd known she possessed. "I want to make sure she's all right."

He was already halfway out the door and she followed behind, stiff-arming the door before it could swing backward in her face. "I'm coming," she stated flatly.

"Kerry, don't—" he threw over his shoulder.

"I'm coming!" She cut him off.

"I don't want to be responsible for you, too!"

"Damn it, Cole. You're not!"

She had to run to catch up with his longer strides. They

reached his Jeep at the same moment. She was going to have blisters from her sandals. Blasted things were brand-new.

Cole threw himself in the driver's seat while she leaped in on the passenger side.

"This is police work and—"

"This is my problem. I did this." She cut him off.

"It's still police work and—"

"For God's sake, let's just go!"

Swearing beneath his breath, he threw the vehicle in gear and pulled into traffic, avoiding the pedestrians and running hard as soon as they were out of the center of town. The Jeep wasn't police issue, so it didn't have lights and a siren. She'd seen that the first time she'd been his passenger.

"This is a side to you I've never seen," said Cole.

"Well, yeah, probably. I've just kept it under wraps. But I don't care anymore. Nick's dead . . . Jerry's in the hospital . . . Diana's been killed . . . I'm not going to sit back and wring my hands. I heard you. I've got to be careful. But I'm not going to be on the sidelines."

"You're not a police officer."

"All right, I'm not a police officer."

He seemed about to say something, then thought better of it.

"Okay?" she asked.

"It'll have to be."

Nina Gudner lived in a small, two-bedroom home on a spacious lot with a small forest of Douglas firs at the back that appeared to have been planted by either her or someone else who'd lived on the property because they were thin and hadn't reached their full height. The drive was gravel, and Cole's Jeep crunched onto the surface next to a police car with a rack of lights on its roof. Whoever he'd called had gotten there first.

As Kerry climbed from the car, she saw the officer climb from behind the wheel. Officer Paige, her hair scraped into a ponytail, looking grim and worried. "Just got here. What do you want to do?" She flicked a surprised glance at Kerry.

"Go to the door. You stay here," he ordered Kerry and the steel in his voice was evident.

This time she did as she was told.

They walked up to the front door, shoulder to shoulder, Cole, tall and lean, Officer Paige a shorter, female version.

They knocked on the door, but there was no answer. In front of Kerry was a single-car garage, its door closed but off-kilter a bit, so that it hit bottom on one side but an ever-widening gap lifted the other side into a narrow slot of view. In that slot she saw a flash of movement. Legs. Hurrying.

Kerry signaled to Cole and Paige, but they didn't see her. "Hey!" she yelled. They both turned around, but Kerry was looking toward the garage. She pointed and they walked back together. Kerry kept her finger leveled to the gap below the garage door and Cole leaned down to look.

He straightened and said in a calm voice, "Ms. Gudner. I'm chief of the Edwards Bay Police Department. I'm here with Officer Charlene Paige and we'd like to talk to you."

The legs froze.

"We know you're in the garage," said Cole.

Then an unintelligible child's voice, full of tears, could be heard. The legs shuffled and hurried around the car. A moment later came the low whirr of the lifting garage door.

Cole and Paige were just outside the door and Kerry was back by the Jeep, but all three of them watched as the door rose and Nina the hypnotist came into view. Kerry had expected her to be more exotic, but she looked like your basic soccer mom: blond ponytail, athletic gear, Nikes. Beside her was a young girl of about seven in blue shorts and a blue and white soccer shirt, clinging to the back of her mom's shirt in fear. A true soccer mom.

"We have a practice," Nina said shortly. "Summer league. I don't have time to talk."

"Mommy . . ." the girl moaned.

"I don't know anything about what Diana Conger saw or didn't see at her apartment that night. Yes, that's why she came to see me. No, she didn't learn anything."

"Nothing?" Paige asked curiously.

"Diana had impressions. Thought she wasn't alone. That's all. If you want anything more, you can talk to my lawyer."

"Your lawyer?" Paige repeated, surprised.

"I have nothing to say." Nina grabbed her daughter by the shoulders and turned her back toward the car.

Cole said, "We wanted you to be aware of our continuing investigation into several recent deaths. We're warning people even peripherally involved to take precautions. We just don't know what we're dealing with."

"Got it," Nina said, tersely directing her daughter to put on her seat belt. She climbed behind the wheel and waited.

Cole walked to her window and she reluctantly rolled it down. "There have been two homicides. We don't know the motive, but if the killer thinks you know something . . ."

"I'm going to stay at my mother's. I'm leaving right after the practice. We're packed and ready. I'm not sticking around."

"Okay. Good," he said. "I was going to suggest the same."

Cole and Paige returned to their vehicles. "Do you mind not calling me Charlene?" Paige asked as she climbed into her car. "My stepfather would never call me Charlie. And whenever anyone does, I hear and see him again. He's out of the picture now, but I don't want to be reminded."

"Duly noted," Cole said.

Paige backed out of the driveway and Cole climbed into the driver's seat. He stared through the windshield at the back of Nina Gudner's Subaru Forester as she started backing up, then threw an arm over the back of his seat and unerringly drove down the drive ahead of Nina.

As soon as they were back on the highway, he said, "I can't have you in this investigation."

"I didn't mean to scare her."

"I think she was already scared, but I can't share information with you."

Kerry stayed silent. She didn't want to risk her burgeoning relationship with Cole . . . but she couldn't stay on the sidelines any longer. She'd surfaced enough from her grief over Nick's death to be angry—downright furious—with whoever was responsible for his death, and Diana's.

They were silent until they neared the motel. When he pulled up in front, she said, "Do you want to come in? I have peanut butter . . ."

He made a sound somewhere between a choke and a laugh. He didn't actually answer for long moments, which played havoc with Kerry's nerves. "Okay," he finally said. "But let's order takeout."

"From Thai Me Up?"

"Sure," he said.

"Let's go in and I'll order."

He switched off the engine and she preceded him to the front door, threading the key in the lock. She pushed into the unit, glad he hadn't just left her high and dry. Maybe she hadn't completely blown it. Switching on the light, she stopped short. Cole had to lightly drop his hands on her shoulders to keep from bumping into her.

"What?" Cole asked, coming up behind her.

"I don't know."

She walked inside cautiously, nerves jangling. Maybe it was because of Nina? Her fear? Nothing seemed disturbed. The only slight difference was that the door to the office was slightly ajar, but with all the renovations and the temporary plywood wall separating her unit from the office, the two weren't as tightly secured as they had been.

"You think someone's been here?" he asked.

"No . . ."

"Kerry . . ."

"No, it's fine, really. I think I'm just kind of spooked. Let's order."

Kerry looked up the restaurant's menu on her phone, they picked out several dishes, and Cole called the restaurant to place the order. She almost went with him to pick it up, feeling a little more of the heebie-jeebies than she'd let on, but she shook that off. While he was gone, she grabbed several plates and the silverware to set two places at her two-person table. She had several bottles of wine stashed away in a cupboard by the back door and walked over and bent down, searching through the lowest shelf, pulling out her best Cabernet. When she straightened she glanced at the back door.

A man stood in the window, staring at her.

She shrieked and dropped the bottle.

Chapter Eighteen

Egan Fogherty was the last to leave the Blarney Stone. He was drunk, sort of. His head was full of wild ideas. But he knew what he knew. Yes, he was bipolar. That's what they told him anyway. He'd spent most of his life denying it, but what the hell. If that was what it was, that was what it was. Didn't make him the bogeyman. He just had a small problem.

And he knew what he knew . . . because he'd followed Diana home, hoping for a little nookie. That was what his mom, rest her soul, had called it, and that's what he wanted. Diana had been willing before; no reason she wouldn't be willing now.

Ah, well.

He'd quit lithium long ago. Well, he'd kept on it and off it, but he'd given it up several months ago for good because it sucked. He was fine. Just fine. Yeah, he sensed things more, or differently, or something, when he was off it. But was that so bad?

He stumbled over toward The Whistle Stop. It was still light out. Eight o'clock and it wouldn't be dark for an hour.

He headed inside and looked over the busy bar crowd. Loud. Lots of people. It almost hurt his ears, but he couldn't go back to his apartment. It was shit. A cramped one-bedroom with a shower with all the power of a grocery store mister.

He grabbed one of the few empty barstools and ordered a beer. Too many hard drinks at Blarney. Those fucking "friends" of his. He'd tried to tell Josie . . . okay, he'd tried to make a deal with her . . . and she got all cold and mad. Still acted like she was pure as the driven snow, but she'd laid it down for Caulfield all right. He was pretty specific about what she'd done for him—mmm, mmm—just thinking about it gave him a boner. Jesus. Right here in the bar. That mouth of Josie's. It was just so pink and . . . he struggled for the word and finally arrived at it: luscious.

And Caulfield's a fucking Uber driver, whereas I'm going to be a captain!

You sure about that, dumb shit?

Egan stared morosely at the bottle of PBR on the counter. No, he wasn't sure, wasn't sure at all. He was in trouble at work. Serious trouble, goddamn it. He hadn't been paying attention a few days back and had scraped the ferry along the pier when he was allowed a turn at the helm. Minor damage, but the captain had been furious, so furious his face had turned into a red ball. Egan had visualized his head popping right off his neck.

How had it happened?

You know . . .

Okay, he'd actually been thinking about Kerry Monaghan that night. He'd started out with Diana in mind, calculating about maybe getting together with her again, but then that had reminded him of Nick dying in her apartment, which was a complete backslide into depression until his brain skipped over to Kerry. She was every bit as much of a chart-topper as the rest of them. Like Josie, she had a nice mouth. Full lips. Red. He just knew they'd taste like cherries.

And that's when it happened. The captain had suddenly yelled, "*Slow down!*" and BAM! SCREEEECCCHHHH! The sound had gone on forever.

Shuddering, he tipped up his beer and gulped it down. Maybe he did need something stronger.

He knew what he knew.

Valuable information. Maybe Josie had been unwilling to trade for it. But there were others . . . others who would pay. . . .

"Jesus Christ, Vaughn. You scared me to death!"

Kerry reluctantly opened the back door to admit her ex. The wine bottle hadn't broken, and she'd picked it up and now held it by its neck with her right hand. She'd been of half a mind not to let him in, but she had the wine bottle and was poised to clobber him if necessary.

"Sorry. Sorry." He held up his hands. "But you won't return my calls."

"We don't have anything to discuss. We haven't for years. I don't know what you're doing."

She hadn't moved from just inside the door, forcing Vaughn to stand at the back-door aperture.

"Do you mind? I don't want to stand here in the rain."

"It's stopped raining."

"Okay, I don't want to stand in the dark."

She moved aside reluctantly but watched him like she would a coiled snake. He stepped inside and she closed the door, throwing the lock even though she worried the danger was already inside. "Were you here earlier?" she demanded.

"I knocked on your door, but you didn't answer."

"I was probably at dinner." He didn't need to know all the particulars about Cole. "Did you get inside?"

"What?" He was walking toward her couch.

"Don't sit down."

He stopped and regarded her in surprise. "Jesus, Kerry. I thought we were at least friends."

"Vaughn, what the hell. We don't talk. We're not friends. We don't even like each other."

"That's not true."

"Isn't it?" She gazed at him with disbelief.

"I'm going to sit down," he said and did. "I guess I didn't know I hurt you that badly," he added almost petulantly when she just stood in place.

She wanted to deny that he'd hurt her at all. She wanted to tell him that she felt nothing for him, didn't ever think about him, had moved on long, long before, but she didn't want to engage him.

"Vaughn, I have someone coming over, so you've got to leave. Say what it is you want to say."

"Who?"

"I don't think there's anything we need to talk about, but go ahead."

"Cole Sheffield? Think you have a chance with him again, is that it? You were sure hanging on to him last night."

"I wasn't hanging on—" She cut herself off. "I don't have a lot of time, so either tell me what you want to talk about or leave."

"It is Cole, isn't it? He's coming by. Looking for a little free something that you obviously want to give."

"I've changed my mind. You can leave now."

His face grew set. She'd seen that look before. He was going to become belligerent. "I came for the money you owe me."

"*What?*"

"I supported you for nearly two years and what did I get? Nada."

"*Supported me?*" she sputtered. "I had a job, too!"

"You didn't make as much as I did," he reminded quickly.

"Oh, puh-leeze. I can't . . . you can't be serious." She was struggling to come up with words, she was so outraged. "I walked out of that marriage with nothing *because I didn't want anything*. You were fine with that. I was fine with that."

"I was never fine with that. You took everything from me."

"Are you loco?"

His face reddened. "You walked out when I was in a down time. Couldn't sell anything because of you. I've been to a lawyer. And I'm coming for what you owe me."

"We're divorced. I owe you nothing!"

"I thought we could talk about this like reasonable people, but if that's the way you want it, I'll see you in court."

"Go ahead. I don't have anything." She half-laughed.

"But you will."

She blinked and stared. He was talking about what she might inherit from Nick? Was that it?

Or did he know about Jerry's will and just assumed because he'd collapsed at the memorial service he wasn't long for this world?

Her anger coalesced into a hard brick inside her. "If you broke in here, I'll have you arrested."

"I didn't break in here. Jesus. Oh, and you'll sic Cole on me?"

"Don't give me good ideas. I might use them."

At that moment headlights washed across the front of the unit.

"Your date?" He sneered.

"Looks like it." She waited for Vaughn to make a move, but he just sat still, as if frozen to the spot. Kerry went to the front door and admitted Cole, whose brows lifted upon encountering Vaughn. "He's just leaving," she said crisply, stalking to the back door and throwing it open. Vaughn's jaw tightened, but he darted a look at Cole, hesitated only briefly, then strode across the room and out the back door. Kerry slammed and locked it behind him.

Cole set the bags of Thai food on the table.

When Kerry didn't make a move to sit down and eat, he looked at her questioningly.

"How hungry are you?" she asked him tightly.

"What did you have in mind?" he responded, surveying the tightness of her body, the anger radiating from every pore.

"This," she said boldly, and walked up to him, placing both hands on his cheeks, pulling his face toward hers, kissing him fully on the mouth. When she drew back, she gazed at him questioningly.

"Okay," he said.

And she clasped his hand and led him into the bedroom.

"Hey, man, you're done here," the bartender said to Egan not unkindly, pulling his glass away.

Egan gazed at the man who seemed to be rotating as three beings in front of his eyes. Squeezing his eyes closed, he opened them wide, but the man kept circling. "Huh?" he asked.

"You got somebody I can call? Or Uber . . . ?"

"Nah, I walk."

"You sure, man?"

"Yeah, yep . . . yep . . ."

He slid off the stool and dug into his pocket for some money. Money . . . He stared down at the crushed bills and threw three twenties on the counter. The bartender swept up the money and made change. Egan left a couple of dollars and staggered toward the door.

Whoa, he thought, swaying a bit. He was pretty bad. It was dark outside and it took him a moment to orient himself. Where the hell was his car?

He chortled aloud. He'd told the shitty bartender that he'd walk. He hadn't added, ". . . to my car." He didn't live that far away. He could drive home.

He stopped, rocked back on his heels, and had to catch himself before he fell over. No one was about. He bet everybody was at their favorite bar.

What time was it?

He reached into his back pocket for his phone. Pulled it out and promptly dropped it.

"Shit."

He bent over to pick it up and lost his balance, one knee dropping to the wet pavement as he tried to right himself. He swore a blue streak. The knee of his jeans was scraped with dirt.

"Goddamn it," he fumed, grabbing up the phone and straightening.

He thought about the captain, his job, *his life,* and he wanted to shriek with fury.

It wasn't fair. It just wasn't fair.

BUT . . .

I knows what I know.

He chortled on that one. "I knows what I know."

But they didn't. Those bastards. He thought about high school, and all the friends who'd treated him badly. They pretended to be nice, but they had all turned on him in one way or another. All of them. But he knew all about them, too. They could try to rewrite history, but they couldn't. He knew why Nick was dead. They all knew, but none of them could stand to face it.

And they'd killed Diana for it.

"I knows what I know."

A bad feeling came over him and he had to really think

about why that was. Oh, yeah. He knew who'd killed her.
He'd seen them. Was pretty sure he had. And he'd bargained
with Josie over that information.

Josie.

He'd always liked her. Maybe loved her a little. But any
of them would be fine . . . Miami, especially, and . . . oh,
yeah . . . Kerry. He really wanted her. He'd been thinking
about her a lot, too. Kerry . . .

Where the fuck was his car?

Oh.

Empty lot near the Blarney Stone.

He stumbled over that way, head down, across the near-
empty street. Even the cars had gone home. What time was
it? Oh, yeah. Meant to check his phone and forgot.

He fumbled inside his back pocket again but kept
moving forward. He was near the Blarney Stone's rear entrance. There were a couple of steps up to the back door
and a wooden alcove to the right. He'd made out with more
than one lovely lady there. He sure would like to bring
Kerry here . . . run his hand up her ass, press her to him.

"Kerry . . ."

Maybe one more drink? With the guys? His *friends?*
Forrest should still be there, maybe Sean, maybe even
Killian.

He headed up the stairs, grabbed onto the rail, and damn
near lost his grip on the phone again. "Fuck," he spit out.

The phone was lit up, but he had to get his face in front of
it to unlock it: 1:48 a.m. Whoa. Much later than he'd thought.
He watched the padlock icon on his phone slip open. Did he
need to use the phone? It seemed like—

WHAM.

Egan's head exploded and he sprawled on the steps.
What? What?

His hand sprang to his head. Something hit him. Something hit him hard! He half-twisted to look upward.

"What . . . ?"

A black-gloved hand clenched around a rock high above his head.

WHAM. WHAM. WHAM.

The rock slammed into his head over and over again.

"Kerry . . . I . . . knows . . ." His eyes rolled around in his head.

Then he collapsed on the steps in a pile of loose, brainless flesh.

Chapter Nineteen

Doctor: *That brings us to Egan Fogherty. You were responsible for his death, too.*

Patient: *He was bipolar. We all knew that. And bipolar people have a high rate of suicide. So he killed himself. I wasn't anywhere around him.*

Doctor: *He was bludgeoned to death.*

Patient: *I heard he was on drugs, too. Another one of Diana's victims. She really had her hooks into everyone. The ones that are still alive probably have massive drug problems. You should check it out.*

Doctor: *The police already have.*

Patient: *Yeah, well . . .*

Doctor: *It's unlikely he bludgeoned himself to death.*

Patient: *Ha, ha, Doc. Okay, it wasn't suicide. He just pissed off a lot of people. Coulda been any one of them who did it. Egan was sick. No one liked him.*

Doctor: *There's proof you killed him.*

Patient: *I doubt that very much.*

Doctor: *You killed both Diana and Egan because they knew what you'd done to Nick and why. Both of them had seen you at Diana's apartment, and they were starting to understand your motivation.*

Patient: *Then why didn't I kill the hypnobitch, huh?*

"Miss Nina"? The one Diana went to see? Surely someone as sick as me would've taken her out, too.

Doctor: *Nina Gudner has always maintained she didn't know anything about what Diana did or didn't recall from their session. But Diana told Kerry Monaghan about it, and when you learned that, you changed focus. You killed Diana to cover up Nick's death, and you targeted Kerry.*

Patient: *Okay, fine. You're gonna say what you're gonna say.*

Doctor: *You felt Kerry was also zeroing in on you.*

Patient (*suddenly furious*): *Egan said she was!*

Doctor: *What did Egan say?*

Patient: *"Kerry knows . . ." That's what he said, Doc. Kerry knows! Diana called her, too. Talked to her, and then she couldn't leave it alone. Hooked up with Cole Sheffield and kept after it. If you're expecting me to be sorry about what happened, you've got a long wait ahead of you. And look what she did to me!*

Doctor: *It's often said that violence begets violence.*

Patient: *That bitch deserved everything she got and more.*

Sunday morning, one a.m. by her bedside clock. As Kerry glanced at the glowing red numbers, she realized Cole's arm was slung over her and she was snuggled up against his side. She closed her eyes and recalled in vivid detail every moment of their recent lovemaking. The memory of his breath in her ear, the beating of his heart, the rhythmic thrusting of his body that she arched to meet, her fingers digging into the muscles of his back . . . Unbelievable. All those years in between and here they were again.

She opened her eyes again and saw her mask on the nightstand. She'd clasped his hand and started to lead him to the bedroom, but they'd practically stumbled in their haste. Ripping off clothes and touching each other. Then ripping off more and falling onto her bed. She'd had no time to straighten up her room. Had had no thoughts of lovemaking.

Her thoughts turned to certain moments of their time in bed together, and she smiled, pressing her face into his chest. He stirred, his hand going to her hair, his fingers tangling in it.

"You awake?" he asked lazily.

"Mmm."

"We left that Thai food on the counter."

"You hungry?" She propped herself up on one elbow and looked down at him.

"For what?" He waggled his brows at her and she grinned. Then she sobered, feeling a bit like a traitor to Nick's memory.

"We could eat in bed," she suggested.

Fifteen minutes later they were seated side by side on her bed. Kerry had a robe tossed over her shoulders and was digging into a white box of massaman curry with a fork. Chopsticks were too tricky and she was ravenous. Cole was in his boxers, leaning back against her headboard, equally engaged in some pad Thai.

"Gonna be a short day tomorrow," he said with a glance at the clock.

"I didn't intend to take you to bed," she said.

"Coulda fooled me."

"I mean, I was planning on having dinner, but then . . . *Vaughn* . . ." She'd told him the gist of their conversation while they were getting their meal. "He just pissed me off so much, and it reminded me of how much time I'd wasted, and I just . . ."

"Kissed me?"

"Yes, kissed you." She leaned in and kissed him again, on the cheek this time.

"I'm sorry about Nina," she said when she pulled back. "I don't want to get in your way, but I want to help. I just can't stand to do nothing. I know you can't share information with me, but how about if I lay out some things? Just my thoughts. What I feel, what people have said. You can nod or shake your head, or not even get involved. I just want to work through some stuff. I need to. My head's full of stuff."

"Okay."

"Okay?" she asked, peering at him closely.

He half-smiled. "Go ahead. Shake something loose. I could use another perspective anyway."

"If it's still any kind of question, I know Nick wouldn't kill himself. Someone killed him. Maybe accidentally, but now, with Diana's murder, I don't think so. I think they're connected."

"You got a theory?" Cole asked, digging around in his white box for a few last noodles of pad Thai, then set the box, chopsticks inside, onto her nightstand.

She handed him her box and fork and he added it to the crowded nightstand top. "Well . . . no . . . I really can't see why anyone would hurt Nick."

"What about Diana?"

"Someone purposely killed her. Went into her bedroom and strangled her."

"Whoever that is could think you know more than you do, that Diana confided in you. You were the person she called."

"She called me twice at three a.m. I talked to her the first time, but the second time no one was there." He didn't respond, and Kerry felt her skin break out in gooseflesh. "Do you think it was . . . Diana's killer?"

"I don't know."

"You're afraid you'll scare me. I think it was Diana and she just couldn't talk . . . because the other answer, that the *killer* called me on purpose, is just too . . . I can't think about that."

"Don't think about it."

She eased into his arms, fitting herself against him. He put his arm around her. She was growing sleepy, she realized. Small wonder. Stifling a yawn, she said, "I think Diana was killed because she was remembering whoever was in her apartment. Going under hypnosis woke something up in her brain. Something she wasn't sure of. She told me that. And she told everybody at the memorial service. It wasn't a secret. I warned her to be careful, like you've warned me. I think she was starting to realize who'd killed Nick, and whoever that was silenced her."

"I agree," he said, giving her more than she'd expected.

"But why Nick?" she asked. "I always thought everyone loved him. His friends, his family. Maybe there's some business associate who thought they got screwed. Chad Worster?"

"Worster has done fine with or without Nick."

His dry tone prompted Kerry to ask, "Is that right?"

"I don't see how Worster could ever have thought he'd been screwed."

"Maybe there's something else there, then? Envy or something we don't know about."

"Maybe," Cole said.

"Nick had been coming back to Edwards Bay a lot lately, to his hometown and his old high school friends. I've met them over the years, but he reintroduced me to them, so when I moved here, it was like they invited me to be part of the group."

"What do you think of those friends?"

Encouraged that he wasn't closing her out yet, she asked,

"You mean, do I think they're involved in his death? I don't know. Maybe."

"Tell me about 'em."

"Well, I like them okay, the ones I know. Josie seems to want to be friends more than some of the others. Diana, yes, she treated me like I was someone to count on. I don't really know Miami. She's generally been with Killian whenever we're out, which is the only time I see her. Egan is . . ." She trailed off.

"What?"

"Pushy. Aggressive? You kind of want to pull away from him. Someone said he was bipolar, so . . . I guess I try hard to be nice, when in fact I kind of want to get away from him. It makes me feel bad to say it."

"You gotta be honest to get to the truth," said Cole.

"I don't know Taryn well either. She's more impatient. I get the feeling she just wants me to disappear. Like I came in and took Nick from her or something. Stole her best friend. She wants to be the expert on him, although everybody acts like Josie and Nick were the ones involved." She shrugged. "I just never thought Nick would have an affair with a married woman. He had a real sense of fair play."

Cole nodded.

"And then there's Forrest . . . and Sean . . . Forrest can be a little friendlier than's comfortable. Not like Egan, but he's got a way of looking at you that's, I don't know. Nick called him a horndog."

"Apt," said Cole with a humph of agreement.

"Sean's more remote. In his own world, in a way. Then there's my boss, Randy. Whenever he's talked about Nick it was almost with reverence. Nick had made it, and Randy, even though he's running his dad's company, doesn't really feel like he has yet. His wife, Angie, is possessive and doesn't like women—at least she doesn't like me, and she got in a fight with someone at the memorial service."

"Who?" Cole asked curiously.

"A woman named Sheryl. Maybe it was Sheryl from the bank? I saw her at the memorial service. She works at The Bank of Edwards Bay and I think she's a friend of Angie's, or maybe was, now. Angie can't stand any other woman talking to her man."

"That's the bank started by Kent Roker's family?"

"I was there the other day with Jerry, adding my signature to his accounts. Sheryl helped us." She shrugged. "And then there's everyone else. Other high school friends who aren't part of the A-Team . . . and the dads. . . ."

Cole grunted. "The football dads. I talked to some of them at the memorial service. They went on about football, mostly. From the era their kids were in school. It's their prime bonding subject. I got an earful about Killian's prowess and his unfortunate ankle injury that kept him out of college ball."

"That was the conversation?" She could hear her own skepticism.

"It's fascinating to them. Nick apparently was partially responsible for the ankle injury." He related the circumstances of the "horsing around" incident that had caused concrete to fall on Killian's leg.

Kerry listened to the words but also his heartbeat. Feeling herself start to yearn toward sleep, she stifled a yawn and said, "It's a lot about high school, isn't it?"

"Appears that way."

"You know, I saw Randy's dad today. Dropped some papers by. Every time I see him, he talks about Randy's girlfriends from high school. I think he thinks I'm one of them. He told me I was a four, which is the highest amount of points."

"Hmm. Sounds like he was trying to compliment you."

"Yeah. But . . . it was creepy."

"Old guys. Glory days."

"Yeah . . ." she murmured.

They settled into each other's arms and fell asleep.

Sunday.

Miami parked on the gravel strip in front of her parents' home and hurried up the front walk. Their house was a three-bedroom ranch in a pocket of three-bedroom ranches on the east side of town, close enough to hear the dull wash off the freeway, which Miami had pretended was the sound of the ocean when she was a little girl. Her great-aunt and -uncle had owned it once and sold it to Miami's parents. They were now living with their daughter, who relied on Miami to give her a break whenever she could. For Miami's part, she enjoyed visiting them. It was warm and uncompli-cated, being with them, listening to her uncle's garrulous talk and her aunt's fussing. She loved them and wanted them to be proud of her. Would they be, if they knew? she often wondered. Their disappointment was one of the rea-sons she'd kept quiet for so long.

The house itself was worth some money now, Miami supposed, and once upon a time it had been her parents' pride and joy. In recent years, however, the wooden fence that bounded it on three sides had weathered and fallen into disrepair, the grayed boards along the south side leaning toward the house as if they were trying to reach it.

Her long black coat protected her from the frisky breeze that threatened to turn into a gale if given enough time as she reached the front steps. She was between the morning shift and the evening, neither of which was normally hers. She'd agreed to cover Toni at the desk in the morning, and a guy named Hal in the evening. In between, she normally would have stayed on property rather than deal with the ferry or the drive from The Pier back to her parents' house, but today she'd felt antsy and, well, it was time to talk to her father and mother.

Unlocking the front door with her key, she yelled, "Mama?" while heading to her bedroom, the smallest of the three. She'd moved back in two years ago, the day she'd recognized she couldn't afford her small Edwards Bay apartment; a temporary solution, she'd told herself . . . She just wasn't willing to accept help from the Keenans any longer.

She tossed her coat on the bed, her small purse beside it. She stared at both items for a moment, thinking about what she actually owned in this world. The purse and her coat were about it, or at least they symbolized how little of a mark she'd made to date. She knew her friends never thought in the same terms she did, but they didn't feel the weight of history either.

"Mama?" she called again, walking down the short hallway. The house wasn't large enough for her mom not to have heard her. She headed past the maple nook table, the kitchen a U-shape to one side, and out the back door to the yard. Her mother, a rain hat covering her wavy, steel-gray hair, was examining her planted tomatoes. She saw Miami approaching out of the corner of her eye and turned and smiled at her daughter.

"You're home," her mother said.

"Just for a minute or two. I'm still taking over Hal's shift. Umm, is Dad here?"

"He's at the store. He'll be home around six. What is it?" she asked, picking up on Miami's tension.

"I . . . I . . . want to, need to, talk about high school." She ran her hands up her own arms. Maybe she should have kept her coat on. The gray clouds overhead seemed to be pressing down on her.

Her mother turned back to the tomatoes. Margarita Miller knew what her daughter was about to say and didn't want to hear it.

But Miami had had enough of lying and covering up. "I'm going to talk to someone . . . maybe a counselor or something."

Her mother continued staring straight ahead. Margarita didn't know the whole story. She only knew the little bit Miami had been able to get out before she was cut off by her father. The subject had been taboo since that day, right before graduation.

"I've . . . uh . . . made a decision. Some terrible things have happened. Nick Radnor, and now Diana . . . I think they both were murdered."

"Murdered?" Her mother swung back to her, her brown eyes wide.

"It's all coming out. Ugly stuff. I'm not going to be able to avoid it. None of us are."

"Well, it's certainly not your fault."

"But I didn't speak up. I didn't tell. And Nick, those last few weeks he came back to Edwards Bay . . . He was going to tell, Mama. He was going to do the right thing. Even with all his success, he was sad. It was all going to come out."

Her mother suddenly shook her finger at her. "You had it the worst. Far worse for you than that Josie girl and the other ones."

"No, I—"

"Yes! *Worse* for you."

Miami thought back to that last year of high school. She'd made mistakes. Big mistakes. She should have said something then. "Worse for Lisette," she whispered.

"You know what I mean. That was a tragedy, no doubt. But

you've been locked into yourself. A prisoner of something I've never understood!"

"That's what I'm telling you, Mama. I'm not going to be a prisoner any longer. I don't care what happens. The truth has to come out."

"Don't say such things."

"I know you're worried about what Dad will say. He's not going to like it."

"The shame will kill him!"

"There is no shame," Miami said, her voice rising. "Not to me. Except that I didn't tell!"

She turned back to the house, her blood on fire. Angry. Good and angry. She held on to it with all she had. She needed to stay angry or she would chicken out, and she couldn't afford to chicken out. Not now.

Sunday. Josie stared out the back windows of her house to the rolling grounds of her backyard and its view of the bay. Her arms were wrapped around her. She'd tossed and turned all night and now had a very sober outlook on her life, which basically came down to: *What the eff are you going to do about it?*

She'd allowed Chad into her house. Had been eager for him to stop by, no doubt about it. Had she asked to get mauled? No. But did she feel guilty? Yes.

She'd poured herself a cup of coffee, but it sat cooling on the kitchen table. Picking it up, she reheated it in the microwave, took a sip, and burned her tongue, then sloshed hot coffee on her hand.

"Damn it!" She suddenly wanted to cry. Instead, she set down the mug and angrily thrust her hand under cold water from the kitchen tap. A few moments later she wiped her hands, picked up the cup, and tried again. Her hand still smarted, but maybe a little physical pain was what she needed to move out of her inertia.

Her cell phone was already on the kitchen table. She swooped it up and called Taryn. "Hey," she said. "I did something stupid and gave a guy the wrong impression."

"What did you do?" she asked.

"I invited him over for . . . some afternoon delight, but changed my mind almost as soon as he arrived."

Her voice sharpened. "What happened?"

"Oh, nothing. He manhandled me some, but then he left."

"That's not nothing, Josie!"

"I know. I just don't want to make a big deal of it. But I want to talk about it."

"You want to go to the Blarney Stone? Find a quiet corner?"

"God, no. And aren't they closed on Sunday?"

"They are. You're right."

"You want to come over here?" Josie asked diffidently. She and Taryn had never been what you'd call buddies.

"Sure. Should I bring baked goodies?"

Josie smiled. "Yes."

"I'll be there in a bit."

Cole awoke before Kerry, kissed her on the forehead, then headed out.

"It's Sunday," she protested as he was getting dressed, even though she knew that didn't matter with Diana's murder, on the heels of Nick's.

"I'll call you. Stay in bed."

She took his advice, sleeping in till after nine, but then she got up, took a shower, conscious of tender places on her body that hadn't been that tender in a long while. She closed her eyes and grinned into the spate of water from the shower head, then dressed in jeans and a gray, long-sleeved T-shirt, though when she looked out the window, she could see the skies were clear and it looked like it might be a surprisingly nice June day.

She went to see Jerry in the late morning. He tried to be glad to see her, but he was mostly cranky. Dr. Stevens had gone from being a savior to a jailor, apparently. "He won't let me leave."

"Maybe tomorrow," said Kerry.

"It will be tomorrow," he responded forcefully.

He'd told Kerry that he'd called Marcia's home phone, which she rarely answered, and had gotten Audra, which had cheered him up for a while, based on how much he'd clearly enjoyed the conversation.

"Audra's thinking about taking sailing classes but said Marcia was worried about the cost. I think I'll give her some money," Jerry informed Kerry.

"Good idea," Kerry agreed.

"Maybe I'll add to her college fund, too, while I'm at it. You know my checkbook's in the top drawer in the kitchen. The one by the oven. Would you bring it to me, because I'm not getting out of this place today."

"Sure," she agreed. She hightailed it out of his room as his expression darkened with his pique.

Kerry spoke to the nurse on duty on her way out. She let her know Dr. Stevens wasn't releasing Jerry until Monday at the earliest, and it could be Tuesday. That meant he was going to miss the lawyer from Barnes & Barnes who was meeting them for the reading of the will. She kept that information to herself, wondering if she should call to reschedule, or at least move it from Jerry's house. She knew Jerry would be extra-aggravated at being in the hospital while she and Marcia met at his house.

In the end she left things as they stood. She spent the afternoon walking around the property and looking into each unit. The tile was finished in units one through eight, but nine through twelve were still in various stages of completion. All the lights were off and the doors locked, so Emilio had taken care of things. No one was on the job today. Kerry locked up and went back to her unit, wondering with more anticipation than was probably healthy when Cole would return.

"I'm going to confront him tonight," Miami said into her cell phone. She was seated in her car, parked outside Edwards Bay High School. "I'm just working up the courage. There's a killer out there . . . and you know it has something to do with what happened in high school. The fucking chart! It killed Lisette, and it's killed Nick and Diana. I'm not going to let it kill me!"

"Wait. Calm down. Take a breath."

"Don't tell me what to do," she flashed. She was crying again. She was always crying when she got close to the truth. "Maybe I won't confront him tonight. Maybe I'll wait till tomorrow. I don't know. I don't know what to do, but I've got to do something soon!"

"Let's talk tomorrow. I want to be there with you."

"Okay . . . okay. But I have to do this! I know you don't understand, but I have to do this!" She clicked off in a fury, then buried her face in her hands, her body racked with sobs of despair.

She was supposed to think the abortion was a blessing in disguise. The cancer had been caught. Her ovaries and uterus removed. Her life saved.

But her baby's hadn't. And the life she was currently living was in tones of gray.

She dried her tears, felt the anger settle in her heart.

She knew who to blame.

Chapter Twenty

Monday morning Kerry woke up by rolling on her back and reaching an arm across the bed, only to find Cole wasn't there. He'd come by after he'd finished up with his duties, which included dealing with the press. Nick's death had created some coverage, but Diana's on top of it had created a growing alarm throughout the community, one Kerry felt keenly as well.

She lay quietly for several moments, feeling her heart surge when she recalled their most recent lovemaking, locking eyes, moving slowly, excruciatingly slowly, as he brought her to climax.

"Mmm. . . ." she muttered, shaking herself out of the memory. Good God, she couldn't lie here all day waiting for him to come back.

Her thoughts slid to the sensual once more. Vivid memories. Laughing to herself, she buried her face in her pillow. Damn it. She'd never stopped loving him. Never. She'd lied to herself. She wished she'd tried harder to hold on to what they had in the past, but she knew Cole's grief over his brother's death had been too big, too all-encompassing, for her to find a way past it. She'd sensed it at the time, then had fallen victim to her own hurt and turned to Vaughn.

Throwing back the covers, she took a quick shower,

giving herself a good soap down. She had a feeling if she didn't, someone would smell Cole on her, and today was the day to finally meet Gil Barnes, Nick's lawyer.

She'd told Randy she would be in later, but she was really dreading showing up for work at all. She was still seesaw-ing on whether to call him to offer her resignation.

She stopped by the hospital on the way to Jerry's house, where she was due to meet the lawyer and Marcia. Jerry gave her his keys and reminded her about the checkbook. Something slipped across her mind but vanished before she could grab on to it, then was lost beneath Jerry's grumbling about waiting to see the doctor. "You tell that lawyer I want to see him," he told her before she left, which she assured him she'd do.

She drove to Jerry's house, pleased to see some of the gray clouds that had started to lift yesterday were almost entirely gone. Maybe they would get a bit of sun. About time.

She parked in front and hurried up the walk, jogging up the front steps. Fitting the key in the lock, she had that same sense of a tugging memory. What? She stayed still, listening to the faint sound of neighborhood voices, the low-grade hum of a distant chainsaw, the light whisper of the breeze, her own breathing. She couldn't grasp it. Shaking her head, she let herself into the house.

It was dark, curtains drawn, so she flicked on a light. Her pulse jumped at a surprise figure against the wall, and her hand shot to her mouth before she saw it was just the shadow from the high-back kitchen chair thrown into relief against the light beige plaster.

"Scaredy-cat," she chided herself, throwing back the curtains.

She looked around the kitchen, then moved the chairs around the table, pulling one away to make more room for the lawyer, herself, and Marcia to be seated. Remembering the checkbook, she found the drawer next to the oven and pulled it open. It was right on top. She picked it up and was just shutting the drawer when the front door flew open—no knock—and sharp footsteps headed her way. Marcia.

"What are you doing?" Marcia demanded.

Kerry raised an eyebrow. "Waiting for you?"

"I realize that," she said scathingly. Her gaze fell on the checkbook. "You're already signing checks?"

"No, this is . . . what do you mean?" Kerry asked.

"You went to the bank with Jerry, what? Last Wednesday. It hasn't even been a week."

"How do you know I went to the bank with Jerry?"

Her lips curled, as if she'd sucked on a lemon. "You told me. Or Jerry did."

"Neither of us told you about our trip to the bank." Kerry's voice was careful.

"Well, I heard it somewhere. What does it matter?" She brushed that aside, adding, "You've really made yourself indispensable to Jerry since Nick died. What are you writing a check for?"

"I'm not writing a check."

"What are you doing with the checkbook, then?"

"Marcia, I'm sorry. I don't think I have to tell you."

A hot pink flush crawled up her neck. "I'm only asking because Audra is Jerry's granddaughter. The only one he'll ever have. I think she has a right to know."

"Well, Jerry can talk to Audra, then." Kerry managed to stop short of reminding her that Audra was his step-granddaughter, and that she, Kerry, could ostensibly have a child and offer up another stepgrandchild.

Bzzzz.

"There's the lawyer," Kerry said instead, stepping around Marcia and heading for the front door.

Gil Barnes was a man in his early fifties whose hair was

cut so short around his thinning pate that he appeared almost bald. He wore a white shirt and a chocolate-colored tie, teamed with a tan sport coat.

He shook hands with Kerry and followed her into the kitchen, where Marcia had placed herself near the table, one leg in front of the other, an elbow thrust out, in a classic take-my-picture pose. Full-on Miss Seashell. She smiled hard at Gil, who greeted her warmly, shaking her limp hand. Marcia had never learned the art of meeting a businessman without making it some man/woman deal.

"Is Mr. Radnor here?" he asked politely.

Kerry explained about Jerry being in the hospital, which she was afraid might put a kibosh on the meeting, but Gil just took it in as they all scraped back their chairs.

"Since Gerald Radnor does not play prominently in Nicholas Radnor's will, I think we'll go ahead, unless either of you have any objections," Gil said.

Both Kerry and Marcia shook their heads.

"Good. Nicholas Radnor initially worked with a law firm in Palo Alto, then transferred his personal business to us, Barnes and Barnes. Mr. Radnor was very specific on what he wanted, which was to wait until after his funeral or memorial service before revealing the particulars of the will."

"We're here now," Marcia said. She'd seated herself across from Gil and was leveling laser eyes on him.

Gil pulled out Nicholas Radnor's Last Will and Testament and slid a copy toward Kerry, who shook her head, especially when Marcia's head whipped around and she glared at her.

"Would you read it?" Kerry asked.

"Certainly," he said.

And he did. He went through the document point by point, but it boiled down to the fact that, apart from a healthy sum set aside for Audra's college, the balance of

Nick's estate was divided between Kerry and the Nicholas Radnor Foundation, of which Kerry was in charge.

Marcia was white-faced to learn that the only reason she'd been invited to the meeting was because of her daughter. Kerry was dumbstruck at the amount. Barnes said there would need to be an accounting of Nick's full net worth, but it was safely in the millions.

Kerry was stunned and could barely hear as Barnes brought up Nick's condo, and that was when she remembered what had been nagging at the back of her mind. Nick's keys. And wallet. His belongings were still in the property room at the Edwards Bay Police Station.

"There is also an insurance policy, which names Nick's father as the beneficiary, if it's found that his death was an accident. The policy doesn't cover suicide."

"Who cares?" Marcia said bitterly.

She pushed the chair back so hard it toppled over. Then she stalked out.

Gil Barnes was slightly bemused by her abrupt exit. "Would you like me to arrange for valuation of Mr. Radnor's estate?"

"Yes. Please." She could scarcely find her voice. It felt wrong. Terrible. Like she was profiting from Nick's death, which she was.

"Ms. Monaghan?"

She blinked back tears, then looked a bit dazedly at the lawyer. "Yes?"

"Do you have a lawyer to handle your own estate?"

"Oh. No. Not yet. Would you?" she asked.

"Certainly." He hesitated. "It's not my business, and I don't know quite how to say this, but it may be difficult to process the insurance claim. There will be an investigation. Insurance companies don't like to part with their money if they don't have to."

"Okay."

"Mr. Radnor . . . was quite . . ." He inhaled and exhaled through his nose, thinking. "Sober. Maybe depressed. I'm not a doctor. I'm just telling you how he seemed when he was at our offices. It was clear to all of us. And his choices seemed as if he had his death very much on his mind. When the insurance adjuster asks, I'll be truthful in describing his state of mind."

"It wasn't suicide."

He didn't respond to that. "There is also a sealed letter I didn't get to mention while Ms. Radnor was here. It's addressed to a Mr. Durant Stipe."

The name took Kerry several long moments to recall, and when she did, she got a distinct shock. *Lisette Benetton's stepfather.*

"I had an incorrect address for Mr. Stipe," Gil Barnes went on, "but we've managed to reach him by phone. He is coming to our offices tomorrow to pick it up."

Her heart was pounding. Had Nick finally found a way to apologize to Durant Stipe for all the wounds, real or imagined, that he'd caused him?

"My brother was murdered," Kerry said. "Maybe that letter could shed some light on what happened to him. Do you know what's in it?"

"No, it's sealed."

They stared at each other, but Kerry could tell she wouldn't be able to budge him. They shook hands and she promised to check her calendar and call his offices to make an appointment. After he was gone, she phoned Cole, but he didn't pick up. She quickly texted him a message that just said *Call me.*

Then she grabbed her purse, made sure Jerry's checkbook was tucked inside it, and headed for the door. She would check with Cole and go to the station to pick up Nick's belongings.

Cole called Charlie into his office. Ben looked at them questioningly, as if he were being left out, but Cole didn't invite him in. A lot had happened over the weekend and Ben had been impossible to raise on the phone, which was business as usual; he was strictly by the time clock, and he always seemed to wangle weekends off. It was Charlie he could count on to work the odd hour and maybe pick up a little overtime. She had a natural mind for puzzling through things, like Kerry did, and she'd noticeably thawed in her don't-mess-with-me persona as they'd recently worked closer together.

"Eileen Conger called again," she said as she perched on the edge of one of the two chairs on the opposite side of Cole's desk. "She's convinced Diana's neighbor, Alan Jenkins, is involved somehow."

"I know. I've checked with him again."

"I told her that."

Cole shook his head. He'd spoken with Jenkins in person, along with other neighbors all around Diana's apartment. Whoever had killed her had done it quietly, sneaking up the side stairway to the second floor without disturbing anyone, and Diana hadn't shrieked or made a sound, unlike when she'd discovered Nick Radnor's body in her bed, according to Jenkins himself.

"I've been talking to Heather Drury pretty regularly," Paige went on. "And Jill Potts, the director from Brighter Day. Ted Perry hasn't been around at all."

"Is that unusual?"

"A little," she said. "You want me to keep on it?"

"Yes, but I also want to do some deeper research into Lisette Benetton's suicide. Her mother died shortly after

Lisette's death. Don't know anything about her biological father, but I'm going to try to reach Durant Stipe, the stepfather, today."

"I'll see what I can find out about Lisette's father, too."

"Okay." He grabbed his jacket but threw it over his arm as he headed outside into watery June sunshine, which held the promise of some real heat by the afternoon.

Kerry brought back Jerry's keys and gave him his checkbook. He'd brightened considerably since earlier that morning, greeting her with, "Doc Stevens is going to spring me from this joint later today."

"That's great," said Kerry, meaning it. "I'm going to have to get going. I've got a lot to do."

"How's work at The Sand Drift?"

"The tilers are back. I have the carpet layers scheduled, and the second set of shower doors are on order."

"Getting to the last things," he said with satisfaction.

"Units one and two are almost there." She thought about telling him she was likely quitting Starrwood Homes but decided she owed Randy that information first.

"Wait!" he called as she headed for the door. The checkbook was flipped open and he was hurriedly writing out a check. He ripped it out and held it out to her. "I want you to take this to Audra."

"You want *me* to take it to her? What about Marcia?"

"The less either one of us see her, the better."

Kerry's brows lifted. Jerry usually kept his feelings about Marcia under careful lock and key. She accepted the check. "Did something happen?"

"Well . . . when she dropped by to see me, she was all het up about you and the will."

Marcia must've hightailed it to Jerry's bedside straight from the meeting with Gil Barnes. Kerry had gone home and made herself some toast and coffee, the effects of another late night, wonderful as it had been, taking their toll.

"She tell you I was a main beneficiary and I'm in charge of the foundation?"

Jerry smiled faintly. "She did bring it up. It was no surprise, really. You were his sister, for once and always. He loved you."

A lump filled her throat and she had to clear her throat.

"Don't pay her any mind."

"Thanks."

He waved that away, then sighed heavily. "It's a whole new world without Nick. Think we'll ever get used to it?"

"No."

He nodded, then waved a hand, pushing off the emotions that threatened to overtake him. "Now, tell me . . . why are you looking so tired?"

She was saved from answering when Dr. Stevens himself joined them. He talked to Jerry for a couple of minutes, but when Kerry tried to sneak out, he asked her to wait up. They met in the hallway outside Jerry's room.

The doctor said, "I'm releasing him this afternoon, but he's going to need care. He's living with congestive heart disease and needs someone to take care of him. I've suggested assisted living, but he's resistant."

"To put it mildly, I'm sure." Kerry was thinking rapidly. "Maybe I can find some temporary live-in care? I'll stay with him tonight and until we figure it out."

"Good. I was going to suggest that."

"Is he ready now?"

"In a couple of hours. We've got some paperwork."

"All right, I'll come back. I've got some things to take care of."

* * *

Josie was propped on her bed, on her laptop, idly surfing the web and checking sites like Monster.com for possible job openings. She'd spent a lot of the last decade just being Kent Roker's wife, and it hadn't done her any good. She'd been unhappy and restless, more involved in a fantasy relationship with a man who was now dead than working on either her marriage or herself.

Meeting with Taryn had put that in crystal-clear perspective. Taryn was practically a man hater, which, though it had salved Josie's conscience a bit about the traitorous thoughts she'd been having about Nick, and yeah, for a while, Chad, she hadn't fully embraced her anger.

"I just need to figure out what I want to do," Josie had finally said, and that was what she'd been doing ever since. She'd almost called Kerry, knowing she might be a better sounding board than Taryn, but she'd decided to try to figure it out herself for a while.

She was looking at the requirements for teaching, or even a teacher's aide, when she heard the garage door go up. Kent? Really? What kind of a business trip to New York had him back by Monday afternoon?

She shut down her laptop, shoved it aside, and waited. She was fully dressed in athletic pants and a loose over-the-shoulder shirt and just needed her canvas mules to face the day, but she hadn't expected Kent, or any, company. In this new self-reflective phase, she'd enjoyed the quietude. She needed her brain to relax. With Nick's death, and Diana's, and Chad's attack on her—Taryn had been firm about her admitting it was more than a "pass"—and Miami's decision to what? Tell secrets from high school? Josie had taken a time-out today.

Josie's thoughts touched on Miami's remarks about the boy who'd spread those rumors about her. Man, had she been humiliated, embarrassed, and furious. Lawrence Caulfield.

Asshole. He'd wanted to be one of the cool kids, for sure, and he'd thought he could lie about Josie to put himself there. He was an Uber driver now, though she thought he'd had a job with Keenan Motors for a time. He'd always sucked up to Keenan. She'd seen him at the memorial service, but she'd ignored him, just like she'd ignored him ever since high school, when he'd spread those lies. He'd tried to apologize to her once, but she'd brushed him aside. She doubted anyone remembered he was the one who'd spread the rumors; they just remembered the rumor.

The chart.

Points scored by members of the football team on the girls they nailed. She wasn't exactly sure how it worked; she'd just heard rumblings about it. Killian's name was at the top. He'd scored with Miami, of course, but she wasn't the only one. There were lots of others, according to rumor. And Sean had been up there, too. And Randy. She didn't know about the girls. At the time, she'd let them all know if her name was on the chart it was a big, fat lie.

She listened to the back door open and felt kind of let down that Kent was back. She needed a little more time to ready herself for what was going to be a difficult conversation. She wanted a divorce. That was the bottom line.

When Kent appeared in the bedroom doorway, she said, "You're back early."

He didn't answer, just regarded her in a strange, penetrating way, which made her stomach drop.

"What?" she asked him.

"Where's Chad Worster?"

"What?" she repeated, her pulse spiking.

"Well, I saw him groping you on the security camera. Thought you might've brought him back to our bed."

Josie could hear her blood rushing in her ears. In a voice that shook ever so slightly, she asked, "What security camera?"

* * *

Cole put a call in to Kerry on his way to the address he had for Durant Stipe. She didn't answer immediately but got back to him within minutes, sounding breathless. "Jerry's being released today," she said, and he could tell she was on speaker phone, like he was, while she drove. "Looks like I'm going to be staying there tonight, maybe longer, until he's settled."

"Ah. I'm being kicked out." He was smiling, remembering moments from the night before.

"Temporarily," she assured him quickly, and then went on to tell him about Nick Radnor's forgotten personal belongings, which she'd never retrieved from the property room.

"I'll put Youngston on that," he said. "He should've reminded you in the first place."

"I'll stop by the station later to pick them up. But there's something else . . ." She told him about the meeting with Nick's estate lawyer, the disposition of the will, and the letter to Durant Stipe.

"I'm on my way to Stipe's place now," Cole said, surprised. "When was the lawyer delivering the letter?"

"Actually, Stipe's going to Gil's office to pick it up tomorrow."

Cole thought that over. He could wait, he supposed, and try to pick up Stipe on his way out of the attorney's office. The man lived east of Seattle and it would be a bit of a drive, and very probably a fool's errand, but he still determined he'd make the trip. He had phone calls he could get to while he was on his way, and the trip would also keep him away from the station and the press, who were hungry for answers about Nick and Diana's homicides he didn't have. "I won't be back at the station till after five."

"Okay."

"Be careful. I'm glad you won't be alone."

"Call me later?" she asked lightly.

"Yep."

He clicked off, half-smiling, thinking of Kerry. Slowly, his smile dissipated. The investigation into Nick's death had spreading fingers, touching others' lives. There was someone out there who'd meant Radnor harm. Someone who'd orchestrated his killing and Diana's. Maybe several someones? Too soon to tell.

With an effort, he tamped down his growing anxiety about leaving Kerry alone. If he could, he'd ship her away from Edwards Bay until he figured out what the killer's motivation was. He opened and closed his hands around the steering wheel, easing tension. He wanted to forge a new life with Kerry. He'd pushed her away once before in grief and anger and was lucky to be given a second chance. He didn't want anything, or anyone, to ruin that.

". . . the bank's security team installed it," Kent was saying. "I talked to them about my own house, and when we built it I added the video system. It goes right to my phone." He held up his cell for Josie to see. On the screen there were a number of small, black-and-white squares that depicted the rooms in their house. She could see the entry hall, where the camera's view aimed down from the ceiling and encompassed the whole area and, if the door were open, the front porch.

She felt cold inside. An iceberg. "You didn't think to tell me this?" she asked. "All the years we've lived here?"

"It never came up till now."

She could almost hear the smile in his voice. The one he was hiding.

He said, "Gotta admit, I was surprised it was this Chad guy. Thought it would be Nick."

"No audio?"

"Nope."

"You have a camera in our bedroom," she accused. She'd noted that "square" on his screen before he clicked off his phone.

"Well, I don't have one in the bathroom."

"Oh, where someone might see your shortcomings?"

He barked out a short laugh, but she could tell she'd scored a direct hit. "You're so funny, Josie. So very funny. That's what I liked about you when we met. Your quick wit. But . . . it's gotten tiresome."

Her pulse was running hard and fast.

He went on, "You think you're in the driver's seat here?" He pinched his thumb and index finger together. "You're this close to being out on your cute little ass."

The initial jolt of fear she'd first felt had drained away. She could feel rage building inside her. She'd been unfaithful to him in her mind. She'd wanted Nick Radnor, had dreamed about him, fantasized about him, planned a fairy-tale future with him. But she'd never acted on those feelings. And this one time she'd nearly cheated, she hadn't been able to go through with it.

"I'd like to see the video of Chad and me." She was a little startled at how hard her voice sounded.

"Oh, you want to relive it?"

"Yes, Kent. I want to relive it. I want to see if it depicts what really happened, or if you're just trying to make me feel bad."

"Playing the victim. Nice move, Jose."

She came off the bed so fast, he took a step backward out of the bedroom in surprise. She was so angry, she hardly knew what to do. She'd never openly defied him. Their marriage had been a slow descent into a silent abyss of distrust and dislike.

She walked up to him. He was in the hall but still stood in front of the doorway.

"I'll leave," she said. "Today."

"Oh, for God's sake." He puffed out his chest, standing his ground now, embarrassed by his own retreat. "We both know you're not leaving."

For an answer, she brushed past him, shaking off the hand he tried to grab her with, and walked through the entry hall and out the front door.

Forrest banged through the back door of the bar into the dim recesses of the Blarney Stone's interior. They'd been closed yesterday, were closed Sundays, as a rule, until business heated up in the summer and they expanded their hours. Sean's idea, which Forrest had objected to, but with the problems with keeping help and well, yeah, smaller crowds on Sundays, he'd gone along. They'd talked of putting in big screens and making it a sports bar, but Sean had resisted that idea, too. He liked the Irish pub motif and Forrest had gone along with that, too. Maybe it was time for some changes around the place.

But at least Sean had been talking about opening next Sunday. Time for the summer crowds, though they were sure as hell having trouble finding experienced people. Maybe Miami would step in, he mused. Or Josie. She might not have any experience at much of anything except for expanding her vocabulary . . . what was that word she'd used to describe Egan? *Oleaginous*. Oily, mealymouthed sycophant, which in itself was a Josie word. She was really kind of a pain in the ass when you thought about it, but he'd do her if given the chance.

The lunch crowd had dissipated and Siobhan was clearing dishes off one of the tables. "Well, finally," she complained when she saw him. "Mike took a break right about the time I needed him. I'd like you to fire his ass, except then who would I have?"

"Sean not here?"

"Do you see him?"

"Well, he could be in the back," Forrest muttered with ill-concealed impatience. Sometimes the lip from the help was enough to make him want to roar with primal fury.

She stopped, thrust out a hip, and propped a hand on it, waiting for him to check.

Muttering to himself, Forrest grabbed the hinged portion of the bar and swung it upward, passed through, and let it bang shut behind him. It sounded like a pistol shot, and, collectively, the leftover lunch crowd jumped.

A bit sheepishly, Forrest said, "Sorry" to the room at large, then disappeared into the kitchen, pissed off anew that Siobhan had driven him to such actions. What the hell. This business was getting to him. And Sean . . . good buddy that he'd once been . . . was in some dark place that made him inaccessible.

He was also not in the kitchen.

He yanked his cell from his pocket and texted Sean: **where the hell r you?**

He waited. No response. As fast as his fingers could tap those goddamn, tiny "keyboard" keys on his phone, he wrote: **I fuckin need help Sib is by herself & havin a shit fit about it.**

Durant Stipe's ramshackle, faded blue house was at the end of a weedy lane in a pocket of weedy lanes on the southern fringes of Woodinville. It had taken Cole about an hour to drive there, and in between other calls, he'd tried to raise Stipe on his phone, so far to no avail. Maybe it was a wild-goose chase. Maybe his time could have been used more productively. He felt a little bad about leaving the other officers to deal with the press, but Charlie had assured him they were in no-comment mode whenever a member of the press caught them coming or going from the station. "Well, maybe Ben's said a few things," she admitted, clearly uncomfortable ratting him out. "But they want to talk to you."

"I'll take care of it when I'm back," he'd told her. He had to admit she'd really stepped into the role of his right-hand woman at work. He wondered if Youngston was aware of how the station dynamics had changed over the last few weeks and how he would react. Not well, he'd guess.

Cole parked his Jeep about halfway down the rutted lane that led around the back of Stipe's house before disappearing out of sight. He could just see the rear end of a rusted Chevy truck jutting out. A dog started baying as soon as he stepped from the vehicle. A large dog, from the sound of it, and he put a hand to the gun on his hip. He liked dogs. Was thinking about getting one of his own and would hate to have to kill one, but he wouldn't hesitate if he was attacked.

The black Lab rounded the corner at a full gallop. Cole stopped short in front of the grill of his Jeep. The Lab took a look at him and skidded to a halt. They eyed each other soundlessly, except for the sound of Cole's adrenaline-ratcheted heartbeat in his ears and the dog's labored breathing.

"Chip!" a male voice barked from behind the house. "Chip! Damn it, dog. Get back here!"

Chip didn't so much as move an eyebrow. He was on point. Ready to attack the interloper.

From around the back of the rusted pickup, the man Cole assumed was Durant Stipe appeared. He walked with a half limp; a hitch in his hip, maybe. Upon spying Cole, he straightened, as if prodded by a hot poker, his steps slowing. "Who might you be?" he asked, his gaze fastening on Cole's hand and gun.

"Chief of Police Cole Sheffield from Edwards Bay. I've called you and left messages."

"Down, Chip. Goddamn it, dog. *Sit!*"

Chip broke focus and sat. He looked back at Stipe, who humped his way toward the dog, putting out a gnarled hand to its black head, rubbing gently.

"Came all the way out here from Edwards Bay, did ya? I got your messages. I don't want to talk to you," said Stipe. "I know Radnor's dead."

"And you got a call from his attorney."

Stipe, who was tall and lean and slightly stooped, his gray hair a tad too long, his brown eyes sharp and assessing, gave a start. "You talked to my attorney?"

"I tried calling him, but we didn't connect. But I know Nick Radnor left you a letter."

"Well, I don't know anything about it."

"Would it be possible to talk to you about your stepdaughter, Lisette Benetton?"

"I said I don't want to talk, didn't I? You want to know if I was screwing my daughter underneath my wife's nose. The answer's no. It's always been no. It's always gonna be no, 'cause it's not the truth. She killed herself over Radnor, so don't ask me to cry tears he's dead." He spat a small brown stream onto the ground, more disdain than tobacco.

"Any idea what could be in that letter?"

"Nope. Not even all that curious. Oh, I'll go get it tomorrow. Find out what the man had to say. But that's as far as it goes."

"You have any thoughts about Lisette's suicide?"

"She killed herself over Radnor. Plain and simple. He . . . had his way with her . . . told all his friends. Then they started sniffin' around like hound dogs. One of 'em was pretty persistent. Acted like they were doing her a favor. I chased 'em off as best I could. But it was Radnor she wanted, and he sweet-talked his way into her pants and laughed at her. She told her mama, and her mama told me. Lisette was shy, but she kinda thought of herself as better than her mama and me. Her dad left when she was a little kid. Moved to Florida and started another family. Lisette pretended it didn't matter, but it did, to her. When she caught the quarterback's eye, she laid right down for him. That's it. That's what happened. I've said it and said it. Her mama told you police officers the same thing at the time, and there you go. I wanted to kill Radnor, but my wife wouldn't have it. She'd lost Lisette. Didn't wanna lose me, too." His mouth worked for a bit until he got it under control again. "So, I left Radnor alone and my charges were dropped, but nobody wanted to believe me. Wife died about six months later. Broken heart. I moved over here." He spat another dark brown stream at the ground.

"Someone killed Nick Radnor."

"So, that's why you're here. And me, the dope, just told you I wanted to kill him!" He laughed aloud, and Chip stood up and started wagging his tail. "Well, I didn't do it. You can arrest me if you want, but it wasn't me. Not sorry he's dead, but it wasn't me."

"I'm not here to accuse you of killing Nick Radnor."

"Yeah? Then what are you doing here?"

"Like I said in my messages, I wanted to ask you about Lisette. Her state of mind. The circumstances before her death."

"What for?" he asked curiously.

Cole didn't feel like telling him about Nick's change of attitude the last weeks of his life, that it appeared to have something to do with regrets he had, that Lisette's suicide might have played a bit part of what had been driving him.

Stipe didn't wait for an answer. "Like I said, her mama died of a broken heart, and I suspect she did, too. Nick dropped her as soon as she gave him what he wanted. Story old as time. I always said he should be the one in the grave. Finally got my wish."

Chapter Twenty-One

It was two p.m. when Kerry walked into Starrwood Homes. She headed straight for Randy's office and could hear he was on the phone. ". . . have to stop calling, Dad," he said in a long-suffering voice. "We're getting the job done. It's hard getting workers to commit. Jerry Radnor's in the hospital, Dad. I told you that! I'm not going to tear him a new one. Jesus. How about if I send Kerry over again? Will that make you feel better?" There was a moment of silence as he listened. Kerry had stopped short outside his door. Her soft-soled shoes had kept him from hearing her approach. "Yes, Dad, she's a four. A-plus."

Angie suddenly came around the hall corner and caught Kerry outside Randy's door. "Eavesdropping?" she snapped.

Randy's voice cut off as if someone had stolen his tongue.

"I came to talk to Randy."

"He's on the phone. What do you need?" Her face looked pale beneath a rather aggressive makeup application meant to disguise that fact.

"Well . . ." She'd felt like she owed Randy a face-to-face, but hearing he was about to have her run interference between him and his dad changed her mind. "I'm tendering my resignation."

"You're *quitting*?" she practically shrieked.

Randy spit out, "Gotta go," and then flew to his office door to stare at Kerry in outrage and consternation. "What the hell, Kerry?"

"If you need me for the next two weeks, I'll be happy to help out."

"Oh my God," Angie cried. "You have control of Jerry's money and here you go! Leaving us high and dry."

Jerry's money? "I don't know what you're talking about."

"Angie, shut up," Randy barked.

"You're a signer on his account. And you're probably in Nick's will, too. You came back to Edwards Bay like you're so friendly, so sweet, but you've really dug yourself into that family, haven't you?"

"Ange!" Randy looked apoplectic.

"How do you know I'm a signer on Jerry's account?" Kerry asked. Marcia had said much the same thing, never explaining how she knew.

"Randy said you met with Nick's lawyer today. This is all really convenient. Your mom marries some other guy and takes you away from the Radnor money, but you sure found a way to get back to it."

"Sheryl. Your friend who works at the bank," Kerry realized.

"She's no friend of mine!" Angie declared.

"Goddamn it." Randy grabbed his wife by the shoulders and pushed her back down the hall, away from Kerry. "Let me handle this," he growled at her furiously.

Angie seemed to finally recognize her husband meant business, but she looked around him to yell at Kerry, "Stealing our workers and then dumping us. We'll sue!" She twisted on her heel and stomped away.

Randy turned back to Kerry. He was angry, his ruddy complexion bright red. "Sorry about that," he said shortly.

"You showed Sheryl too much attention and now she and your wife are at war. Dangerous, Randy."

"It'll pass." He waved that away. "But you can't leave. I need someone . . . stable." He shot a dark look over his shoulder in the direction in which his wife had disappeared.

"I'm not entertaining your father, Randy. Tell him thanks for the A-plus, though," she couldn't help adding.

He started, as if she'd pricked him with a pin. "He was just joking."

"He told me the same thing. What is this ratings system?"

He laughed, but it sounded tight and uncomfortable. "Oh, nothing. Stupid stuff from high school." He exhaled. "You're really quitting?"

"Yes."

"Because you came into money?"

"Because it isn't working out here."

"Nick's will?" he asked, ignoring her.

"It's you, Randy. You and Angie. You're impossible to work for. That's why I'm quitting."

"If you stay on, I'll make it worth your while."

"Randy . . ." She had a lot of things she wanted to say but decided it was better if they were left unsaid. "I'm going to clean out my desk" was all she said and turned back to her office to do just that.

Josie sat in her car at the red light. The world looked oddly hazy, as if through a distorted lens. Seismic changes in life could do that. She'd walked out without anything and really wasn't sure she could even go back for her clothes. She didn't trust herself not to make up with Kent. As angry as she still was, that was the nature of their relationship. She'd never challenged him quite like that before, though. That was a new wrinkle. If—

Beep. Beep.

She came out of her reverie and drove through the now-green light. Was she really doing this? Walking out on her husband?

You've already done it, Jose.

But could she go back? Would she go back? He'd betrayed her in a way she hadn't believed possible. Yes, she'd betrayed him, too, but she hadn't been able to go through with it. Didn't that count for something? Besides, he'd *really* betrayed her.

The thought of what his security system had caught. Their lovemaking perhaps? *On his phone!*

She nearly rear-ended the vehicle in front of her. The Uber sticker on the back window filled her vision. Her eyes shifted to the driver. He wasn't aware how close she'd come to smashing into his bumper.

Well, hell. Lawrence Caulfield. She started laughing when she thought of the power his lies about her had held all these years. It had all seemed so momentous at the time, but now, in the wake of Kent's *security videos* . . .

"You need a drink," she told herself, shaking her head.

She drove to The Bank of Edwards Bay and headed for the ATM. She put her debit card in the slot and punched in her code. The machine bleeped, warning her that her card was no good, and then flashed a red light at her, as if it were thinking, her card inside its mean little jaws.

Kent.

She held her breath and was relieved when the card slid back to her. But it wasn't working. She'd walked out without any of her belongings apart from the clothes on her back and now she had no access to money. Apart from a few dollars in her purse, she was frankly destitute. The house was in Kent's name. And so was the Prius she was driving.

Well, shit.

* * *

Kerry helped Jerry into the house. He could walk on his own power but was weak enough that he clung to the railing as he slowly moved up the few steps to his front door, Kerry hovering around behind him. "You sure you don't want a wheelchair?" she asked.

"No."

"I just don't want you to fall."

"Just help me into the house, honey."

As soon as he was settled into his favorite chair, Kerry headed back to the car for his remaining belongings and the folder of paperwork and his prescriptions, which she intended to fill as soon as he was settled. She stole a glance at the time. After four. She wanted to call Cole, but she wanted to do it out of Jerry's earshot.

She brought everything in, fussed enough over him to get his dismissive hand flap, then pulled out his checkbook and keys from the pile. She kept the keys for herself but slipped the checkbook back in the drawer on top of another familiar ring of keys, an extra set to The Sand Drift motel units.

A loud clatter and Jerry's sudden yell sent her scurrying to his chair.

"You okay?" she asked in alarm, looking him over.

"I just dropped the damn remote."

She glanced down and saw the remote on the floor, its back popped open. One of the batteries had sprung out. Collecting it, she snapped it back in and tried to reattach the plastic back. It wouldn't latch, its tiny, plastic clip having broken off.

"It might still work, but . . ." She held out the remote and detached piece.

Jerry took the remote and tried to switch channels,

grunting when they changed with ease. "Don't need it, I guess."

Kerry put the tiny piece of plastic on the counter, then closed the drawer she'd left open when she'd raced to Jerry's side. He called her over again, asking for some water. She brought him the water and told him she'd make him some tea, which she did.

Fifteen minutes later she was able to leave. She tried Cole's number and got his voice mail. Knowing she didn't have much time, she drove to the police station, hoping he would be there by now. Instead she found only Ben Youngston, who took her to the property room and pulled out Nick's belongings—his wallet, keys, and jacket—and handed them to her with a flourish.

"Thanks," she told him. "Is Cole going to be back soon, do you think?"

"He doesn't explain himself to me, but then, he doesn't have to. He's the chief."

Kerry nodded. TMI, but okay, whatever.

She next went to the pharmacy and filled Jerry's prescription, nearly tapping her toe with impatience. Finally she had the pills in hand and returned to his house, where she found his head lolling on the back of the chair, mouth open. "Jerry!" she half-shouted in alarm, to which he woke, startled.

"Sorry," she said on a short laugh. "I'm not too good at this."

"You're fine," he told her, giving her a smile.

She'd planned to go back to the station again to wait for Cole there, but now changed her mind. She'd just be watching the clock, and anyway, she'd told the doctor she would keep an eye on Jerry. She rummaged through his cupboards, concluded they were barer than her own, and settled for some Campbell's Chicken Noodle Soup, which she and Jerry ate with faintly stale saltines as they watched the news together.

She received a text from Cole at about 5:30: **Caught in traffic. Didn't think it would take so long.**

I'm with Jerry at his house, she texted back.

Will call when I'm back was the answer, and then her screen went black. Damn. She switched it off and switched it back on, and the screen slowly came back to life.

"Did you get Audra her check?" Jerry asked.

"No, but I could do that now."

"Yeah, go. I want her to have it. Suppose I shoulda given it to Marcia, but I didn't want to."

"I won't be long."

At six p.m. Sean finally had the audacity to stroll through the back door of the bar as if he owned the place, which he didn't. He only owned half. "Nice of you to finally show," Forrest said acidly.

"I had some things to do."

"Radio silence all day, pal. I texted more than once."

"Didn't mean to hurt your feelings."

Sean brushed past him, which really pissed Forrest off. "You didn't hurt my feelings, but you made it damn difficult to get anything done around here. We're short-staffed, remember?"

"I know."

Sean held up the hinged part of the bar and gently let it down behind him. That pissed off Forrest some more for no good reason, other than he was already pissed off and it added fuel to the fire.

"We're gonna have to make some changes around here," Forrest told him.

"You wanna buy me out?" Sean came back fast. He gave Forrest that hooded look that seemed to drive women wild.

"Yeah. I do," Forrest snapped, calling his bluff.

Sean calmly named a figure, and added, "The sooner the better, if you're serious, because win, lose, or draw, I'm leaving Edwards Bay as soon as humanly possible."

"Bullshit."

"No bullshit." He wagged his head from side to side. "I'm through with this place. I'm taking my . . . my meager possessions and heading cross-country."

"Where? Again, bullshit. You're not going anywhere." Forrest felt a pang of alarm.

"I'm through here, Borland. All done."

"Because of Radnor? And Diana?"

"And other shit, too." A customer came up to the bar, a good-looking woman with a lot of cleavage and luscious, bee-stung lips that couldn't possibly have been made by nature. Sean smiled, and she practically melted into the barstool. Probably already wet for him. Fuckin' A. Life just wasn't fair most of the time.

"I'm not letting you leave, buddy," he warned.

To which Sean just shrugged, as if the decision had already been made.

Kerry more than expected Marcia to be home when she got to her house, but when she rang the bell, it was Audra, a skinny, coltish, dark-haired girl with blue eyes like her mom and a huge grin of greeting, who answered.

"Mom's late," Audra informed her, as if Kerry had asked. "She's late a lot. It's no big deal. I can handle being alone."

"I see that."

Audra might be only nine, but she had always acted older than her years. She'd asked for Kerry to identify herself before she'd opened the door, but then had flung it wide when she'd learned who it was, grinning delightedly.

"I have something for you from Grandpa Jerry. He wanted me to give it to you," Kerry said.

"So Mom wouldn't see it?"

Out of the mouths of babes . . .

"It's for those sailing lessons you wanted, and a college donation besides," Kerry said, handing over the card with the check.

Audra opened up the envelope and her eyes turned to saucers. "That's a whole lotta money!"

"College is expensive," said Kerry.

"I don't have a bank account. I did have a savings account once, I think, from Nick . . . but I don't think so anymore."

"If you want, I can take you down to the bank sometime and we'll get you started."

"'Kay . . . today?"

"Well, how about later this week? I'm staying with Grandpa because he just got out of the hospital."

"Oh, I know! Mom wouldn't let me go see him."

"You might want to call him and thank him."

"Yeah, before Mom gets home," Audra said, pulling out her own cell phone.

"I was going to say before you forget, but okay."

She put the phone to her ear. "I like being alone. I wish she'd leave for more than a weekend next time. She's always looking over my shoulder like I'm doing bad things on the internet, which I'm not."

Kerry frowned. "When did she leave you alone for a weekend?"

"Oh, don't worry. I was with the neighbors, so it was cool. She just got back." She sighed dramatically.

"She was gone this last weekend?"

"Yeah. I don't know where she went. Somewhere. She told me to call or text her on her cell if there was a problem, but I didn't. Oh, hi, Grandpa," she said, turning away as the call connected. "Aunt Kerry's here. She just brought me the check. Thank you, thank you, thank you! Wow! And how are you? Mom said she'd bring me to the hospital, but she never did. Maybe I'll come see you soon? Tomorrow? Great! If Mom won't bring me over, Kerry will, right?" She looked to Kerry for an answer. Kerry nodded, distracted by the fact that Marcia had left Audra for parts unknown this past weekend and never mentioned it. Was it some kind of secret? It wasn't as if Marcia owed Kerry any explanations, but it seemed odd.

Kerry had to shake herself out of her suspicions. There was probably nothing to it other than that Marcia didn't like sharing with Kerry. Nick's and Diana's deaths, coupled with Cole's admonishments to be careful were making her see diabolical plots everywhere.

Still . . . huh.

Taryn had just seated herself at the end of the Blarney Stone's bar with a good view of Sean when Forrest entered through the back door, letting it slam shut behind him, making sure everyone knew he'd arrived. She was determined not to think about what had just happened with Killian. He was a bastard, had always been a bastard, would always be a bastard. The fact that he'd humiliated her when she'd asked for a job interview after that fucker in accounting had brown-nosed up to Dan and together they'd trumped up totally false charges against her, offering two weeks' severance pay and a boot out the door, was bad enough. Killian had then compounded the problem.

"Siobhan's on a cigarette break," Forrest declared to Sean

and anyone else within earshot. "Since when does she smoke, huh? It's all bullshit."

"Give her a break," said Sean, which warmed the cockles of Taryn's heart, alleviating her fury a bit. A guy who would actually stand up for a woman. How many of those were left in the world?

"Yeah, where's Mike?" Forrest demanded. "He's here and then he's gone. Do you see him? I don't see him."

"Siobhan'll be back soon," Sean said levelly.

"She practically took my head off about how many hours straight she's been working. We gotta get this fixed, Sean. We gotta get more people."

Taryn felt mildly impatient with Forrest, who always had to be the biggest, loudest son of a bitch in the room. Sean was the only good guy left from high school. The only one.

Sean gave Forrest a sharp nod as he shook up a martini for the woman with the big lips a few seats down the bar from her.

The back door opened again and Josie stumbled in, looking as if she'd seen a ghost. Taryn was mildly shocked. What was this? Had something else besides Chad's attack happened to her? She slid off her stool.

A bloodcurdling shriek from outside suddenly electrified the room.

Taryn looked around quickly. Josie feinted toward the wall as if she'd been hit. Everyone else turned to stare at the back door as it swung shut and latched. Sean nearly overpoured Big Lips, sloshing a drop on the polished bar.

"What the . . . ?" Forrest was openmouthed.

He snapped to and headed toward the back door. Taryn was immediately on his heels. Outside she saw Siobhan stagger out of the side alcove and down the porch steps to collapse on the gravel lot at the base of the stairs, dropping a smoldering cigarette as she fell.

"What the fuck, Siobhan? You trying to burn the place down?" Forrest growled as he crushed out the smoke.

"HE'S DEAD!" she shrieked, pointing to the alcove.

Taryn looked to where she was pointing. All the hairs on her arms were standing on end, adrenaline kicking in.

"Who?" Forrest gulped, stepping carefully toward the alcove. A long shiver glided down Taryn's spine as she carefully followed. She had to look around his portly body to see.

Tangled up in stacked outdoor furniture were a pair of blue-jeaned legs, the feet enveloped in tattered black Nikes. Egan Fogherty's Nikes, she thought. He'd had them forever. Never wore anything else. But then she saw that Egan's dull, dead eyes were staring at her accusingly. Her whole body shivered.

"Oh, Mama, Mama, he's looking at me," Forrest whispered, pitching forward. He clunked his head against the fir planks and sprawled out cold next to Egan's body.

Taryn, who'd left her phone on the bar, cried to the gathering crowd, "Would someone call 9-1-1?"

Sean, who'd apparently been the person out of the bar behind her, whipped out his cell phone and did just that.

He really was a good guy.

Chapter Twenty-Two

Cole checked in with Charlie as he was nearing the Edwards Bay city limits. Before his trip to see Stipe, he'd been wrestling with which avenue to take next in the investigation into Nick Radnor's and Diana Conger's deaths but had since decided to go with his gut, which meant back to the beginning, back to high school.

"I got a call from Jill Potts, Brighter Day's director," Charlie informed him. "She said it's spaghetti night at the center and Ted Perry rarely misses it. If he shows, she wanted to know if she should tell him we're interested in talking to him, but I thought I'd go over there and hang around, see for myself . . . unless you have something else you'd like me to do?"

"Nah. Go ahead. I've got a few interviews I want to make. Think you should take Youngston or Spano with you?"

"Youngston's gone. Big date. Perry isn't dangerous. I've got this one, Chief."

"Okay."

Cole thought about the football dads, specifically Carroll Keenan, Millard Blevins, and Bart Borland—Killian, Sean, and Forrest's fathers. He'd sensed their sameness, their bonding views, at the memorial service. They all seemed shaped by events that had happened over a decade ago, ones that still seemed to resonate. He'd told himself he was making too much of it. So a bunch of dads liked to remember their sons' glory days. Where was the harm? But there was something there, and it had to do with Nick Radnor . . . and maybe Lisette Benetton. Was she Nick's one-time girlfriend . . . or a conquest he'd thrown aside, according to Lisette's stepfather? But Stipe had good reason to want to throw shade on all the Edwards Bay students and parents from that year, if his protestations of innocence were true, and Cole was inclined to believe him.

Jerry Radnor didn't really fit in with the football dads even though Nick had played quarterback for the team during those years. His mind touched on Cecily Wright. Her husband, Conrad, had wanted Alan to be on the team, hang out with those guys, but Alan was a tennis player. Neither of them were part of the close-knit football player cult.

But Randall Starr Sr. had been part of the group, Cole reminded himself. The man's health was failing some, so he hadn't been at the memorial service. His memory was iffy, too, according to Kerry. He needed to ask her more about him.

He didn't like the picture that was developing of high school players and their dads and the death of a shy, pretty girl who'd thought she was too good for her roots, according to her stepfather, and who had subsequently ended her own life. Something rotten there.

His cell phone buzzed. Charlie again. He punched the button to answer.

"Chief, Jesus, Chief! It's Egan Fogherty!" she sputtered before he could even say hello. "He's been killed. Bludgeoned to death. Behind the Blarney Stone restaurant . . ."

* * *

Charlie had just been finishing her meeting with Jill Potts at Brighter Day when Ted Perry appeared for the spaghetti dinner. Potts pointed him out to her and she waited until he'd gotten his tray and settled onto one of the benches at a table before approaching him. He'd chosen a spot with no other diners around and clearly wanted to stay away from the rest of the crowd, though most of them were engaged in what appeared to be a camaraderie of like circumstances. Perry regarded them all suspiciously behind lank, greasy hair and a dour, angry glare, and when Charlie slid onto the bench across from him, he pretended not to notice her, too. She was glad she'd changed from her uniform to civilian clothes: jeans, a long-sleeved gray T-shirt, and a pair of beat-up sneakers, a purposeful choice designed to put him at ease, if she could.

"Hi, Ted," Charlie said. The twenty-one-year-old startled at hearing her speak his name but still didn't look up. Jill Potts had said his attitude was mostly a disguise to hide his insecurities, which were many. He'd been kicked out of an abusive family at eighteen and hadn't assimilated well anywhere else until he'd connected with Justin Drury. Perry had been looking for a tribe, a group, a friend, and he'd felt he found that in Justin. Justin, however, had been more of a problem than a help.

Charlie saw his hands wrap around his tray, as if he were getting ready to get up and leave.

"Don't go," she said. "I just want to talk."

He hesitated. "Don't have anything to talk about."

"I want to know about Justin Drury."

He went still. Stopped as if she'd hit him with a magic freeze wand.

"Ms. Potts said you and Justin were friends."

His gaze shifted to the director, who was in the room,

chatting with some of the diners. She clearly had a good rapport with many of them.

"He didn't come here," Perry said.

"To the shelter? I know. He lived at home with his mother."

"He don't like her much, that mom of his. Too strict." He focused his gaze on his food again, relaxing his fingers around the tray. "He's dead?"

"Yes."

He licked his lips. "Overdose?"

"That's what it looks like, though he was found in the bay."

He finally glanced up and stared her in the eye. "I don't use drugs, ma'am . . . if you don't count weed anyway. Or a few pills here and there . . . but I'm not an addict. Neither was Justin. He just . . . had to make a living, y'know? And who's gonna hire a teenager for that kinda green? Nobody. Like he said, ya gotta live on the margins. Make it where you can."

"He was a dealer?"

"Nah, nah, well, kinda. Yeah. But that wasn't me. That's not what I do. If Potts told you it was me, she's a liar."

"She didn't tell me you were a dealer."

"Justin had his reasons, y'know? And I don't know how he fu—messed up. He wasn't that kinda user, y'know? He just used a little, and I know you're going to say you can't just use a little, but he did. That's what he was doing. He didn't overdose. Not Justin." Perry's eyes now pleaded with her to understand.

"So what do you think happened to him?"

He didn't hesitate. "Somebody killed him. One of his customers."

"Do you know who those customers are?"

"Uh-uh." He shook his head quickly.

"Ted, I'm not sure I believe you," Charlie said.

"Well, too bad. I don't know 'em."

"Any of them have a problem with Justin?"

"Nope."

"If they killed him—on purpose, not accidentally—would you want them to be brought to justice?"

"I can't help you, ma'am." All pretense of tough guy had disappeared, and he suddenly looked young and scared.

"There was an overdose that happened about ten days ago. A man named Nick Radnor. Someone used a hypodermic needle on his neck." She marked her fingers at the right side of her own neck, and his eyes followed as if pulled by a string. She'd been straightforward to that point but decided to wing it a bit. "Nick Radnor believed in Brighter Day. He was a big donor. Maybe he knew Justin . . . ?"

He shook his head.

"Maybe . . . Nick was looking for someone to procure some drugs for him?"

He stopped shaking his head and began picking at his fingernail, his meal forgotten.

"Justin was found in the bay a few days after Nick's death."

"Justin didn't do it! He wasn't like that!"

Charlie was a bit surprised by his sudden vehemence. She specifically hadn't said whoever had killed Nick had done it on purpose, though Perry's tone and paranoia spoke to his own belief.

"We think Radnor's death was a homicide."

"It wasn't Justin!"

"But maybe one of his customers? Maybe someone who helped Justin OD and into the bay?"

His eyes rolled wildly in his head, as if he were looking for an escape. "I can't talk to you no more. They'll know it was me."

"Who?" Her cell phone rang, but she ignored it.

"I don't know! I told you that!"

"But you know some of his customers, don't you? You just don't want to name them."

"I don't want to die!" he hissed at her, then clambered off the bench and practically ran out of the room.

Charlie got up to follow him, but her phone was still buzzing. She headed across the lunchroom, yanking out her phone in the process. Ben.

"Yeah?" she answered a little shortly.

"Egan Fogherty has been bludgeoned to death outside the Blarney Stone. I'm on my way over. Call the chief. . . ."

Sean stood outside the perimeter of rescue vehicles and personnel. Egan was dead, but the EMTs had first taken care of Forrest, lifting him onto a gurney; he was passed out cold. He came to in the back of the ambulance and was now sitting on its bumper, talking to Ben Youngston. The medical examiner had arrived in the coroner's van and the crowd of gawkers was growing. Youngston finished with Forrest and looked around, clearly enjoying being in charge. He'd been a pain in the ass in school and he was a pain in the ass now. His going into law enforcement was an almost expected choice. Either that or a one-eighty into criminality.

Killian showed up, his expression grim and careful. He said a few words to Ben, who ate it up, Killian being the king and all. Sean thought about how Killian had blown him off at the memorial service, assuring him there was nothing to worry about. Well, there was plenty to worry about. Whether Killian wanted to admit it or not, this harkened back to the God-awful ratings system he'd initiated in high school and they'd all played. When Sean's dad had learned of it, things had only gotten worse. The dads getting in on the scoring. Rating their sons' dates . . .

Ugly high school memories. Totally toxic shit.

He sidled up to Killian and said, "We need to talk."

Killian ignored him. His attention was on the second gurney, now heading toward the coroner's van. They'd draped a blanket over Fogherty, but his beat-up black Nikes were visible. "What do you think happened?" Killian asked, still not looking at him.

"I think somebody's got it in for us," Sean said.

Now Killian looked back at him sharply. "All of us? Who?"

"I don't know. Do you?"

He snorted.

Sean added, "This has to do with the ratings system."

"Where do you come up with that? Your dad's the one who still has the chart. He told me that himself, so what does that mean, huh?"

Sean could feel the angry flush that rose up his neck. "Somebody smashed in Fogherty's head. That's a fact. My old man might be a pain in the ass, but he didn't kill Egan."

"Well . . ." Killian shrugged that off. "When do you think it happened?" he asked, his gaze on the guys slamming closed the van's doors.

"I don't know. Coulda been today. More likely yesterday, because we weren't open."

"Like premeditated?"

"Maybe," said Sean.

"It can't be the ratings system. Who would do that? Makes no sense."

"Like I said—"

"Don't be an asshole, Blevins. None of us would kill Radnor and Fogherty over the chart. What would be the point?"

"I didn't say it was one of us, and you're forgetting Diana."

"You were the one who just said it was because of the ratings system."

"And she was on the list," Sean reminded tautly.

"Thought you were making this out to be some kind of revenge or something," Killian scoffed. He was starting to lose interest. "Nobody's going to kill Diana for that. She didn't even score that high. Radnor committed suicide, and who really knows what happened with Diana. She's always been a mess. Probably did it to herself somehow. And Fogherty? The poor shithead was bipolar. We all know they have a high suicide rate."

Believing he'd made his point, Killian sauntered away.

Sean watched him go, his lips drawn into a thin line.

They don't kill themselves by smashing a rock into their own head, asshole.

By the time Cole got to the Blarney Stone, the crowd had dissipated. He put a call in to Kerry, but it went straight to voice mail. He'd tried a couple of times already with no success, so this time he left a message. He didn't want to tell her about Fogherty over the phone, so he just said he'd run into an unexpected emergency, which would probably freak her out as well, but he didn't want to lie either. He just wanted to see her in person.

The crime scene team had finished their examination of the area and were packing up. Yellow tape ran across a protected side of the porch where the body had been found. Youngston was standing by, arms folded across his chest as if daring anyone to get past him.

Cole said, "Are Blevins and Borland inside?"

"Yeah, along with Taryn, Killian, and Josie."

"They were all here when the body was discovered?"

"Killian came later."

"Have you talked to anyone?"

"The waitress who found him. She's a wreck. And Forrest, who passed out when he saw Egan." He smirked. "Had to grab him out of the ambulance. They're all inside. The A-Team."

Cole heard a thread of resentment in Youngston's voice. Against the A-Team or himself? Probably both, he reasoned. He'd heard that same thread a number of times since he'd become chief. Cole had a bone to pick with him over neglecting to give Kerry Nick Radnor's belongings, but he let it go. He hadn't followed up on it either, so maybe it was both of their faults.

"You can head back to the station now," Cole told him. Ben seemed about to argue, then gave an insolent shrug and left.

Cole entered the Blarney Stone to find the A-Team hovered around the bar with Sean pouring drinks and Forrest sitting glassy-eyed on the far end. If there'd been other patrons at the time of the discovery of Egan's body, they were gone now. It was empty apart from the high school friends. He asked them if they'd seen anything and they collectively shook their heads. They gave him a rundown of where they'd been inside the bar when Siobhan, the waitress, had screamed, and Killian said he'd still been at work. They didn't have much to offer or were unwilling to talk in front of one another. What Cole needed were some one-on-one, in-depth interviews with them, along with Mia Miller and Randy and Angie Starr.

"I'll be calling you in the next couple days to get some more information," he told them, watching their reactions.

"Haven't you talked to us all enough?" Killian Keenan challenged him. "If there's really a killer out there, it seems like you don't want to look for him."

"What do you mean, 'if'?" Josie demanded. She was

hanging on to her drink as if afraid it would sprout legs and run away, although it looked like she had yet to take a sip.

"I mean, Fogherty was bipolar. . . ." He held out his hands, palms up, clearly believing he'd made a major point.

"He didn't commit suicide," Sean said shortly.

"Shit, no. His head was smashed in," Forrest said in a subdued voice.

Killian looked about to argue, but, maybe seeing there wasn't much of a rebuttal to those facts, he subsided.

Josie shuddered and picked up her drink, taking a careful swallow.

After a few more questions that elicited nothing new, Cole left them to their own devices. He called Kerry, getting her voice mail once again. His final call was to the ME, de la Fuentes, for a full report.

Time had dragged all evening. Kerry's eyes had traveled to Jerry's wall clock every ten minutes or so. She'd been telling herself that Cole would call when he could and had forced herself not to stare at her phone, so she'd purposely left it in her purse. She'd watched several game shows and sitcoms and finally, when it was getting dark, she couldn't stand it one second more. What had happened?

When she pulled her phone from her purse she realized it was totally dead this time . . . and her charger was at the motel. Her battery, which had been slowly losing its ability to hold a charge, appeared to have given up the ghost. She just hoped the phone would still work enough to make it till the next day, when she could figure out what was going on with it.

"Jerry, I'm going to head back to The Sand Drift to pick up my phone charger and an overnight bag." She'd meant to pack her bag earlier, but inside her heart of hearts she'd hoped to have some time with Cole alone at the motel. That looked like it probably wouldn't happen now.

"Go on ahead."

"I'll be right back."

When she was in her Mazda she tried to find her car charger, but she had a distant memory of taking it out of her console for some reason. She would have to wait till she got back to her apartment.

She was anxious to talk to Cole. She should have asked to use Jerry's cell. She knew he had one, though it hadn't been with him at the hospital and she hadn't seen it in his catchall drawer with the checkbook and keys.

She started down the hill toward Edwards Bay proper, her mind on Cole. She turned onto the street that led to the motel, her mind flicking to a particular moment in bed when she'd felt his tongue rim her ear, which made her smile.

She turned the last corner and gasped in shock, standing on the brakes.

Every motel room was lit up, every light turned on, a spectacle of illumination bursting from every window.

Chapter Twenty-Three

A cold shiver slid down Kerry's spine. She took her foot off the brake and carefully drove around to the back of the building, heart thudding. She pulled into her parking spot and saw a dark figure on the back-door steps.

She inhaled sharply and blasted on her brights to illuminate the intruder.

Vaughn.

"Jesus."

Her galloping heart started to slow. She was instantly mad. She switched off the ignition and slammed out of her car. Vaughn, shading his eyes with his hand against the glare, came down the steps to meet her.

"What the hell are you doing?" she demanded.

"I just stopped by. You won't take my calls, so what was I supposed to do?"

"My phone's dead," she said, her voice withering.

"Well, fine. I didn't know."

Her headlights automatically switched off and she and Vaughn would have been in the dark except for all the lights blasting from every room of the motel. Vaughn walked toward her, stepping through the lighted square from the window in her back door.

"Did you do this?" she demanded.

"What?"

She pointed to the rectangular blocks of light that marched down the backside of the motel from each of the windows built into the showers.

"No. How could I? What do you mean?"

"Somebody did it and it wasn't me. You were here Saturday, when I thought someone had been in my place."

"Well, it wasn't me. I don't have a key, remember? I didn't break in. Looks to me like someone's playing a prank on you."

He sounded so disgruntled that Kerry, who'd been sure the culprit was Vaughn as soon as she'd seen him on her back porch, took a moment to reconsider. She still thought he was lying, but if he wasn't . . .

"I'm going inside," she said tersely.

"You want me to come with you?"

"No . . . but you can stand on the back porch while I enter."

"You mean if somebody attacks you?"

"Yes, Vaughn. If somebody attacks me."

Maybe it wasn't his fault, but it felt like his fault. She unlocked her door and carefully went into the kitchen. She glanced around quickly. On one of the open shelves stood a thick glass vase that tapered down to about two inches in diameter near its base. Grabbing it, she held it in her right hand like a cudgel.

She then quickly searched through her apartment, as well as the office. A distant part of her mind recognized that Vaughn was perfectly happy letting her search for the intruder by herself. Fear for his own safety? Or the foreknowledge that no one would be there?

Returning to the kitchen, she saw he was still on the stoop, not a toe inside. Fear for himself, she decided.

"I'm going to get the keys and go through every unit.

But first . . ." She fished out her cell phone from her purse, went into the bedroom, and plugged it into the charger on her nightstand. She next went back around the plywood wall into the office and opened the safe, pulling out the master key. With it in hand, she went to the plywood partition, barked at Vaughn to lock the back door and meet her around the front, to which he obeyed. She then peeked through the blinds that covered the window in the office door to the still brilliantly lit outside of the building, assured herself that no one was lurking there, and let herself into the dark evening. She'd lost any fear of Vaughn and just needed someone as backup.

As soon as Vaughn appeared, Kerry slipped the master key into the lock for unit one. She entered carefully, Vaughn behind her, his cowardice never more evident. She saw the main rooms were empty except for the tile saw and the shower door tilted against the wall, ready for installation. She stepped carefully toward the bathroom, again finding no one about. She switched off the bathroom lights, then retraced her steps to the door, dousing the rest of the apartment's illumination as well. They went systematically through the same routine through each unit, the remodeling progression becoming more basic till they reached unit twelve, which was still at the Sheetrock phase. By the time Kerry had turned out the last light, Vaughn had regained his aplomb . . . and attitude.

"One of those friends of yours playing a prank on you," he said again, as if that settled it.

Though there was something in what he said, she felt argumentative. "Two people I know are dead. Somebody wanted to scare me."

"A prank."

They walked back to her rooms together, now the only unit illuminated.

"You should get security cameras," he said.

"You got that right."

"Look, I'm sorry for coming down on you like that last weekend," he said as they circled to her back door. Kerry used the master key to unlock her place as well. It made her realize she should have separate locks to her place and the office.

She put the vase back on the shelf as Vaughn, who was again hanging by the back door, having not been invited in, added, "Kerry, I'm broke. I need help. The IRS is coming after me and I don't know what to do."

"At the risk of sounding like Captain Obvious, your finances are not my problem anymore."

"I know." He held up his hands and hung his head. "Believe me, I know."

"I've got other issues, as you can plainly see," Kerry said.

"Are you going to make me beg? You're going to make me beg. Okay. I'm begging. I just need a loan. Don't tell me you don't have any money. I know you don't yet. But you will. Soon. You're Nick's beneficiary. All I want is fifty thousand to get me on my feet."

"*Fifty thousand!* Who told you I'm Nick's beneficiary? I didn't even know till today!"

"Marcia said you were going to be. She didn't believe that woman who said Nick was giving it all away to that shelter. And see?" He held out his hands to her. "You just said it's true."

"Vaughn, I'm not loaning you any money!"

"Thirty thousand."

"Zero. Thank you for helping me out tonight, but I don't owe you anything, no matter what you think. And we aren't friends." She tried to close the door, but he stuck out his toe to hold it open.

"Don't make me call the police."

"Five minutes. That's all I ask. Please."

"I've . . . got to check my phone."

She left him and strode back to the bedroom, checking her cell phone.

Nine missed calls. Cole, Vaughn, and Josie.

She immediately called Cole. She heard Vaughn come inside and she whirled around to stare at her open bedroom door. When he appeared, he lifted his hands in surrender to her full-on glare.

"I really don't want to have to take you to court," he said, as if it were her fault.

"Then don't. But if you have to, go ahead. Sue me. Do your worst."

The call to Cole went to voice mail.

"Kerry . . ."

"Vaughn," she warned right back.

He clearly wanted to argue some more, so she pretended Cole had answered. "Hi, there," she said warmly, even though she'd cut the connection to his voice mail. "Sorry about the phone. Think I'm going to have to get a new charger. Hope it's not the phone itself. Yeah, come on over. Vaughn's here, but he's just leaving." She pretended to listen, then said, "Okay, see you soon." She clicked off and said to Vaughn meaningfully, "He suggested you make yourself scarce."

"He threatened me?"

Kerry didn't disabuse him. "You can stay if you want. Meet him face-to-face."

"Fine. I'm leaving. Just think about it, Kerry. I need a little help, that's all. Let's not make this messy."

"Get a job, Vaughn."

When he was gone, she locked the back door behind him, then rechecked the front door. The master key was on the counter and she put it back in the safe.

Keys . . . Emilio had a set of twelve, one for each unit, and so did Jerry. . . . There was no evidence of a break-in, so how else had the intruder turned on all those motel room lights?

Kerry left her bedroom light switched on and turned off most in the kitchen, just leaving on the under-cabinet lights. It was creepy to think someone had come in to her place, seen her things, her lifestyle. Renewed fear raced through her veins. There was a killer out there. Cole had warned her to be careful.

But turning on all her lights?

She called Emilio, who was shocked about the lights and fell all over himself saying the keys had never been off his person. He kept them in a zippered pocket of his pants, so no one had had access to them.

The intruder was unlikely to have used the unit keys in the safe or the master key. They would have had to get inside the office to access the safe, so that didn't wash. The only keys susceptible were Jerry's and she'd seen them in his drawer this afternoon.

But not this morning . . .

Her pulse jumped as she thought back. The keys hadn't been in the drawer when she took out the checkbook. She would have seen them. But later, when she put the checkbook back in, they'd been there, kind of tucked beneath other items. Now she wondered if they'd purposely been shoved down in the drawer to make it seem like they'd always been there. Whoever had taken them hadn't counted on Jerry asking for his checkbook.

Marcia.

When Kerry had gone to the door to admit Gil Barnes, she'd left Marcia alone in the kitchen for several minutes, more than enough time to replace the keys. Marcia had taken them. Marcia, who was mad at her for being Nick's beneficiary.

As Kerry thought about it, she grew certain Marcia was behind the *prank*.

And where did Marcia get off telling people she was going to be Nick's beneficiary? What the hell was going on with her?

Josie stumbled out of the bar to her Prius, unlocking her door and flopping into the driver's seat. She wasn't drunk. She hadn't even finished one drink. But she felt discombobulated to the extreme.

She stared straight ahead, hands on the wheel. Her cell phone suddenly buzzed in her back pocket and she scrambled around to grab it without accidentally turning it off.

Oh, shit. *Chad.* She'd put his number into her contacts list.

She didn't have time for him today . . . or ever. She let the phone ring until it finally stopped. A minute later she heard a *bing* that said she had a voice mail.

To hell with him.

She sat a moment longer, then realized with some surprise that Chad's call had snapped her right out of her funk. Her spurt of fury had blown away the miasma of fear that had overtaken her. Was that right? Miasma. She thought it was.

Be an English teacher. Go to school. Get a degree. Become what you want to be.

She switched on the ignition and then stopped. She didn't have anywhere to go. A moment later she turned the engine off again. The headlights stayed on a minute longer, then switched off as well. While she was sitting, Miami's rust bucket of a Camry from several decades back drove into the lot. Josie felt a pang of regret that she'd never asked her friend anything about her finances. She'd married Kent and moved into another income bracket and never considered Miami's circumstances. How selfish.

As Miami climbed from her driver's seat, Josie got out

of hers. Remote-locking the Prius, she hurried toward her friend. "Hey," she called as Miami started up the back steps.

Miami glanced back and hesitated, though she looked as if she wished Josie hadn't caught her.

"You heard about Egan?" Josie asked, her eyes traveling toward the taped-off alcove.

"Killian told me. I just got off work . . . I just . . . can't believe it."

"I know."

"Josie . . ."

"Yeah?" The way she said her name, in that charged way, made Josie slightly nervous.

"I'm going to tell about the rating system, and other things. I've made a determination. I was going to do it last night, but I changed my mind. I chickened out."

"What are you going to tell? That the guys had a chart?"

"Oh, you know it's more than that," she said bitterly. "I'm picking up Killian. He's drunk. He's been doing that a lot lately. He's either drunk or he wants to run off to Mexico with me."

Josie half-laughed. "Doesn't sound like that bad of an idea."

"Oh, I'd run away if I could, but I can't. Too many responsibilities. And I would never go with Killian," she stated darkly.

"Isn't he your boyfriend?" Josie asked, but Miami had already opened the back door and let herself into the bar.

Josie stood on the porch, uninterested in returning to the A-Team. She wheeled back to her car, thought about it some more, then switched on the ignition again and aimed the Prius for The Sand Drift Motel.

Cole's phone caught Kerry's call when he was in the middle of an argument with Youngston, who hadn't taken kindly to being reprimanded about not giving Kerry Nick's belongings, so he couldn't answer it.

"She never said anything," Youngston declared. "What am I, a mind reader?"

"I told you she was coming in and we discussed it. And I told her to check with you on the way out."

"Well, she never did."

"I'll take some of the blame. I should have followed through. Let's just do better."

No reason to flog a dead horse. Youngston was the kind of guy who wasn't going to go out of his way to help anyone beyond what he was assigned to do. He let that argument go and went back to discussing the Fogherty homicide with the squad room. He'd ducked the newspeople outside, whose clamor had only risen with this newest development.

"We've got a serial killer," Charlie said.

"Looks like it. But there's a motive to these killings. It's not just an urge by a sick predator," Cole said. He wanted to phone Kerry back but needed to speak to his officers. They were all jumpy. Needing reassurance themselves. He did take the time to text her: will call soon.

"What motive?" Ben asked.

"We don't know that yet. Charlie has a list of friends and acquaintances of Nick Radnor and also of Diana Conger. Egan Fogherty's intersect with them. We've spoken to most of the people on the list at least once, but now I want some serious information. Where they were when each of these deaths occurred, I mean within minutes. Until I hear differently, all of these deaths are homicides. No accidents. No suicides. Something ties them together. Find out if there are any discrepancies in anyone's story. I don't care how small. A stranger didn't pick out these three people at random. Somebody knows something. I want to find out what that something is."

Charlie said, "Do you want to divide the list?"

"Yep. I'll take the Keenans and the Borlands, Bart and Forrest. I'm also going to talk to the press."

"Good luck with that," Spano said, grooming his mustache with his fingers, a nervous habit.

"I'll take Marcia Radnor," Ben put in casually, at which Dave Hoffman, the quietest officer on the force, couldn't hold back a snort.

"What?" Cole asked sharply. He was feeling tense.

Charlie's tongue was at the roof of her mouth as she rolled her eyes toward Ben. Hoffman ducked his head, as if he wanted to disappear. Spano looked as lost as Cole.

"Somebody tell me," Cole snapped out.

Charlie said, "Ben has been seeing Marcia Radnor."

"Seeing?" Cole repeated.

"Like dating," Charlie added. "That's why he couldn't be reached this weekend."

Ben sent Charlie a scorching glare, which she shrugged off.

"Is that true?" Cole asked.

"And if it is?" Ben countered.

"Then you're not interviewing Marcia Radnor. Spano, you're on for her. Ben, you take the Blevinses, Sean and his father . . . what's his name?" Cole asked.

"Millard," Charlie said.

"Right. Okay. Hoffman, I'm putting you on the Starrs, Randy, Angie, and Randall Sr., who's in an assisted care facility, Callaway . . ."

"The Callaway Center," said Charlie.

"Charlie, take Josie Roker, Mia Miller, and Taryn Whitcomb. I'm hitting you with three, I realize, so if—"

"I can do it," she broke in quickly.

"All right. Find out their whereabouts, what they thought of Radnor, Conger, and Fogherty."

"We know the drill," said Ben.

Cole ignored him. "When we're done, we'll move on to more names."

"Are we working tonight?" Ben asked in disbelief. They were already into overtime.

"We'll pick it up in the morning, but if you do find out something tonight . . . we'll find the overtime. Let's get this guy."

Charlie was already reaching for the phone as Cole headed out to talk to the press. Cole hesitated before pushing through the outer door, stopping to put a call through to Kerry. This time she answered on the first ring, and before he could say more than "Hi," she said quickly, "My phone isn't working too well. It's sort of charging right now. Just wanted you to know in case we get cut off."

"Man, I'm glad to hear your voice. When I couldn't reach you, I was getting worried. I called Jerry. He told me about your phone, but I still was worried."

"Well . . ." And then she told him about coming back to the motel, finding all the lights on, and walking the grounds with Vaughn Campfer.

He suddenly realized she didn't know about Egan Fogherty. He'd wanted to tell her in person, but time was passing. He said, "Stay there. Don't move. Don't let anybody in. As soon as I'm done here, I'll be there."

"I need to be back with Jerry."

"Better idea. Go to his house. I'll meet you there."

"Okay."

"Be careful," he said with real feeling. "There's . . . more bad news, I'm afraid."

"What?" she asked, a thread of alarm in her voice.

"It's Egan Fogherty." Quickly, he told her what they'd found behind the Blarney Stone.

"Oh my God, oh my God . . ."

"Just get to Jerry's. Call me when you're safe. On his phone, if yours isn't working."

"Okay."

"I . . ." *Love you.* He pressed his lips together, berating himself for not saying what was in his heart.

"Cole?"

"Yeah?"

"The lights? I think Marcia was behind that. I think she took the keys to the motel from Jerry's house. Maybe she had his house key and could let herself in? I don't know, and I don't know why she did it either, but I'm pretty sure it was her."

He thought that over. Thought about Ben's weekend with Nick's ex. "Whatever the case, be extra-careful," he said now.

"You too," she said, then clicked off.

And then he walked outside into a night sky studded with stars and news vans and people and cameras from every local station.

Kerry was packing her overnight bag, eyeing her phone charger with distrust, becoming convinced it was a phone issue rather than a battery one. Not what she wanted to deal with.

Knock, knock.

She nearly fell to the ground at the rap on her front door, she reacted so strongly. Remembering that she'd thrown the lock and pulled the chain, thank God, she tiptoed to the peephole . . . and saw Josie on her front step.

For a moment she hesitated. *Egan Fogherty had been killed. On the heels of Diana's and Nick's deaths.* Cole had told her to go to Jerry's. But Josie . . . ? Josie was harmless, wasn't she?

She chewed ferociously on her lower lip. Damn it. Call

her crazy, reckless, stupid . . . anything you wanted . . . She yanked back the chain and unlocked the door.

Josie stared at her for a moment, then her eyes filled with tears. "I didn't know where to go. I left my husband. And now Egan's dead!"

Kerry practically pulled her inside, glancing behind her to the moonlit night before slamming the door and locking it once more. "I'm just on my way to Jerry's house. He got out of the hospital this afternoon and needs someone with him."

"Oh." Josie looked around dully. "Do you mind if . . . could I stay here tonight, on the couch maybe?"

Kerry hesitated. The thought of leaving someone in her apartment . . . but Josie . . . those tears were real. She couldn't be that good of an actress. "If you don't mind being alone," said Kerry.

Josie smiled crookedly. "Turns out I've been alone for years. I just didn't know it."

"Okay. Well, there's something you should know." She told her about the lights blasting from the units. "I don't know why they did it, other than that it was meant to scare me."

"Did it? Scare you?"

"For a bit. But honestly, now I'm just kinda mad."

"Do you know who did it?"

"I've got a theory."

"Who?" Josie asked, but Kerry shook her head.

"If it's who I think it was, it was definitely out of spite, nothing to do with Nick, Diana, and Egan."

"Then someone should stay here to guard the place, don't you think?" she asked, which was the opposite reaction of what Kerry had expected.

"Okay," Kerry said. And reiterating what Cole had said to her, she added, "Be extra-careful. There's a vase in the kitchen that makes a good club if you need it."

* * *

Josie watched Kerry leave. She walked around the small apartment, almost envious of Kerry's warm little space. She saw the vase on the open shelf and picked it up, hefting it in her hand. Woulda been handy to have when Chad was forcing himself on her.

Chad.

Josie pulled out her phone, deliberated for a moment, then hit the Voice Mail button, pressing Play on Chad's message. She braced herself for a half-assed apology, maybe, then was surprised, stunned even, when she heard what he had to say.

What the hell?

Immediately, she punched in Kerry's number, but of course she didn't pick up. She'd just left and was undoubtedly still driving, probably didn't want to answer yet. Josie left her own voice mail on Kerry's phone, then clicked off.

With time on her hands, she walked into Kerry's bathroom and looked at herself in the mirror, seeing the tiny brown dot in her green-blue eyes, the flaw. She thought back on her attitude toward her friends less than two weeks ago, the bitchiness that had been an overlay atop every word and thought. It was embarrassing now. So mean.

She thought about Egan Fogherty. She'd only seen his body on a gurney, but it had been enough.

"You need to be a better person," she whispered to herself.

And that was when Kerry called back. "You have a message from Chad?" she asked.

"He left a message on my phone that I just listened to," Josie said. "Apparently no one told Nick's cleaning lady about his death and she showed up at his condo. When she went inside, she was confused that things had been rifled through, as if he had been robbed. When she couldn't reach Nick, she called Chad. He went over to Nick's and saw what the woman meant. Someone went through Nick's drawers and closet."

"Huh." Kerry absorbed that. She'd just arrived at Jerry's and was still sitting in her car. "Did they use a key, or how else did they get access?"

"Chad didn't say."

"Who . . . why?"

"I don't know. I just thought you should know," said Josie.

Kerry thought about Marcia, about the keys she could swear had just materialized in Jerry's drawer. Had she gone to Palo Alto this weekend?

"Chad called you with this information?" Kerry asked, slightly baffled.

"Yeah, well, that's a long story. He owed me an apology and gave me one of sorts. Kerry, do you think these were robbers who knew Nick was dead and targeted his house?"

"Maybe," she said dubiously.

Headlights came up behind her. "Josie, I gotta go," she said and clicked off.

The car behind her parked along the sidewalk in front of Jerry's house as well. The headlights switched off, but no one got out of the car. Kerry's pulse ran fast and light. All of Cole's warnings flashed through her mind.

She froze in her seat, hands on the wheel. Were they here for her? Should she leave? Just take off?

She was still deciding when the driver's door opened and Kerry saw Marcia step onto the sidewalk. Kerry quickly scrambled out as well.

"What were you doing out here just sitting in your car?" Marcia asked.

"Trying to figure out why you turned on all the lights at The Sand Drift."

"What do you mean?" she asked cautiously, but her whole body had stiffened.

"The keys, Marcia. You took the keys to the motel from Jerry's drawer. You were pissed off about Nick's will and tried to scare me."

"I don't know what you're talking about!"

But she did. Her body language practically screamed her guilt. Kerry added flatly, "How'd your weekend in Palo Alto go?"

"Wha—wha—?" Marcia actually took a step backward, as if receiving a blow.

"Breaking into Nick's condo. Even before the will was read. What did you take, Marcia? What did you *steal*?"

"I didn't! I didn't take anything!"

"That's not what the cleaning person said," Kerry embellished.

"It wasn't me! I didn't want to! It was my ring. Nick bought it for me and I threw it at him, and I wanted it back!"

So that was it. Kerry exhaled. "Oh, Marcia."

"It wasn't my idea! I just went along with it, because Nick owed me, and I knew, *I knew* it was going to be you who ended up with everything. I knew it."

"So you decided to break in to Nick's condo and take your ring back," Kerry said coldly.

"It was Ben's idea! Not mine! Ben's! I just told him about the ring. He's the one who broke into Nick's condo! It's his fault!"

Chapter Twenty-Four

Kerry hadn't expected Marcia to confess so readily, but Nick's ex had never been able to hide her feelings. "You and Ben broke into Nick's condo and stole your ring," she reiterated.

"It was my ring. And we—he—didn't break in. He used a key."

"But you gave him the key," Kerry accused.

"No!"

"You had to, Marcia."

She shook her head. "No . . . no . . ."

"He didn't just come up with it out of thin air." *Oh, shit. Yes, he had.* "Oh . . . he used Nick's keys," she realized. "They were in the property room, and I didn't pick them up till later. He had ample time to make a copy, in case I suddenly remembered. And that's how you got into Jerry's house. Nick had a key to his father's house."

"What are you doing?" Marcia screeched when Kerry suddenly pulled out her phone.

"Calling Cole." Damn. Her battery life was dissipating like smoke.

"No. Don't. Kerry, please." Marcia grabbed her hand, as if she was going to snatch the phone away from her.

"Ben's an officer of the law, Marcia. Maybe that doesn't mean anything to you, but it does to me, and it will to Cole."

"He'll lose his job!"

"Yeah. And he should."

"No, no. Please. I'm sorry. I'm so sorry. I just wanted my ring back. That's all I wanted. Don't be so hard. You're so damn hard! I just wanted . . . Nick back." She suddenly buried her face in her hands and began full-body sobbing. "I love him! I still love him. And now there's no chance, *no chance* we'll get back together. It's all I can do to get out of bed in the morning. Whoever killed him took that away from me. The chance. If I find out who it is, I swear I'll kill them myself."

"Cole," Kerry said when he answered.

"Hey," he responded warmly, though he sounded somewhat distracted. "Can I call you back?"

"Yes . . . I just need to tell you something."

His voice sharpened. "Is someone crying?"

"Marcia," she answered, then she told him what Marcia had just said about Ben Youngston.

Cole clicked off and slowly pocketed his phone. He'd given a terse report to the press about Egan Fogherty's death: The victim had been found behind a local bar. It appeared he'd died from a head injury. Foul play was a definite consideration. He had no proof that Fogherty's death was related to Nicholas Radnor's and Diana Conger's, but the three victims had been friends. The questions had gone on from there, but he'd kept the report purposely vague. He needed to catch a killer, or killers, and the fewer details on Fogherty's murder available to the public, the better chance he had of snagging the perpetrator in a lie.

He was also half-convinced the football dads were involved. Had they stabbed Nick with a hypodermic, strangled

Diana with a scarf, or bludgeoned Egan with a rock . . . ? He couldn't quite put that picture together. Yet. But they were in the mix somewhere.

But now this about Ben . . .

He'd been on his way to the Borland home to interview Bart Borland, who'd grudgingly agreed to speak to him, but now he changed direction, heading back to the station. He called Borland and told him he would set the interview for another day, and the sigh of relief on the other end of the phone spoke to how much the man was dreading seeing the law.

From the moment Miami had left Josie outside the back door of the Blarney Stone and pushed through into the nearly empty establishment, she wished she hadn't come. She had a lot on her mind, and though she needed Killian with her tonight, seeing him perched on the barstool, looking as if he could fall off, made her groan inside and wish she'd rethought the whole thing. But she needed to get it done. Off her chest. Bared to the world. Free of all the secrets and pain.

"Hey, Mia," Sean greeted when he saw her.

"Hey, Mia," Killian mocked with a snide giggle. "C'mere, *Mia*." He patted the seat beside him. "Come sit by me. Come sit by your man."

Miami reluctantly obeyed, taking the seat between Killian and Taryn. The two of them had never been simpatico, and now Taryn sent them both a disgusted look as Miami sat down.

"My name is Mia," Miami pointed out as Killian fiddled with the hibiscus flower behind her ear. She ripped it off and set it on the bar.

"What can I get 'cha?" Forrest asked.

Miami looked from Forrest to Sean. "Pinot gris."

"Got it," Sean said, practically pushing Forrest out of the way.

"Hey," Forrest protested.

"Well, *Mia*," Killian went on, wearing his usual smirking smile. "What are we gonna do the rest of the night? We're having a wake here, but nobody's really sorry Egan's dead, are they?"

"Shut up," said Taryn at the same moment Miami declared, "That's not true."

"Isn't it?" Killian shifted his glare to Taryn. "You say something, bitch?" Before Taryn could respond, he turned to Forrest and Sean and spread his arms wide. "You know she got fired today?" He cocked his head in Taryn's direction. "Guess Jefferson Motors finally realized what a liability she was. She came over to Keenan Motors and asked for a job, but we didn't have room for deadweight. Sorry."

Sean slid Miami her glass of wine and they caught eyes for a second. Killian, even through his drunkenness, spied the exchanged look. "Babe, you got a problem with what I'm saying?"

Miami took a long swallow. She'd dealt with Killian for so long, she knew what pushed his buttons and what didn't. She'd loved him as a teenager, or thought she had. She didn't love him anymore. "I'm not looking forward to going to your parents' house tonight, but we need to."

"Oh, really. You don't want to go because of Egan?" His tone belittled her.

"Because of Nick, Diana, and Egan," Sean put in.

Killian's dark head swung his way. "You say something, shithead?"

"Yeah. I did." Sean didn't back down, just kept his blue eyes focused on Killian, the challenge unmistakable.

Miami took a breath, as did both Taryn and Forrest. This had never happened.

Killian pointed a finger gun at Sean. "Aren't you the one who's afraid it'll all come out? How you fucked all the girls you could and put their names on the charts? Tried to give them all A-pluses when they were just a bunch of dogs."

"Killian," Miami warned. Her face was hot with embarrassment and anger.

But Killian had Sean in his sights. "You were sure worried at Nick's memorial service. Afraid it'd all come out. And you got a right to feel that way, 'cause I've got all the facts on you, buddy. How about Lisette?"

"I think you've got me mixed up with yourself," said Sean.

"That wasn't you humping on her when she was dead drunk on Forrest's couch? Pretty sure it was." He leaned forward and added in a stage whisper, "And I've got the pictures to prove it."

"Oh, Killian," Miami moaned, feeling ill.

Sean said quietly, "There are no pictures 'cause that's not how it went down. And I didn't have sex with her against her will."

Killian suddenly stood up and leaned threateningly over the bar. "Neither did I, asshole. She wanted it. Wanted to be on the chart."

"Bullshit," said Taryn.

"Fuck you. Nobody ever wanted you." He rounded on her.

"Hey," Forrest said nervously.

"We all did it," Killian reminded them. "All of us." He made a circle with his finger that included them all. "And Nick, too. Perfect Nick. But I was the only one who got the prize." He suddenly threw his arms around Miami's neck, and for a moment she thought he was going to grab her breast. "We all did it," he repeated. "Truth comes out. You know it does." His gaze slid from Sean to Forrest and then back to Sean. "And when it does, how's everybody gonna feel about your little enterprise here? Bet it closes in three months."

"A lot of it was lies," said Sean.

"Yeah," Forrest admitted.

"Nobody got Josie, and her name was there," Sean reminded.

"You still talking?" Killian's face was turning red. He couldn't stand being argued with, couldn't stand being wrong. "Caulfield did."

"And Caulfield lied," said Miami.

"Oh, you're gonna believe Josie, now? That stuck-up bitch?"

"Yes."

He turned to her. "What is this?"

"We're all just trying to get used to the idea that somebody killed Egan. Right outside our door," Sean said heatedly. "And Nick and Diana."

"Who do you think that was?" Taryn asked, her eyes on Killian.

"Don't look at me," Killian muttered, stumbling to his feet. "You know he was going to tell, don't you? Nick."

"Yeah, I know. He talked to my dad about the chart," Sean said. "Wanted to see it. Who was on it. What kind of things had been written."

"Did your old man give it to him?" Forrest put in, his mouth slack.

"Jesus Christ," Killian said in disgust.

Sean said, "No. He didn't give it to anybody."

"But you saw it?" Taryn asked. "Recently."

"I don't want to minimize what we did or anything, but it's just a chart. Doesn't say anything. Just names and dates. Not enough to kill over."

"Don't be so sure." Killian wagged a finger in front of Sean's nose. It was all Sean could do not to bat it away.

At Sean's cool, assessing look, Killian demanded, his voice rising, "You think I did it?"

Forrest looked fearfully at his business partner. "Let's cool it down around here, okay?"

"Fuck that." Killian stepped back, his thighs smacking into the barstool he'd shoved aside. In a fury, he picked it up and hurled it across the room, where it smashed onto a table that, in turn, smacked into the wall. The force broke off one leg and made the dartboard tremble. "Fuck you all," he growled and headed for the back door, swaying.

Miami immediately got up and followed him, but Sean, with more speed than forethought, caught up with her before the door banged shut behind Killian. "You don't have to go."

"I've got to see his parents."

"Why?"

She gave him a meaningful look and reached around him to pull open the door. He seemed to think about it for a moment, then followed her outside into the night.

In the odd quiet that followed inside the bar, Forrest asked Taryn, "You think people'll really stop coming?"

"When they find out what sick bastards you all are? Yeah, maybe."

"Thanks for the vote of confidence." He gazed at her with a mixture of worry and fear. "You want a drink?" he asked hopefully.

"I'm sick of all this."

"Me too. That's why you should drink."

But Taryn slid off her stool and headed out as well. Forrest had always been a little needy. But it was Killian who was the true asshole.

Miami drove Killian in dead silence, at least on her part. He was making snide comments about all his "friends." Ha.

That was a joke in itself. He didn't have any friends . . . and he didn't have her anymore.

Sean had grabbed her arm for a moment, just after Killian had slammed the passenger door of Miami's car and slumped down in the seat. "Call me when it's over," he said.

"I will."

"And then we'll tell him."

"What if he's . . . what if he *killed them?*"

"He didn't."

"How do you know?" she'd whispered.

"I just know."

"I love you."

"I love you." He stepped back and said, "I'll be back at my place."

"Okay."

"I could come with you."

She'd smiled and shook her head as she walked around to her side of the vehicle. The last thing she needed was for the Keenans to be faced with Sean as well.

Now she followed the road to a winding cul-de-sac. At the farthest arc four McMansions faced the bay, each with a spectacular view.

Carroll Keenan had been waiting for them, standing by the front door under the portico. Another one of the required Keenan meals that were usually on Sundays. Last night, however, Miami had been unable to attend. She'd backed out, unable to go through with the truth about what had happened in high school, but today she was stronger. Egan's death had done that. Stiffened her resolve. Bad things were coming down like rain. The Keenans had no idea what was coming. Neither did Killian, for that matter.

But it was time for the truth.

"We here?" Killian suddenly asked, straightening as Miami pulled through the portico along the semicircular drive and parked her Camry next to the row of new, sparkling Jeeps.

"We're here," she agreed. She stepped into the coolish night. The stars overhead were bright and hard, a stiff breeze having blown the clouds away. She could smell the bay. She sensed she would remember this moment a long time. The before.

She smiled at Carroll as she walked toward him. Carroll looked past her, to where Killian was practically pouring himself out of her vehicle.

"He's drunk," Carroll observed.

"Egan Fogherty was murdered," she said.

"You're not drunk."

"No."

"You don't even seem particularly . . . moved."

"I'm scared," she admitted, but realized she'd developed a surprisingly stiff backbone somewhere along the way. Sean had helped do that for her. Their secret feelings had been bubbling beneath the surface a long time before they'd finally acted on them, tearing off their clothes at his apartment one of the few nights she'd been free of Killian, who normally stuck to her like glue. Since then, they'd grabbed time together whenever they could. Both of them had been late for work more times than either wanted to admit.

Miami and Carroll entered the foyer, which soared two stories to a dome-shaped skylight. Miami looked up through the glass at the stars again. She thought about how nervous she'd been when Carroll had approached her at work and given her his and Faye's blessing to marry their son. She felt light-headed as she headed toward the dining room. Faye entered through a side door wearing a dark blue dress and the necklace of pearls she sported at every family event. She probably wore them to bed as well. Miami had never seen her without them.

Miami could hear Sally, the caterer, in the kitchen, and she appeared a moment later with four cocktails, Maker's Mark for Carroll and Killian, gin and tonic for Faye, pinot gris for Miami. Miami accepted her glass but didn't drink from it. Her fingers were clenched so tightly around the wineglass's stem, she thought there was a chance she could break it. With an effort, she loosened her grip and took a sip. There was a distant buzzing in her ears and it felt a little as if she were looking at the three of them down a long tube. The periphery of her vision seemed to be closing in.

"I have something to say," she said in a breathy voice.

"Wait till we sit down, dear," Faye said. "My, my, you look as if you've seen a ghost."

"Don't have anymore," Carroll told his son scathingly, to which Killian lifted his glass and drank thirstily, holding his father's gaze.

"I can't have children," Miami said, unwilling to wait a moment longer. "I had a hysterectomy shortly after graduation. I had ovarian cancer. I also had an abortion, which is how the cancer was found."

"What?" Killian shifted his attention to her. "What?"

Faye inhaled a sharp breath and clasped her pearls with her free hand. Carroll eyed her carefully.

"My parents never wanted me to tell. They were afraid of you all, afraid of your power in Edwards Bay."

"They're not afraid of me," Killian disputed.

"I wasn't really talking to you." She turned to his father. "Sorry, Mr. Keenan. You might have had another football player if our baby had lived."

"You aborted Keenan's baby?" Carroll asked, his face reddening.

"*What?*" Killian looked at her like she was batshit crazy. He struggled to process. "What the fuck . . . sorry, Mom . . .

hell are you talking about! We always used protection. Every time!"

"Yes, I know," said Miami.

"So, you're lying . . . or . . . it wasn't mine?" He looked at her and realized she was staring down his father.

Carroll Keenan made a choking sound, then pulled himself together and started a slow clap. "Nice performance."

"It was your baby," she said.

"Now listen, Mia," his father began, but Miami cut him off.

"You're not going to advise me to call you 'Carroll,' are you?" she demanded harshly. She'd practiced this scenario so many times in her head, it was like being in a play. He was right about the performance. She was acting, but she wasn't lying. She'd been meek all her life. Meek and afraid. And though her stomach was currently tied in knots, her resolve was firm. She wouldn't back down now for anything, and in that vein she turned to Faye, who was standing by gray-faced and slack-lipped. Miami suspected her gin and tonic was about to slip from her grasp. "It was one night when we were all underage drinking. I was asleep on your couch. I came to and he was inside me. No condom. Killian's right. He's always been a stickler for birth control, but not his father apparently." She turned to Carroll. "When I found you atop me, you said it was because Killian said I was the best. More than a four. Top of the chart."

"I told you I accepted you!" Carroll sputtered. "I said you could marry my son!"

"Because of the mood of the country," Miami said, looking directly at the man who'd raped her. "#MeToo's scared you, I'll bet." She set down her drink on the pressed silver tablecloth, a little amazed at the steadiness of her fingers. "So now I'm going to take this matter to the police. Maybe they won't do anything about it. Maybe it's been too long, or they won't believe me. I don't know. Or maybe they will do something."

"Lies!" Carroll decreed in a booming voice.

"Oh, Carroll . . ." Faye whispered. "With a high school girl?"

"*Lies!* She's . . . always been a goddamn lying whore!"

"Dad?" Killian squeaked out, staring in horror.

"She's lying. All these years later? It's all lies. You know it's all lies!"

"We were at that party at the end of the year," Miami said to Killian. "Where you and Nick got into that fight. Nick blamed you for Lisette's death and he had you on the ground."

"That was horseplay!" Carroll declared. "The concrete fell on his—"

"Shut up, Dad." Killian glared at his father, then at Miami. "Nick attacked me and I got my foot caught and he yanked me around, tore up my ankle."

"You attacked Nick," Miami corrected. "And your ankle was an accident, or maybe just deserts. And I came back home with you that night. We didn't know how bad your ankle was. We just were trying to hide that we were drunk from your parents. You passed out and I slept on the downstairs couch, but your dad came downstairs and found me."

Silence fell. And then Killian suddenly leaped toward his father and they crashed against the sideboard. Faye screamed and Waterford crystal rattled behind the hutch's glass doors. The impact knocked those doors open and crystal goblets, bowls, and silverware smashed to the hardwood floor in the most God-awful crash and clatter Miami had ever heard.

Killian and Carroll had broken apart, breathing hard. Faye was standing amid the twinkling shards of glass, her hands raised as if she were involved in a stickup. Killian went after his dad once more, slipped on glass, and slammed into him, and they both went down.

"Shit," Killian muttered, lifting an arm that held a piece of crystal sticking out.

Sally had come to the kitchen door and stood there in wide-eyed shock, her mouth an O of disbelief.

Faye clutched her pearls with both hands and turned tear-filled eyes to Miami. "You filthy slut," she cried out.

Miami turned and left.

Kerry put her cell phone away and asked Marcia, "What are you doing here?"

"I wanted to see Jerry," she cried, tears still streaking down her chin. "I just wanted to see him."

"Well, I'm going inside." She almost left her standing on the sidewalk in front of the house but said instead, "You want to tell him what you've done, then come on in."

"I can't tell him. It wasn't my idea," she moaned.

"Then tell him that, too," Kerry said in disgust, and Marcia, after a few moments, followed after her up the steps and onto the porch.

Cole was glad to see the press had dispersed by the time he got back to the station, but when he entered he learned Youngston wasn't there. Charlie was, though.

"Ben called Sean Blevins, I think, before he left. I'm not sure he got an answer," she said.

Cole nodded, but his anger at Ben was a rock inside his gut. He'd worked hard on his appearance of impassivity over the years since his brother's death, had been determined not to let anyone see his pain or emotion ever again. But he was having a real hard time hiding his feelings right now.

Charlie went on, "I left messages on Mia, Josie, and Taryn's phones, asking them to call me. None of them picked up. I did just get a call from Jill Potts at Brighter Day, though. I pushed Ted Perry about Justin's customers and he wouldn't say anything, but now he wants to see me. He doesn't have a phone, so Jill called me. I think I'd better talk to him while he's willing."

"You're heading to Brighter Day tonight?" Cole asked.

"Might as well."

As Charlie got ready to leave, Cole pulled out his cell and put a call in to Youngston. He'd hoped to confront him at the station, but clearly that wasn't going to happen.

"Yo," Ben answered, his tone and demeanor meant to irk Cole, which it did.

"Where are you?"

"Doing what you said, Chief. Investigating."

"Are you with one of the Blevinses?"

"No, I'm at the Wrights with Adam."

"The Wrights?" Cole asked. He could hear a television in the background.

"Oh, Cecily called, looking for her keys," Charlie whispered. "But Adam hadn't brought 'em in. She just couldn't find them."

Ben seemed oblivious to the fact that Cole knew about the break-in to Nick's apartment and Kerry's home. His blood boiled, but he forced himself to stay cool. He clearly hadn't spoken to Marcia yet. In fact, it seemed like he was off work and just hanging with Adam Wright, who was in the same graduating class, the same one as the A-Team. "Okay, I'll be right there."

"What? Why?" Ben sounded alarmed.

Cole clicked off and followed Charlie out the door.

* * *

". . . and I just wanted to be with him," Marcia said, achingly sad, "and I couldn't be. It was over and I threw the ring at him, and I just wanted it back. Ben had the keys, so . . ." She shrugged, crying softly.

Jerry was seated in his chair. He'd turned the sound down on the television and now he looked at Kerry. Kerry immediately worried she'd made a mistake inviting Marcia in, given Jerry's iffy health, but he'd shown remarkable fortitude. It was almost like Marcia's misery was a tonic. Her crime could be forgiven beneath her love for his son. Or maybe it was just a relief to see Marcia acting like a human being with a heart for once. Whatever the case, Marcia's appearance had done Jerry more good than harm.

Kerry's cell phone gave an aborted ring. She looked down at the screen. Josie.

Then the screen went blank. The damn thing was toast.

"Could I borrow your cell phone, Jerry?" she asked.

"It's not charged."

"You want mine?" Marcia asked with a sniff.

"Do you mind?" Kerry hated to be beholden to her, but, for the moment at least, Marcia was a pathetic puddle.

Marcia handed it over and gave her the access code. Kerry immediately called Josie back, but she didn't answer. She struggled to remember Josie's number so she could text her . . . and failed.

She had a bad feeling about it. "Josie's at the motel and she called me, but she didn't answer. Do you mind if I leave for a few minutes?"

"I'm perfectly fine," Jerry told her with his usual hand flap.

"I'll stay," said Marcia.

"What about Audra?" Kerry asked.

"She likes being by herself." As Kerry started to protest, Marcia lifted a hand to stop her. "But there's a sitter with her tonight. I wanted to . . . see Jerry . . . and talk about Nick. And I wanted to see you, too."

Kerry thought she might have been telling the truth about Jerry, but that last part was definitely a lie. But it didn't matter.

You shouldn't go out. You promised Cole you'd be extra-careful.

But she was nervous about Josie. And it wasn't that far to the motel. And she had Marcia's cell phone.

The motel was quiet and dark except for the windows of her unit as she arrived. She pulled into the back lot in her usual spot and saw Josie's Prius. No other cars were around. The workers had left neat piles of lumber and there was a stack of tile beside some of Kerry's gardening paraphernalia, but their tools and machinery were safely locked up. Nothing looked out of place.

She went to the back door and found it locked. Good. Josie had taken precautions. She rang the bell, but when nothing happened, she slipped her key in the lock and twisted the knob.

"Jose?" she called softly when she entered.

Nothing. The room was empty.

Was she in the bedroom?

Kerry hesitated, then tiptoed across the kitchen. Something caught her eye. Something different.

She glanced over the kitchen, and it took a moment before she saw the glass vase was gone from its spot on the shelf.

She turned back just as Josie came flying toward her.

Crash!

The vase smashed into her head and Kerry crumpled to the floor.

Chapter Twenty-Five

Patient: *Okay, Doc. It's confession time.*

Doctor: *You admit to all the killings?*

Patient: *You know serial killers use one methodology. They kill their victims the same way every time, or try to. They go with what works for them, what makes them comfortable.*

Doctor: *That's not what you did.*

Patient: *Nah, I guess you could say I fell into the job by accident. I didn't intend to kill Nick. I didn't want to. He forced me to. By lying to everyone. Pretending to be something he wasn't, and when I figured it out, I had the hypodermic needle with me, so . . . I just did it.*

Doctor: *And Diana?*

Patient: *Saw me. Started remembering. She would've recalled in time. I saw her at the memorial service, wearing that scarf. Again, I didn't really plan to kill her. I just knew she was going to be a problem, so I followed her home. Her balcony doesn't really latch. I learned that the first time I was there. Jiggle it right, you can get in.*

Doctor: *You didn't plan to kill her.*

Patient: *I knew she had to go, but . . . she was still wearing the scarf. I just ran forward and pushed her against the wall and grabbed the ends of her scarf and pulled it tight around her neck. It took a while. A lot harder than you think.*

Doctor: *You took her belongings.*

Patient: *Okay, yeah. I took her purse and keys. Just scooped them up. I just did it to make it seem like a robbery gone bad, but I left the cell. Too easy to trace unless you take the battery out. You know, serial killers often keep things.*

Doctor: *Trophies.*

Patient: *I already had some things of Nick's, so yeah, trophies.*

Doctor: *Did you take something from Egan?*

Patient: *I would've liked his Nikes. Couldn't get 'em. But Doc, I'm really not a serial killer. Not really. So I don't need a trophy from all of them.*

Doctor: *What do you think you are?*

Patient: *Nick and Diana and even Egan . . . They weren't really my aim. If Egan hadn't seen me right after I left Diana's carrying her purse, I would have left him alone. No one listened to him anyway. But he saw me, and though he didn't know the purse was Diana's, he figured it out. He was the one who told me Kerry knew. I believed him. She didn't know, as it turned out, but I spent a few pretty sleepless nights while she and Cole were screwing like rabbits. The chief of police was glued to her. I kept thinking she would tell him, but she didn't* because she didn't know! *Finally, I had my chance to take care of her, and you know how that turned out.*

Doctor: *You used a large rock to kill Egan.*

Patient: *That's what I'm saying about methodology. Mine was different every time. I based it on availability. Kerry was the only one I really planned for, but that didn't work out the way I envisioned.*

Doctor: *What was your end game?*

Patient: *To stop it at its source.*

Doctor: *It?*

Patient: *You already know the answer to that, Doc. This whole Q&A . . . you just want me to corroborate all your theories for you. Make it easy for a conviction. Well, you're going to have to do a little bit of work. This interview is now over.*

Cole pulled up to the curb in front of the Wright home, the nose of his Jeep about a foot into Cecily's driveway. The last time he'd been here he'd dropped Cecily off in front, but this time there weren't any parking spaces on the street. Other residents were home for the evening.

A text came in on his phone: It's Kerry. I have Marcia's phone. Mine died.

He grunted and texted back: Got it.

He was about to go around the driveway and garage to those front steps when a side door to the house opened and Ben came through, Adam following after him. Both men looked ill at ease as they met Cole on the driveway.

"What's going on?" Ben asked Cole.

"You're not working on the case," Cole observed.

"It's after-hours, for sure."

Adam said, "We were just getting ready to go out. Just checking on Mom first."

Cole said to Ben, "You talked to Marcia lately?"

"Marcia?" Ben asked with feigned innocence.

"Your recent . . . date?" Cole felt a vein pulsing in the side of his head.

Adam laughed and looked at Ben. "You dog. You didn't tell me you were dating Miss Seashell."

But Ben wasn't laughing. He was watching Cole carefully, with the same regard he would give a poisonous snake. "I have been seeing a little of Marcia."

"But that ring on her finger. That was from Nick."

Ben licked his lips. "I guess. She's got a lot of rings."

Cole cut to the chase. "You and Marcia went to Palo Alto with Nick's keys from the property room and broke into his condo. Marcia took back her wedding ring and you helped her. Maybe you took something else. We'll have to see."

"I don't know what you're talking about," he tried to bluster.

"Yes, you do. And you did this, you risked your job, for what? Love?"

Adam stared at Ben in wonder.

"I don't know who you've been talking to."

"Marcia," Cole declared coldly.

The garage door started lifting and they all three looked over.

"Marcia told Kerry what you did. And that she gave you the keys to The Sand Drift units and you turned on all the lights, trying to what? Gaslight Kerry? Just so Marcia could get back at her?"

"That's not true," he said uncertainly.

"It is true," Cole stated, realizing only too clearly that Ben had done exactly what Marcia asked. "And you're out of a job. Don't come back. Take it up with the union."

The engine of the car in the garage turned over and its lights came on.

"Mom?" Adam said, looking worriedly toward the vehicle.

"Is your mom in the car?" Ben asked.

With a screech of tires, the Volvo suddenly shot backward. Cole leaped one way, Ben and Adam the other.

Cole blasted his shoulder into a small rock wall as the Volvo smashed into his Jeep, thrusting it into the road. He heard a scream from the other side of the driveway. Oblivious, Cecily backed all the way across the road, took out the neighbor's mailbox with a screech of torqued metal, then motored on down the road toward town.

Shit, Cole thought, slowly getting to his feet. His shoulder was wrenched, something strained, maybe broken.

On the other side of the driveway Adam was blathering, "I knew it. I knew it. I knew it! She can't have a license. Goddamn it! She can't have a license!"

Ben lay on his side, his leg twisted at an impossible angle. "Help," he whispered.

Cole gritted his teeth against his own pain, found his phone in his back pocket, dialed 911.

Charlie showed up at Brighter Day and was admitted to the dining hall, where Ted Perry was hunched once more at the end of one of the benches, and once again Charlie slid onto the bench opposite him.

"You wanted to tell me something?" she asked.

"I wanted to tell you about her."

"Her," Charlie repeated.

"The customer. The one who wanted the heroin. I only saw her once, er, twice, I guess. Justin didn't want me to know his customers. She seemed so nice, but I think she wasn't."

"You don't know her name?"

"Uh-uh. But I think she killed him." His words were so soft, she could scarcely hear them. "And she's gonna kill me if I tell."

"We're going to make sure that doesn't happen."

He gave her a look wise beyond his years that said she couldn't promise any such thing.

"What did she look like?" asked Charlie.

"Pretty," he said after a moment. "Not like you'd think a killer would look."

* * *

Kerry came to slowly. She'd been lost in a hazy twilight, not completely out, not completely in. She could hear voices. Raised in anger. Several voices. One of them she recognized as Josie's. Another one—male—was roaring, "Fuck you, fuck you, fuck you!"

BLAM!

A gunshot?

Josie's terrorized shriek rose to the ceiling and rang on and on, filling Kerry's ears. She shivered from head to toe. She was lying in the bedroom, in front of the bathroom door. The voices were in the kitchen.

"You shot me," the male voice cried in shock. Killian.

BLAM, BLAM, BLAM!

"Oh, God . . . oh, God . . . oh, God . . ." Josie moaned. "He's dead. He's dead. He has to be dead!"

"Nobody deserved to die more," a hard female voice pointed out.

Taryn.

It wasn't Josie who'd come after her. It was Taryn, Kerry realized dully. She'd just thought it had to be Josie.

"What are you crying for?" Taryn yelled now. "Would you cry that way over *Chad*?"

"I don't know what you want," Josie blubbered.

"We're together in this, right?"

"I'm not . . . I can't . . ."

"You asked for my help. I came over. I even brought you *muffins*."

"But Kerry . . . you hit Kerry . . . and you shot Killian."

"Kerry knows too much . . . for that matter, so do you. Didn't expect you to be here, but now you gotta pick sides, Josie. Are you with me or not?"

Silence.

"Josie," Taryn warned.

"I'm with you," she said in a small voice.

"I don't believe you."

"Taryn, I can't . . . we need 9-1-1. Killian . . . and Kerry could be dying."

"That's kind of the point, isn't it? Kerry knows about me. Egan said so."

"I don't . . . know if—"

"All we have to say is Killian came after Kerry because she knew he'd killed Nick and Diana. He hated them both. Everyone knew it. So that isn't even a lie. And Egan got in the way and even solicited you for sex, so Killian killed him, too."

"I don't know if Egan was really telling the truth about Kerry. I don't think she knows about you. He fabricates all the time."

"Fabricates. There you go again." Taryn laughed indulgently. "Josie, we should have been best friends in high school. I was so jealous of you, y'know? You and Miami and Lisette. I wasn't sorry when she killed herself. When Nick nailed her, she zoomed up to a four. But then she had sex with all the guys and her popularity tanked. Four to zero. She just gave it up for anybody."

"That's not true . . ."

"Yes, it is. Killian had her. And Sean. Maybe even Forrest and Egan and God knows who else."

"That wasn't the way Lisette was."

"She was a slut and so was Miami. You, though, you only had sex with Caulfield."

"That's not true either. I don't know what's happening. You know all that isn't true, right?" Josie's tone had changed from terror to pleading for reason.

Kerry lifted her head, which was pounding like something was hammering from within her skull. She squinted against the pain. The first thing she saw was Marcia's cell phone, which had apparently skittered from her pocket when she was dragged into this room. She tried to reach for it, fighting a groan. Taryn wanted her dead. Believed she'd seen something she hadn't.

"If Kerry knows, don't you think Cole knows, too?" Josie asked.

There was a long, low moan. Killian.

"Shit. He's still alive."

"No, wait, wait! Don't shoot him again. If you want to pin this on Kerry, let it play out. You called him over here to take the fall. You gotta make it look real."

"I don't want to listen to him anymore."

"Just . . . please wait . . ."

"Are you fucking with me, Josie?"

Kerry's fingers touched the edge of the phone. She tried to clasp it, but it slipped from her grasp. Her hands were slick. Blood. Her blood. Dripped from her head onto her hand.

"No, no. I'm not," Josie assured her.

"Yes, you are. You're fucking with me. I shoulda shot Kerry instead of listening to you."

"No, I—"

Bang!

Kerry cried out, a soft peep, but it wasn't heard over Taryn's sudden burst of laughter. Josie? She'd shot Josie?

But the text that came in next was a loud trill of notes that sounded as if they were pealing from a bell tower. Marcia's phone.

Kerry cringed, tossed the cell out of reach, and played dead, but not before seeing Cole's message: I'm at Jerry's. You on your way back?

Footsteps running toward her. Kerry lay still, mouth open, pretending to take in struggling breaths.

Then a crash from the kitchen, frantic footsteps, and the bang of the back door.

"JOSIEEEEEE!" Taryn shrieked in horror near her ear, and then she was chasing after her.

Kerry struggled for the phone once more, working her way over to it, finally grasping it and painstakingly typing: **Motel. Taryn killer.** "Be careful," she whispered, hitting Send and collapsing back, spent.

"Get yourself to a hospital," Marcia practically screeched when she saw how weak Cole's arm was, recognized his pain.

"I'm fine," he bit out. He was still angry with her for a lot of things, not the least being Ben's and her illuminating the motel unit.

He'd tersely told her what had happened to Ben and that he'd sent Hoffman out to track down Cecily to stop her from further havoc and danger. Adam was going to look for his mom, too, after waiting with Ben for the ambulance, while Cole left to ostensibly take care of himself, though he was more anxious to connect with Kerry since she'd left him the message that she had Marcia's phone.

"You aren't fine," Marcia said, going into caretaker mode.

He ignored her and texted Kerry another message. **I'm at Jerry's. You on your way back?**

A text came in. Cole jumped on it, but it was from Charlie: **Perry said Justin's killer was a woman ... heroin customer. Can recognize her.**

Cole pushed aside the dull pain in his arm and thought hard. Justin's death was a homicide and the killer was a woman? Was it connected to Nick's death? The "heroin customer" who'd bought from Justin just days before the kid had died? Everyone had used "he" and "him" in connection with Nick's killer, even the hypnotist, though that had been Diana's supposition at the time.

But Justin's killer was a woman?

That his friend, Ted Perry, could recognize? Ted Perry of Brighter Day.

"Shit," he muttered.

He could almost hear Taryn giving her speech at Nick's memorial service, lauding Nick's philanthropic goals, saying he was leaving everything to the homeless shelter.

"You need a doctor," Marcia said.

He punched in Charlie's number. "It's Taryn Whitcomb," he said as soon as she answered.

"Our killer?" Charlie asked in surprise.

"We need to pick her up and find out. Tell Spano and Hoffman to get to her apartment."

"On it. What about Ben?"

"He's . . . incapacitated. I'm on my way to the station."

He was in the Jeep, rolling, when his cell phone beeped its text sound:

Motel. Taryn killer.

"JOSIEEE . . . JOSIEEE . . ." came Taryn's singsong voice from outside.

Josie was alive.

Gathering all her strength, Kerry got to her feet. She swayed. She couldn't move her head without dizziness. Marcia's phone slipped from her grasp. She bent down to pick it up and nearly fell over. She staggered, and her foot hit the phone, sending it shooting away once more. She had to get out while she could. Had to hide somewhere; she didn't have the strength to run.

But where?

She stumbled into the living room, was blasted by the

lights. Killian was sprawled on the kitchen floor, staring up at the ceiling with a surprised look on his face. Dead.

With an effort, she pushed on the plywood wall to access the office, squeezing through, biting her lip so hard to keep from crying out that she drew blood. The fingers of her right hand were red with rivulets of blood. She left bloody marks on the keypad as she pushed in the code to the safe. The whir of the safe door as it opened sounded like a helicopter to Kerry's ears. She reached in and grabbed the master key, shut the safe door once more.

She was moving on autopilot. At the office door she slumped against the blinds that covered the glass panels.

"Who the fuck are you?" Taryn asked, just feet outside her door. Kerry jumped about a foot then froze in fear.

Blam!

Male screams of pain.

Blam!

Cole!

Silence.

No . . . no . . . not Cole. Taryn knew Cole. Not Cole. *Not Cole.* She heard Taryn's footsteps run away and disappear and then, farther away, down by unit twelve maybe, or even around the side to the back . . .

"JOSIEEEEEEE . . ."

Kerry unlocked the office door and let herself outside. The cool air fanned her face, woke her up a bit. Her movements sounded loud, too loud. A stampede of sound. She stumbled toward unit one, nearly falling. The body caught her up and she toppled, only saved by her hand connecting with the motel's new shingled siding.

Who had she tripped over?

She covered her mouth with her hand and looked down. She could see the circle of black on the white skin of his forehead. The moon was a sliver, casting almost no light, but she recognized her ex-husband.

Dead. Dead like Killian. Vaughn hadn't left when she told him to. He'd needed money, so he'd stayed.

Oh, God.

Please, please, please let Josie get away. Please . . .

She held the master key in a death grip. If she lost it now, she'd never find it again. She moved her way to the door of unit one, her hand braced on the siding, where she suspected she was leaving a bloody trail. Nothing she could do about that.

She threaded the key in the lock and turned, feeling blessed when the tumblers clicked and the door opened. New hinges. Quiet hinges. She let herself inside. Cole had the message. He would be here. He would save them. She closed the door, twisted the lock, and turned around, smack into something hard that slammed into her waist. She gasped, clapped a hand to her mouth, her heart galloping.

The tile saw.

"JOSIEEEEE . . ." she heard outside, coming closer again.

She moved behind the tile saw to just outside the bathroom door. She could see through the rectangular window above the shower/tub combo to faintly lighter sky beyond, lit by distant stars.

And then she heard footsteps stop outside unit one's door.

"Josie," Taryn said with triumph. "Nicked you after all, didn't I?"

She'd seen the blood.

Kerry shrank to the wall, crouching down. If Taryn had a flashlight . . . but the curtains were drawn. New curtains. Just installed.

Crash!

Kerry gasped as a rock smashed through the front window of the unit. An arm came through, fighting the curtain, groping for the door handle. "How'd you get in there?" Taryn asked. "Sneak a key?"

Cole. Hurry . . . hurry . . .

She had nothing to defend herself with.

She reached around her, hoping for a forgotten piece of wood, or metal, or anything, but this unit was the only one carpeted. Damn near finished.

Her frantic fingers encountered a cord. The cord to the tile saw. She slid it through her hand until she reached the prong. Fumbling along the wall, she landed on an electrical outlet.

Her eyes were on the door. She could barely see, but she could hear, and the reaching hand found the door latch, which snapped back with a soft *nick*.

Panicking inside, Kerry willed her jerking fingers to connect the prongs to the outlet.

The door flew inward, banged against the wall. Taryn switched on the light and illumination blasted Kerry's eyes. Now that she could see, she was looking down the barrel of a gun.

Blam!

Sheetrock exploded beside Kerry from the bullet as she instantly ducked and flicked the switch on the tile saw. Its whining screech and blurring saw deafened. Taryn said something Kerry couldn't hear. If she could, she'd shove the damn thing at her, but as it was, there was nothing she could do but make a loud distraction. The safety mechanism wasn't working and the blade kept spinning without Kerry's hand on the control.

"You bitch!" she saw Taryn's mouth say.

And then she suddenly pitched forward. One second she was standing, the next her head came forward into the blade. Her ear shredded.

Kerry screamed and so did Taryn, staggering backward, clutching her head, falling to the floor.

In the doorway stood Josie, bleeding from somewhere near her own ear, a rake held in her hands like a baseball bat.

Kerry's senses swam. She sank back and unplugged the saw. As the screeching sound wound down, she saw Cole rush into the room, holding his own gun on Taryn, who was writhing, holding her ear and screaming.

Josie still held the rake, standing over Taryn. She wouldn't let go even when the paramedics arrived to take them all to the hospital.

Clasping Cole's hand until her gurney was lifted into the ambulance, Kerry's last two memories were of Josie taking her rake into a second ambulance and Cole whispering in her ear that he loved her.

Chapter Twenty-Six

The hospital discharged Kerry late Tuesday afternoon. Cole had been seen to in the ER, treated for a cracked scapula and wrenched ligaments. It had been suggested they strap his arm to his body, but he'd refused and was now in a shoulder sling with stinging words of warning ringing in his ears. Now he was with Kerry as the nurse pushed her wheelchair into the hall.

"How's Josie?" she asked Cole as they neared the front doors.

"Lucky. Grazed by a bullet at near point-blank range. She moved in the split-second before the shot. She's probably going to have some PTSD. So are you, for that matter."

"No. I'm fine. I'm grateful. So grateful."

Kerry had escaped with a large knot on her head and a line of twenty stitches over her right ear, which would necessitate a very strange hairstyle for the near future, but she was lucky. No bleeding on the brain and only a mild concussion.

Cole clasped her hand and squeezed, their silent signal to each other that they were there for each other.

"What about Killian . . . and Vaughn?" she asked, though she already knew the answer.

Cole shook his head and Kerry nodded, swallowing against a dry throat.

They returned to Jerry's house, more so Jerry could see them than for any other reason. Marcia had stayed the night, but Jerry had shooed her out in the morning. "A little goes a long way," he said of his one-time daughter-in-law. "Besides, she needed to relieve the babysitter. She's bringing Audra over this afternoon."

Once Jerry was satisfied that both Kerry and Cole were going to be okay, and he'd assured them he, too, was fine, fine, definitely fine, they headed to Cole's place, where both of them got cleaned up. Kerry, having picked up her overnight bag from Jerry's, changed into fresh jeans and a long-sleeved, gray T-shirt she gingerly pulled over her head. Cole was also in jeans and he'd buttoned on a dark shirt carefully over his shoulder.

"Hurt?" she asked him.

"I'll survive."

Taryn was still in the hospital. There was no ear to stitch back on.

"You talked to her this morning," Kerry said.

"Some. She's meeting with a psychiatrist. She's had a break with reality."

"Think she'll go to prison?"

He shook his head.

"Did she say anything about Nick? They were friends. She adored him. I don't understand how this all started."

Cole moved to his couch and Kerry came with him. "I've got a few minutes before I talk to the press again. Charlie Paige has been front and center for me, but she needs a break. The media's hot for this story."

"Well, sure," said Kerry. "Can you tell me what Taryn said?"

"Yeah."

When Cole had entered her hospital room, seeing her

head swathed from one side to the other, he'd felt a bit sorry for her. Even with all the crimes she'd committed, she'd looked pale and vulnerable lying in the bed. But her attitude had disabused him of that feeling almost immediately.

"Yesterday was a bad day," she said, and then she told him about being let go because the "asshole who sexually harassed me" finally got to her boss. She was thinking about suing the company, and it hadn't helped when she'd tried for a job with Keenan Motors and Killian had laughed her out of the place.

"I always meant to kill him," she admitted. "Way back in high school, I told myself if no one else did it, I would. He's the only one I wanted to get."

"But you killed Nick and Diana and Egan first."

"You know about the rating system?" she asked, ignoring his comment. "I was heavier in high school. Some of those guys didn't think I was worth putting on the chart. Miami was at the top, and Lisette. They were Lady-Killerian and Nick's girls. Everyone wanted Josie, too, but apart from Lawrence Caulfield, who's a liar, they're right, she stayed out of it. Diana was rated like a two. There were other girls on the chart, too. I mean, the A-Team weren't the only fours. Some of the guys wanted to add Miss Seashell, but she was a couple of years younger and another one of Nick's conquests anyway, so . . . Killian had lots of girls, and his dad got involved with rating them. All the dads did. They haggled over which of us were fours . . . Nick said they bet on their sons, which girls they would nail next. If a girl took a long time to give it up, she scored more points. Too easy, well, bottom rung."

"How do you know all this?" Cole asked her.

"Well, Nick. He was guilt-ridden. Couldn't hardly talk about anything else at the end. He was going to tell the world about it all. He didn't even look at me like that and I'd gotten myself in killer shape. Killian even told me that

I'd gone up a few spots, was almost top tier. Totally sexist. I knew he had to die, even though it felt good."

"When was that?"

"Last year. He never got over it. Neither did his dad, or Sean's dad or Forrest's. They never really quit playing the game. The only one who did was Nick."

"Then why . . . ?"

"Everything was fine. Nick and I were good friends, but we were really falling in love. And then Diana sneaked in there, and I could tell . . . I could tell Nick liked her. He said she was herself, and that we shouldn't judge her. She turned his head, even made him laugh a time or two. She was just like that. All sex and drugs and Nick . . ." Her chin trembled at the memory and she gazed out the window. "Diana had given him a pill at The Whistle Stop. I don't know if he even knew at first, but he was going with it. And then he went home with her, and she was so out of it, she didn't even know! My cousin's diabetic and I had a syringe, and I'd scored some smack earlier. I just . . . kind of knew."

"From Justin Drury?"

That stopped Taryn for a moment. "How'd you know that?"

"Did you kill him, too?"

"He tried to shake me down, the little shit. I didn't want to hurt him. I didn't want to hurt Nick! I wanted Killian, but others kept getting in the way. Egan too. And Kerry . . . she knew about me. Egan told her."

"I don't know where you heard that, but it's not true."

"Egan told me."

"Kerry didn't know you were the one who'd killed her stepbrother and the others until you attacked Josie at her apartment."

"Josie. I thought she was Kerry. And she met me at the door with that vase in her hand, like she was going to clobber me, so I wrestled it away from her. I thought both she and Kerry knew. I scared Josie, but I knew she thought guys were the problem, so we were a team." Her face darkened. "Until she turned against me."

"You brought the gun?"

"For Kerry," she said. "When she came to the door, Josie and I were hiding in the bedroom. I knew Josie wanted to yell out, so I told her I wouldn't shoot Kerry but she had to stay silent. I kept to my promise, though she did yell out when I kit Kerry with the vase. I smacked Josie with the vase for that, too. I think I broke one of her perfect teeth."

Cole had seen Josie, who, besides the bullet streak along the side of her head, had indeed suffered a broken incisor.

"And then I called Killian. He was drunk and raving about Miami and his father and an abortion? Said he was gonna kill 'em both. He's the one who got the gun for me a couple of years ago, when I asked for it. Said I needed it for protection. It's funny now, huh. Don't you think? I told him Miami was with me at the motel."

"What happened when he got there?"

"Well, he was pissed when he realized Miami wasn't there. He started yelling and was mad and I was sick of it, and I wanted him dead for so long . . . so I just pulled out the gun and shot him. A bunch of times. And then . . . the cell phone rang . . . and I ran to grab it, and Josie got away. She wasn't with me after all! I started chasing her down, but that guy was there and he saw me, so I had to kill him, too. Kerry's ex-husband. Guess he didn't know you were in the picture?"

"So you intended to kill Killian, but the others just got in the way."

"I'm just telling you a fable, Mr. Chief of Police. Just something you want to hear."

"What?" Cole asked cautiously.

"I'm just talking. None of it's true."

"Other people's accounts suggest it is."

She shook her head, smiling.

"Why did you call Kerry at three a.m. after you killed Diana?" Cole asked, but she merely shrugged and spread her hands.

Now Kerry said, "I think Taryn likes to keep people guessing. I don't know if you're going to get much more out of her."

He exhaled heavily. "You may be right. She stayed with the story, then suddenly switched to another reality. We've learned a cousin of hers is diabetic and that's where she got the hypodermic idea. She probably got it for Killian, but then Nick betrayed her with Diana."

"It's terrible," Kerry bit out.

Cole nodded and silence pooled between them.

After a few moments Kerry shook her head and said, "I can't believe Vaughn's gone, too. And Killian."

"If you hadn't stopped her, she would have killed more of you."

"You said Josie and Miami and the rest of the group are meeting at the Blarney Stone this afternoon?"

Cole looked at her in disbelief. "You're not thinking of going, are you?"

"I'd like to see them. Make sure they're okay."

Her hazel eyes silently begged him and he was no proof against them. "All right. I'm going to the station, but I'll be back soon and we'll go together."

Josie sat at her kitchen island, drinking a cup of tea her newly solicitous husband had made her. Actually, solicitous wasn't quite right. Predatory was closer to the truth. He was lying in wait, watching her like a hawk, keeping her in his sights . . . all the clichés that boiled down to the fact that he thought he had her now. The wounded bird come home to roost.

He'd been waiting for her when she was checked out of the hospital. She'd let him take her home and he'd slept in the spare room last night, giving her the bedroom. His conversation had been all soft and sweet. Prince Charming. But he was waiting . . . She'd worried that she might go back to him, that he would convince her to give their marriage another try. But that was before yesterday, before she'd been shot at and lost a tooth. Her tongue probed the shattered incisor. She had a dentist appointment tomorrow.

Currently, Kent was telling her about the calls he'd been receiving from damn near the whole world, it sounded like. Everyone wishing her a speedy recovery. Everyone wanting to know exactly what had happened. Who the heroes were. Who the villains were. How close a friend she was to Taryn Whitcomb, and did she have any idea, any inkling, about Taryn's murderous soul?

Miami had called, a brief conversation during which they'd checked with each other, making sure they were both basically okay. Miami said she'd tell Josie all about her bout with cancer and how its discovery had come about, the abortion and Carroll Keenan. Josie in turn said she had a lot to tell her, not only about her experiences at the motel with Taryn, but about what was happening in her life. They planned to get together next week for a one-on-one.

But for now, decisions needed to be made.

As if recognizing the time for a serious discussion was nigh himself, Kent leaned back against the counter across from where she was sitting, clasping the quartzite edge as if bracing himself. "So . . . we should probably talk about a few things . . ."

"Like what? Closing off my debit card? I imagine the credit card suffered the same fate."

He laughed apologetically. "I just put a hold on them. They're already reinstated."

"My name isn't on the house, or the car."

"Well, no . . . we should have done that, but we never did."

"You took care of everything," she said matter-of-factly.

He hesitated, clearly finding Josie's terse questioning a new and probably unpleasant characteristic in his previously affable wife. "We can fix that." He spread his hands.

"How are you getting along with your folks these days?"

"Fine," he said cautiously, clearly wondering where this was going.

"They've never liked me. They've kept you on a tight string financially and emotionally all the years of our marriage, and you've bowed to them all that time. I'm not even sure why you married me, although maybe it didn't matter. Whatever power play you and your family are in was there before me, and it will undoubtedly be after me as well."

"I think we need to talk about you and me, not my parents."

"That's the point, isn't it? It isn't just about you and me. It's about them, and their money, and your position in the community, which could be threatened by this scandal."

"You weren't a part of that whole ratings thing," he said quickly.

"I knew enough about it that I should have done something. It's not okay that I didn't push. Somebody should've opened this up years ago."

"Oh, for God's sake, Josie. When did you become Joan of Arc?"

"You just don't want me to be part of the scandal. Kind of proves your parents right, huh? You marrying beneath yourself." She slid off her stool and walked out of the room.

"Where are you going?" he clipped out.

"To the ATM, to see if you've really reinstated my card." She picked up her purse and cell phone.

"When are you coming back?"

"Good question. I'll let you know when there's an answer." She headed toward the garage and realized her car was still at The Sand Drift. She hesitated, but had no intention of going back inside and ruining her exit. Pulling up the Uber app on her phone, she headed outside through the garage door to wait by the curb.

When she saw the Uber vehicle approach she nodded to herself. Fate.

Lawrence Caulfield got out and opened the back door for her. "Hi, Josie."

"Hi, Lawrence." She climbed inside and they pulled away from the curb.

"I'm probably the last person you want to see," he said.

"Oh, not the last person, but pretty close."

"Where to?"

"The Sand Drift and my car."

"I'm sorry for everything that happened to you and the rest of your friends. Nobody can get their head around it."

"Thanks."

"And I'm also sorry for being such an asshole in high school. I don't know what was wrong with me."

"Try malignant narcissism," she said, which pretty much ended their conversation till they reached the motel.

"Hope you're okay," he said as she got out of the car.

"I am, Lawrence. Thanks for asking."

"I've actually got quite a few investments, you know," he said quickly, before she could close the door. "Been making shitloads . . . er, tons . . . of money. I just drive Uber because I like it."

"Hmmm."

"So if you ever need anything . . . ?"

"I'll figure it out on my own." She smiled, shut the

door, walked away, and thought, *Once an asshole, always an asshole.*

She climbed in her Prius and aimed it toward the Blarney Stone.

Miami pulled into the Blarney Stone's back lot and could scarcely find a parking place. She had to wedge into an iffy spot by the tree and another car. Luckily, she had the oldest vehicle in the lot, so it was up to the other drivers to avoid her.

As soon as she stepped out of the car, she saw a man do the same from his, several over, a Ford SUV of some kind. She knew who he was because they'd been hounding her wherever she went. A reporter. Wanting another angle on all the details of her alleged seduction by successful businessman Carroll Keenan, the father of her murdered fiancé.

Alleged seduction? Fiancé? Try rape and former boyfriend.

Former boyfriend. When she thought of Killian, she mostly felt numb. She couldn't believe he was gone. She felt terrible, no doubt. He'd been a huge part of her life for so long, she couldn't remember being without him. But she also felt lighter. Relieved of a terrible burden. If that made her a bad person, so be it.

"Hey, Ms. Miller. I'm Thomas Williams from KST—"

"I know who you are. I have nothing to say."

"Carroll Keenan, who's grieving the death of his only son, is denying your accusations concerning the seduction you allege happened at his home when you were in high school. If—"

She shut off his voice by running up the back steps of the bar and banging the door shut behind her à la Forrest Borland. Despite all the cars in the lot, there were only a handful of people inside, courtesy of the sign that read "Private Party" she'd seen taped to the door on her way in.

She looked around. Her friends were there. The balance of the A-Team anyway. Angie Starr rushed over to her and gave her a full-body hug.

"How did you ever keep that secret so long?" she breathed. "Did Killian know? Are you still cancer-free?"

"Ange," Randy warned.

"I just want to make sure she's all right."

Miami looked past her to Sean, who had been leaning his elbows on the bar but straightened as soon as she showed up. She'd been with him almost every minute since she'd left Killian's house. They'd been together when the news about what had taken place at the motel came in, but she'd insisted they split up when she went to warn her parents of the shitstorm that was undoubtedly on the horizon. Sean had told his father, who had scrambled to find the chart and burn it before it hit the airwaves, blubbering that it had all just been in fun. Sean had walked out on him, as his mother had the night after Nick's memorial service, embarrassed by Millard's remarks and attitude during the event. Sean had told Miami that he looked back on those days in high school in mortification. Yes, he'd made a fumbled pass at Lisette Benetton, which hadn't gone well, but it was because he'd had a crush on her. She was shy and cute and feeling low after Nick Radnor's rejection. Nick hadn't been in love with her, but Sean had. Puppy love maybe, but he'd kissed Lisette, and when she hadn't initially pushed him away, he'd taken things too far too fast. That was bad enough, but what he'd done later, telling Killian to put his name on the chart beside Lisette's, was the real crime. He'd spent years in self-flagellation, putting up a shield that had become his cool attitude. For herself, Miami had been living in a kind of purgatory, burying what had happened with Killian's father, living essentially half a life that she somehow felt she deserved. She hadn't told Sean the depth of what had happened until recently, and then he'd wanted to be with her when she confronted the Keenans, but she would have none of it. She'd needed to confront Carroll Keenan herself, which had led to the debacle at their house the night before.

Now Sean pushed his way between Angie and Miami and held Miami in his arms. She laid her head on his shoulder, and they both looked at their friends.

Forrest goggled at them. "So . . . you two . . . how long has this been going on?"

"A while," said Sean.

"Nick's death . . . and Diana's and Egan's . . . made it impossible to keep it a secret any longer," Miami admitted. "We all saw how life can be taken away."

"Like Killian," Forrest said. "That's just a mind-bender, isn't it?"

The back door slammed open and shut as Josie came in. They all commented on how good she looked, even with a bandage on the side of her head. Was she okay? Amazing she'd escaped that bullet. And the rake? She probably saved Kerry's life! Was she really okay? Really?

"Yep," was all she said.

"Grey Goose martini?" Forrest asked.

"Make it a double," she said with a faint smile that turned into a chuckle when Forrest brought her two glasses.

"Sean's going to sell me his half of the bar. Hopefully the Stone'll survive this," Forrest said as the back door opened once more and Kerry and Cole joined them. "We're all here now," he added. "What's left of us."

Kerry said, "I was never really part of the A-Team."

"Neither were Cole and Angie," Forrest agreed, "but close enough. And I wouldn't turn Miss Seashell away."

"She's home with her daughter," said Kerry.

Randy gave Kerry a somewhat awkward hug in front of his wife, who did manage a nearly inaudible, "I'm glad you're all right."

"Thanks," Kerry said, a bit dryly.

"What about Ben?" Randy asked.

Everyone looked at Cole, who explained that Ben had had surgery on his leg, which had been broken in two places. Cecily Wright had been collected at a grocery store and had been flummoxed by Officer Hoffman and her son suggesting she couldn't drive home. When she'd seen the damage to her car, she'd instructed Hoffman to find the person responsible for hitting her.

"Adam is looking for an assisted living home for her. Maybe Calloway Center," Cole said.

Josie said, "Got a motel room for me, Kerry? I'm leaving my husband."

"You sure you want to stay in one after last night?" Kerry asked.

"Yep," she said.

A silence followed. Everyone knew enough about what had happened with Taryn to almost not want to talk. Forrest poured them all a drink, and they lifted their glasses to those who were gone.

"And to those of us who remain," Forrest added to a chorus of "Hear, hear."

That evening Kerry sat on Cole's couch, watching the news. All of the A-Team's faces were splashed across the screen as the news of the rating system, Miami's accusation against Carroll Keenan, and the string of homicides went nationwide. She was almost glad her cell phone wasn't working, although she'd managed to get it running on a hit-and-miss basis as long as it was plugged in.

"You still watching?" Cole asked when he arrived from

a trip to the police station. Her answer was to switch off
with the remote, to which he said, "I have something for
you," and handed her an envelope.

Her stomach lurched when she saw the name on its face:
Durant Stipe.

"Nick's letter?" she asked. "How'd you get it?"

"I had Charlie wait outside the Barnes and Barnes offices. When Stipe came outside, he was reading the letter.
She told him she was from the police and he thrust it at her
and told her to give it to me."

Kerry unfolded it carefully.

Dear Mr. Stipe,
    *I can never undo the harm I caused you and
your family. I cared a great deal for Lisette. I was
weak and craven not to stand up and speak against
the terrible wrong some of my classmates and their
fathers placed upon the young women of our class.
I am dedicating the rest of my life to making
reparations. I wish with all my heart that Lisette
was still alive. It may be small comfort, but I am
changing the name of my foundation to the Lisette
Benetton Foundation. My sister, Kerry, will make
sure funds are appropriated for charitable causes.*
                    With sincere and heartfelt regret,
                    Nicholas Radnor

Kerry slid into the comfort of Cole's arms. "He *was* a
good guy," she said.

"Yeah."

"He just never had a chance to do all the things he
promised."

"But you can."

"Yes, I can. But it would be better if you and I did it together, right?"

Cole smiled and kissed her lightly on the lips. "Right. I want to do everything together."

"You do?"

"Mmm-hmm. A lot of lost time to make up for."

"I think Nick would like that," Kerry said. "I think he'd like that a lot."

Connect with

U **s**

Visit us online at
KensingtonBooks.com
to read more from your favorite authors, see books
by series, view reading group guides, and more.

Join us on social media

for sneak peeks, chances to win books and prize packs,
and to share your thoughts with other readers.

facebook.com/kensingtonpublishing
twitter.com/kensingtonbooks

Tell us what you think!

To share your thoughts, submit a review,
or sign up for our eNewsletters, please visit:
KensingtonBooks.com/TellUs.

Romantic Suspense from
Lisa Jackson

Absolute Fear	0-8217-7936-2	$7.99US/$9.99CAN
Afraid to Die	1-4201-1850-1	$7.99US/$9.99CAN
Almost Dead	0-8217-7579-0	$7.99US/$10.99CAN
Born to Die	1-4201-0278-8	$7.99US/$9.99CAN
Chosen to Die	1-4201-0277-X	$7.99US/$10.99CAN
Cold Blooded	1-4201-2581-8	$7.99US/$8.99CAN
Deep Freeze	0-8217-7296-1	$7.99US/$10.99CAN
Devious	1-4201-0275-3	$7.99US/$9.99CAN
Fatal Burn	0-8217-7577-4	$7.99US/$10.99CAN
Final Scream	0-8217-7712-2	$7.99US/$10.99CAN
Hot Blooded	1-4201-0678-3	$7.99US/$9.49CAN
If She Only Knew	1-4201-3241-5	$7.99US/$9.99CAN
Left to Die	1-4201-0276-1	$7.99US/$10.99CAN
Lost Souls	0-8217-7938-9	$7.99US/$10.99CAN
Malice	0-8217-7940-0	$7.99US/$10.99CAN
The Morning After	1-4201-3370-5	$7.99US/$9.99CAN
The Night Before	1-4201-3371-3	$7.99US/$9.99CAN
Ready to Die	1-4201-1851-X	$7.99US/$9.99CAN
Running Scared	1-4201-0182-X	$7.99US/$10.99CAN
See How She Dies	1-4201-2584-2	$7.99US/$8.99CAN
Shiver	0-8217-7578-2	$7.99US/$10.99CAN
Tell Me	1-4201-1854-4	$7.99US/$9.99CAN
Twice Kissed	0-8217-7944-3	$7.99US/$9.99CAN
Unspoken	1-4201-0093-9	$7.99US/$9.99CAN
Whispers	1-4201-5158-4	$7.99US/$9.99CAN
Wicked Game	1-4201-0338-5	$7.99US/$9.99CAN
Wicked Lies	1-4201-0339-3	$7.99US/$9.99CAN
Without Mercy	1-4201-0274-5	$7.99US/$10.99CAN
You Don't Want to Know	1-4201-1853-6	$7.99US/$9.99CAN

Available Wherever Books Are Sold!
Visit our website at **www.kensingtonbooks.com**

More from Bestselling Author
JANET DAILEY

Calder Storm	0-8217-7543-X	$7.99US/$10.99CAN
Close to You	1-4201-1714-9	$5.99US/$6.99CAN
Crazy in Love	1-4201-0303-2	$4.99US/$5.99CAN
Dance With Me	1-4201-2213-4	$5.99US/$6.99CAN
Everything	1-4201-2214-2	$5.99US/$6.99CAN
Forever	1-4201-2215-0	$5.99US/$6.99CAN
Green Calder Grass	0-8217-7222-8	$7.99US/$10.99CAN
Heiress	1-4201-0002-5	$6.99US/$7.99CAN
Lone Calder Star	0-8217-7542-1	$7.99US/$10.99CAN
Lover Man	1-4201-0666-X	$4.99US/$5.99CAN
Masquerade	1-4201-0005-X	$6.99US/$8.99CAN
Mistletoe and Molly	1-4201-0041-6	$6.99US/$9.99CAN
Rivals	1-4201-0003-3	$6.99US/$7.99CAN
Santa in a Stetson	1-4201-0664-3	$6.99US/$9.99CAN
Santa in Montana	1-4201-1474-3	$7.99US/$9.99CAN
Searching for Santa	1-4201-0306-7	$6.99US/$9.99CAN
Something More	0-8217-7544-8	$7.99US/$9.99CAN
Stealing Kisses	1-4201-0304-0	$4.99US/$5.99CAN
Tangled Vines	1-4201-0004-1	$6.99US/$8.99CAN
Texas Kiss	1-4201-0665-1	$4.99US/$5.99CAN
That Loving Feeling	1-4201-1713-0	$5.99US/$6.99CAN
To Santa With Love	1-4201-2073-5	$6.99US/$7.99CAN
When You Kiss Me	1-4201-0667-8	$4.99US/$5.99CAN
Yes, I Do	1-4201-0305-9	$4.99US/$5.99CAN

Available Wherever Books Are Sold!

Check out our website at www.kensingtonbooks.com.